Jim for thee,

Mister Moffat's Hill

Other books by Stan Moore

MISTER MOFFAT'S ROAD
A historical novel about David Moffat's railroad
from Denver towards Salt Lake City, set in 1902.
Mik Mas and friends help Moffat to
overcome unforeseen barriers.

OVER THE DAM
Mik Mas uncovers and works to stop eco-vigilantes
in today's Summit County, Colorado.
Fiction (overthedam.com)

SEESAW: HOW NOVEMBER '42 SHAPED THE FUTURE
A fresh look at the crux month of WWII.
Nonfiction (seesaw1942.com)

Mister Moffat's Hill

Stan Moore

Many people have given input and criticism which has been invaluable. Particular credit goes to the final editor and cover artist, my long-patient wife, Kiki. Her opinions and judgment have helped me over many a tough stretch. Any errors are mine alone.

Design by Jack Lenzo

To those who built the road and operated trains over Rollins Pass. The men and women of the Denver Northwestern and Pacific Railway Company showed remarkable ingenuity, determination, and loyalty.

And to David Moffat, without whom Colorado would be a poorer place.

Who is Who

(in Mister Moffat's Hill)

Rollins Pass. A passage over the continental divide in what is now north central Colorado. For thousands of years, wild game, Native Americans, and European settlers have used this route to cross the Main Range. A railroad was built over it starting in 1904. As of 2017, Automobiles can drive the old railroad grade to the top from the west. From the east it is driveable to just above timberline but not to the top.

Karat Top Mine. A precious gem lode boomed by speculators located somewhere in northwest Colorado or south central Wyoming.

Mik Mas. A Denver water lawyer become 1904 railroad man.

Cam Braun. Construction Foreman for the Denver Northwestern and Pacific Railway. He is a family man and devoted railroad builder. Braun is a valued employee and relied upon by senior officers of the company.

Johanssen. A railroad yard dick and operations worker, a gandy dancer.

Ella Queue. Labor agitator, animal rights advocate and entrepreneur. One time employee of the Union Pacific Rail Road. Prefers to go by the single name Ella.

Dale Smertz. Labor agitator and Union Pacific employee. He has some locating engineer and railroad construction experience. Life and business partner with Ella.

Josephus Eggers. Troubleshooter and troublemaker for hire. Always on the lookout for business opportunities and schemes. Has found a home in the Rocky Mountains.

Steuben Wentz. Security chief for construction operations of the Denver Northwestern and Pacific Railway.

Charity Hovus. Life and business partner with Eggers. A woman who seeks out business prospects and opportunities. She is adept at using the tools and people at hand to achieve her goals.

A few of Mik's sketches of the road and its territory

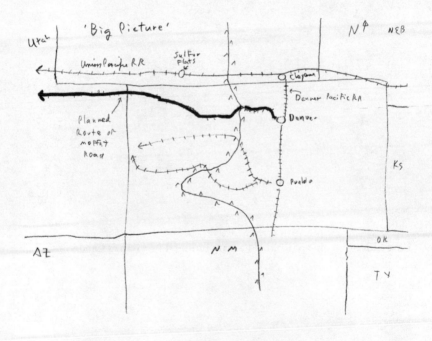

Big Picture: Shows the planned route of the Moffat Road. Across southern Wyoming see the trace of the Union Pacific RR. Also, City of Denver, Denver Pacific RR to Cheyenne, and some other railroads in the area.

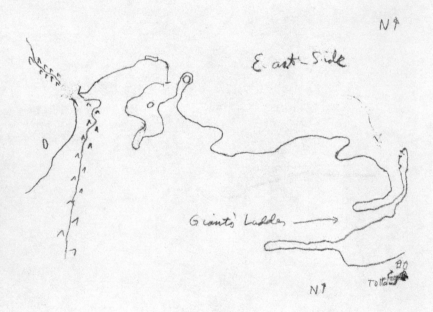

East Side: East side of Rollins Pass including The Giant's Ladder.

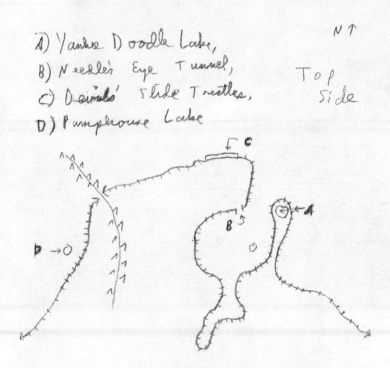

A) Yankee Doodle Lake,
B) Needle's Eye Tunnel,
C) Devil's Slide Trestles,
D) Pumphouse Lake

N ↑

Top
Side

Top Side: Shows the section above timberline, with the loop around Yankee Doodle Lake, Needle's Eye Tunnel, Devil's Slide Trestles, and Pumphouse Lake.

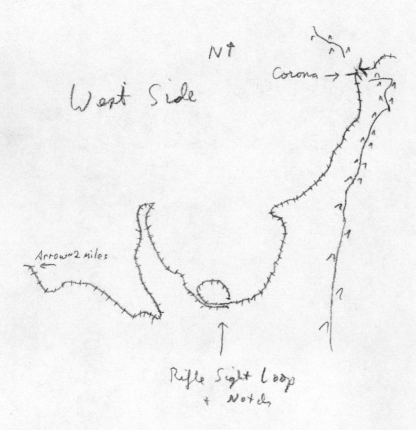

West Side: Shows the Rifle Sight Loop and the winding grade down towards Arrow.

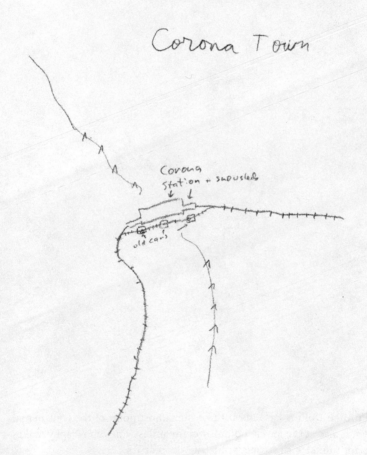

Corona Town

Corona
Station + snowsleds

old cars

Corona Town: Home to some, shelter to many.

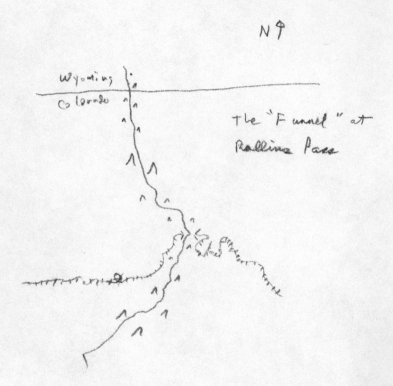

The Funnel: Rollins Pass sits at the easternmost point of the continental divide; it is also at the lowest point for many miles. The topography makes for a giant funnel with strong winds and deep drifts.

Contents

I

Prologue

Expecting a challenge or worse at any moment, Mik was extra alert. He moved, wary as a rabbit in coyote country. Around him the crags loomed darkly. Joe and the woman were, he was sure, armed. Mik had left his horse loosely tied and ready for a getaway. Before taking a step he made darn sure his revolver was loaded and close to hand.

Dawn smeared the east but it was still dark enough to see a comet. Its arc made him think of crossing over and back from the twenty first century. That was about a year ago. Friendships, months of building a railroad, and adventure such as this made him glad that he decided to return to 1904.

His foot scuffed a stone little bigger than a peach pit. A peculiar shine rose from it even in the poor light. He leaned down to pick it up.

II

HE COULD GO BACK.

Michael 'Mik' Mas stood on the side of Eldorado Mountain. With one last look he drank in the cliffs, trees, and mountains. Cam and Johanssen were walking a road up the hill, talking and gesturing, completely unmindful of him. Looking down the hill he saw a couple striding the other direction, intent on each other. A final deep breath let him savor the clear 1904 air.

Then he stepped back through.

The step was into what he hoped, believed, to be the portal. He didn't pretend to understand. Several months back he had come through the other direction. It had delivered him from the twenty first century to 1903. He sure as heck hoped that stepping back through now would work in reverse. Home, his wife Sula, and modern Denver were over there.

The destination was good, desirable. He knew that the transition would be in no way comfortable. It would be a pummeling.

As he stepped in, each of the five senses got slapped. There was the penetrating head buzz. Light and his entire field of vision wavered. A gust of sound assaulted his ears, kind of like a wave hitting the beach, but not as pleasant.

Even his nose and mouth got brassy, dry sensations. A sense of weird un-connectedness hit him. It was almost like he was coming apart molecule by molecule. Thoughts too came apart, an odd sense that different parts of ideas and awareness were drifting away. When he felt he could bear no more, a rush of disbelief and near panic piled on. The four or five minutes it seemed to take were, he later decided, probably only four or five seconds.

However long the transition was, when he came out it took a few moments to feel whole again. He thought, *I have done this five or seven times. It really doesn't get any easier or less disagreeable. Will I ever get used to it?*

The sensations bowed him but Mik was still standing, clearing his head with a shake. He was feeling better by the second. Being back in the twenty first century, the first thing he did was pull out and power up his phone. He wanted to check the time and date. The phone lit up, a good sign. The usual chirping and vibrating were reassuring. Familiar territory!

Judging from the surroundings, he was home or close to it. He looked around and saw the familiar foothills southwest of Boulder. Everything was as he remembered—condition of the road, where his car sat, the big green Denver Water pipes coming out of the mountain.... His location added up.

But something on the phone made him look again. By the time shown he had been gone from here for only a little. The display clearly showed that only twelve minutes had elapsed. What on earth?! Mik was staggered. He literally almost lost footing, he was so surprised. He distinctly remembered noting the precise time and date as he shut the phone down, before he stepped back in time. Twelve minutes' difference is all that it showed.

He knew he was back. But he had been there for weeks, months. But here, virtually no time had elapsed. What the...? Well, he figured, a portal in space-time was unbelievable to start with. So he shouldn't be surprised that time measure was all screwed up too. He just had to accept. There was no way to rationally explain any of it. Mik shrugged, smiled, and started to walk towards his car. Two steps later he stopped. Twelve minutes? His wife wasn't expecting him here until the next day. If a minute or two here was a week there, an hour here was about a year in Moffat's time.

A free pass, that is what he had. He could go spend time railroading virtually as long as he wanted, and it would have no impact! Free time, literally time out of time, was on offer.

Two courses of action were weighed in his mind, all in a fraction of a second. Yes, he really wanted to see his wife, to tell Sula about this incredible experience. He might even write a book about it. But at the same time, he had made new friends. His work, his new calling, was helping to build a railroad, shaping Colorado's future. Somehow sculpting a grade into a mountain and laying rails on it was satisfying. Knowing that the train using them would ease and enrich peoples' lives was rewarding. Building a railroad that was still in use a hundred years later was fulfilling in ways that practicing law never could be. And it was only twelve minutes!

Mik Mas did not hesitate. He simply turned around and stepped back through to 1904.

STEPPING THROUGH WAS NO EASIER GOING BACK THAN COMING forward. Coming out, he again shook his head and looked around. No car was parked down the way and there were no big green Denver Water pipes coming out of the mountain. The terrain was familiar, though, and he knew the road he stood on. Like any newly cut road, the edges were raw and no grass or plants had grown up. The surface was not graveled or smooth, just rocky dirt.

This road was designed for horse and wagon. There were many like it scraped into the land. Crews needed access to the railroad grade being built across the mountain above. Supplies had to be brought in but bringing them all up the rails was simply not practical. Thus many wagon access roads were cut. The formal name of the railroad being forced through the mountains was 'The Denver Northwestern and Pacific Railway'. Only accountants and lawyers called it that. Most Coloradans knew it as 'The Moffat Road'.

Mik was comfortable at this spot. He had walked past here, this very place, many times. It was located between his boarding house and the construction camp at tunnel four. He knew the camp was gone, moved. The camp at tunnel four had been relocated. It had been literally picked up and moved in the past days. Having been called away, he didn't see it happen.

The Great American Chase, 1840-1920: Trains running on tracks laid ever on by working men who first tore a level road out of the country side. This vast coordinated waltz among loggers, dynamite handlers, gandy dancers, tunnelers, surveyors, supply clerks, engineers, financiers, bridge builders, and countless others would continue. In this case, until Salt Lake City was reached or the money ran out.

Mik glanced out at the prairie, the Great Plains which rolled off to the east. They looked a lot like the ocean looked when viewed from the side of a Hawaiian mountain. The impression flew through and out of his mind. Just as well. If anyone here knew about the Pacific island chain of islands known as 'Owhyee', it wasn't much. No one would recognize the state of Hawaii. Some probably knew that there had recently been a coup unseating the King there, and a government favoring Americans had taken power. Not a lot of Coloradans were aware of that smattering of current events. He knew he had better lei such references aside.

Motion on the road below caught his eye. Striding down the hill, maybe fifty or sixty yards away, backs to him, were two people. Both were dressed as men, in work shirts and denim trousers. It was easy to see that one was not a man, or at least did not walk as a man. The hair and more also the gait was of a woman. The image stuck in his head. After all, one didn't see many women dressed as men, nor men swaying their hips like this one did. The main thing was that they walked away, towards Eldorado Springs and who knows from there.

Swaying hips aside, their gait and posture seemed cheery and carefree. They looked at each other, talked, and smiled or laughed. The two could almost have been friends or lovers walking in a city park.

Mik watched them a moment then turned. Looking up the hill, he saw more motion. As far above as the couple were below, strode two men. Their pace was purposeful. They were nearing a bend and would soon be out of sight. One was burly and dark complected. The other was as tall but paler, not quite an albino. He was wiry, not stocky.

A long gun was in over second man's shoulder. It was a shotgun, broken open. No doubt he could bring it over and use it in a moment if need be. Their body language was not carefree, rather focused and businesslike. They talked not as folks out on a lark, but as men with work to do.

Ah, Mik thought. *There's Cam Braun, my friend the foreman. Who's that with him? He's a company dick, what is his name? Johnson? No, Johanssen.*

Mick glanced back at the now distant couple. *Good riddance to bad rubbish.* The thought came to Mik out of nowhere. He was glad to see the last of that pair! He turned and started up to catch the men.

III

THE TWO MEN TRUDGED UP THE HILL. THERE WAS NO CHAT, NO need to fill the quiet or make time pass. As with most men, their talk was utilitarian: to gain or trade information. Gradually words came. Living and working in the mountains made them extra strong, fit, and accustomed to the air. Even so, the elevation and exertion made for extra breaths and a calm rhythm of conversation. The pace was relaxed, almost carefree, but the subject was not so much.

These men lived and worked on the edge of the law. Not as law benders or breakers, rather as enforcers. They didn't patrol city streets or pursue cattle rustlers. Their work was to organize and keep order among hard men and women. Rock workers, rail layers, camp cooks, dynamite men, pleasure girls, land grifters and mule drivers were all in their flock. These were the people they worked with, knew, and occasionally had to punish or expel. One man did his share of this work as a boss, the other as a cop.

The big foreman spoke. "It is good to see the back of those two and I'm damned glad for it! That man and woman are nothing but trouble. Their type is always hanging around and trying to slow our progress. They will do most anything— file bogus land claims, stir up the workers, claim animal cruelty. They cause problems wherever and whenever they can. Trouble hangs on them like stink on a skunk."

For about a dozen paces, each thought about the pair and their actions.

Johanssen: "Yah. I was glad to run them off of our road."

Cam expected just such a pearl from the security man. He let it go by and went on. "And that silly woman. Why dress in men's clothes but then not try to conceal her womanhood? What is she hiding, what is she trying to do? And what sort of a man consorts with and supports such a woman?"

Johanssen didn't really know the word 'consorts' but figured it out. Cam sometimes used high falutin' words. That was alright, the man was hard but fair.

Being worked up, Cam couldn't help but repeat himself. "What kind of a man would put up with that dressing nonsense? I tell you, wherever those two go, they are nothing but trouble. Good riddance!" He smiled in recollection, but it was not a warm or friendly smile. Had the man or woman seen it, they would have quailed.

"I know I run on about things, but I have to say it. I hope never to see that Ella Queue and Dale Smertz again. I hope you succeeded in getting rid of them, Johanssen. Maybe they will get the message to go somewhere else. California maybe, or Idaho. Someplace far, the further the better." He glanced at the lanky blond man who smiled. Johanssen carefully held, almost fondled, the shotgun he had used to make sure the couple left the property.

The weapon didn't waiver as Johanssen spoke. These sentences were a normal day's worth of talk from him. "I think we are shut of them. But you never know, anyone odd like them may not get it in their heads. They might hang around. We think they are hooligans, nothing more. But they probably consider themselves professional spies or worker do-gooders or something."

Cam nodded. "Good point, Johanssen. I think we probably had better warn other railroad men about them. I'll have Steu put the word out to the Sheriff and others." He paused, thinking about the company security manager. Steu was supervisor of security. On the street he was called a railroad dick. The image of Steu, a big strong man who knew the streets, came to mind. He pushed that image back and came back to the present. He'd see and talk to the man soon. No need to daydream about it.

Cam wondered about Mik and said so.

"Say, I wonder where Mik is. He hung back down there after we ran those two off. He seemed a little distracted." Cam didn't stop to think that Johanssen probably had never heard that word. He went on. "I hope he is feeling alright. Said he had some business to take care of. Probably, he had to get rid of some coffee. I can't imagine there is any other business up here that needs taken care of."

Johanssen snickered and Cam smiled faintly.

The two people that Johanssen had just escorted off wouldn't leave their minds. Johanssen relived the morning, the hours when he had encouraged them along with his shotgun. They had been caught red handed on company property where they had no business being. Now, with them gone and no one to escort or surveil, he could relax. The man was fit with a Nordic look. Actually, Cam figured him for an out of uniform soldier. His careful handling of the weapon, precise gait, and ramrod posture made him a likely candidate for one of Teddy Roosevelt's recruiting posters.

With no one needing intimidation, he didn't brandish the gun. The weapon was now broken open, riding easily on Johanssen's shoulder. If by chance they met a rattler or a bigger opponent—a cat, a mama bear, or a very unlucky troublemaker—he could close and use it in just a moment.

"He'll be along," guessed Johanssen. Glancing over his other shoulder, his eyes brightened. "Matter of fact, he is coming up the hill behind us. He's just a little back."

MIK STRODE OUT, TRYING TO CATCH THE PAIR. HE TOO FELT the altitude and steepness of the road. Plus, he had almost run to catch up. As he neared, he called. Being a little short of breath, his words sounded kind of wheezy.

"Hey, you two! Wait up." They coasted to a halt. After stopping, the two of them looked back down the road at him.

"What's cooking? Are we glad to get rid of those two? So I bet you're glad to be done escorting riffraff out of the road's property, Johanssen. And Cam, I know you're glad to be done doing chores for the suits on Sixteenth Street."

"Yeah, errand boy work isn't for me. I preferred not to go to Hot Sulphur Springs just to deliver papers for filing by the County Clerk. But Mr. Sumner said it had to be done. It put the road on sound footing to extend tracks through Gore Canyon. Now, done it is, and I am damn glad!"

'Mr. Sumner' was the railroad's chief engineer. He worked on Sixteenth Street in Denver. The 'work' Cam mentioned was to deliver a deed for the railroad. Cam was given the job because he was loyal, smart, and tough. Being a line foreman, he knew how to get things done and could handle himself in a scrape. The job entailed some legal maneuvering to get a deed recorded in a small mountain town. Sumner figured, correctly, that there were people trying to stop him and Mr. Moffat from filing the deed. But they wouldn't be looking for a foreman to be carrying the legal papers. They would expect some officer or a courier to make the run.

Cam quietly handled the job. He didn't do it entirely alone. Mik helped. He and a man named Joe Eggers teamed up to divert the attention of troublemakers. The man and woman down the hill were among those who needed to be diverted. They dearly wanted to get their hands on the deed. Mik made sure that they didn't.

Relief showed on Cam. "Speaking for myself, I am eager to get back to railroad work. I'll take iron and dynamite any day over paper! Since I was away, I was out of touch. I needed to find out what has happened on my stretch of road. Me and Johanssen were just catching up on things, the job and stuff, as we walked."

He glanced over at the happily armed security man, and explained to Mik. "Maybe you put two and two together. Just in case you came up with five instead of four, here's what happened."

The joke was lame but he grinned anyway. He nodded Johanssen's way. "Steu and him met those two agitators up on the grade. They were coming towards camp, walking on the grade like they owned it! Needless to say, Steu bounced them. He sent Johanssen along with his shotgun just to be sure them two Harriman spies really left. If they have any sense, they'll not show their faces around here again. Anyway, that is what was going on when you and I met him and those two."

He paused again, trying to read Mik's expression. Then he went on. "You know, when we ran into all of them as we came up the road. After I got back into town and the two of us met up. We had just called on the Prudens to give condolences for Seth's passing and all."

Mik gave him a wondering look. "Yes, of course I remember. Sad business, that. So now we're done with the deed and can get on with building a road."

"I figured you were prodding beauty and the beast along with the .410!" Mik addressed Johanssen, not really expecting a response. It was a relief to make a joke of it. Smiling, he continued, "So you got the honor and pleasure of running those two skunks off, huh?"

Johanssen nodded, a satisfied look on him.

Cam looked at Mik. "Anyway, let's get going. The new camp was moved from tunnel four when we were gone. I know the new spot and am eager to see it." He was back in railroad mode now, ready to run tracks through the mountains. Those around him knew he would push hard, demanding more and better of them.

He changed subjects again, from rail to people. "You said you had some 'business you needed to attend to' back down where we met Johanssen, Mik. Did you get it done?"

"Sure, I just had to take a quick break." *I think 'break' is the word*, Mik thought. *I just decided to stay here for now. If I can get back to work I'll be fine.*

Mik didn't say anything more. He tried to avoid thinking about coming and going like that. The whole thing was too complicated, eerie, and agonizing to dwell on.

Cam was satisfied with the answer. He went on. "I look forward to seeing the new digs. We, the Denver

Northwestern and Pacific, are making good progress on this road. At the rate we're going, we'll have the grade and track up to the Main Range before snow flies!"

The three started up the road.

Cam talked. He wasn't sure just how conversational Johanssen or Mik were. Well, he knew Johanssen wasn't a talker, period. Mik sometimes was, sometimes not. Either way, he sure felt like conversing. Some fascinating item he had seen in the papers was his subject.

"You know," he said, "I read about two brothers named Wright. Couple of bicycle makers back east somewhere. Apparently they got tired of bicycles. They invented a machine, metal and fabric, with one of those new gasoline engines. I guess it is almost a mechanical bird. And they flew it, under control, took it off the ground and got it back down. On their first try, they went quite a ways in the air and brought it back to land without crashing the machine or the pilot."

He glanced at Johanssen who was half listening. Mik seemed kind of preoccupied.

"Exciting times we live in. Who knows, maybe some day there will be big sleek flying machines and other fanciful things. You and I will be able to climb in one and go to another city in hours instead of days. Wouldn't that be a hoot!"

Mik heard and grinned knowingly at the idea.

For a man with a Louisiana sharecropping background, Cam was fairly well read. Speaking to him, one wouldn't know that he grew up poor and had only four or maybe five years of classroom education, he wasn't sure. For him, such a background was unpleasant. He tried telling himself it was nothing to be ashamed of, and that he had done well. In fact, he only half believed that and didn't talk about it.

Out here in the field it wasn't easy to keep up on current events, or anything else. Worthwhile reading material was hard to come by. Living and working at the forefront of a railroad being imposed upon the unwilling Rocky Mountains was truly isolating.

Talking eagerly to newcomers and travelers helped him overcome this lack. And he made a point to read newspapers even if they were days or weeks old by the time they came to him. Most of the men and women up at the construction sites weren't interested in life outside the work camp. Having only the Johanssens of the world to converse with didn't make for long interesting discussions. Cam knew that even short exchanges were rare unless you were talking tunneling or track or some such.

Foreign railroading came to mind. "Say, I read that a new road is being planned. It will run from Berlin in Germany to Baghdad in the Middle East. Work has started and rail is being laid. There is no railroad now to Baghdad. I guess Germans are engineering the road and supervising the work. It will open up the entire region for trade and travel. So we aren't the only railroading pioneers at work!"

Johanssen made a contribution. "Yah, those Germans, they are good engineers. I wonder why they don't stick to building railroads in Germany? I'm glad I'm over here, away from Germans. They are always doing something, building or causing trouble for someone."

Cam made another attempt. "I read that there is unrest in Russia. I guess the people don't like their king. They call him the Tsar, not king. In any case, the people want him to give up power. They want the legislature to have the power not the royals. There have been riots I guess, unheard of there.

People there have plenty of reasons to be unhappy. Many are hungry. And both their Army and Navy just got whipped by the Japanese. The citizens aren't happy about that."

"Yah, those Russians. They run Finland. My grandfather tried to do business in Finland. They made it hard on him. There were all kind of rules and laws. Also payoffs and beatings. He couldn't make it. Finally he quit trying and sent his family over here. That's why I'm here. Yah, those Russians."

Cam went on as if Johanssen hadn't shared his background. "All in all I'd say that our system is pretty good. At least you and I won't get thrown in jail if we say we don't like some senator or the President. And the big money men, the trusters like E.H Harriman, they can hire and fire. They can make business hard for competitors like Mister Moffat. But they can't have him or us sent to exile in Alaska or somewhere. Or have us shot. In Russia a nobleman can have a commoner jailed or shot on his word."

He turned to look at his companion. "You know, Johanssen, your grandfather was right to get out from under the Russians in Finland."

Johanssen had listened but not really heard. Politics and current affairs baffled him. He responded halfheartedly. "Uh, yah. I guess so."

Mik was silent through this dialogue, lost in thought.

This type of exchange reminded Cam again how he had come to rely on his friend. Mik was one of the few who seemed to care about such things and liked to discuss them. It was good to talk with someone who could look beyond the construction camp. Cam enjoyed that. As long as work came first and the job got done, it was ok to read newspapers and talk current events.

Before long the steepness of the road eased. The hikers came out on the top of the dirt access road. There it made a T, running straight in to the rail bed. Where they stood was at the edge of the wide flat and level rail grade. It was a monumental sight, a pretty one to Cam's railroading eye. They took a few moments to admire the work of the crews. The grade pulled their eyes first to the left, south. There the roadbed sloped gently down. It was the mandated two percent grade, changing two feet of elevation for every one hundred feet of travel. The fine wide road gradually and consistently fell towards the plains and ultimately Denver. Looking to the right, north, it climbed at the same rate. Cam knew this superb stretch of road grade would soon have rails and it would carry people and freight. Through the mountains trains would go, all the way to Salt Lake City and even beyond.

No rails or ties were to be seen. But the grade was finished and ready for them. Soon, maybe even in hours, ballast would be laid. Ballast is the layer of gravel between grade and the railroad itself. Ties would be set on this base, one every two feet or so. True railroaders like Cam knew that the ties would be set nineteen and a half inches on center. Then rails would be laid on the leveled ties and spiked in. Voila! A railroad!

Before long engines would be hauling loads of building material up to the head of rail. The new steel highway would be put to good use. And not long after that those engines would be bringing people up to the mountains, passengers and day tourists. Freight would move: Goods and supplies would go in and coal, ore, lumber and cattle would come out.

The iron rooster, Cam had read somewhere. Apt name for a locomotive, strutting, preening, billowing smoke and noise, ready to show its stuff to the world!

But for now, the men stood and looked up and down an untracked, wide flat road. After a quick breather they walked north towards the new camp. Construction camps on a railroad have a short life. Work progress constantly compels their relocation. Camps are always chasing the head of the work and fleeing the laying of rails. The crews' latest temporary home was now about two miles up the way, just past tunnel six.

This stretch of the railroad was a challenge and a labor of love for Cam. The man was absolutely crazy for railroading, building grade and laying rail. He was a hard driving, demanding boss. His thing was, get your work done well and efficiently. He didn't care how you spent your off time as long as it didn't interfere with your job performance. The job was the thing.

For Cam opening up country and making life easier and better for the people there was satisfying, almost joyfully so. The main drawback was, working up here kept him from town and his family. It was hard to be separated from his wife and children, but God, he loved the work.

For a few moments he considered the future. Not the work that needed done today or this week, but months and years out. He remembered the beginning. It was back when David Moffat, banker and Denver civic leader, filed incorporation papers. The company was to be called the Denver Northwestern and Pacific Railway Company. Mr. Moffat intended to build from Denver to Salt Lake City, standard gauge, direct through the mountains. He announced his plans and that he had eastern investors. Somehow that financial backing shortly evaporated. The road went on anyway.

Cam had been one of the first hires. His job started, as did the road, at Utah Junction. Cam sometimes wondered why it was named Utah. Maybe for the destination of the road starting there. It was about two miles north and a little east of downtown Denver. From that spot he and his crews built north and west. Cam had seen it all and supervised most of the construction.

This part of the route, the climb out of Denver, was his favorite. At least so far. He especially liked the way the grade conquered the approach to the mountains. It climbed northwest by west out of Denver up to the south side of a high plain running down off the mountain. It was an area probably five by three miles, flat and boulder strewn. Some unimaginative soul named it Rocky Flats.

This high plain between Boulder and Golden was the preface to the cliffs and canyons of the foothills. Moffat's railroad skirted it on the south. Then the road gained elevation by a big sweeping 'S' turn. From there the route climbed across the east face of Eldorado Mountain, a foothill visible from anywhere in the area. Northwest of Denver and southwest of Boulder, it had a distinctive cliff shaped like twin ears on top. Up on the side of the mountain, the views from the grade were huge. One could see almost to Kansas and Wyoming.

This Eldorado Mountain stretch had buttresses of cliffs. They ran perpendicular to the rail route and appeared every few hundred yards. Almost all of them were too thick and high to make a cut through. Tunnels had to be drilled. The rock was solid granite, firm and strong. Even so the tunnels called for some shoring. There were occasional cave-ins, almost unavoidable given the nature of the work. And there were a few unexpected springs. If inadvertently tapped into while drilling a tunnel, the results were wading or even a swim. All of this tunnel drilling work was done with hammer, chisel, muscle, and dynamite.

The tunnel crews relied on the surveyors to get them started right. A matter of a few feet one way left, right, up or down could make a big difference in the outcome. Starting at the precise correct spot made all the difference and ensured that the two ends of the tunnel would meet up square. Seldom did workers tunneling from both ends find themselves more than a few inches off. The grade, the steepness of the railroad bed itself, had to be part of the calculations and tunneling work.

After crossing the whole east front of Eldorado Mountain, the route turned west up the valley of South Boulder Creek. At that point, it was still high above the waters. The road climbed at the prescribed two percent. Eight or ten road miles to the west, about three miles as the crow flies, they met up. The road climbing west got to where the creek came, falling east.

It was an important but unnamed junction, this spot where the road met up with South Boulder creek. From there, the entire the job got easier for a while. The grade would simply follow, that is run parallel to, the creek all the way to its headwaters at the base of the continental divide. In most of that stretch the topography was kind. There weren't too many crags and no cliffs that needed tunneling through. The open gentle creek valley made for a fairly easy run to the main range.

The foreman reflected on the job up to this point. Cutting a road to these specifications made Cam feel like an artist. He loved molding the mountain to proudly and safely to carry the finished railroad on its side.

At gut level he considered himself a sculptor on a grand scale. The name Gutzon Borglum of course meant nothing to Cam. That man wouldn't begin to shape Mount Rushmore for another twenty plus years. Not that it could happen, but Cam would have been proud to compare his work to that of Borglum. His work was utilitarian, not historical and patriotic. But Cam Braun justifiably felt that he was every bit as much an artist as did the man who carved faces on a South Dakota cliff.

Not that he focused on it, but Cam knew that his work would endure and be admired by generations. Such froufrou wasn't of interest. He just loved being outside, hearing the clink of holes being drilled for dynamite, watching the land being transformed before his eyes. And he knew that the railroad was good for people, good for Colorado.

The foreman's sojourn into the job and his history with it did the trick. He forgot all about delivering papers and enduring troublemakers. The job at hand took over his concentration. *Soon, we'll be done with all the tunnels through these cliffs. A week or two after that we'll have grade cut and dressed, with ballast, ties and rail laid. We'll be running trains up to the great divide soon. Then we start up and over. That's what I want to do, build over that pass. The backroom boys can decide where to put their tunnel while we're doing that. That will take them several years, and I get to build road and run trains over the hill while they do! I can't wait!*

As they rounded a corner the new camp appeared. They saw tents, temporary corrals, stacks of material, and a flimsy shed or two. The scene was busy with wagons and people going about their business. Every person was intent on a job. The sight reminded Cam of an anthill, with apparently overlapping and useless activity. But he knew that chaotic it was not. It was actually planned and directed, and each individual was focused on their part of the big picture.

As they walked down in to camp, Johanssen split off to report to his boss and Mik went to the tunnel face. Cam went toward his office tent. Everyone recognized it by size and by a peculiar shade in the coloring. Plus, he had the only tent in Colorado with a wobbly wooden gargoyle over the door, he was sure! Few workers noticed it or even knew what a gargoyle was. No matter, that was a fun small luxury he allowed himself. He was eager to get in and see what was going on. As he went along, he stopped workers, quizzing them.

"Norby, what is the count on tunnel braces? And is there anything I need to know about the dynamite magazine?"

"Ciano, rations. How many day's rations do you have on hand? Where is the water supply for this new camp?"

"O'Leary, go get me the specs on tunnel progress. And give me a thumbnail on the geology of them. Any loose areas or other problems?"

"Bingham, does everyone have a place to sleep, their own cot in a tent?"

By asking the right questions he assessed conditions and job progress. He had a thirst to get current with his real job. Running the construction of a railroad, not delivering papers was the thing. Getting up to speed didn't take long. Soon he knew where each crew was and what they were working on. And he knew what hot spots and concerns were developing, both on and off the grade.

Once Cam felt confident that he had a handle on the work of the day, the week and the month, he relaxed. A bit. There were no problems or issues his supervisors couldn't handle on their own. With that under control, he stepped back. He wanted to think big picture. Seldom did he allow himself to consider the entire road, its future and other aspects. Still, from time to time he felt it a good thing to do.

The foreman knew the projection, the timetable, was to have rail laid to the base of the Main Range by year's end. Where would the road go from there? The plan was for a tunnel to go under the Range, under the continental divide. It would spit the road out somewhere near the headwaters of the Fraser River. But a tunnel there would be miles long, a big and time consuming job.

Sure, Cam thought, *we have driven tunnels through rock ribs all the way across Eldorado Mountain like nails into a pine board. Dozens of them, straight and true, from several hundred feet to half a mile or longer. But a six or eight mile tunnel, thousands of feet under the surface, is a different animal. It will take a lot of time and money to build. That will be some big job. And ventilating that hole will be a challenge in itself. Running a coal burner produces lots of gas and cinders, enough to choke an engineer. Not to mention being hard on passengers! They'll have to find a way to move bad air out and good air into that tunnel....*

He knew that the plan was to throw a road up and over the Range. It would be a temporary fix. Like a hose strung while a water main was being installed. The road over the range would be used for only two or three years until the tunnel under the mountain was completed.

Having been up to the headwaters of the creek a time or two, he had some ideas. He figured the tunnel ought to be started through at the head of the valley, before the meadows petered out. More to the point, he wanted the road over the top to start there. Getting over to the Fraser valley would call for switchbacks and a tunnel or two. And likely there would have to be a few stretches steeper than two percent. But what the heck, it would be a temporary road. They could relax the specifications a bit if they had to.

Yes, Cam loved his job.

IV

WHEN MIK HAD LOOKED, HE FELT THE COUPLE WALKING DOWN the hill acted happy and unburdened. It was hard to say why, but it was an accurate read. The couple really were cheerful and carefree.

Dale and Ella were enjoying a windfall of good news. An hour before this they were sad. They feared their jobs were in trouble. It felt like they had been outmaneuvered, outsmarted, and had failed in their primary duties. In fact they were afraid their boss in New York would make an example. They were pretty sure they would be humiliated then fired.

But of a sudden it changed! Their lives went from being limited with murky prospects to just the opposite. This surprise came not from a boss or circumstances. It came from an enemy. Maybe not an enemy, but the man was at best a business opponent. He offered information which completed the puzzle. What he told them made sense of a jumble of confused facts and occurrences. As things fell into place, their outlook changed. In an abrupt moment, they found themselves secure in their jobs.

Enjoying and sharing their pleasure kept them focused on each other. Neither of them really saw Mik standing up the hill. They certainly didn't witness his momentary disappearance. As far as they knew, he was just standing up on the road where they had left him. Dale Smertz and Ella Queue—although she seldom used her last name—were in their own sunny little world.

If you asked, Dale and Ella would say they were sales representatives for a sewing machine company. This 'job' let them travel the country and talk to all sorts of people. Actually they didn't work selling sewing machines. They worked for a railroad. Their job title for the Union Pacific Railroad was 'troubleshooter'.

A more accurate description of their work would be 'troublemaker'. Their job was to deal with local issues before they became problems big enough to come to the attention of people in the New York offices. The problems they dealt with usually involved competitors to the UP. And they 'dealt with' these competitors with no holds barred. Their goal was to weaken or make the competitor go away. Occasionally the work involved satisfying or silencing noisy customers or suppliers. But most of their effort went to slow or eliminate competition.

The nature of their duties required confidential communications with New York. Just recently Dale and Ella thought they had a big problem. As the job went on, there were 'coincidences'. Enough of these occurred that they feared their messages were being read. By whom, they weren't sure. It certainly seemed that one of their competitors knew what they were up to, down to small details. The company they focused on and feared was the Denver Northwestern and Pacific, the one that Mik, Johanssen, and Cam.

And why were the couple so happy now? They had just learned that no one was reading their mail and telegrams. At least no one in Cam's outfit was. Probably the only person reading them besides the recipient was the telegraph operator. This entire situation they just uncovered was, in fact, bittersweet. No, their telegrams weren't compromised. That was good.

Even so, they had flat out failed. Not so good. David Moffat's new railroad was not stopped, not really even slowed. To their chagrin it was progressing nicely as it built north and west from Denver.

Dale and Ella had been hard at it. They had worked a number of ploys and schemes. Their meager achievements weren't due to lack of effort and planning. They had spent hours, together and separately, surveilling construction camps. Ella had tried to stop a flow of work horses to them, with scant result. The two had taken long bumpy stagecoach rides over Berthoud Pass and back, buying up rights of way and filing mining claims and homestead papers. They had talked with and agitated local ranchers, workers, land owners and others. Still, meager were the results. The two had barely slowed the competitor's operations.

There was one big idea, an innovative scheme. Sitting in the little mountain town of Kremmling Colorado, Dale came up with a plan. The thing was to file for some specific property rights. He wanted to obtain the rights to a plot all the way across a canyon. If they got the property, it would literally put a stopper in the way of the railroad. He communicated the essentials of the idea to New York. There was a big canyon just west of town, Gore Canyon. This deep narrow gorge carries the Colorado River. If he could block access to it, he could cause real problems.

It would have been a good chokepoint for Dale and Ella to grab the competition by the neck. The folks in New York agreed and came up with a full-fledged plan, a way to stop Moffat there. They tried to block the canyon. They proposed to build a power plant and dam.

It didn't work. They got outmaneuvered by Moffat and company. Actually, the outmaneuvering was done by Cam Braun and Mik Mas. They managed to file a deed showing prior claim to that part of the canyon. The power plant idea was strangled in the crib.

How did the Moffat people know to file such a deed? Ella knew that New York would not be happy. She knew it was just a matter of time before word of their failed efforts got back east. Her boss—their boss—and others all the way up the line would learn of her and Dale's failures. Even the lofty Mr. Harriman, owner of the UP and a very powerful man, would probably hear. And she knew that was not good. No one wanted an unhappy Edward Harriman. Ella saw that they were dealt a weak hand by events and by New York. Things worked out badly but they couldn't really be blamed for the outcome.

Still, Ella was wary. She was pretty sure New York wouldn't make an example of them. But for the life of her, she could see no good reason to hang around and find out. They should leave town, she thought, just get out and away and go somewhere. If she (or they) stayed in Colorado, it should be somewhere new doing something different. Let someone else get in the ring and spar with the Moffat people. She was tired of it.

The two walked easily down the road. She glanced at Dale. Time to bare the soul, as little as Ella wanted to.

"We fell on our faces. We did not stop or even slow the Moffat operation. They are making good progress. At the rate they seem to be going they'll have rail up to the foot of the main range soon, this year. Heck, Dale, we didn't slow them down for even a day."

Thinking, she scowled and continued. "I have liked working at the Union Pacific. It is a fine company. I enjoy having an expense account and being able to come and go as we please. I hope we keep it all. We sure tried, but the job was just too big. No one, even Mister Harriman, seems able to slow down the Moffat people. We—you and I—put out a lot of effort and covered a lot of miles. But we sure have darn little to show for it."

A jab of pain shot across the bottom of her foot. She stopped, hopping in surprise and discomfort.

"Ouch! I have a rock in the shoe. Stop a minute and let me get it out." She hung on to a roadside tree, took the shoe off, dumped out the offending pebble, slipped the shoe back on. "That's better. You know that the people in New York will be unhappy, maybe even angry. They have no idea the size of the country or of the problems and barriers we faced. It wasn't really our fault. Maybe someone sees the difficulty of the job. I guess there is good reason that they haven't fired us. At least not yet, anyway. But they might get rid of us, make us an example."

She stumbled again. Her trousers were long and her rolled up cuffs were unrolling. She noticed but ignored the fraying cuffs when she put her shoe back on. Now that fabric grabbed at her ankles and almost tripped her. Pausing to roll them up, she complained.

"These damned trousers! Sometimes I wonder why I bother. I'd probably get further with my work if I dressed as a woman. The thing is, most women's clothes are tight and uncomfortable. And they're confining! I would have trouble getting around on a railroad grade in a dress with stays and corsets. All of that stuff is designed to make one sit still and look dainty. I don't like to sit still or be dainty. But I sure am tired of canvas trousers and scratchy shirts!"

For almost as long as Dale had known her, she wore not dresses but men's clothes. Why, he had never figured out. Nor had he ever summoned the nerve to ask her. Besides, like she said, wearing trousers let her get around on the job much easier than a big dress with hoops and all.

Ella pretended to ignore her clumsy pirouette, simply hitching her pants up. She heard herself whining about wearing men's clothing. It grated on her and probably on Dale as well. She made a decision. It was time to go back to wearing women's clothes. Maybe she could find some fancy trousers to wear with a stylish blouse, to be comfortable but not weird and frumpy.

Wardrobe decisions made, she continued with more suggestions for their future.

"I think we ought to go somewhere else, outside of Boulder and Denver. Maybe stay away from railroads for a while. At least we ought to steer clear of these local roads. You know the dicks talk to each other and have traded information on us. If we lay low, it will let the dust settle. And the folks back in New York will have time to calm down."

An idea flew through and she smiled. "I know, Dale, let's head south. Wouldn't it be nice to forget winter for a while? Who wants to wear heavy coats and gloves and constantly cut firewood and stoke the fire and all that?"

She pantomimed a big shiver. "Let's go down to where the circuses spend their winters. Don't they go to Texas or Arizona territory or somewhere like that? Somewhere balmy and pleasant? It'll be warm there. No snowstorms for us!"

Loving and helping animals was important to Ella. It was every bit as important to her as detesting and harassing company bosses. Whenever possible she tried to do good for animals. Someone had to, she figured.

Visiting the circus might be a way to get out of town. It was a way to make a new life and career. She warmed to the subject.

"Dale, we can enjoy the change in scenery and weather. And our faces and names will fall out of the local scene. Maybe we can make contacts with some circus folks. I'll bet they are an interesting crew. And they know how to make money off of people. We could learn some new schemes and moves...." Her smile brightened. "Plus, we can work to improve conditions for the animals. Many circus animals are not well treated, you know."

Now warmed up, she was off and running. "Imagine, we could help to care for and train animals. Monkeys, elephants, horses, maybe even a tiger or lion!"

Ella was a sharp eyed, calculating labor agitator and worker advocate. The woman knew how to size up a business or labor situation and get things riled up. Her softness for animals was good and bad. It wasn't unusual for her to win over a landowner, convince him not to allow the railroad to run over his land. And in the next breath, to lose him by criticizing his handling and treatment of farm animals. This was a problem. She knew it and tried not to, but often she couldn't help herself.

Dale rolled his eyes. He had heard this story many times. She was always trying to take advantage of people and always trying to help animals. Or so she said. Circuses, animals, or leaving the area were of absolutely no interest to him. He had been thinking of his response since she mentioned going south. He volleyed back.

"And do you have any idea where these camps are? And aren't the circuses out on the road putting on their shows this time of year? Will anyone or any animals even be there? How would we get there?"

He smiled, not wanting to be too harsh. "I know you are soft for any four footed pal, Ella. But let's look at this. Suppose we can find a camp and the circus is there. Do you really think we could just waltz in? Drop in and start telling circus people how to run their business? What would you do if some stranger stopped you in the street and tried to tell you your business?"

Unpleasant memories came to mind. They were of being on the receiving end of shoves, fists and kicks. After a short pause, he asked softly, "Surely you realize that circuses have their own version of railroad dicks?" A railroad dick was the security guard. Railroad dicks were not gentle when they ran people off of trains and out of the switching yard.

Dale drove it home. "You know they have men who would love to get people like you and me into a dark alley. Then they would 'persuade' us to forget about their circus and their animals. You know they would make us leave town. Those guys will be all over us as soon as we show up. Hell, they probably talk to the railroad dicks and would know we are on the way. And meet us when we show up."

He didn't like having to come on strong. From past debacles, he knew that when Ella got on a toot about animals she was hard to stop. The best thing to do was hit hard at the idea, right away. Otherwise she wouldn't easily give up her well-intended but strange crusade.

He looked at her and smiled. Time to take the edge off his words but get the message through.

"I see your point, and maybe sometime we can go south and help circus animals. But it takes time to develop the contacts we would need. We have a good start on that here. We are finally getting to know the lay of the land here in Denver and Boulder. Maybe we should put that to good use. And we can do that now, today."

He paused, gauging her reactions. "But first we should lay low around here. Let's fade into the woodwork for a while. If anyone wonders what happened to us, it would be best if they simply can't find out."

The arguments made sense. She hated to admit it, but they did. Deflated, she shrugged. As usual, he was on the money.

"You are probably right, Dale. I didn't think about how we would go find the circus camps. And you called it about their security men. They talk, and I'm sure that circus guards are cut from the same cloth as railroad dicks. Bullies. Maybe the circus is a project for another time."

She paused, thinking. "And you have a good point about working with people we know around here now. Before I thought of the circus, I was thinking too that we need to lay low for a while. And while we do that, we need to find or create new opportunities."

He nodded. "If we are quick about it we can still tap our UP expense account. We should empty it out." His face brightened.

"Tell you what, let's ask them to wire more money. The worst they can do is say no, and if they put some in we're better off."

He stopped to enjoy the view out over the prairies, drinking it in, then went on. "But we need to get going on that. I'll wire them as soon as I can when we get to town. We need funds until we can find some other source."

Ella too stopped. She made a comment apropos of nothing. "The prairie out there looks like the shore."

Dale was deep in thought and barely heard her. "And like I said, we ought to move fast, in case it does get cut off. Then we hang around here, or in Denver, or one of the mountain towns, and see what develops."

"Yes, alright, you are on to something. So you will handle getting money into the expense account, right? Let me know if you want me to do something."

She perked up, another idea coming to her. "Hey, you mentioned mountain towns! We could go see what is happening in one of the mining towns. Maybe Leadville. Or Cripple Creek. Lots of gold mines and lots of gold. That means a ton of money floating around. And lots of workers who need help. And animals. I'll bet things are wide open in those towns."

She didn't remember, or maybe she never knew, that Leadville was a silver mining town. Silver mining was essentially over, done. Leadville, Creede, Aspen and other silver towns were now declining. Silver had lost its price support from Congress ten or so years back and the industry never recovered. Gold was still in demand. She wouldn't really have cared even if Dale had explained all that to her. Ella Queue was off on another toot.

"There must be some way to help out the miners, and make some money. We need to put a stick in the eye of those big mine owners." She thought, but didn't say, *And the animals in the mines need someone to care....*

Dale thoughtfully nodded. "Maybe we should at least consider mining towns. They offer lots of opportunities. For that matter, you know there are other mining districts to be discovered or developed. Maybe there are miners who need a grubstake—we'll have money...."

Now he was on a toot of his own. "The real action, the real money, is at the towns not the mines. The stores in them supply everything to the miners, from food and liquor and women to shovels and dynamite. Lots of money goes through those places, lots of it. People and supplies come in, ore goes out."

He scuffed at a rock in the road, kicking it to the side. "Like you say, no reason we can't get our share of some of that money floating around. For that matter, there are many kinds of mining: coal, silver, copper, shoot, maybe even gems, garnets and diamonds!" He grinned at that last thought. It was absurd. Wasn't it? *What the heck*, he thought. *You never know. Look how that man Rhodes cornered the diamond market in Africa. Now he is richer than Croesus. Even richer than Harriman! You just never know about new opportunities....*

Ella was thinking along similar lines. A wolfish smile lit her up. "And there's high grading."

"High grading? What's high grading?"

"You really don't know? I'm surprised, you of all people! High grading is when a miner secretly takes ore out of the mine in his lunch bucket or tool box. After all, it is his, isn't it? He dug it out, not the mine owner. So the miner brings out a pocketful of rich ore. He quietly takes it to an assayer who buys it for a discount. The miner makes money, the assayer makes money, and the owner gets shorted. Isn't that just the thing!"

Dale saw the possibilities. "The question is, how can we get in on that action? That could be a good plan for us. Do you know anything about assaying Ella? Do we know someone who does? We'd be newcomers. We would need to play it safe. You know, get ourselves established, have an assayer to work with, get some assaying knowledge."

She grinned at the thought. Ella loved to see the little guy do good and the big guy get the shaft. "Maybe we can make good, honest money at one of these camps. Let's go and see!" The more she talked, the more she liked it. Gold dust was swirling in her head. This would be better than visiting any circus camp!

She paused, coming back to earth. Reluctantly she agreed. "You're always right Dale. We don't know enough to go to a mine town. Alright, for now, we play it safe. Let's go stay a few more nights at our hotel in Boulder," she said. "But from there, we'd better have a plan. Maybe we can stretch things out, maybe not. Let's be ready to move on, somewhere somehow. For at least tonight, Mr. Harriman and the Union Pacific can put us up in grand style."

They grinned and walked a little faster.

Dale's thoughts turned to a serious appraisal of 'what next'. *We really had better steer clear of any railroad for now. Except for some of the people we met, and we need to keep contact with the ones who could prove useful. Actually, I like Ella's idea of mining—lots of money changing hands, men willing to spend it, probably not a lot of cops. There won't be a bunch of yard dicks harassing us like along the railroads. And Ella, maybe Ella will start dressing as a woman. I'm tired of her canvas trousers and wool shirts, and I bet she is too. Matter of fact, I'll suggest that. A change of costume will help us blend in.*

V

JOSEPHUS EGGERS WAS RESTLESS. HE HAD NO REASON TO BE. Joe—no one but his mother called him Josephus—liked his job, his work. He couldn't complain. It had treated him well, providing freedom and a good living. All in all, life had treated him better than he had a right to expect, and he was grateful.

Maybe his vague discontent was because he felt the years mounting. He started life near the bottom rung of the ladder. Granted he was mid-way up the ladder of success, but he wanted to reach the top rung. The universal deep blackness somewhere ahead caused him to take stock. How many more chances would he have to prove himself? To show that the kid from a shack below the Canal made something of his life?

For years his job had given almost complete independence. Not long back he had been given a new territory loosely defined as 'the west'. Priority setting and new projects were pretty much up to him. He worked when and where he saw fit. Expenses were covered by an ample account kept full of dollars by some clerk in New York City. What did he do? The job was to make things better for the Union Pacific and worse for any and all who stood in the way. Objects of his attention were other railroads, landowners, labor groups, suppliers and the like.

His relationship with his boss was ideal. They seldom communicated. It was a good setup: Joe got things done and the boss stayed out of his way. It had been years since Joe had seen him. A New Yorker, the man was far from Colorado, in mindset and in miles. Joe was happy to be accountable to such a remote boss. There was one man higher up the line that he always kept in mind, Mr. Edward Henry Harriman. He was the big boss, the owner, the hurler of lightning bolts. Harriman could make or break a man with a nod, and he had been known to do so.

All in all, thought Joe, it wasn't a bad job. In fact it was a good one. He was glad to have it. And yet....The west was full of opportunities. There were many, he came to see, that were closed to him as a representative of the Union Pacific. Many people out here did not care for the UP. They were reluctant to do business with or accept investment from an employee of that railroad.

He liked the Rocky Mountain area, the West. The unlimited prospects called. At first he paid scant attention. The more they called the more he listened. He couldn't shake the vague but growing desire for change that dogged him.

Eggers thought back to his childhood. He hailed from upstate New York, near the Erie Canal. Like most, he was born broke. First job was pulling on the reins of a mule which was towing a barge along the canal. He was excited to be a 'canal man'. But the allure of looking at a mule's hindquarters wore off quick. The thought of a lifetime of that drove him to seek better. Talking to everyone he could, he kept eyes wide for a job, any job off of the canal. As soon as he could, he left.

The young man became a gofer at a railyard. It was little better than smelling mule droppings. But he studied and learned and anticipated and gradually found himself better off. Joe loved this leading edge of technology: the steam engine and the railroad system. Ever open to a better offer, finding one didn't take him long.

He knew right away that his life wasn't going to be spent oiling wheels or rebuilding boilers or even driving a train. The future for him was people. His forte was meeting, assessing, using, and doing deals with people. Joe found he liked and was good at a variety of tasks and duties. He could close sales, oversee development, troubleshoot, put together land deals, make 'confidential' arrangements with payment above or under the table, you name it. Figuring out the right people to work with and delivering for them was the ticket. That was the way to money and influence.

One thing led to another. And, now, here he was, a man defining his job and his hours for a powerful national company. The money was good and he didn't have to account closely for his time or whereabouts. It was almost ideal. Base of operations for him wasn't grimy Cleveland or congested New York City. Boulder Colorado was his home. But there was so much more one could do, so many ways to grow and improve. And make more money.

His good job be damned! Other ways to get along and grow were coming clear in his head. Some real possibilities were starting to come clear. Well they should: he had been kicking around ideas and plans for quite a while. Poking and prodding, all the day he considered options and locations.

Now things were starting to make sense. He found a practical, workable means to make the transition to independence. The way was cleared to move away from his job at the Union Pacific. And he could do it at the time and place of his choosing.

Eggers was ready. The plan was to leave the UP and go to one of the new Colorado railroads. This time he wouldn't be an employee. Being an investor and advisor was the intent. Even as a kid walking behind a smelly mule's tail alongside the Erie Canal, Joe had dreamed. He fantasized about being part of an organization like the Denver Northwestern & Pacific.

On the street and the switching yards, this railroad was called the Moffat Road. It was being built even now, from Denver through the Rockies. Their plan was to run standard gauge tracks from Denver through to Salt Lake City. No spindly, inexpensive narrow gauge road for them. They would lay tracks at four feet, eight and half inches apart, not the thirty six inch spread of the narrow gauge. The road's chief owner and sponsor, and the road's namesake, was David Moffat. The plan was efficiency driven. Moffat wanted to be able to interchange cars with eastern and western roads. A standard gauge road let him do it quickly and profitably.

Moffat was a wealthy Colorado businessman and Denver civic leader. A part of the Denver business scene since the 1860s, his life embodied success and achievement. He treated his people well, had a good reputation, and had amassed a pile of money.

The coast was clear for Joe: He could leave the UP on good terms, and with a parting success. It was important look good to the people in New York, to leave on amicable terms. If things didn't work out in Denver he wanted to have that goodwill to fall back on.

He wanted to help Moffat's new railroad. It didn't really matter to Joe that New York had been and was even now paying him to impede the progress of that road. Business was business. He was ready to change sides. The important thing was his own wellbeing. If he played it right, making strides in his personal fortune and social standing would follow, sure as bulls chase cows.

The last few weeks at the UP had been, well, interesting. He had managed to thread a tricky and ambiguous needle, to fuzz things up. By all appearances he was working diligently to stop or slow Moffat as he was paid to do.

Appearances are just that, not realities. The opposite is what he did. He managed to steer two of his colleagues' efforts aside without seeming to do so. And he did it while leading them to believe he was in their corner. That unlikely couple was Dale Smertz and Ella Queue. They had genuinely tried—rather ineffectively, he thought—to stop or slow the Moffat Road through western Colorado. Between their lack of finesse, his behind the scenes dealings, and circumstance, their work had come to naught.

Joe made sure that he would be the hero to New York. It looked like he almost overcame the odds and they looked the buffoons. Dale and Ella got no credit, even some blame, from New York. It was the best of both worlds.

So now, Joe could part ways with the dear old Union Pacific Railroad. And it would be done positively and agreeably. No bridges burnt, no hard feelings. And things got even better. He was quite pleased and proud of the way he had smoothed his own way in Denver. Joe had actually made some friendly contacts in the region. Granted, they were merely business associates, not true friends. Still, they could prove useful and they were not hostile.

Some of them were well placed in the new railroad, Moffat's Denver Northwestern and Pacific. Chief among them was Horace Sumner, the Moffat road's head engineer. And further down in the organization, but every bit as valuable, he knew and had done some work with Cam Braun and Mik Mas. Their jobs weren't high in the formal order of things. Joe had been quick to see that they knew people and spent time at headquarters. They had knowledge and influence.

Such dreams and goals were always at the back of Joe's mind. Today he had taken steps to make them real. He had spent his day in Denver hanging around Sumner's office in downtown. It was the Moffat Road's headquarters and its nerve center. That might sound kind of snooty, but it was true. The office was connected to all the construction camps and stations by telephone. Imagine, Mr. Moffat paid to have telephone lines strung and maintained! Every one of the twenty or so locations was connected to headquarters in the business district. Modern communications were wondrous. With a phone handy, most any problem could be handled.

The plan for Joe's day had been simple, actually more a hope than anything. He wanted to get a glimpse of Mr. Moffat, maybe make his acquaintance. Naturally, David Moffat was wary and skeptical of new 'friendly' faces. The man was not only a railroad entrepreneur. He was also a bank president, mine owner, and investor. He owned or controlled such important things as water delivery and the Denver tramway system. Such a man's time and person were safeguarded. Joe figured, make the contact first, then shove his foot in the door later.

No luck today, no sightings or talking to anyone of interest. All Eggers saw was routine comings and goings of clerks and messengers. Nothing out of the ordinary seemed to be happening. Patience was hard but necessary.

It was quitting time anyway. He decided to head back to Boulder. His suite there was in a hotel in downtown, near the station. The space was provided by his New York expense account. Joe knew that was on borrowed time. For all intents and purposes he had already quit the job. His heart wasn't in it. But he continued to accept the paycheck. And he continued to use and enjoy the advantages and allowances that went with it. Pretty soon he would have to formally resign. Then the benefits, the prestige, and the support of the country's largest railroad would be cut off.

That would be a big change for him. He was used to being able to wire New York if he needed information or money. It was so easy. Working on his own was a skill he knew he'd have to relearn. So tonight, he intended to take full advantage of the UP's hospitality. Thoughts of that kept him occupied as he walked into Denver's Union Station and got in the ticket line.

"One round trip to Boulder." The tone of voice was peremptory, almost rude. Joe almost felt bad for a moment. The sales clerk behind the ticket window hadn't done or said anything out of line. No matter. The man was apparently used to such treatment. He responded mechanically.

"Dining car or coach?" He took payment, handed out the ticket, and was on to the next buyer before Joe was two steps away.

The station's usual hubbub was for many a tonic, soothing and energizing. Passengers came and went. Train whistles blew. Conductors and porters called and talked. As ever, an aura of coal smoke and cinders floated in the high ceilinged room.

Usually this orchestra of travelers and machines renewed and refreshed Joe. He loved the sight and sound of trains.

And the people. Fun to speculate on where folks were going and why. For some reason this day the Union Station concert hall and its instruments didn't make a symphony. Today he heard a cacophony. The whole scene got on his nerves.

Sitting and waiting for the train was more of the same. He was glad that he managed to grab a seat near the door out to the tracks. Conversations that he couldn't shut out swirled around him. "Are you sure all of our bags got put on board?" "Do we have time to go eat a meal before our train leaves?" "...I've found that if I twist the reins just so, it..." "...better sit still young lady, and I don't want to hear..."

He relaxed on his hard seat and opened his mind. Daydreams of new and old acquaintances, some shifty but some reliable tumbled around. Semi formed thoughts and memories of business deals chased each other. Some were successful, others went sour.

Soon his train was announced. He awoke from his woolgathering and stood. With a step he joined the crowd. People went to where their train awaited or would soon arrive. Being an old hand he was able to stay at the front, ahead of all but the most assertive travelers. He was one of the first to reach his car and quickly climbed the steps, surveyed the car, and took a forward facing seat. And he made sure it was near the exit.

Getting a forward facing seat was more than nice, it was essential. Others had learned it was unpleasant for them if he had to ride facing backward. It was ironic, Joe being a railroad man and all. On short trips his stomach didn't get upset enough to revolt, just queasy. On longer trips he had gotten quite sick if he had to face backward. More than one unfortunate fellow traveler could testify to that.

As he waited for departure, Joe tried to recapture the elation he felt earlier. His thoughts slowed. They started to flow gently, positively. Even before the conductor cried 'All Aboard', before the car lurched and the train moved, he was feeling better. His thoughts turned upbeat. *I positioned myself pretty well, if I do say so myself. I will make a neat exit from the UP. I have friends in Denver. If I play the cards right, I can invest in the Moffat operation. Or maybe I ought to look around. Nothing says I have to stay in railroading. Maybe I should at least think about doing something else.*

He looked out the window. Not only the train but ideas and brainstorms were starting to roll now. *Mercantile stores and land development are good ways to make money too. Look at who made real money in the Pikes Peak gold rush—the people who sold to the prospectors and miners did better than most any man drilling, panning, or hauling ore. And land sellers did even better than them. Heck, town plats were being filed all over, and many lots were sold. Maybe some of the towns never grew but the developers' bank accounts sure did. But....Mining is the biggest thing here. Gold, silver, coal, what other riches are hidden under Colorado's ground?*

On impulse he had picked up a newspaper at the station. The Rocky was the oldest and best newspaper in the region. He stopped musing on riches and opened it. News of labor troubles was prominent. Strikes, tent cities, pitched battles, scabs, management and labor skirmishing and maneuvering. And wars: American boys in uniform were fighting in the Philippines and Cuba. The Boers and British were going at it in Africa. German and French ambassadors were trading bristly messages over some place called Tunisia. Joe wondered what was worth fighting over in Tunisia. On the other side of the globe, in Asia, the Russians and Japanese were doing their best to kill each other. A couple of banana republics were fighting over a border down south. *Nothing new under the sun*, he thought.

Events closer to home were more interesting. There was an article about two Ohioans who had built a flying machine. They had actually put together a working machine of metal, fabric, and wood. It was powered by one of those new 'internal combustion engines'. Joe admired their ingenuity and their courage. One of the men had taken it up into the air, flown under control, and landed it back on the ground in one piece.

That caught his attention, and his thoughts leaped. *A flying machine! That is right out of Jules Verne! What's next? Going to the moon?* His moneymaking antenna quivered. *Too bad they are in Ohio, so far away*, he mused. *That aeroplane will be a money maker for someone, you wait and see! I'll bet right now a dozen or more men are copying their design, trying to make it better and sellable! And look at this, a world's fair planned next year in Saint Louis. Celebrating the centennial of the Louisiana Purchase. That deal was a stroke of genius for Jefferson. It sure made America. I'd like to go and see that show. Maybe Mister Moffat would like to have an exhibit. I could sure make a name for myself if I can convince him to do that.*

Joe idly scanned the rest of the paper. There were dozens of reports from all over, most of them one or two sentences and of little significance. A typical one, from 'your correspondent in Saguache': 'Rancher Jonas Burley reports his calving season went well with almost no die-offs, and he has high hopes for a good hay season.' These, he scanned very quickly. He wasn't paying close attention to them.

Buried on page nine was a small article. Being a bit larger than most, it caught his eye. When he saw that the lead was 'Copper' he almost skipped it. The story was of some man in southern Illinois. Apparently he salted an area with showy copper bits. Just chunks of native copper and high grade copper ore. Then he had boomed it, talked up the field, the industry, the coming need for copper. That had attracted a fair number of investors. Last seen, he was hurrying out of town 'to tend to his sick mother'. Needless to say, he took the investors' money and left the ore samples. The article gave a description and asked that the local Sheriff be notified if the guy turned up.

Joe read and reread it, then looked in the distance, thinking. *Hmmm. I guess there are several ways to mine. There is the mining of ore from the earth, and then there is mining of money from investors. More power to the guy!* The next article was smaller. It was about diamonds, some guy who was convinced there were diamonds in northern Colorado. He wasn't looking for backing, at least not yet. Apparently he simply wanted to spout his knowledge. *Diamonds? What? This is gold and silver country, Colorado. What's with all the news about other minerals?*

He again looked up and off into the distance. Something clicked. Maybe there was an opportunity here.

VI

DALE AND ELLA HIKED QUITE A WAYS, ALMOST TO ELDORADO Springs. The conversation over immediate plans continued. One thing was, getting to Boulder quick was important. The pair walked past the Pruden place, unaware that Cam and Mik both roomed there. They hoped to hitch a ride along the road from town east towards Marshall and Boulder. Before long someone driving a wagon headed their way.

Dale waved; the team slowed then stopped.

"We're trying to get to Boulder. Any chance you're headed there?"

"Yup. I work for Klinky. He runs the stables in town." The man nodded over his shoulder, indicating Eldorado Springs. "You're in luck. Today I have room for two passengers. It'll cost you twenty five cents each."

Ella said sharply, "Two bits? Way too much. A nickel."

Klinky's man looked her over, unsure if the speaker was in fact a she. The person had a woman's voice and face but dressed like a man who carelessly threw on whatever was in the closet. Live and let live, he thought.

"Make it a dime each and you have a ride."

He held out his hand and Dale reluctantly dropped the coins there, not saying a word.

"Hop on. Usually I do not have room. Today I do since I have to go into town—Boulder—to bring back horseshoes and other smithing supplies. One of you can sit on the seat next to me, the other can ride in back. I need to go straight to the ironworks but can drop you somewhere along the way."

Ella inspected the horses, expecting to find them uncombed, too thin, or poorly shod. She actually walked around the team. Dale took the opportunity to climb onto the seat next to Klinky's man. As the wagon was well maintained and shipshape, she nodded to herself in unexpected pleasure. The teamster noticed and also took in her approving glance at him.

Then she climbed in to the back of the wagon. It was no trouble when like now she wore canvas trousers and a man's shirt. Good thing she wasn't trying to clamber on wearing skirts! Of course, she reminded herself, if she was in skirts she would have the seat in front, no question. Dale's eye was on her as she sat and got comfortable.

Almost as if it hurt to say it, Ella complimented the driver. She spoke just loud enough for him to hear.

"It is nice to ride with a caring owner. The team of horses looks good."

Dale was quietly relieved that she approved. Occasionally, even when begging a ride, she saw a rib, or a sore foot, or some other problem with the animal. She was not shy about bringing it to the driver's attention. No matter that it wasn't really her business and she had no right to pass judgment. Her duty, she believed, was to right injuries or misdeeds done to an animal, any animal. Of course this was a bottomless stack of wrongs. Sometimes for her trouble, they got paid in kind. More than once they had been kicked off the wagon and had to walk wherever they wanted to go. To Dale's relief, that wasn't going to happen. At least not today.

He himself was not heartless or unmindful of animal cruelty. It was just that he preferred picking his battles. Only under threat to his own well-being would he try to police others' acts. He believed and lived, 'go along and get along'. Dale's focus was trying to get and stay ahead, and to prove wrong those who considered him a loser.

Right now he was just glad to be riding not walking. It had been an exhausting day. An early start with stealthy a walk up the hill only to be met by armed railroad dicks wasn't exactly relaxing. Insult to injury, they pushed and poked and ran him off their property. But as that happened it came out that what they feared most hadn't happened. Lows and highs, highs and lows, the story of life....

The sounds and rhythmic jostling put him at ease. From childhood he enjoyed the creaking of a moving wagon and the clip clop of the horses. He could have fallen asleep, he was so relaxed. His mind flowed and he looked things over, especially the last week or so.

He was happy to be free of the Moffat project. Honestly he couldn't see what harm Moffat's business did to the Union Pacific or Mr. Harriman. Who cared about another railroad? Colorado was a huge state and there was room for many. Dale wondered, if the Union Pacific cares so much, why didn't it do more in that part of the country? It made no sense. For now, he was glad to be out of that picture. He and Ella were done. Let someone else try.

Pondering that, Dale wasn't so sure stopping them would be easy. The Moffat operation had a lot of momentum. Crews were scraping grade, laying track and surveying the line of work at a good clip. The company had grade going up to the foot of the Main Range, maybe even a bit farther. If crews hadn't yet started laying rail, they soon would. Yes, before long the Moffat's men would put iron up and over the Great Divide. And the plan was to punch a tunnel through the mountain at the same time. The man and his project had lots going right.

Considering options, Dale hoped to find a job like he had with the Union Pacific. Likely it wouldn't be the exact same thing. Maybe he could do something for another railroad, or a mining company, or a townsite developer, or some other outfit. Frankly, he liked the independence his job gave him. And he loved being able to swashbuckle among the hayseeds. That is how he thought of going out to the country to buy up land or options to prevent a railroad. Maybe he could do the same to keep a mine or a townsite or a factory from coming through to completion.

It was fun to provide information to your boss on the competitors. It was even more fun to make trouble for those trying to take your business and customers. Why try to build something, be productive? It was much easier and loads more fun to try to stop others from doing so! Not that Dale and Ella would care, but there was a young Texan about to be elected to Congress, Sam Rayburn. He would spend a career there, ending up as Speaker of the House. Rayburn made many good quotes, one of the best being: 'Any jackass can kick a building down, but it takes a carpenter to build one.' Dale and his sidekick preferred the jackass to carpentry.

Keeping things totally legal seemed a waste of time and effort to Dale. Even so, he was careful not to be flagrant. Breaking big laws, those involving prison time, was to be avoided. Even the small ones he broke with discretion. He never got involved in beatings nor had any part of hurting or injuring an animal. Company assets or a person's property, now that was a different game. Articles, mere things, were fair game. Stretching the truth, claiming expenses when none were incurred, trespassing, vandalism, theft and so forth, were all perfectly acceptable. One just had to be careful.

No matter how he sliced it, Dale had had enough of the railroad business. He nourished a hope, possibly in vain, to keep some kind of job with the UP. After all, Mr. Harriman owned mines, hotels, and other businesses as well. But if it didn't work out, if he had to leave, well, he had some ideas.

Right now, I just want to prop my feet up and relax. Can't get to the hotel soon enough for me. Maybe me and EQ can celebrate. Images of pleasant intimacies ran through his mind. He stifled them, returning to business. *The thing is, where to next? I want to have some plans made. Don't want to just float and wait for things to happen....*

All these thoughts whirled fast, coursing through his head before he had even gotten settled in the wagon he had just climbed onto. He sat on the front seat and faced towards Boulder. As he squirmed to be comfortable, he acknowledged his companion and partner.

Agreeing with her quiet assessment, he softly said, "Sure, Ella. This team looks like it'll take us into town just fine."

He smiled, hoping he sounded sincere and more concerned than he felt. He wanted her in a good mood. *Who knows*, he thought. *Maybe her good mood will last. And maybe tonight we can enjoy a fine evening and night.*

He continued, ignoring the wagon driver. "You know, EQ, maybe we ought to see what that Joe Eggers character is up to." Dale had the habit of calling his partner 'EQ' rather than Ella when he was trying to sell an idea. He wasn't aware of the habit. She was. When he started a conversation with 'EQ', she went on alert.

Dale knew that Ella was wary of Joe. He himself sort of liked and almost trusted the guy. He would have been surprised and hurt to learn that the feeling was not mutual.

"Why see him, Dale? What good can come from it?" She watched the scenery slowly go by for a moment, thinking.

"I have to admit that he hasn't done us wrong. At least so far. But I don't think he has done us any favors either." Ella couldn't decide if he was friend, foe, or someone to be ignored. The jury was still out: she didn't dislike him but had no warm feelings either.

"I just don't know, Dale. If anything, we should keep our distance. Maybe keep an eye on him, stay in distant touch. But I don't want to get too close, at least right now. I'm still thinking he didn't do all he could for us."

Truth be told, Joe Eggers was not particularly reliable, even to his 'friends'. The man was not a friend to them. Nor was he an enemy. He was out for one person only, and that was Joe Eggers. To him people were just pawns. They were to be moved around as chess pieces. How they got moved and used depended on Joe Eggers' aims, needs and whims at the moment.

The more Ella thought about it, the clearer it became. She continued. "Dale, that Joe Eggers is a user. He is just out for himself. He would use us in a second. I think he probably is or has, and we just haven't discovered it yet."

"Well, I don't think so." Dale paused, turning the idea around and over, considering. "I can't see that he has played us. But if he has, let's turn the tables. We can find out what he is up to. If we can use him to make money or gain some advantage, well, we do it."

He glanced at her. "Rather than just let him be, let's find out. Isn't it better to know what he is up to anyway? That way we can use that knowledge for us?"

"I'm not so sure. Like we discussed, we should just disappear for a while. Certainly, we ought to stay away from any of our recent contacts. At least for now. Let's do that for at least a few days. See what happens, let things blow over." She paused. "Heck, we used to go to the field and not talk to anyone in New York for over a week and they were alright with that. So now we can go silent for a while, six or eight days. Lay low and watch, see what is going on. And then we can report to New York like nothing new is happening."

Joe frowned but Ella continued. "We're pretty sure no one is reading our mail. There is no reason we can't stay on. We can continue to work for them, or appear to continue to. At least that keeps us on the expense account and maybe we can find some things out. We can always leave at any time if the whole scene blows up."

Dale was taken aback by her adamant refusal to look up Joe Eggers. Usually she went with his lead on such matters. He had to agree that it made sense to go with her. It couldn't hurt to wait a few days. Plus, she liked it when he agreed. Privately, he intended to explore other opportunities as well. With her or without her.

"If you really think that is the way to go, Ella, alright. But I think we should keep our eyes open too."

Klinky's man half listened to this give and take. The horses knew where to go and didn't need to be steered. They had walked from the stable into Boulder and back many times. For the driver, it was a boring ride. A conversation, even a droning one he wasn't part of about a man he didn't know was alright. At least it helped pass the time. Soon Boulder loomed on the horizon.

"I need to go to Twelfth and Pearl. Where do you want me to stop and let you off?"

"We're near there and can walk. Thanks."

Even as Dale agreed with Ella, he was thinking of ways to branch out. *And I will find Joe Eggers and follow him like a hound dog. He has money and knows how to make money. Ella may be part of that or not. Let's hope she is, but if not, well, we'll just have to see.*

VII

Lurching, the train left Denver on time. After clearing the crowded railyard the engineer opened the throttle and picked up speed. The sights and sounds of train travel melded and formed a cocoon for the passengers. Joe relaxed, unconsciously enjoying the car's motion, rocking and clacking over the rails.

Several sets of tracks were laid to the north and west. The engineer, conductor, and yard master made sure the right signals were given. Switches were turned, shunting the train along the right route. As usual, each was adjusted without flaw. The engineer and his engine went onto the tracks running through the coal town of Marshall then to Boulder and points beyond.

Somewhere Joe had learned to estimate speed while riding. After a few moment's watching and figuring, he guessed their speed at twenty two to twenty eight miles per hour. *There is something soothing about the motion of the engine and the cars,* he thought.

He knew for a fact that he was sitting in a railcar, moving at a good speed. But as he lazily watched, it felt for all the world that he was the stationary one. The countryside could have been most anywhere. Farms, irrigation ditches, small towns, mines, and teams of draft animals pulling wagons came and went, each in its turn. These structures and features appeared on the horizon, small and hard to discern. The image or item grew, sometimes moving or showing activity as details became clear. With a silent whoosh each thing appeared to sweep quickly by Joe sitting still in the train. Then its size gradually changed, this time in reverse. The feature got progressively got smaller until it disappeared. Joe enjoyed the mirage and was able to unwind. He actually dozed a little.

It was not a deep sleep. Details of past business deals came and went. The background of trains sounds and passengers talking melded seamlessly into the dreams. Sometimes the subconscious musings made sense and sometimes they didn't. His partly awake mind also churned over ideas and schemes of opportunities and possibilities. All in all it was a pleasant nap. The train stopped in Boulder. He opened his eyes refreshed and excited for the future. As he headed for his rooms he considered plans for the evening and what to do in the coming days.

On entering the hotel lobby he paused and looked around. Joe never forgot that he was born poor. He momentarily and gratefully savored the nice furnishings, the hubbub of nicely dressed travelers, and the staff ready to serve his every need. The prospect of his expense account going away nattered and worried him slightly. Then he heard his name being called. The desk clerk was holding out an envelope.

"Mr. Eggers, Mr. Eggers! I have a letter for you. It came special delivery." The clerk behind the desk dramatically waved an envelope as Joe approached.

"Thanks," as he glanced at it. No return address on it, and that kind of surprised him. He expected it was from headquarters in New York. The letter went into his inside coat pocket; he'd read it when he got to the room. He smiled and asked, "Are there any other messages? Any callers?"

"Yes, in fact you had a visitor. A tall gangly man, said he knows you.... Ah, please excuse me for a moment." The clerk took a minute or two. Service was important. He felt he had to answer the questions of an imperious, gray haired woman whose pinched face made her look the maiden aunt. Joe knew the type, a person who couldn't or wouldn't wait. The clerk clearly knew how to handle impatient customers. He put her at ease and off she went. She glanced at Joe as if to say 'Of course I am important enough to step in front of you'. Joe couldn't help but notice her smirk. Knowing she wanted a reaction, he didn't give one.

Seeing that wordless mini drama, the clerk smiled conspiratorially. "A man was looking for you. A tall rangy chap. Wouldn't give me his name. In fact he just left. I'm surprised you didn't bump into each other at the door. I asked several times but he wouldn't state his business or leave a calling card. Said he'd come back. Like I said, tall and gangly. He seemed intense and in a hurry. Talked and acted like an intelligent fellow."

Nodding, Joe acknowledged. "Alright. Let me know if he comes by again please. I'll be in my room for a while. If I go out I'll let you know."

Walking to his rooms, he thought hard. *Tall and gangly? I wonder if it is that Dale Smertz fellow. Not good, if he's coming around. He was waving a gun when I last saw him. I really expected that he and his 'partner' would be long gone by now. They should be on the way to another state or country. Or to jail. I hope it isn't Smertz. I was starting to get concerned when I last saw him.*

It looked as if I might have to use my cane on him. Let's hope he has calmed down. Maybe he wants to apologize? I doubt it, but maybe he has cooled off and is rational. Well, I'll have to keep my guard up if he is lurking around here.

He entered, closed the door and dropped his bag. Starting to take his coat off, he remembered the special delivery. The coat came off and he slid it onto a hanger. Before hanging it up he pulled out the letter. Curious, Joe looked it over front and back. He wasn't expecting news. Few people knew where he was or how to get hold of him, and he liked it that way.

What was in this envelope? In his experience good news didn't require mail. Welcome words usually came in person or via telegram. Special delivery mail was different. More often than not, it brought sad news or unwelcome demands. He took a deep breath and opened it up.

This letter didn't have bad news. Nor did it tell him a long lost uncle had left him a fortune. It did surprise him. And it brought new concerns. The largish handwriting was familiar and oddly warming.

Dearest Joe,

I hope this letter finds you well and prospering.

Why have you not written? I feel terrible that I haven't heard from you. I could have written sooner and I truly wanted to. But I just couldn't bring myself to sit down and do it. Joe, darling, we parted too abruptly. Even before you left, Joe, I missed you. And it hurt that we made no plans to see each other. I feel bad for not writing before this. I know, I think of this every day, that we have much in common, my dearest. You and I have been through much together. We have enjoyed many adventures and successes over more years than seem possible.

Surely there are more good times and opportunities in store for us. I don't want our life to die, to be cut short, to waste away. I can't let that happen without trying to see you again.

Joe, dear, I am coming west. If the trains run on time, I will be arrive there the same or the next day after you get this.

I can't wait to be with you again!

Charity

Mixed feelings boiled up. Joe was taken aback, apprehensive, and excited by this news.

Charity Hovus and Joe Eggers. Longtime friends, sometime business partners, occasional adversaries, on and off lovers. Images and memories rushed at him. He savored for a moment then stopped. He was awash in memories of languorous kisses and morning sunshine. That, she expected him to home in on. He knew that was her intent and fought it.

Thoughts raced and tumbled. *She is the last person I expected to hear from. I figured she had found someone there in the city. She was dead set on not coming west, determined to stay in New York. I wonder what she has been up to. What does she have up her sleeve? Something unpredictable, I'll bet. It will be good to see her. But it has been several years. Why now? If she wanted to stay with me or hear from me, why hasn't she been in touch? How did she find me? What is she up to, I wonder? It will be good to see her!*

The more he thought about it, his curiosity built. Yet he was wary. There were no coincidences in life, he was sure.

Why had she reappeared? What made her leave the lush rich easy life she no doubt led in New York City?

His mind drifted back. Their parting hadn't been bitter, but it wasn't with hugs and kisses either. Perhaps the way to describe things before he left New York was vinegary. They had talked unpleasantly before he left. She didn't want to leave the east coast for Denver. Nor did she want him to go.

"Oh Joe," she said, "Who cares about some silly new railroad. And nobody knows who Donald Moffley is. Why does it matter what he does?"

"He is David Moffat, not Donald Moffley, and I care. More to the point, Mr. Harriman cares. The boss wants to know what he is doing. And he wants me to look into making adjustments."

"Adjustments? What adjustments? To what?"

"Adjustments means I need to find ways to slow him down, to cause problems for his railroad. Or stop him. That is what is important here. Mr. Harriman does not want David Moffat to have an easy time of it. He wants me to go out there. And you could come with me. I wish you would."

Charity didn't miss a beat. "But you have a good job here. New York City is the best place on earth. Why would anyone want to go out there? Joe, you'll have to dodge buffaloes and risk flying arrows. Why, those poor people don't even have electricity yet!" Her limited knowledge and attitudes fit in well on the east coast.

She didn't want Joe to waste time in the western hinterlands, Mr. Harriman be damned. Trying to disrupt David Moffat's new railroad was of no more interest to her than flying to the moon. No, Charity said, she would not go with him. She simply saw no future, no reason, no advantage to be gained.

Charity Hovus was not even interested in learning about Colorado. She would stay in New York City. Her intent, as she told Joe in a huff, was to have her own life. If he was going to run off to the wild west, she would simply stay and be alone. At least until she could cultivate other contacts and opportunities. They both knew what that meant.

Those words, uttered emotionally, meant that Joe and Charity would no more be partners, friends, and lovers. Her parting words were definite. They stuck in his craw even now: "I want to stay in New York where I am comfortable. I love the culture and the excitement. I love the rich men and old established families in this city. Denver is just a cow town. I won't go there. I simply will not."

She stepped back, not offering a hug or even a handshake. "May you have the best of luck. Good bye, Joe Eggers."

Solo travel was new to Joe. At first he was lonely and missed Charity and New York. Unlike his former friend, he kept his eyes and mind open. It didn't take long. He found that he liked the blue skies, dry weather, and immense vistas.

And the people were genuine. He really liked that. Maybe they didn't have the history and the old money of the east. What they did have was an open friendliness, and most everyone was cordially ambitious. There was opportunity for everyone. People didn't stab you in the back and take your ideas. No need; they had their own. The prospects were literally unlimited.

Soon memories receded. Charity didn't come to mind often. When she did, his reaction wasn't 'I miss her', it was 'she missed out'. Before long she faded entirely from his day to day thoughts.

Dreamily, he pondered what his fine raven haired ex-companion was doing, inviting herself to come west....

A knock on the door brought him back to Boulder Colorado. His fond and not so fond memories of Charity paused. Maybe it was her! He hoped that she wanted the same reunion and welcome that he did. That made him feel shallow in a way but in a way it seemed fitting. Seize the moment and get the most from the other person, that's how they had operated when they were together.

He glanced around the room. It was clean, and his belongings were more or less organized and tidy. The bed was freshly made up. If it was her, he hoped they could be together soon....

A man's voice followed the last rap on the door.

"Mr. Eggers, Mr. Eggers. Are you there? I need to speak with you."

Joe stood still, trying to decide if he should answer or not. Who was it?

"It is Dale Smertz. Can we talk? Please."

Joe wondered, did he really just want to talk? Or did he intend to finish what he threatened last time they met?

The man paused, hoping for a response. "I know you are in there. I saw you come in and go up the stairs. Mister Eggers, I am sorry I lost my temper with you a few days ago. I lost control of myself. I am ashamed to say I was so angry that my mouth ran away. And it took me with it. I am not proud of what I said and did. I did not mean a word of it. Surely that sort of thing has happened to you?"

Joe still waited, trying to decide.

"I am here alone. I am unarmed. And there are some things it would be good for us to talk about. Or maybe I should say, things you would like to hear about. Please open up, Mr. Eggers. I am standing back from the door. If you want, crack the door and take a look. Please."

Joe wanted nothing to do with Smertz. The guy had been a patsy and was a loser. Joe didn't respect losers. And he was nothing but trouble. Last time Joe had seen him he acted almost insane. Angry and ranting, he was nearly violent. Still, he said he was alone. And he claimed to have something Joe would want to know.

Another rap. A voice, imploring and coaxing. "I know you are in there Eggers. I saw you come into the lobby and watched you go in to this room. Open up. If you want, I'll stand in the hall rather than come in while we talk. Once I start you won't want me to stay out where anyone can listen. I'm alone and just want to talk. If you don't like what I have to say you can go your way and I will go mine. No further contact and no hard feelings."

Dale actually had nothing earthshaking to say. He wanted to see what Joe was up to. Maybe the two of them could cut a deal. He would do or say whatever it took in order to get that done.

Joe pushed aside a sudden image of Charity and fixed a picture of Smertz in his mind. Striding over to the door, he picked up his cane, just in case.

VIII

As the weather warmed Moffat's crews worked apace. Summer months were prime for building. The 1904 season had been productive but the end was in sight.

"It has been a stemwinder of a summer for us." Cam squinted out over the rails after this observation.

Mik couldn't disagree. The iron was now up into the high country. Trains were running from Denver clear to the foot of the Main Range.

"It sure has been. Say, I'm not sure who had the idea for the snow cars. Whoever the genius, it was a big hit!" Someone had the brainstorm to pack a couple of open cars with snow from up on the mountain. They took the cars down and the snow was featured in Denver's Fourth of July parade. Snowballs flew in fun during that parade, and people were delighted.

"Yup. Reading about the road reaching the Main Range is one thing. Seeing snow and being hit by a snowball is another!

The conversation meandered and rambled.

Mik talked even though Cam only half listened. "...months ago. We—you, me and the crews—really have accomplished a lot. We've come a long way since Steu ran those two troublemakers off. Remember that? Not long after I got shaken up with the blast on Tunnel Four?"

Cam remembered his friend's confusion and odd behavior all too well.

"Yes, that I do recall. You seem to have settled down, Mik. It has been good to have you back!"

Mik went on, ignoring the questions and memories the scene brought up. "We haven't seen those two oddballs again, have we? The man and the woman who dressed as a man, always making problems and trouble. Maybe they finally went away."

He continued, enthusiastically recapping what every crew member and most Denver citizens knew. "After that little encounter, we got the stretch across Eldorado Mountain done. Then we turned the corner west and finished grade all the way up South Boulder Creek. And laid rail. That stretch wasn't nearly as difficult. It went faster and easier. So now it is late summer, and here we are at the foot of the main range!"

Even as Mik said these things, he was aware that everybody knew them. Still, he couldn't help but brag on everything they and the crews had accomplished. With reason, he and they were proud of their achievements. Other railroads had attempted to approach this part of the continental divide. None had gotten this far. Everyone expected this to be another road that 'almost got there'. No one thought David Moffat and his crews would get this far, even in five years. And they had done it in just over two years. The Moffat Road was on a roll!

Trains were regularly scheduled from Denver. They were running up and down the line, consistently if not profitably. Now, everyone knew, things were about to get even more difficult. The Road was about to go over a 'hill'. Some hill! The Continental Divide was more than a small rise. The rails would be topping out at well over eleven thousand feet above sea level. The standard gauge road being built would be among the highest through railroad routes in the world. It would certainly be the highest in North America.

A crewman signaled he needed to talk with Cam. He went over and they moved further away.

Mik stood with his back to the Main Range, the mountainous wall carrying the continental divide. He looked east down the beginning trickles of South Boulder Creek. Above and behind him it gathered water from small tributaries, tarns, beaver ponds, and ice fields. About where he stood, the valley opened up. The creek widened as it bubbled and coursed, chirping and foaming as it wended its way east.

Looking back, he considered the view up towards the crest of the continent. The continental divide ran pretty much north and south here. High as the ridge was, here the divide was lower than most any other place in Colorado. There were still snowbanks up there among the rocks. The scene could have been on a calendar. He enjoyed it for a few moments.

Before long there would be new snow. Despite the calendar winter would come soon. For that matter, snow could fall up here any month of the year. In July or August snow was just a flurry or a dusting. But by early fall it would be accumulating, count on it. The peaceful, sunlit scene before him was fleeting. In a few months it would be a windswept, savagely cold, deeply drifted slice of hell.

He looked again at South Boulder Creek as it ran down the center of the valley. Parallel to those chortling waters, up the valley proudly came a set of railroad tracks. They ran a steady four feet, eight and one half inches apart. This was the industry custom called standard gauge.

It was unusual to see standard gauge tracks high in the Colorado Rockies. Many trains in the Centennial State did not run on standard gauge. The norm was narrow gauge with the tracks set at thirty six inches apart. The use of this gauge gained traction, so to speak, early in Colorado, even before statehood in 1876. The reasons were several: narrow gauge was less expensive to build and operate than standard; it could take tighter turns and climb steeper grades. For these reasons, narrow gauge tracks ran all over the mountainous state. At first there were few standard gauge rail lines.

David Moffat was determined that the Denver Northwestern and Pacific Railway would be a standard gauge road. He wanted to offer passengers the improved stability and ride that a standard gauge road offered. And the businessman in him liked the greater carrying capacity of the engines. A standard gauge road could haul more tons of freight per pound of coal burnt. He liked that profitable ratio. Plus with standard gauge cars he could efficiently interchange cars. Freight wouldn't have to be unloaded from narrow gauge to be reloaded on another railroad company's standard gauge car running to other markets.

The steel rails coming up the valley ran true. It was almost as if they were eager to carry people and freight west. The stream they ran along meandered a bit but the rails did not. Their objective since leaving Denver was the Main Range of the Rockies and they pointed straight at it. Fresh from the mill, the rail's tops were shiny from contact with locomotive wheels. Their sides still glinted because they were too new to have grown a layer of rust.

Everything else was new too. The grade the rails laid on still showed where it had been cut through the land. Visible on down the valley, it was a fifty to seventy five foot wide scar that ran for miles. At this altitude most of the cuts into the hillside were really little but raw rock. Here and there were patches of poor bare soil. New grass or bushes slowly sent out roots. Due to the short growing season at this altitude, it would take several seasons for the plants to take hold and cover the scrapings and diggings.

With beauty enough for Thoreau, nature sat in her sun filled, evergreen clad majesty. There were many other valleys at the foot of the continental divide with peaks towering all around. Through them many a trout filled stream rushed down the slopes, carrying waters to distant seas. Yet the view here was unique. Every man and woman on the crews and in the camps reveled in that fact. In all the world, not even a handful of mountainous Edens had an intrusion like this.

The steel road, those ties and rails laid on a flat base, made a statement. To nature and the wilderness it proclaimed, 'Make way for people and commerce. We mean no harm but will have our way.' Those tracks, that road, were due to the vision and will of one man, David Moffat. Of course he didn't swing a hammer or haul rail himself but without him it would never have been built. All could agree, it was a fine engineering and construction achievement. To have usable rails pierce the mountains and to come this far was a feat to be admired and praised.

Mik gazed out at the craggy scene, thoughts flying. A train could come here from Denver. For that matter, a train could come from New Orleans, or San Francisco, or New York. In one swoop it could arrive at the foot of the Main

Range. It wouldn't have to change rolling stock or disgorge passengers for a ferry or change cars for different trackage.

Such rail service would open up the country. It would enable settlement and help people to provide for themselves. And, soon the train would go further. Ultimately a fine set of tracks would go over or through the mountains to the headwaters of the Colorado River and all the country beyond!

Cam returned, satisfied that his crews knew what they needed to do today.

"Well Cam," Mik paused to again congratulate himself and others. "We sure made things move fast, punching tunnels and laying rails. We have, what thirty or so tunnels between Denver and here? And it has only taken about two years to do it! I laugh at the naysayers. Those who thought we would never even get tracks out of Denver, much less way up here are eating crow." He had to stop and look around, again, at the magnificent scene.

"And now the fun starts! We're poised to put a full-fledged railroad over to the headwaters of the mighty Grand River. Or the Colorado River. Which is it? I can't keep the name straight."

Mik wasn't confused or making fun. He was simply not current on the latest developments. There was, or maybe would soon be introduced, a Bill in the Colorado State Legislature. It would propose to rename a stretch of river. The running waters that ran from near Grand Lake in the central Rockies to the confluence with the Green River in east central Utah were called The Grand River. The waters of those two rivers, the Green and the Grand, then formed the Colorado River which ran on through the Grand Canyon to the mighty Pacific. Anyway, there was talk about changing the name of the Grand River stretch, to call it too the Colorado River. The State of Colorado wanted to claim the headwaters of the main river in the southwest United States. Long story short, this political gamesmanship was the reason Mik was not sure of the name to be found on a map.

He finished the thought, redundantly. "Anyway, we've all done good work on this here railroad!"

"Yes," nodded Cam. "We had a tough spot here and there but we have pushed things pretty well and fast, I agree." He looked soberly at his friend. "And you had a tough spot too, Mik. You darn near bought the farm back when the dynamite went early in Tunnel Four. I still see some effects of that blast in you." He grinned. "Heck, it took me weeks to retrain you. Sometimes I swear you didn't remember anything about railroads or life here in Colorado. Occasionally it seems like you still don't."

"Sometimes it seems like that to me too, thought Mik. "Well, Cam all in all I am doing alright. Can't really complain. " This wasn't a subject he wanted to delve into, but he couldn't think of a way to change it.

They watched workers busily extending the finished road. From where they stood they could see crews finishing grade up the valley. Behind them crews spread ballast, gravel to level the grade and provide drainage. Following closely were crews seating ties. The rail laying machine was not far behind.

Back in the late 1860's things were different. At that time the Union Pacific and Central Pacific were racing across the continent laying track towards each other. They started thousands of miles apart. The UP came from Omaha building west and the CP from Sacramento heading east. They worked feverishly making road, each wanting the bragging rights of having laid the most miles to get to where they met. That meeting took place west of Salt Lake City in 1869. At that time the job of laying track was brute human labor and not much else. Ten or twelve man crews hauled each twenty foot rail up by hand and set it. Another crew spiked it in while yet a third crew approached with another rail.

Now the process was mechanized. Cam and Mik watched the track laying machinery and the supporting crews at work. When every part functioned as designed and intended, it was a smooth and precise if noisy process. On this day things moved along well and track was methodically coming their way.

A short way up the valley, behind them, was a cache of equipment and supplies. There were tents and even a few small hastily erected buildings. This settlement was to be the construction camp. In it men would live and supplies would be assembled and distributed. From there the next stretch of road over the divide would be built.

There would also be work on the tunnel under the divide. Exploratory work and surveying would be done here. Perhaps even excavation work on the tunnel itself would be run from this site.

The line over the Hill would be temporary. At least that was the thinking from headquarters. It would be a quick fix. Quick in this case meant six or eight months to build the line which would be operated for several years at most. It would be maintained and units would run over it until the tunnel was driven under the mountain. The trick would be to build a road good enough to function and last for several years, but not to spend more time and money than needed to make it so. A fine line to walk!

As to the tunnel, the engineers were already at work. They and the money men were trying to decide where it would be and when to start work. There were several spots being seriously considered. All would start somewhere in this headwaters region. As to the actual financing of it, that was Mister Moffat's bailiwick. No doubt he had that part of the job lined up and ready to go.

Cam turned and looked up valley. "Here comes Steu. I wonder what good news our security chief has about supplies, trespassers or agitators." He grinned, knowing site security was well in hand. Like Steu had told him once, darn few would come all the way up here near tree line just to make trouble. That was more likely to happen down in town.

Most of the commotion these days was caused by four legged critters not two legged ones. Gnawing mice, the occasional aggressive moose, or a hungry bear were known to cause problems. Not even one hobo had yet come looking to cadge a meal or hole up in the warm shelter of a railcar.

Mik too knew that the head of security was good at his job.

"Steu goes to great lengths to keep things moving smoothly, supervising and managing. Still, I think he likes to keep his hand in the rough and tumble of security work. He seemed to enjoy it several months ago, when he ran off the loco woman who dressed in canvas pants and her gangly sidekick. The guy she was with looked half starved, almost ready to meet the undertaker! Seriously, since those two agitators got the boot, things have been quiet. At least I haven't seen anyone lurking around. And I haven't heard of someone trying to throw a wrench in the works. Have you?"

Cam nodded. "No, things have been going well. Almost too well. I am waiting for something to happen, to hit a snag of some kind."

Mik couldn't disagree. "The hill will be snag enough. Up to here you and your crews have made good progress. This next stretch will be a challenge. A challenge to build and a challenge to keep running over the winter."

Out of the corner of his eye he saw several deer bounding across a clearing. They held his attention for a moment, then he continued.

"Maybe people—other railroads—see that this road is shaping up. It is succeeding and will be a well run, profitable venture. Hopefully the big boys, the Goulds, Rockefellers and Harrimans, have turned their attention elsewhere. Is it too much to wish that everyone just leave us alone, not to try to stop us? With luck they'll go pick on someone else and leave us be."

Cam smiled. "Good luck on that. With or without opposition, we have our work cut out for us. In any case, this is a day to remember. We have done one hell of a job." A buck with a nice set of antlers crossed the clearing after the deer, and Cam admired him for a moment.

"Here we are high in the Rockies! And we did it in months, not years. We did it while the naysayers and nannies told us it couldn't be done, while some of them tried to stop us. And I'll bet that some east coast financiers are kicking themselves now. I'll bet those fancy suited men who didn't believe enough to invest now wish they had. They may be sorry but I'm not!"

He paused for breath, and realized he had said quite a bit, none of it original but all of it true. It felt good to get things off his chest.

"Mik, you will tell your grandchildren about seeing this day. And more to come. Now we start building up over the Hill."

Oh yeah, thought Mik. *You have no idea the stories I will be able to tell. Not that anyone will believe them, but I will have some good tales!*

Steu had been walking towards them all this time. He neared the two coworkers.

"Hello, Cam." He then nodded at Mik. "Mik, how are you?" The big security man was also in a jovial, self-congratulatory mood. "Quite a day, isn't it? In less than a week, people will be able to ride the rails, our big wide standard gauge rails, from most anywhere in the country clear to the foot of the continental crest. This is some accomplishment we have been part of, isn't it?!"

The two nodded. "Cam was just saying the same thing." Mik's grin faded. He contemplated the serious task awaiting the crews.

"The fun is going to get more intense. Now comes the hard part." He turned and looked north and a little east, up the pile of mountains Cam's crews would tackle next. The entire complex of hills, ravines, valleys and lakes to be crossed by their rails would shortly come to be called 'The Hill'. Cam and Steu followed Mik's eyes. They couldn't see people up there. But they knew the surveyors and locating engineers were already at work. Those crews of men were finding a line for the railroad, then surveying and marking it.

"Seems to me we won't have to dig many tunnels on this stretch, if any. At least for the next few miles, there don't seem to be the cliff bands. Not like in the foothills above Denver. But we sure have a lot of elevation to be gained in a short distance. Probably will need to go with a grade steeper than two percent in a few places. Maybe up to four if we have to. The altitude and steeps are daunting. It is tough enough now, and this is summer. I shudder to think of winter."

Mik studied the terrain, trying to imagine where and how it would all come together. He drank it in deeply, wanting to remember exactly how it looked before the crews started to sculpt the land.

He pointed. "So we will start there. It sounds so easy. The suits on Sixteenth Street say, 'Just cut grade and build a line up and over.' They should come up here! It is not so simple. Just look at the amount of altitude to be gained, in a short distance! If I were doing the locating work, I'd throw a long series of switchbacks up that hill there." He pointed with his chin across and a little ways down the valley.

Cam looked across and nodded. "Yes, switchbacks and loops galore. And no doubt there will be a tunnel or two, but we won't have a dozen. We will do a lot of gyrations and make many adaptations before we're up and over."

The distant look in his eye saw...snow. "Avalanches will be a problem, and snow drifts. We'll need to be able to move snow, lots of it and quickly. Snowsheds will have to be built. Probably a big trestle or two." A determined look came over his face. He seemed to tense up, then stood a little taller, as if facing a challenging foe. Steu and Mik could hear his excitement and passion for the work.

Steu grinned. "Now Cam, stay with us. I know you are already scraping grade, filling small drops, building snowsheds, and spiking rails in your mind."

Cam sheepishly agreed, nodding. "This is just such a damn fine, fun job, building this road. Every day, I look forward to it. There is nothing better than watching the road grow and get longer!" For a railroad foreman, he was being very eloquent. The man was actually expressing feelings and emotions!

Steu threw cold water on Cam's poetry. "Well, for now, Cam, let's stay practical. I have stock and equipment over there." Steu pointed at his construction camp. "Right now we have quite a bit on hand. There are enough items and goods to supply us for several weeks, easy. So, the question is, should we keep accumulating supplies? I know we'll build road through this summer season, as long as the weather is fine."

He stopped. He was ninety five percent sure he knew the answer, but asked anyway. "The question is, are we also going to build all winter? Or should I plan, this fall, to hole up until spring? Just save and preserve the supplies on hand? Not worry about more being brought in?"

Mik almost blurted his thoughts: *The railroad will have to run year round! We can't generate any income if it doesn't. The sooner we get it done, the better.* He was trying to think of a half tactful way to say this.

Cam beat him to it. His dreamy grin disappeared and he was all business. Steu was a little taken aback by the steel in the answer.

"Of course we will build every day. We will move ahead regardless of weather and conditions. We need to get tracks over and start hauling freight. Ranchers and towns on the other side of the Hill need the road. And, even before we get to Salt Lake we need to generate income. No money coming in, no profit. No profit, no railroad or railroad jobs! The sooner we can start hauling and generate income, the better."

He took on last searching look up the hill where his men would carve the road. Then he turned and spoke to Steu.

"Don't hole up. What we have, what you have here, is just one more construction camp. A temporary construction camp until we move the rails forward. This is not a major base or way station. You need to continue as you have been. Protect the camp and the works. You have done this well since we laid tracks out of Denver. But understand that whatever the weather or other challenges, we will go on with the work. We will cut grade, lay rail, and run regular trains over them. My men will start up the hill. Today."

"I assumed as much. Still, better to ask. I just want to be sure I am pulling the right direction."

Cam continued, almost like he hadn't heard Steu. He was again happily immersed in the details and the immensity of the job.

"At the same time we are cutting grade here, engineers and surveyors will continue their work. They'll be out reconnoitering and marking the route up and over." He stopped and looked at his friends. "It is also time to decide where to locate the main range tunnel. With luck we can get that determined soon. And start digging it. Sooner the better! Once we start, we can get a big old tunnel done in a few years. Then we can use the pass with its steeps and snow drifts as a back up only."

Cam glanced at Mik. "That is all fine talk about the future. For now, we need to get things started. Come on, Mik."

With that, he headed for the camp. He had a railroad to build!

IX

"I THINK I'LL GO BUY A PAPER." DALE LEANED OVER AND TIED his shoes. "I haven't seen one for several days. While I'm out, Ella, is there anything you want me to pick up? It is easy and convenient now that we live in downtown Denver. Lots of stores around."

"No, Dale, thanks. But several times I have seen that guy at the newsstand hit his dog. Watch to see if he is mean to that poor pooch."

As he left the room, he mused that Ella's soft spot for animals came out at odd times. He barely knew the man in the newsstand, and he had never seen a dog around. But Ella somehow had homed in on that. He reminded himself to keep an eye out for the mutt.

"Morning! I need a Rocky, please. Say, how is your dog?"

"Not my dog. My son's. He left town, headed for Cripple Creek. Being an old softy, I agreed to take it. That cur turned out to be a handful."

The newshawk held out the morning issue of the Rocky Mountain News.

"Here's your paper. That'll be a penny."

"Anyway, the dog missed his owner like crazy, and acted out real bad. I tied him up, even had to smack him a few times, but still he got away. Haven't seen him for several days. My guess is that he is out looking for my son. Maybe someone has taken him in now. I hope he isn't one of those stray dogs you see around."

He thought a moment. "You know, someone ought to set up a shelter or temporary place for dogs like that. You know, keep them safe until someone wanting a dog comes and takes it. That would be the kind thing to do." He looked over Dale's shoulder. "Next! What can I do for you?"

Dale strolled away, glancing at the paper. Nothing earthshaking on page one—no bank robberies, shootings, kidnappings or wars. At least no new wars were starting up. The big news was Moffat had his rails nearing the top of the Main Range. 'Rails to the clouds' was the headline. It looked to Dale like the Moffat Road would be over at the headwaters of the Grand River—or was it now the Colorado River?— before snow started to fly.

He thought back to some of the ranchers he had talked to over in that part of the state. Oh well, he and Ella had tried.... As he neared their rooms, Dale wondered whether he should tell Ella the dog had run away, or leave it that he saw no dog. He decided for full disclosure.

Her reaction was enthusiastic and unexpectedly positive. "That is a wonderful idea! A shelter for homeless animals. I should have thought of that. Thank you, Dale for telling me about that. It is too bad about the dog running away, but if the newshawk was hitting him he is probably better off.... You know, Dale, if we ever make it big I will use my money to start such a refuge for stray animals. I will take in dogs and cats, and maybe big animals too."

MIK STOOD ABOVE TIMBERLINE. HE WAS ON THE EAST SIDE OF the continental divide just below the crest of the Main Range. A few months back he had been standing with Cam and Steu. Then they were several miles away and at a lower elevation near the head of South Boulder Creek. Their view was out over what would become Rollins Pass, where the Road's serious climb started. At that time, the three had enjoyed the dramatic scenery and shared the crews' exultation in getting tracks laid that far.

What Mik really remembered about that day was their talk on how to build the road over the Hill. And now, several months later, they had done it. The road started up with a giant set of switchbacks called the Giant's Ladder. It gained the heights overlooking the valley. The rails then snaked around to the northwest. They broke out of the trees, approached timberline, and passed a few lakes and ponds as the climb continued.

Today Mik stood next to one of those pools named Yankee Doodle Lake. This grandly named body of water was in the transition zone where heavy timber became small trees then tundra. A few clumps of small trees were to be seen, and low willows sheltered behind rocks and in swales.

Sitting right at timberline, Yankee Doodle was an alpine tarn two or three acres in size. The mountains around were reflected in it. A whisper of breeze lightly stippled the surface. The surface moved just a little bit, so that the reflections were not mirror perfect. Mik watched the reflections of mountains, clouds, and trees swaying on the water. It reminded him of a fancy French artist's work, with soft lines and impressions not crisp images.

A Colorado day was running its delightful course. Mik knew there would be bright sun and blue sky in the morning followed by scattered afternoon showers. A few storm clouds would form then clear away for a fine sunset and starlit night. Up here the unfiltered light was bright and forceful enough to make one squint. The late summer sun was already well on its journey through the sky.

From the shore Mik looked down the hill. The newly laid rails coming up and around the lake were dazzling white daggers. They danced momentarily with the sun's rays. They bounced the light back into the heavens. It was almost as if the rails were shouting out their conquest of the mountain. Those steel ribbons made an arc, a huge hundred and eighty degree path around a lake. They came up from the south, circled the north side, and headed south again. Were the rails a boa constrictor, they could easily squeeze the lake dry.

Mik sketched himself a map. Whenever he wanted to be sure, he drew a diagram. It helped him see things as they were, not as he wished or assumed. Yet another look at it confirmed what he saw.

People riding the train up from the valley floor would see the trees become shorter and less stout as they climbed. Big trees yielded to small trees which gradually faded into shrubs. These low woody plants in turn disappeared bit by bit. About that time, the passengers would see the lake. Mik was unsure of how the name, Yankee Doodle Lake, got stuck to it. Probably there was a fourth of July connection. It was likely an interesting tale but he doubted he'd ever hear it.

The tiny lake with a fancy moniker kind of intrigued him. In Yankee Doodle country back east it would be too small to rate a name at all. Out west, a body of water this size merited respect. Its surface floated, as Mik remembered for some reason, at ten thousand seven hundred and eleven feet above sea level. 10,711! Over two miles high. Where he stood, the rails were higher than most any other railroad on the globe.

That was plenty high. But the Moffat Road wasn't yet close to the top of Rollins Pass. From around Yankee Doodle, the grade and rails had to climb nearly a thousand feet to reach the pass. It would take four or five miles of road. Five miles to gain a thousand feet is a significant and steep hill. Reaching the crest above, to the north and west was the goal. From there the summit itself was an unremarkable saddle. It sat between the tops of two mountains at eleven thousand, six hundred and seventy one feet above the sea.

From that point the tracks would drop to the west. Starting at almost two and a half miles above the sea, the trains had plenty of altitude to lose. The engineers driving would start and do their best to stay slow. Creeping, they would come down through the barren tundra to timberline, down over and through valleys and gulches and along ridges.

After fifteen or sixteen track miles, they would reach an open valley. At first it seemed much the same as other valleys the rails came through to get there. But there was one big difference. This valley sat on the west side of the divide. It carried not South Boulder Creek, but the headwaters of the Colorado River. The waters here ran to the Pacific, not the Atlantic.

On reaching the valley, the tracks would run north and west along the creek. A few miles from where the tracks first reached the valley bottom was the ranching and logging town of Fraser. People there were ready, even eager, for the latest transport technology. Without a railroad they depended on horse drawn wagons and stagecoaches, or walking. Ranchers were keen to ship cattle to market. Loggers wanted to get parts for mills so they could cut timber into lumber to be sent to the city. Merchants were looking forward to a steady supply of the latest goods and products at reasonable prices.

Mik pulled out his sketches. After brief study, he shoved aside thoughts of Colorado River headwaters.

He had more than enough to do here on this side of the pass. Aside from the steep climb needed to get to the top, there were other issues. On this east side of the pass, Yankee Doodle Lake was the best opportunity for a locomotive to take on water. There was one spot, Jenny Lake, about half a mile south. It was in the middle of a switchback leg and for a full locomotive it was at a tough spot to stop and get going again. This problem was simple to describe. But it had all sorts of ripples and ramifications.

A steam locomotive needs fuel and liquid every bit as much as a person. In an engine, coal or wood is burnt, firing the boiler. The heat from the fuel boils water drawn from an on-board tank to make a constant supply of steam. The steam drives pistons which turn the drive wheels. The steam cools, condenses, returns to the tank, and is reused. But the amount of water in the tank is diminished in the process. If the engine runs long enough, the water tank will go dry.

This is the reason steam locomotives needed to take a watering stop every ten or so miles all across the country. Every railroad was routed to have ample water, conveniently available. Full water tanks were essential to keep a train system on the move.

The terrain over the Hill did not lend itself to train operations. The engineers laying out the road did the best they could with it. Taking on water at Yankee Doodle Lake was critical. Doing so meant the engines could pull that final nine hundred and sixty feet to the top, with enough left to reach the next water tank down the other side. At least that was the intent and hope.

If an engine did run dry before getting over the top, problems: First was the loss of power and momentum before the summit. Then the unit made a short coast to a cold halt up on the side of the mountain. This meant someone would have to haul water to it. Then they would have to restart the boiler which was a big dirty job, even on a good weather day. Often it meant someone had to climb into the firebox and reset the grates. In cold, snow and wind it was hell. Plus passengers were stranded, cold and angry. Not to mention, the engineer and crew would have to explain to the bosses why it happened. Woe to the engineer who repeatedly failed to fill tanks and needed rescuing. He would not stay employed on the Moffat Road.

Mik was deep into the issues of water and steam engines. Something would have to be done about the supply between Jenny Lake and the first tank down the west side. What, no one was sure. Water had to be made available along the way.

In any case, the tracks looped clear around Yankee Doodle and headed south again, climbing towards another switchback. He referred again to his diagram. That switchback, about a mile south and west, set up the final part of the ascent. It ran around a small knob and turned back northerly. That switchback lay under the summit of the continental divide.

Sometimes that summit glowered, sometimes it smiled. This morning, it smiled.

Summer above timberline sure doesn't match summer any-where else, he thought. *It is unique, beautiful, soft then harsh, and almost spiritual. Here, now, it is summer. The sun is hot even though there are still snowbanks around. But when Old Sol ducks behind a cloud things get chilly real quick. Like a door being closed.*

He mused on a summer day's the mercurial nature, up high in Colorado.

Yes, it is like a door being closed, I guess. If a cloud shadows the sun it gets chilly as quickly as if someone darkened a room by slamming a door.

He considered other challenges of working in this hostile environment.

And it is dry up here. The air, the plants, the rocks, all dry. Thirsty, everything is thirsty.

This made him realize he himself was parched. He pulled out and swigged from a heavy canvas water bag which was damp and sweaty. His thoughts ran on. *It is hard to remember to drink lots of water. And it isn't particularly convenient. Someone should invent a portable, light, unbreakable water container. That sounds impossible but maybe somebody will. It would be better than the clumsy water bag or heavy metal canteen we have now. I would love to be able to carry a small unbreakable jar or container around, drinking when I want to.*

He returned to the jobs at hand. *And the physical conditions here are challenging as all getout. Air is thin. It is not easy to work at this altitude, just clawing out grade. It sure doesn't help that we have had to shovel out some huge snow drifts and banks just to get down to where we can start to work the grade, much less lay rail.*

Mik's brainstorming stopped as Cam approached. The foreman was not drinking in the view. He was deep in thought. What concerned him at the moment was gradient, ballast, the supply of ties, crew size, and a dozen other tasks and problems. He was always juggling long lists. Not paper lists, mental ones. They were of the tasks, priorities, tools, and people that needed to be managed, supplied, started and stopped. For all the job's demands, Cam reveled in the detail and in getting things done.

"The grade is ready there up above Yankee Doodle and the switchback. There is a stretch of steeper grade above the switchback, at four percent and not that long." This was unique in the stretch from Denver to here. Mr. Moffat's aim was to keep the climb (and fall, for that matter) at two feet for every hundred feet forward.

Cam went on. "The steep stretch just couldn't be helped. We had to get the road up to the top of the ridge above us. We can't stay low because there are cliffs on the other side. Building through them would have been expensive and difficult. So we decided to run the road along the top of them."

He looked up at the giant range above them and grinned. "Steeps come with the territory I guess. We just have to live with it. If nothing else, when service starts, we can run a pusher."

He wasn't really trying to communicate to Mik, rather he was just completing a thought. Mik knew about pushers. A pusher was an extra engine used to help get a train over a tough stretch. It was easier to keep a train moving than start it moving. Railroaders had found that it paid to use more than one engine to keep a train moving, especially on steep or tightly turning stretches.

"But I'm getting ahead of myself," exclaimed the big foreman. "Right now I want to give the grade its final prep and lay ballast and set ties. And put rail put down! Get trains up to the top of the pass!"

He paused, gathering his thoughts. "I think we can move the contraption." His use of the term 'contraption' was half affectionate, half frustration. It referred to the Roberts Track Laying Machine.

He continued. "Yup, it is time to start the Roberts Track Laying Machine out past Yankee Doodle and the switchback. It is time to make the summit push!" He grinned, excited and tense.

"That contraption is really something. It is a big machine, so complicated it sometimes breaks down. But it does lay rail well, true, and fast. It sure is better than forty Irishmen muscling twenty or fifty foot lengths of rail one at a time."

The Roberts was in fact quite a sight. It looked like a hybrid of a clipper ship on rails with a deck full of iron. The machine had a big boom in front like a bowsprit on sail ship. There were rails stacked on a platform to the rear. That supply of rails was constantly being used and replenished. Cam's 'contraption' would set rails down on ties, true and straight, ready for a crew to spike them down.

When all the parts were working, it was a noisy productive symphony. A steam engine chuffed, rails clanked as they were put on the rear of the platform from another car. And they clanked again when they were spit out the front in place, precisely onto the grade. A swarm of men then nailed each one down. The entire rig moved forward and the steps were repeated. The moving parts of the machine were powered with steam from an attached locomotive. The Road used a locomotive for this that had an engine too small to pull or push even a small train of cars up the mountain. The Roberts truly was productive and consistent.

Cam gave this rail laying report to himself mostly to be sure he hadn't forgotten or overlooked anything. Sometimes he found it useful to run through lists out loud—it helped him to keep up. Frankly, also he was speaking to Mik on purpose. The reason was that Mik now acted as a roving get it done man.

Mik nodded. "Yes, the track is coming up the mountain fast. Is the line from Tolland up to here holding up to the traffic? I was a little concerned with the turns, the outside of the grade on the big switchbacks particularly."

Switchback, every railroader knew, was just a fancy way to say U turn. He went on. "Those are some big turns on the Giant's Ladder. Is someone keeping an eye on them? Over and above the usual maintenance inspections, that is?"

He thought of an old sketch he made of the Giant's Ladder.

The Giant's Ladder was the picturesque name given to the road as it climbed out of the South Boulder Creek valley up towards timberline. It was a series of long climbing straightaways with big sweeping switchbacks. Straightaways and switchbacks were the way to climb a hill yet keep the grade steady and manageable. They were also relatively easy to survey, build, and maintain.

If one stood across the valley and looked, the reason for the name would be evident. The switchbacks did look like rungs of a huge ladder. The valley floor there was about 9000 feet above sea level. The Giant's Ladder ended at the end of a ridge, above 10,000.

There was one short tunnel part way up the ladder. Mik suspected that little tunnel would be daylighted before long. Others agreed. No need to maintain a tunnel and risk collapse if it was short and in suitable terrain. Daylighting was the process of 'de-tunneling'. That is, the roof of the tunnel would be taken off. Actually, the roof was collapsed in and the debris carried away. The tracks then would run through a cut which allowed daylight. A hole through a hill was re-sculpted to be a slot cut into it. In any case, with one tunnel or none, the Giant's Ladder worked. It effectively surmounted the climb out of the valley and delivered the tracks to Yankee Doodle Lake.

Mik's questions on the condition of the rail bed continued. "Keeping the grade precisely even for those big 180 degree turns was tricky. Like I said, I want to keep an eye on the fill under them. It was a job to bend the rails exactly, but we got it done."

Mik glanced at Cam and repeated his question. "So, how is the road down the hill holding up?"

"So far, no problems. The track is carrying the construction traffic alright. As always, every inch of the road bears watching. That's true now. It will be doubly so when the weather gets cold. A steady run of more frequent and heavier loads will tell. If there is going to be a problem, we'll see it quick."

Cam paused, thinking. "On the question of the durability of the road. There are some other issues we want to keep in mind: Some of the culverts. We put them in quick. After all, Mr. Moffat intends to use this road for only several years while he drives a tunnel under the mountain. I hope he is right; he usually is. I just hope he isn't being too optimistic. We may have to use this road for longer than just a few years." He wouldn't second guess the owner lightly and his doing so made Mik think.

Cam went on. "I think cheap drainage may not prove the best way to go. Will what we put in last? I'm not certain. They'll do for two, three seasons, maybe more, sure. But those culverts may need to be shored up or replaced. Up here with the freeze thaw everything will have to be watched because everything will wear out quicker than down below."

Mik didn't disagree. "Yes, I think you have something. Things like that will be doubly important with the road being above timberline. Conditions will get more difficult and we'll have to build out much more durably."

The area above timberline was subarctic. Everyone knew that building and running a railroad there would present challenges. Some of those challenges were known and some would be learned as they went along. Problems had to be taken as they came. The thing was to prepare as well as possible and go from there.

Mik shaded his eyes and looked out past Yankee Doodle and Jenny Lakes. "As I look south, the road climbs about several hundred feet in a mile or so, then turns back north. From there it climbs another several hundred feet. At the spot just above us", and here he looked straight up the hill, "is the last tunnel on this side of the divide."

He thought of his sketches, and pulled one out, matching it so it faced the same direction he was looking.

The road climbed in this upper stretch at a steep grade for a short while, well above Yankee Doodle. It ran high on the mountainside heading northeast. The lay of the ridge called for a turn out near the far end. The turn needed to be a little more than ninety degrees, hooking left. A cliff came down on that corner of the ridge. A tunnel was cut there. It was aptly called the Needle's Eye. It was made to be wide enough for a train's safe passage. From down at the lake looking way up, it looked tiny, a narrow little slot at the end of a sewing needle, awaiting thread. Up there, standing and looking through it, all one saw was sky. It was truly out at the edge of space.

Something basic, something he should have thought of, occurred to Mik. "Good God, I never thought about this. Will the Roberts Machine will fit through that tunnel? The Needle's Eye? Or will we need crews to manhandle rails in that stretch? If not, what will we do for the rest of the way? Disassemble, move it through, reassemble?"

Cam shrugged, glad he had anticipated the issue. "Of course it will. Its dimensions are the same as a full size train. We can get it through. Heck, we can't not use it going on over the Hill. We still have one whale of a lot of track to lay from here to Salt Lake City."

He thought again, and added, "I'm sure, but I'll have someone double check. I sure as hell don't want to run it up there just to have to return it here. If that happens, there will be a lot of explaining to do!"

As Mik asked the question about the Roberts, he marveled. All the details that went into making this enterprise work! He was sure the locating and construction engineering specs allowed plenty of room in the tunnels. After all, a locomotive and huge cars sometimes carrying protruding freight had to go through them with clearance. No doubt allowance had been made for construction equipment. Still, better to measure twice....

X

WELL BEFORE CHARITY HOVUS WROTE THE LETTER TO JOE, she knew it was time to move on.

It was time to shake off the cobwebs. The New York scene was losing its allure. It felt so, well, so old world and stodgy. It seemed like there was nothing new. No one she knew had come up with a fresh idea. She hadn't heard of anything exciting and intriguing for quite a while.

Restless and ready for a change, she decided to create a whole new life. No more attending teas with people she didn't care about, held in buildings crammed one on top of another. No more inane conversations. Away with spending her days with wily, talented women who were shackled and stunted by marriage and custom. No more deadly boring talks about the season's fashions. And she didn't care who was seeing who in the open or on the sly. The latest theater openings would be left to others. Charity Hovus was ready to go achieve something, something famous or maybe even infamous.

It was intoxicating. The future opened up. She could do whatever she wanted. It didn't take long to decide. She would travel across country alone, convention be damned. Joe Eggers was out in the west, in Colorado. They had been good together. Charity wanted to be with him again.

Calling in old favors, she made preparations. And she brought to fruition a long considered plan. This was a scheme she had mulled over, picked at and tweaked for a long time. Unconsciously, she had crafted it so that Joe would be the ideal partner to work it. He didn't know it yet, but he was the man. This was going to be good!

To start the plan, Charity had to obtain the raw materials. That was sweet in itself. She set up a meeting with an associate. Daringly, she summoned him to her rooms. By now she really didn't care if her actions looked improper. Just wait!

"Alright, Charity. You win. Here." The man thrust two items at her. She held them carefully, feeling and examining. They were cloth bags of fair size. Each was about big enough to hold a pair of shoes. The fabric was high quality, thick and soft. Seams were securely sewn with no loose ends or weak spots. The drawstrings were fine cord, not simple string or yarn. The strings were pulled tightly closed and securely knotted. The contents made them bulge.

He had hawk's eyes. He was a predator wanting to take prey but holding back in fear. "This is full and final payment. Now give me what you agreed to." He fiercely grimaced, as if in pain. More likely he was restraining himself from saying or doing more. "Then you take these and you go. And I never want to see or hear from you again. Or to hear that you are even in this city."

"Why, thank you, my friend. Is this all of them?" She gave him a vicious, fake smile as she hefted them, one in each hand. To her pleasure they were heavy, so much so that lifting one handed was difficult. To be safe she set one down and used both to lift the other. Her expression oozed from vicious to avaricious. Greed and pleasure showed on her face. "My, it hefts like they're all here."

Pulling on the string, she opened and set it on a table. Then the contents spilled, slowly at first, into a pile on a table. She looked through, carefully assessing and feeling as she went. The man looked on. He fought to stifle his anger as she took her time. Saying nothing, he succeeded in keeping his hands at his side. Her sorting took a while, probably longer than necessary. The feel of them captivated her. At last she was satisfied. Charity refilled the bag, again eying each item, one by one. The inspection was repeated with the other bag. Satisfied, she retied it and checked the drawstring on the other. Then she looked over at the man.

"All right. Everything we agreed to is here. You and I are square." She opened a drawer and took out some letters, ten or a dozen of them. They were bundled with ribbon. "These are for you." He grabbed and riffled through the packet. As she handed them over she couldn't help herself. "Well, not really for you, but for your 'friend'."

One last jab was too hard to resist. "You should count yourself lucky. Lucky that I ended up with them." She smiled again and this time it was actually a friendly gesture. "Better I than someone else. Like a reporter. Or your wife. Or her mother. So...." Here, the smile iced up. Now her eyes were those of a predator and she brazenly eyed the prey. She focused on the man, hungrily and exultantly. "So, you and I were able to make an arrangement."

They looked at each other. He glared. Her eyes softened and brimmed with a victor's gloat. "Good to do business with you, sir." She stood, tightly holding the bags. "We agreed on a swap, goods for goods. You will stay around here and I will not. You need not worry. You and your friend are in the clear. You have the letters and I will forget what they say. Your secrets are safe with me. I will be leaving the city shortly."

She was lying. These last sentences were for his benefit. She had made copies of every letter and would make full
notes of this meeting. Probably she would never use them out
in Colorado, but one never knows....

Transaction done, she curtly nodded and flicked her eyes
towards the door. "Good day. You can see yourself out."

Charity's plan was coming together. For some time she
had worked towards this one last detail. Now she had the vi-
tal ingredient.

If things worked the way she intended, this would be
a good play. The plan was to use these new assets to persuade people to give her money, big piles of money. Inside
these bags were hundreds of money magnets. She had long
dreamed of and sought such a thing. And now she had it.

It was clear she would have to leave New York. The main
consideration was having connections wherever she landed.
Charity needed to know who had money, who was seeing
who, who owed who, and so on. Her network in New York
provided that information, but that was scant help. Such
knowledge and connections could be developed in any new
city, with time. Patient she was not. The question was, who
did she know who was established in a city or a region? Did
that person live where she could use the goods?

That was when she came back to her long time, on and
off relationship with Josephus Eggers. Joe had been out in
Colorado for at least a year or two. Rumor had it he was
striking out on his own. A person doing that was pretty well
established with a network and other connections. Just the
thing!

It was an easy decision, and it made sense. Just go to Joe
in Colorado! Simply making the decision was exhilarating. It

was sweetened by the anticipation of seeing him again. His surprised face danced in her imagination. Plus, it would be fun and fresh to start over. Visiting new places, making new friends, learning new activities and associations would be good, challenging but good.

Time to go. Charity slipped the two bags into a carpet bag. And she kept it in hand when the bellman entered. He smiled. He anticipated a good tip from this rich looking woman. "Yes ma'am. Take your trunk and suitcases to the train station? Tell me which rail line I should deliver them to? Of course, they will be waiting for you."

ONCE OUT WEST, SHE DECIDED TO GO BY CHARI, NOT CHARITY. This was the first step in reinventing herself. Frankly the name Charity brought to mind a prune faced maiden aunt, which she was not. It didn't take long to realize that she liked the friendly and easy ways of her new city. She came to wish that she had left New York long before.

Several months after the fact she thought back on her trip to come west. At first she disliked this new city. Being a typical easterner, she had been ready to dodge arrows and buffalo. It was astonishing that she wouldn't be living on the frontier. In fact, Denver boasted street lights, electricity, central heat, and brick buildings. It had pretty much everything New York had except for the shore and the crowds.

The days of travel were fatiguing. It was good to arrive because she was really tired of being on the go. True, with trains you could go coast to coast in a week. That was really fast, much faster than walking or riding in a wagon pulled by oxen. Reading about transcontinental train travel was inspiring and romantic.

The reality was gritty, not romantic. A trip from New York to Denver meant days sitting in one seat inside a rocking car. Even before the first breakfast, the experience had lost its charm. Cinders and coal dust swirled endlessly around the passenger car. The food offered was adequate in amount, mediocre in quality. The worst were the passengers. She had had it with the attitudes of some travelers. Women's looks condemned and men leered. Of course many, most people didn't care if a woman traveled alone. But a few passengers showed their disapproval, and that was tiresome.

It could have been the worse. She had money and she had a plan and she had memories. During the long days chugging across the prairie, it helped to draw on memories of Joe. Recalling their adventures and achievements helped the miles to go by. She was glad of it all. The two of them had had some good times together, enjoying and appreciating each other. Working some lucrative schemes had given them some big payoffs. And then one day he left and went west. He said he would write and he did, once. New York just wasn't the same. She hoped coming west was the right thing to do.

When she got here to Colorado, things started pretty well. She had written Joe that she was on the way. It was no small relief that he was receptive when she showed up.

He was at first cordial, even warm, and oh so correct. As she hoped and encouraged, he was soon passionate. They got themselves settled in rooms, living as a married couple. Money was not a problem. Chari had some ready funds but didn't have to use them. Joe seemed to have an income and plenty of assets. On her he spent freely. Chari didn't ask questions. Neither discussed their income or its sources. If she needed something he cheerfully ponied up. Sometimes he would simply buy her a dress or a nice dinner. This helped her start to make contacts in the city even as he expanded his.

Of course there were a few clouds on the horizon. Weren't there always? Occasionally she fretted, try as she might not to. Doing that was like using a ladle to try to fill a bucket with a hole in the bottom: never ending and of no use. Even so, sometimes she found herself ladling away....

Her latest concern surfaced from time to time. Her thoughts burst out unbidden..... *Was coming to Denver the right thing to do? Was it smart to come out here to work my plan? I had good contacts and sources back in New York. Did I make the wrong move? No, I had to leave. That was the agreement and that lout would have harmed me. He would harm me here if he could.* Chari was taking stock of her life. *I am sure Joe and I make a good team, like old times. He seems to have the touch still, but, I don't know. It was the right thing, I think. The plan wouldn't be credible back east, and besides there is nowhere we could set it up. Too many people back there. We need somewhere people don't go and haven't thought to look....*

Her mind changed gears. She sighed and looked in the mirror. *I still look pretty good I have to say.* Chari primped and poked, her mind suddenly diverted from second guessing. Her move and her plan took a back seat.

Joe walked into their suite, interrupting her admiration.

"Hello, Shay." Whenever he called her Shay she knew he was in a good mood. Things were going well for him. She knew that right now if he wanted something, it was her. In this mood, he wouldn't ask any special favors of her. He wouldn't ask her to go meet a prospective business partner.

There would be no dinner to try to charm a contact or future investor.

He had once asked, pleaded, for her to do some other less than pleasurable chores. That wouldn't happen tonight. Given his apparent stature in Denver' business community, such a request would never come up again.

Had someone asked him about his use of 'Shay', he wouldn't have connected it with wanting something of her. To his oblivious self it was just a friendly nickname. He was off on his own pleasant journey today.

"How are you this afternoon? Didn't you have a meeting for the Young Girls' Temperance Society Scholarship Fund? Or was it the Committee to Establish a Stray Animal Asylum? Was the time well spent?"

"Neither. I spent the afternoon with 'The Miners' Daughters'. They want more statues of heroic miners along the streets." She rolled her eyes.

Grinning mischievously, he cooed. "Ah, The Daughters. You are running in high society, woman! And how did you get along with those rigid, dry old biddies? Lots of good contacts and acquaintances to be made there. And no doubt you charmed the socks off some of them. Or maybe I should say, they welcome you as a most trustworthy, solid citizen of the city."

He looked at her, hoping for a nod or smile or something. Feeling coy and hard to get, she just gazed at him, half cool and half in heat. Joe was nonplussed and intrigued.

"I'll bet you were ready for a drink not long after you got there!" He guffawed at the image of the committee sitting around primly sipping lemonade. And it was delicious to imagine that she wanted to spike it with bourbon as they chatted.

In fact, Chari's meeting hadn't gone particularly well. As the new girl on the block, she found herself shunted to a minor committee, something about telling the story of the mines in the schools. Like she wanted to spend time with spinster school teachers! But Chari didn't want to tell him about it that right now. Matter of fact, the whole statue thing was dull as chalk.

They had agreed she should get in on these groups. They needed to build on his credibility and standing, and of course to make contacts. But she was coming to think it was a dead end. Their purpose was to find people with money, spendable money. Not many members of the groups she had fluttered around were willing to invest. She suspected that many of those women had money. But persuading them to part with even a modest amount would not be easy.

Suddenly Chari wanted to talk. Temperance and statues were not the subject at hand. She wanted to discuss them. He had little idea of the import of this one little word, 'them'. She wanted to know, what did he feel? About the future for her and them as a couple? When? Granted, she also wanted to talk about their business plans. And she wanted to talk about them.

Chari wanted to dance that eternal fascinating and frustrating tango. The woman understands and talks about practicalities while the man imagines great schemes.

This had all run through her head in a moment. She dropped her gaze and sighed.

"Oh, things went all right I guess. The meeting was well attended. I'll have to collect my thoughts and tell you about what was said. Long story short, I think it will turn out a waste of time. But we can discuss that later."

She turned and walked close to him, almost full frontal contact. He could almost feel her against his chest, his legs, but not quite. Shay looked him in the eye. It was tantalizing, as intended. It took only a moment to get his full attention before she continued.

"But, Joe, we need to talk. About the future."

Joe, of course, shuddered inside but didn't move or show it.

"I haven't asked about your money, Joe. It seems you are well set. Well and good, and I won't pry. But I do have one question."

He nodded, and tried to ease forward an inch to close the gap between them. She edged back and to the side, losing all touch but keeping eye contact. He was skewered and he knew it.

"You have said you have some money invested in Mr. Moffat's road. You are apparently thinking of putting more in. Is that wise?"

"I think so, all in all. Research and observation tell me it is a good proposition. Why, what did you hear?"

"Those women at the meeting may or may not have money. I can't tell yet. But I am sure they know where it flows in this town and how it is being invested. What I heard this morning sounded some alarms. They weren't major but were enough to make me wary." She paused, making sure he was with her, listening to her.

"Joe, be careful. You may want rethink things. Especially if you are ready to put more money in. The rumor is that the financiers in the east—New York and Boston, even London—won't lend money to him. To Moffat. Even with the exceptional progress in making grade and laying rail, the road has problems. The big banks won't put any money up.

Apparently, Mr. Moffat is having to use his personal fortune. He simply cannot raise any other funding."

Her questions went from the general to the specific and personal. "Does he have enough money to build an entire railroad? Most important, what happens to your stake if he runs out of money?"

She paused, pretending to think, her eyes still pinning him. "Maybe I should say not when but if he runs out of money. Maybe he'll line up some outside financing yet. But why is he being shunned by financiers? And we need to think about how that affects us?" Chari wasn't sure if he noticed how the premise changed from affecting 'him' to affecting 'us'. He did but he didn't; she set the hook well.

Joe was flabbergasted that she had picked up such news at a society ladies' meeting. Of all places to talk finance! He covered his surprise, simply gazing back. "From what I know, your rumors are true. He is using his own money. Of course since he owns banks and mines galore, he has plenty. I have heard his fortune is more than ten million dollars."

Surprise rounded her eyes. "Ten million will buy a lot of railroad!"

He nodded. "But only so much. As of now, I believe he has no outside financing, at least so far. Jay Gould and E. H. Harriman are behind it. You know, the robber barons back east. We used to work for Harriman. Heck, I met him once." Joe stopped, remembering how careful he was to stay in the background at that meeting.

"It is those men and others like them. They have their own railroads. And they have put the squeeze on eastern bankers. They don't want Moffat's railroad to succeed. They don't want the competition. If they can bleed Moffat white and kill the railroad, so much the better. That may not be good for Colorado and Denver, but that is not their concern. They are looking at what is best for them."

"Oh Joe! The new railroad seems like such a sound and well placed investment. What will we do? Do you think we should put more money in? Can we get out what you have put in?"

"I expect it will turn out well yet. The tracks are well into the mountains, up to the foot of the main range. The plan is to soon throw rails over that part of mountain crest. In fact that line is a-building right now. And they will run the road under it via a tunnel too. Plans are being made for that but far as I know, no work has started. At the rate they're building, before long they will reach the coal fields of north-western Colorado. Those are big and the seams thick, by all accounts. When they start hauling the coal to the Denver area, the line will make money."

She was glad to hear there was a plan. Still, she was concerned and was going to ask to ask another question. She didn't have the chance.

"But as we talk, I've decided not to put more into it. Not now, not until prospects become clearer. In fact, Dale and I are…."

"Dale!" Chari's reservations about the Moffat Road were nothing compared to her dislike of Dale and his sidekick Ella. They were no better than snake oil. She had to find out about this.

"Joe, I am concerned about this Dale character, and his—friend? Companion? Partner? Whoever or whatever. Ella. Do those two ever pull their own weight? I'm not sure since I don't know what you are having them do. Far as that goes, I'm not sure they have been totally honest. Do you really want to do business with them?"

The fact that she and Joe didn't tell them everything didn't occur to her. If so she would have justified it. "So tell me, just what are you and Dale doing? What has he, or have they, contributed to the effort? Maybe we need to talk about that. You aren't paying them are you?" A million questions and suspicions arose; she couldn't spew them fast enough.

"Now, Chari, you and I have always worked as side by side partners. You have your friends and contacts, I have mine. We work together often but have our own lives too. We do not own each other. You know that we each have our own networks and projects. I don't ask too much about your people and plans, now do I?"

"Well, I suppose not." She calmed for a moment, then hurled an objection. "Still, I think those two are leeches. Tell me, what have they contributed compared to you?"

"As I was trying to tell you, Dale and I have a plan. We're investigating an opportunity in northern Colorado."

He stopped and dramatically looked into her eyes. It worked; she was riveted, looking and listening. "Keep this to yourself, do you promise? No hints, no discussion. Don't mention it even to me when anyone else is around. Do you understand?"

She was surprised at his intensity. He waited for her to nod agreement which she slowly did.

"I understand, Joe. As you ask."

"Thank you, Chari. This is important. It must be kept quiet." He waited for her attention. "There are thought to be precious mineral deposits in northern Colorado."

Chari rolled her eyes. "No kidding, Joe. Mineral deposits. That is a secret no one else has. I'll zip my mouth!" With that she drew her hand across her mouth, dramatically sealing it.

He smiled. "Sarcasm doesn't become you, Shay. These aren't just any mineral deposit. They are semi-precious gem-stones, and possibly even precious jewels. I have learned the formation's probable location, which no one else has. It turns out that Dale has some engineering background. The plan is for us to go investigate their potential soon."

He didn't mention that the precious stones were said to be diamonds. Nor that Dale's 'engineering background' was useless for a mine. His experience was in surveying and road construction, and even that was limited. He hadn't done any of that for years. Still, it was more engineering than Joe knew.

It wasn't that that he didn't trust Chari. He trusted her more than most anyone else on earth, he really did. From hard experience he knew that she sometimes had trouble keeping a secret. No need for her to know too much at this stage. Heck, the whole thing could turn out to be nothing but smoke. There was no reason to spread the word until he was sure what the word was. He and Dale hadn't talked about it, but he imagined that Dale hadn't told Ella too many de-tails, for similar reasons.

Chari giggled, then laughed, deep belly laughs.

"Joe, I have a secret for you." She mimicked his tone of voice and his demand. "This is important. It must be kept quiet! No hints, no discussion. Don't even talk about it with me when anyone else is around. Do you understand?"

He was taken aback, offended at her tone. He almost stormed off. She apparently had something up her sleeve. Even if she didn't he wanted to keep her in a good mood, so he agreed.

"Alright, alright. I will keep whatever you say to myself."

Chari went to her closet and dug around in a suitcase from the back. She walked out with a heavily laden bag made of fine fabric.

She looked him in the eye as she dumped the contents on a table.

"Here is the plan."

XI

WHILE CHARI AND JOE WERE PLANNING, OTHERS STOOD astride the mountains some fifty miles west. There, things were quite different.

What Cam looked out over could have been a scene from a Jules Verne novel. He truly enjoyed the Frenchman's fantastic scenes and adventures in alien worlds. He almost mentioned him, but didn't. Cam would have bet a month's wages that Johanssen had never read a novel, much less 'science fiction' by Verne. The Swede was a good reliable man. Reading fancified tales of future worlds was not how he spent his time. Still, Cam couldn't let go of the comparison.

"Look out there, Johanssen. Here we stand atop the continent, looking down on the Atlantic and Pacific. Not a tree for miles, just scrawny grass and tiny flowers. Cliffs and rocks everywhere. Snowbanks from past winters. Not a sign of life but for us and our shanty."

His description of their building was facetious. The 'shanty' was in fact a very big structure. It was a station at a rail stop aptly called Corona. Corona is Latin for crown. This station literally crowned, sat on top of, Rollins Pass. It occupied the highest point of the rails, more than two miles above the world's ocean shores. The entire structure was long and rambling. It was tall but there was no second story, no rooms above the first floor area. From end to end it was about four hundred feet, and width was about eighty feet at its narrowest.

On both ends it tapered to a snow shed. A snow shed is just that, a long narrow structure. It has walls and roof but no floor. Keeping snow off the tracks and work area is the sole purpose. The central part of the building, running the length of the structure over the tracks, was built high enough to accommodate locomotives. The main part of the raised building was wide enough to accommodate two tracks. Seldom would two trains be inside but it did happen. In the center of the building, right at the top of the pass, were rooms and offices. They were built out on both sides of the train shelter area.

Cam thought of Mik's sketchbook, and he was sure it had one of Corona Town.

What Johanssen saw didn't fit with what he knew about the word 'shanty'. The Swede mutely watched and listened, trying to keep up. The foreman continued. "And we built a railroad up here! Up to the top of this wasteland. We leveled grade and laid rail and now we run trains! Some days I feel like we are on the moon, the surroundings are so hostile and isolated. We have surpassed nature. Why, we even have telegraph and telephone communication with Denver!"

This stretch of the road had not come easy. It ran from Yankee Doodle Lake up to the top of the Hill. By the map, it was about five miles of track; as the crow flies the distance was just about one mile. Altitude-wise, the lake sat just under a thousand feet below the pass. To get here, the engineers, surveyors, and crews had to invent new ways to do things.

This was as harsh and demanding an environment as had ever seen a railroad.

The top of the road had steeps. There were stretches of up to four percent grade for a half a mile or more. That section led to the Needle's Eye tunnel. Past that tunnel, the road took a big turn north then west around the end of a ridge. There, unavoidable cliffs were encountered. They were smooth and tightly up against the slope. The mountainside was so steep that the engineers decided not to cut grade or make tunnels. The solution: two gigantic trestles. They went along the side of the mountain for a hundred yards or more each. Huge steel beams supported the two long trestles on the side of the cliffs. Before long the cliffy area got the name 'Devil's Slide'. God help any engineer who had a derailment here. He and his passengers would tumble a thousand feet to the Devil.

Those miles from Yankee Doodle to Corona had more than steeps, a tunnel, and trestles. Virtually all of that stretch was shelf road. The grade was cut out of the mountain. The steeps swept up above and down below the road. The rails literally ran along a narrow shelf cut into the side of the peak.

Cam thought of Mik's diagrams, and remembered the one of this stretch.

Overall, Cam was humbled but proud. The whole project was one heck of an engineering and construction feat. The crews had reason to be proud. And Cam was the one who had managed those crews in their day to day building work. No one else in the country could make such a claim. Even the Central Pacific Railroad had it easier when they built road up and over California's Sierra Nevada from Sacramento back in the 1860s. They had to go through mountains, yes, but they didn't have to climb over eleven thousand feet above sea level to do it.

He gave a shiver, hoping he would never have to face a derailment on this road. Cam tried to think of something positive, or at least different. "Hey, Johanssen!"

Johanssen was not a lightning thinker. He was still trying to get his head around Corona Town being a shanty. It made little sense to him, and it was a relief to slide his mind away. He swiveled and looked at his companion. "Yah?"

"I hear there was a scrape last night. Some pushing and a few skinned knuckles, right?"

"Yah. I wasn't there but I guess Steu got it settled. I don't know what they were fighting over. I hear it was just fists and shoving, no more. Whatever the beef, it wasn't real serious."

Cam had been ready for the construction challenges. The steeps, the tunnels, the grade, the weather, all were something he and the crews could understand, anticipate, and overcome.

But people problems were different. The building of this road was a pioneering effort. The crews were of course inventing and using new techniques. They were also forced to develop answers to unheard of problems in an environment no one had ever worked in. Turns out, the isolation of the workers multiplied the effects of altitude. It was challenging just to work the rock, trestles, and grade up where the air is thin and the sun is dry and hot. Hard work at sea level, above timberline it was more tiring and demanding.

On most railroad projects, the crews can go into town and see the girls, have a beer, let off steam. Not up on Rollins Pass. The nearest 'town' was Mammoth, or maybe now it was called Tolland. Whatever the name, it was an hour and a half or two hours away. When you got there you found it was not there: it was a settlement of four or five buildings. Next down the line was Rollinsville, another hour's ride, with fifteen or eighteen buildings. Neither was a suitable place to see new faces and blow off steam.

Denver was six or seven hour's ride away. The crews really had no place to go. It was hard on young men to work in cold dark isolation and be forced into each other's company. Getting along with coworkers is sometimes difficult even under ideal conditions. These conditions, everyone knew, were far from ideal.

Cam and Johanssen chuckled, knowing how these minor disputes went. They shrugged it off, part of the job and all that. The two turned to the day. The tasks at hand deserved more attention than did the previous night's scuffle. Johanssen went one way, Cam another, both at work. At least outdoors, they could enjoy the refreshing, crisp clean air. Locomotive cinders were carried away on the winds, off to Kansas or Nebraska.

The air was not clear and brisk inside of the station building. It was cleaner than a London fog. At least most of the time it was. The atmosphere was warm. At best the room could be called stuffy. There were a lot of good things about living right by the train tracks. One was, getting coal was not a problem. The stoves in Corona never wanted for it. The trains brought a continuous supply of fuel. At least as long as one was inside, the rooms and peoples' toes would be warm.

Steu and Mik were inside. The smell was a combination of sparring gym and campfire. They were used to the masculine mixture and their noses didn't even register it. Truth be told, they were savoring the balmy comfort.

"So, Steu, tell me, did you get the dispute settled?"

The question was asked kiddingly. 'Dispute' was probably too highbrow a term. 'Shoving match' or 'rassle' was more like it. Mik didn't care. Steu knew what he meant. The drama the previous evening was enjoyable, at least to most. Routine can be boring as a sermon. Something like the fight at least broke up the ho-hum, twelve on twelve off routine.

Everyone was curious about it. Mik was in a position to find out, so he did. He hit the security chief with the question as soon as he saw him.

Crew complaints go with work sites. Everyone was aware of them, Steu more than most. He had yet to see many smiles on the men's faces. A good bit of the sourness, he figured, was normal. A man griped and vented when working hard far from his wife and family. It wasn't of much concern. Even back down the hill when the tracks were close to Denver, he heard lots of gripes and whining.

Up here, even cheerful workers struggled with the conditions. Grumpy workers complained and moaned. It was too dry, air too thin, too cold, too hot, too something. They didn't care for the housing. Bunks were hard and blankets thin. Food was plentiful but damn was it plain and boring.... Steu took all this for what it was, grousing. It seemed to him that a job with a dry warm place to sleep was better than a tent or sleeping on the ground and plain grub had it all over no grub.

Anyway, last night, evening time, there had been a fight. Whatever sparked it was something small. It could have been about position in the chow line for seconds. Or maybe someone's favorite seat at supper was already taken. Location of bunks or cots was always a bone of contention. Whatever the spark that set things off, it probably wouldn't even have raised eyebrows down in town. But up here....

Steu grinned ruefully. "Yep, I got the two men, both Swedes, separated. After a minute or two I got them speaking to each other again. Not warm and friendly but at least it was words not fists."

He shrugged. "As head of security I thought there was nothing new under the sun for men to fight over. I was wrong."

Rolling his eyes, he overacted as if auditioning in vaudeville. "That is what started it. One rolled his eyes when the other talked. Made him mad and there you go!"

Mik nodded. "This altitude plays tricks with the mind. Take a job that isn't difficult or complex down on the plains. Up here it can seem darn complicated. Almost like the feet above sea level pile up on the brain or something." Mik wasn't quite sure that made sense but he was on a roll. "I don't mean just physical exertion. Most quirks and habits you can overlook down below. But the same thing will drive you mad up here. Just listening to some coworker whistling can drive you batty."

"True that." Steu stifled a grin and hummed the opening bars of a Christmas carol, ostentatiously not looking Mik's way.

"Very funny." Mik gave as good as he got. He picked up an India rubber ball and started bouncing it vigorously. Up and down, up and down, it soon created vibration and noise. He focused on the ball, concentrating on bouncing it harder and faster.

Cam walked in. Seeing one friend loudly humming and gyrating to "Joy to the World" and the other maniacally bouncing a ball on a desk, he burst into laughter. He lightheartedly considered joining in.

"Mountain fever!" He shook his head, grinning. "At least you two aren't hurting each other." He looked at Steu and smiled. "But your high notes are kind of screechy." Both men stopped, looking sheepish but grinning and feeling better for the antics.

"It looks like some guys I know could use a few days off. I think you both ought to take the next train down to Denver." Neither man reacted.

"Seriously. You should get out of here for a few days, while you can. Winter is coming. Storms, blizzards, cold, big drifts. I won't be surprised to find us folks here at Corona Town snowed in. Sure as Teddy gets his bear, that will happen to us. For a few days is all, I hope. It could be for a week or more, who knows."

Corona Town was Cam's quirky name for Corona Station. It wasn't much to look at, but it was home to man and train alike. The only reason it existed was David Moffat's dream. The inhabitants of the unimpressive weathered building took pride. They lived and worked in the highest train station on the continent, maybe in the world.

Yes, Cam thought, *step out the door and turn west, the snow melt will run to the Pacific. Turn east, the snowmelt will run to the Atlantic.*

Snowmelt. This brought a problem to Cam's mind.

"Mik, change of subject, before you go pack a bag. Think about water. We really need to do something about the water situation. We can carry water up here for people—drinking and washing. Or melt snow up here for that matter." He glanced out at the snowbanks that remained from the previous winter.

"But that won't work for filling the tanks for engines' boilers. Too slow and it would take too much coal. Plus, there's not enough snow to feed them all. What we need is a reliable supply. We need to find a nearby lake. Or maybe find a way to make one. It just needs to be near the tracks, preferably above them. I guess that is a tall order since we are already above almost everything else." He paused, smiling at the accidentally profound thought. "If not above, we can pump it up from below. Main thing is find a place we can store water. Then run a pipe up or down from it to the tracks. That way we can water the engines. No water, we have no..."

Steu and Mik joined in, mimicking Cam. They had heard this spiel many times. "... engines, no railroad, no jobs, no wages." They smirked.

Cam kind of frowned and paused a moment. "Very funny. Alright, so what to do? Come winter we'll have to push snow off the tracks. That means extra locomotive time which means extra water. That question is an annoyance now, but it will become a big problem."

Mik agreed. "Yes, Cam we all agree. We do need a reliable source. And you're right. We can haul coal up to fuel a pump if need be. So even if we find or build a lake below the grade we can pump it up to the tracks." As he spoke, a map of the area was running through his head. He was unconsciously evaluating and ranking sites for a water facility.

Then he had a flash of a restaurant in Denver, with a big steak and a fresh salad. He stopped thinking about watering locomotives and the subtleties of above timberline terrain. "Alright, Cam. I will pack a bag and take today's train down to town. Agreed, I could use a few days off. Steu, how about you? No offense, but I'm glad you stopped your yowling."

XII

MIK WAS GLAD HE DECIDED TO COME DOWN THE HILL. THERE were only small number of male faces and personalities up there. The routine got old and sometimes annoying. The job was great but the grind of twelve hours on twelve hours off wore on you. Still, it was his good fortune to be building a railroad and to be doing it through the Colorado Rockies. Any job could get tiresome sometimes. Having a break was going to be nice.

What he liked about the mountain part was the quiet and the openness. He couldn't get enough of the vistas and the vast spaces. Living and working in a plain wood building set atop an alpine pass was darn near ideal, so far. The weather wasn't real cold up there yet but soon would be. When it was too cold to step out for fresh air, life would be much more challenging.

Denver's lights and restaurants beckoned. For this trip he had only a short 'to do' list. First item was to hang one on. That was never fun to do alone. His wife Sula was on his mind. He really wanted to see her. It had been months for him. But for her, it had been an hour or two. How could he see her, talk with her, hold her? She was near but far, not even born yet. That mix of ideas, emotion and science made his head spin. He shoved the whole mishmash out of his head.

Then there was Juli. Mik met her by chance at company offices on Sixteenth Street. She was niece of an associate of Moffat. She had recently moved here for her health. Before he left Corona he agonized. He wanted to see her again. It was a struggle and he lost, or maybe he won. Anyway, he sent word to her. A perk of the job was sending telegraphs at no charge. So he did. He looked forward to some time with her.

Juli was, well, he didn't know what she was. Was she his on again off again flame? Lover? Friend? A person to be used and discarded? He didn't know and right now he didn't care. He had to work up in the mountains and she had her own life. But she seemed ready to see him whenever he was able to get to town. Discussion, tears, fights, and stubborn silences had brought them to an uneasy agreement. He would work out on the road and come to Denver as often as he could. She would live her own life, keep a home and work in Denver. They would meet up as often as mutually desirable. The last time he came to town she hadn't met him right away, and he was worried about that. He hoped the telegram would get her attention so that they could pass a few nice days together.

The train rocked along at a steady twenty miles per hour. Not bad, he thought. "Steu, what are your plans for the next few days?" Mik tried to take his mind off of Sula and Juli and homesickness and jealousy and lust and loneliness by talking to his friend.

"See the wife and kids. I'll hunker down at home. Eat good food and enjoy being with her and my family. It sure will be good to see them. I like my work but sure miss my son and daughters." He thought a moment and grinned. "Maybe I can move them up to Mammoth. Shoot, my three kids would darn near double the size of the class at the school there! How about you?"

"Try to meet up with Juli."

Steu knew the story of their troubled arrangement. Sometimes, and this was one of them, his contacts told him more than he wanted to know. She apparently was out on the town much of the time when Mik was up the hill building the road. He really didn't want to know what that was all about.

"Oh. Hope that works out."

He was afraid he might say too much, so he looked out the window and changed the subject.

"I love how the road runs here, so high up on the side of Eldorado Mountain. Look, you can see down a thousand feet! There's the big swimming pool in Eldorado Springs. If I had my binoculars I could watch people diving into it. And look out there. On a clear day like this we can see halfway to Kansas, or even Nebraska. To the north I'd lay odds that we can see all the way to Wyoming. That view is a real bonus for passengers. I'll bet no one thought of that when laying out the route!" He smiled.

"And the stop at the hotel, the Crag Hotel, where we just were. That is a good spot for people to get out of Denver into the mountains. And so convenient—the train stops right by it!" The Crag Hotel was on a ridge that overlooked Eldorado Springs. The view there was spectacular and it was a popular tourist spot.

The afternoon eastbound rattled and rolled gently. Mik savored the rhythm as he considered Steu's words.

"You know, you're right, Steu. This stretch of the road is good for city people to escape. And it does have good views. The whole thing is a tribute to our surveyors and crews. Every one of the tunnels the train came through was a real engineering and construction feat. I mean, really, it is one heck of an accomplishment."

Steu nodded, glad he had diverted Mik's attention from his Denver plans.

He added more train talk. "I hear the engineer throttling the engine back. Keeping the speed down. The road here is unrelenting. It has enough grade that if he got going too fast, it could be trouble." He grinned. "Not that our engineers would ever let that happen!"

After a moment's silence, he went on. "Hey, not to beat a dead horse, but I recently heard a good song about that. About a train going fast and trying to stop. The engineer heroically stopped it before a major crash but got himself killed in the bargain. It was called, what was the guy's name? Korri James or Casey James or something. Casey Jones! That's it. A great story, but a little unsettling for us railroad men. Casey Jones, if you get a chance, read it."

Mik drank in the views. Before long the train stopped at the town of Plainview. Calling it a town was probably stretching things. The settlement held fifteen or so houses. Sitting up on the southeast side of Eldorado Mountain, the views out over the Great Plains were truly panoramic. Plainview had one other distinction: It was the first stop after coming out of the mountains and the last one before going in. He looked out at the few buildings.

"I see there is a store here now, and a post office. Plainview is on the map! Hey, there is my friend Charlie Pruden, coming out of the store. It's probably his place. He is the type to grab an opportunity in Plainview."

Steu absently nodded. "Yeah, I heard he has the post office as well as the store. He should do alright here. Some people will want to buy things they forgot to pack, or have used up and need. This is a good location. A small general store should do well. After all, this is the place to get off the train after or before the mountains."

With a blast of the horn and a lurch, they started moving. The two friends looked out the window in solitary anticipation. Denver waited, with restaurants, hotels, stores, and other attractions.

MIK AND STEU PATIENTLY AND GLADLY ROLLED TOWARDS their friends and loved ones in town. The atmosphere was different down in Denver. Ella and Dale were arguing.

They were at sword's point, figuratively at least. That was a good thing for Dale: if a sword had been available, Ella was becoming angry enough to wave it around. Sitting in their rooms, she frowned at Dale. She couldn't believe it. Things had started calmly enough.

"Dale, don't you think we ought to think about plans? Try to figure out where we are, and where want to go, and how to get there?" She paused, hoping for a smile or at least a nod.

"We're still on the UP's payroll. For now. But who knows how long that will last? We need to look ahead. I think we ought to hit some mining towns. Money flows like water in them, I hear. Surely we can find a way to get a small part of it! I'm not greedy, I don't want it all, just some of it!"

She wanted to talk about business and plans. He had plans and business to talk about too.

"Talking about plans? Matter of fact, Joe and I have been thinking about mining. I think you're on the right track. We're looking at a new mine...."

The conversation was deteriorating. Ella was no fan of Joe Eggers.

"You sure have been spending a lot of time with Mr. Fancypants Joe Eggers. Why? What are you doing? Do you have something planned? Does he really need to be in the picture with us?"

Ella skewered him with her most intimidating glare. "Why won't you talk to me about it? What you are up to? You and I are partners, remember? Aren't we?"

She softened her look. "Dale, we really should talk. You and me. We are in this together, are we not?"

She didn't know but wouldn't have been surprised that Dale and Joe had heard rumors of diamonds. People in her circle were always alert to potential business deals and schemes. Something with the sizzle of diamonds would hook any one of them.

It was more complicated than two men hearing rumors. At first look it seemed there were several outside sources of the rumors. Not so. Joe skillfully provided an echo chamber so Dale heard what seemed like numerous reports and tales. But in fact Dale heard only from Joe. Of course, Joe didn't mention that he and Chari were the source. Dale took Joe's rumors as fact.

Ella would have been hurt and suspicious if she knew more of the story. The two men had quietly explored the opportunity. Joe supposedly knew about a likely outcropping, up north somewhere. Dale did some quiet research, nothing specific but an overview on the northern tier of Colorado. There seemed to be a near total lack of filed mineral claims.

It was hard for the two of them to keep this all a secret. They had what looked to be a promising outcrop in a place with no claims or other activity. Joe volunteered to handle the claims paperwork. He had no intent of doing so but it led Dale along. Knowing that claim documents and legal standing papers were supposedly in process made Dale comfortable.

The two of them discussed how to proceed. They agreed that for now, they would tell no one, not even their companions. Somehow Joe failed to mention that he and Chari had already discussed the whole situation. Dale kept the agreement and told Ella nothing.

Ella was still in the darkest of dark about all of this. She was trying to find a ray of light. Something was up, she was sure. "I have been hard at work, and am happy to list out what I have done." She looked him in the eye. "Unlike you, Dale Smertz."

She continued. "I made amends with New York. I was able to slide us right back into our old jobs." She let it go that he did nothing but she did all the work to keep their jobs. "It doesn't seem to me that you have done much. At least nothing that you are willing to tell me about. I have followed and reported on the progress of the Moffat Road, much as that bores me. Remember, that salary and the expense account is what gives us money to live on."

She waited for him to pick up on that. She wanted to learn if or how he had money coming too. He didn't say.

She continued, with some pride, "And while I have done this, I have also been working to ease the condition of the road's animals. Some were mistreated but I stopped it. And, I've even managed to cut our expenses and put us on a sensible footing. Thanks to me, you and I now have a paying operation."

Neither the glare nor her appeal to the partnership had produced results. She softened her stance but still looked pointedly at her companion. "Dale Smertz, I hope you tell me I am wrong. But as far as I can tell, you have brought in zero money. And I know you have spent some dollars."

She flounced around the room and sat down, still looking right at him. "All I can get out of you is, 'Joe and I are working on a deal. It is a good deal, but I can't tell you about it'. So it is time to talk. Tell me, Dale, just what is going on?"

Dale realized he had to say something. He didn't want to keep secrets. He was afraid to raise hopes. And he didn't want to give fodder for gossip. He knew that Ella wasn't above talking out of school. If word of diamonds got out too soon they would lose out.

"Aw, E. I'm not trying to hide anything. It is just that these are sensitive matters. I really am working on bringing in some money. Big money." He paused, and decided to give her part of something.

Putting on a sincere smile, he continued. "When this deal we are working on comes in, we will be in tall clover. We'll have serious money. Molly Brown money." Molly Brown was the flamboyant wife of a mining tycoon. The fortune she enjoyed was large and lavishly spent.

"Right." Her eye roll spoke volumes about past money matters. "I've heard that before. I remember town plat schemes, railroad shares, and something about cornering the market for water. Each and every one of them was a grand scheme. Each was supposed to get us into 'tall clover' and give us 'serious money. And that doesn't even include the ritzy hotel next to a drawbridge." She glared.

"So, Dale, tell me about this no-fail, get-us-rich program."

Damn, Dale thought. *The diamond lode has to be kept secret. But she is about to blow her top. What do I do now? I have to say something.* He relented.

"Ella, what I am about to tell you has to stay with just us. You can't discuss it with anyone, not a friend, not a sister, no one." He realized that sounded dramatic and silly. "Not that you would, I know that. But it makes me feel better to say that up front. Keeping this under wraps really is important." He read her expression. She was curious but not offended. Driving it home, he added, "Do you understand why I say this?"

No, I don't understand, she thought. *This is probably another wild scheme which will cost money and will bring nothing but trouble. I guess I'd better just get him to talk.* Her outer look, her demeanor was another story. She contritely looked down. "If you say so, Dale, I'll do my best to keep it under wraps. I'm sure it is good, but let's talk. Maybe I can offer some thoughts on it too." She paused, looking at him with doe eyes. "So, what's the big secret?"

She was thinking even as she soothed him. *After he spills, I can decide just what he has. We'll see if it is good or lousy. From there, we'll just have to see. I'll have to see if I want to get involved or keep my distance.*

Relieved but wary, Dale opened up. "E, this is good, it really is! Listen to this. Joe and I found a diamond mine! It is in the hills, up north." He realized he had oversold and backtracked a little. "I mean, Joe found it. But he brought me in. He and I are going to be partners."

Sheepishly he back pedaled more. "Actually, it isn't a working mine. I understand that it is a formation, a geological formation. No one knows about it right now and we want to keep it like that." He read her reaction. It was muted. He couldn't tell if she was still skeptical or if she was taking it in and mulling it over. Hopefully she bought it, but he didn't want to seem excited.

"But a mine it will be! It seems that there are outcrops that likely will give paying ore. Joe says sometimes one can find gems on the surface. I can't wait to get close so I can and see for myself. Right at the surface! Imagine how it will be when we can dig in! And like I say, the best part is, no one knows about it!"

Dale considered this to be fact. Like most true believers, he was very was convincing.

Her thoughts tumbled. *Diamonds! If this is a real lode, and we can keep a lid on it....Just think of how that Britisher Rhodes cornered the diamond market in Africa. He is rich as Andrew Carnegie, or Mister Harriman, maybe richer. IF it is really an undiscovered diamond lode, that is. And how did these two find out about it if no one else knows? Are we someone's mark? It sounds almost too good to be true.*

Hardheaded, practical questions followed: "So how do you propose to tap this? 'Finding some outcrops up north' is well and good. But, how do you move forward? How do we develop the property?"

She paused, thinking further out, past just moving rocks and so forth. "And how do we deal with competition? Who else might know about this? How do we keep claim jumpers and other snoopers away? Is it far out in the country? Or is it near a town or ranches?"

Her eyes widened. "We know what Mister Harriman is trying to do, how he is trying to stop Moffat's railroad before it gets going. Don't you think the African diamond cartel— what's it called, DeBeers—will try to do that to us?"

Dale picked up that she went from 'how do you move forward' to 'how do we develop the property'. He was elated but his kept his face blank. No point in irritating her with a triumphant grin. If she turned against it, trouble. But if he didn't gloat, he was pretty sure Ella would stay on board. She would work hard to see that the plan developed and played out.

He stayed cool and shrugged, trying to look uncertain and open to her advice.

"I guess the thing to do is...we need to find investors. Investors who will be happy with a minority stake. We need people who can keep their mouths shut. Opening a mine a big expense, too big for us. We have to get seed money somehow."

Ella smiled. "Sure, Joe. First thing is, I need to see this 'mine' and the 'evidence' that there are diamonds. I want to see if this place is what you think it is. If it is what Mister Fancypants says, then we can figure out how to move. I have some ideas like you two do. And probably his lady, what's her name, Cheryl? No, Charity but she likes to be called Chari. I'll bet she knows something about all this. But first let's see just what we really have with this so called mine."

She squinted like she had just had a thought. "Say, how did you find out about this, if it is so secret? You are no geologist, and far as I know, Joe isn't either. For that matter, have you ever seen a diamond up close? In the rough or cut and polished? Isn't it awfully convenient that this supposed site is littered with evidence? You didn't pay anyone for this place, did you? Who told you about this?"

Dale looked startled at the questions. Some of them had been at the back of his mind but he had ignored them.

Ella smiled, having made her point. "I hope it is the real deal, Dale, I really do. It may well be. Let's just go have a look for ourselves."

Even as she was talking, she had a plan. Her thoughts raced. *What we will do—what I will do—is simple: convince the*

Moffat people to build a spur to the mine. Having access will give us the way to move the goods. More importantly, it will give us credibility. Better yet, I'll get a competitor involved, the UP or the Gould people or somebody. The thing is to start a bidding war. Mr. Harriman would be very interested in this. Someone will want to invest. Or buy it outright. But first, I want to take a look.....

XIII

Time flowed on and the days shifted. Mornings were aloof and still with dropping temperatures. Leaves and grasses, green all summer, were now turning red, gold and russet. Cam loved fall colors, the more because soon they would die away. Plants that grew vigorously all summer would soon be dark, rice paper like ghosts. Buffeted by winds and buried by snow, they would lay and wait.

Hours of daylight diminished; sunrise and sunset were a few minutes closer every day. Summer ebbed into fall with the perpetual flow of seasons. Down on the plains farmers reaped crops and ranchers drove cattle to market. Schools closed. Children of all ages set aside their books and multiplication tables. Everyone was needed to help cut wheat, pick fruit, and fork hay into barn lofts. Most of the students would return to class in a month or so. Gathering the bounty and readying for the cold months took precedence over book learning in the fall.

High above timberline the animals readied themselves as well. Cooling temperatures and shorter days triggered their instincts. All summer, grasses and leaves had been harvested and stored by pikas and marmots. The animals that didn't spend the summer storing food caches were starting to leave.

Some flew or migrated south. Others merely meandered to lower elevations. All sought more hospitable surroundings.

Wild animals weren't the only ones to undergo these changes. The cool and short days would affect people and their lives. They too would adjust their routines and practices. Humans wouldn't up and fly south en masse. Extra layers of clothes would be brought out and readied. Coal, firewood, and food were stockpiled.

Rather than musing on seasonal trends, Cam enjoyed the view. The vista was extraordinary atop Rollins Pass. He looked at Corona Station, with affection and exasperation. The structure sat atop the continental divide in as low a swale as the trainmen could find. It looked like a cross between a shantytown and a house put up by a builder who just couldn't quit. Also there were train cars parked on a siding. The cars were seconds, units too worn to be carrying. Broken springs and cracked axles were common. In a past life they had carried people and freight. In this life they were storage sheds or bunkhouses for the staff and passing rail crews.

The whole motley blend just kind of grew when the rails reached the summit. Year round it sat among snowbanks. Scores of men called it home. Visitors and transients on trains passed daily. And an epic summit it was, truly dividing the continent: spit east or west and it'd end up in the Atlantic or Pacific.

For all the talk about water up here, it was dry. Not Kansas dry; liquor was not unavailable. The place was desert dry. As yet there was no reliable source of drinking and usable water. From the first day tracks were laid here, water had to be brought in. Taking an engine out of paying service and using extra coal, every few days a full water tanker was brought up the Hill.

Soon snow would accumulate, deep and soft. Then the crews could get water by melting the snow drifted up against the buildings. There was no firewood to harvest up here. Melting snow for domestic meant hauling in coal.

All in all, Corona was warm and hospitable. A good stopping point on the railroad from Denver, it was more than just welcoming. It sometimes gave lifesaving shelter. But this friendliness was not achieved easily. Everything had to be brought in, everything but the rocks, the views and the silence. These harsh realities would be brought home repeatedly in the coming snow season, Corona's first winter.

Cam stood outside, enjoying the space and the solitude. Thoughts turned to Corona. This *is more than just a station. It is really a town. Corona Town. We live here for better or worse, nursing the rails and the trains and the people riding them. Me, Mik, Steu, Johanssen, the telegraph operator, the gandy dancers, the relief crews, cooks.... Sometimes, passengers. Sometimes livestock, stranded on the way from Middle Park to the stockyards.*

"Hey Cam!" A yell jerked Cam from thoughts of winter and the layout of Corona Town. Steu stepped out of the covered station area. He walked towards Cam, figuring that his friend had been getting a breath of air and daydreaming a bit.

The door behind him slowly closed. As it did, smoke leaked, almost billowed out. No cause for panic or excitement because there was no fire, nothing aflame or being destroyed. It was just that a train had just arrived. The coal exhaust from the steam locomotive filled the station. It then escaped, wafting out every door, window, and crevice. Of course it also billowed out both ends of the snow shed.

"Damn, look at that smoke. I can't get used to it. It's a wonder that we don't all have pneumonia and miner's cough."

Cam, hacking, turned at the greeting. "Speak for yourself, Steu. I have an annoying throat tickle and cough. Can't sleep more than a few minutes at a time. My ribs hurt, I cough and gag so much."

Smoke plumes were striking, almost beautiful, the way they came from every which way, especially the ends of the snow shed. It made him wonder if a forest fire or a volcanic eruption looked like that, only bigger. Cam forced his attention from smoke to Steu. The man was already in the middle of telling about something.

"...got back from a few days in town. I ate a lot of good food and we got to see some friends." He picked up a rock and tossed it away. "And I didn't think about security or crew fights or hobos once! It was good to have a break in the routine. And it was nice to have clean air to breathe all night. The wife and I had a great time. " He paused, a half smile on his face, reliving the 'great time'.

Then he returned to the present. "And how is Cam Braun doing? Are you ready for a break yourself? Do you need a change from wind, boulders, and smoky buildings?" He eyed his friend with a smile but a serious expression.

Cam ignored the question. Steu realized Cam wasn't ready to talk about himself.

"Hey, what have you heard about the tunnel? I thought the plan was to drive one under the divide down near Mammoth. But in town I heard talk about several smaller tunnels up higher. What gives?"

Cam thought a moment. "I'm not sure myself. I know there was some consideration of shorter, higher tunnels. But I heard the final plan is for one longer tunnel down lower. There is survey work being done for a tunnel about two miles up the valley from the start of the Giant's Ladder. Far as I know those other ideas are off. You'd have to talk to Mr. Sumner or Mr. Moffat to get the story. Not that they would give it to us"

Steu nodded. "I just wondered. Either way we have our hands full. Challenges aplenty here on Rollins Pass."

He shrugged. "I am not a builder like you are, Cam. Still, I'm a railroad man. And I have watched and learned from you. You are always looking at the road. So, on the ride, feeling the train rock and roll as it hauled me back, I looked hard at the road. Every inch—well, maybe every yard." He smiled sheepishly.

"Anyway. The drainage was handled well, even elegantly I thought. But, I think there are some spots which may need attention. There are some culverts at the loop between Jenny Lake and the stretch up to the Needle's Eye. I think they need a look. That side hill is steep. We sure don't want a washout or failure along there. Could some of those culverts be crumbling already?"

"Yeah Steu, I think I know which ones you mean." Cam nodded wearily. "We were—are—in a hurry to get over the hill. We tried to put in good work. In our haste we didn't always build as well as maybe we could have. Don't get me wrong, the work was not shoddy. But maybe things were was done a hair too quick, if you know what I mean." He turned and faced Steu, as if facing his colleague would help him to define and understand the problem.

"We scrimped a little on bed and on some of the drainage structures. You have a good eye, Steu. We have a crew out looking at how the road is holding up. Especially I want them to look at drainage structures. If need be the culverts will be shored up or repaired. That job is on the short list. I want the road and its underlying structures in top shape before the ground freezes for the winter. Once that happens doing major work will be very difficult. I expect a hard frost any day and the freeze won't be long after that."

He paused. "Do you have any specific spot in mind? Something I should have the crew check?"

"No, just a general impression. I don't want to tell you how to do your job. I just wanted to mention it." Steu felt relieved that Cam had gracefully acknowledged him and the situation. He changed the subject, back to looking after his friend.

"I did have a good few days in Denver. Good to see the lights! You know, Cam, you really ought to go out. Take the time to see your family now. I think the winter up here is going to be a siege. For us all but especially for you and your crews. Go while you can. The rest of us can handle things for a week or so."

Cam was torn. The road was his baby. No one could look after it like he did. But Steu had a point. Winter was going to be long and tedious, with a dash of danger thrown in. He thoughtfully nodded.

"You know, I think you're right. I miss my family. I'll telegraph Denver and set it up. If I button things up, probably I can catch the run back to Denver this afternoon. I'll make a list of open items for you to keep an eye on."

"Sure. Go, enjoy your wife and kids and warmth and clean air. Take in the things you can do in town but not up here. We can handle things. I promise we'll give you your railroad back in at least as good a shape as it is now!"

Several hours later, the train from Rollins Pass coasted into the town of Plainview. The conductor announced that they had just come through the 'tunnel district'. He may or may not have known that the man responsible for building them was riding along. Cam was amused and gratified that the stretch had a catchy name. He and his crews had worked hard on them.

None of those passageways were just big, long holes in the rock to Cam. They were artful sculptures of the landscape, enabling and helping the railroad. They had to be dug to allow the road to go where it went. They were uniform, safe, and blended in to the countryside.

The little settlement called Plainview always had people coming and going. It was interesting to speculate. Why did people get off or on? By now, the place had a post office/store and a few houses. It was not and would probably never be a major town.

The train sat, taking a drink from the big water tank, its engine chuffing and belching smoke. Cam relaxed. He was half dreamily planning his time off, looking out over the view of plains to the left, mountains to the right. *You can see forever up here*, he mused.

A man came into the car. He seemed intent, in a hurry, and he scanned around looking for a seat. With a start, Cam realized it was that fellow Joe Eggers! He first intended to ignore the man entirely. Before he could corral his tongue, it blurted. "Eggers. What are you doing up here? I thought you would be gone from Denver by now."

On a whim, he almost moved over and asked Joe to join him. Then he got control of his tongue. Cam eyed the man. Then he realized it was better to talk with him and find out than guess or be surprised later. With an hour's ride before he got home, he figured he might just as well talk to someone. Scooting over, he made room.

"Have a seat."

Surprised at the encounter but not showing it, Joe smiled. In truth he would have preferred to have only his thoughts for company. With no way to gracefully refuse, down he sat.

As he did so, both men warily prepared for a cautious interaction. Each considered the other a friend of convenience. He was not a reliable ally, merely someone you could maybe team up with, temporarily. A person to be worked with if need be but not to be trusted too far.

"Thanks." Joe paused, unsure what to say. *What the heck*, he thought. *If anyone knows the plans for the Moffat Road, it is he. I'll see what I can learn. It never hurts to know people.*

"So, Cam. I can call you Cam, can't I?" Cam nodded, watchful and alert. "Cam, we did good work in sidetracking that odd couple. I was glad to work with you and your friend Mik. From all I can see, you got done whatever you needed to do while we occupied the tall man and the woman in canvas trousers."

He paused, hoping he had Cam's interest. "So where does your road go now? I understand it is over the Hill—that's what you call the pass, right? So you're over the Hill and now it will go on past Steamboat Springs, to the coal fields."

"Yes, that is Mister Moffat's intent. He sees hauling coal from the mines as a good steady source of revenue. But that is just a midpoint. The goal remains to reach Salt Lake City."

Such an opening was unexpected, so Joe was quick to exploit it. "Ah yes, mining. Hauling coal will be a good thing for your road. Mining is the source of all riches. Colorado has sent many precious metals out to the world. Tell me, Cam, do you think there are other minerals and wealth to be gotten out of the earth? Up in the Colorado mountains?"

XIV

SITTING AND MAKING SMALL TALK ON THE TRAIN IN PLAINVIEW, Cam didn't expect a question about mining. What was Joe getting at? The guy had no apparent job or income but somehow was involved in business. His loyalty and honesty were unknowns. Cam was on vacation, but this got his wary curiosity up. *I'll play along and see what he has up his sleeve.*

The question, '...do you think there are other minerals and wealth to be gotten out of the earth? Up in the Colorado mountains?' echoed. By intent he answered as if he semi-understood it. Ticking items off, flicking his fingers up, he laid out a list.

"There are plenty of riches in northern Colorado. Petroleum. Oil wells have been drilled and are producing even now. There are forests of timber, more trees than you can count. The country is ideal for cattle. And people will come to take the cure at the spas near Steamboat. Not to mention the springs at Hot Sulphur, and the big one in Glenwood springs, where the Roaring Fork River flows into the Grand River. Or is it now called the Colorado?"

None of this brought a reaction from Joe, so he continued. "And there are other minerals, almost certainly. Exotic ones like tungsten and nickel. Lead, iron, and other trace riches have been found. The state abounds with them. That is common knowledge. Why do you ask?"

Joe shrugged. "I talk to a lot of people. There are rumors and stories and schemes. And there are also authentic finds and opportunities." He paused, waiting for a question or better, a nibble.

"Opportunities, you say?"

Joe tried to set the hook.

"Yes, I have heard of several new gold finds up there. I have reason to think some are viable." Joe glanced around. No one was near enough to hear. Even so, he lowered his voice. Cam expected to hear a hot tip on a specific gold mine. What he heard next caught him off guard.

"I also hear of another sort of precious mineral find, possibly of rare gems. It is unique for Colorado. I think it may be huge." Joe paused, looking meaningfully at his seatmate.

"If you are interested I will keep you informed. But I need not tell you to keep what you learn under your hat. If it pans out, we don't want every wanna-be prospector trampling the area. And if it isn't real, we don't want to look like fools. I have no reason to think it will not work out, but hope for the best, plan for the worst as they say."

Cam stared. A vision of cupped hands holding gold nuggets wouldn't disappear from his brain. Doubts about Joe's loyalties faded in the rich amber glow they threw off.

"Yes, do that, keep me informed. You know where I can be reached."

The train rolled and conversation flowed. Approaching the city, lights got brighter. The engineer coaxed his engine and cars to the station and stopped. This wasn't Union Station. The terminal they stopped at was several blocks from the main one. Not right downtown, it was still near the center of Denver. The men talked some more and Cam saw an acquaintance. The two parted, shaking hands.

JOE KNEW HE HAD A HOT PROSPECT AND WENT HAPPILY OFF TO tell Chari.

Chari fumed. "It was too early to start spreading rumors, Joe. Why did you tell him anything?"

"It is not too early. We have Dale and Ella in on it, thinking it may be a legitimate lode. They are no doubt whispering about it here and there. I told Braun nothing, really. Just that I had heard of a possible precious mineral find in the north."

He laughed. "You should have seen the dollar signs in his eyes. He is in for whatever we want. If we ask, he will give us money. Better yet, he can probably give us introductions to others in the Moffat organization." He smiled knowingly. "Such a connection would be better than five or six money investors.

Ice in her voice reinforced the frown on her face. "I'm not convinced it was the time to bring him along. But I guess it is done. Now, about Dale and Ella. I do not want them any further in on this. What they know, they know. But not anything more. Especially, they are not to know of our activities, do you hear?"

It was her plan, and she had the goods. So he merely nodded. Joe himself wasn't entirely sure they could be trusted. So her edict was fine with him. Wanting her to feel comfortable, he brought their status current.

"I have told Dale, little by little, that there may be a diamond lode up north. He doesn't know where. I've mentioned that there may be true riches. And that he is one of my trusted friends who may have a chance to get in on it. And I imagine he has told this to Ella. The two of them seem to be partners."

"But you have told this Cam Braun no particulars yet. That is good. He will magnify things in his mind, and like you say, maybe he will give us a doorway to other investors."

The starch in her voice softened. She smiled, her expression a mix of greed and dream. "It is time to move to the next stage. Let's us go find a good spot near your outcrops, and prepare things. Then maybe we choose some people to see the ground. What do you think?"

"I'll get a wagon for tomorrow morning."

THE TWO WOULD BE GEOLOGISTS GOT AWAY FIRST THING. THE blacksmith renting the team and wagon was told they were going out of town.

"And how long will you need this rig for?" The blacksmith was thinking of a commitment he had to rent a rig later in the month.

"Oh, well, we're heading south as you know. We will return as soon as we can. Likely in ten or eleven days."

"Alright then. We won't look for you before a week is out. Have a safe trip." The smith watched as they took off.

Soon they had driven out of town, away from the crowds. Joe looked around to be sure no ranchers or others were around. Hauling on the reins, he swung the rig in a big u-turn to head east then north.

The drive took all of the day. As the sun was about to kiss the horizon the spot they sought turned up. It was ideal.

Chari was mind numbed by the jogging and clip clop through hours of nondescript surroundings. Joe drove over a small hill and she came alert. "This is the place. We have a flattish area with craggy outcrops. They're volcanic rock of some sort, ideal to be the source of gems."

Joe nodded. "And I like that there is water and shelter for the horses. That creek, or brook, is small but looks to be perennial. The aspen grove over there will give shade and break the wind."

"Another thing," interceded Chari," is that the whole thing is overlooked by a nondescript but uniquely shaped hill. The place is distinct. We can find it from any direction. That is essential."

"And we have seen no one since just after leaving town. This spot is isolated. I'll bet we're forty miles from any town or ranch or settlement."

The two did their business. Each carried a small bag and walked a field in their own pattern and direction. The bags were empty when they returned.

Morning broke early. Joe arose, started a fire and made coffee. Taking a cup in hand, he approached the wagon. "Morning, Chari. I think, since we're up here, we ought to reconnoiter today. We don't want to find out later there is a ranch over the hill!"

"Makes sense. We may find a better way to get here."

After several days learning the area, they headed home. The blacksmith was pleasantly surprised. "You're back. It has been only several days. How are things out south?"

"Oh just fine. We got our business taken care of sooner than we thought. No use staying out if we got done what we wanted."

The smith inspected the team and rig. The horses walked soundly and didn't act thirsty or hungry. The wagon was in the same condition as when it left. He was impressed at how well the couple had taken care of the animals and gear. Not everyone did.

"Come back any time you need a wagon. You are welcome here!"

Several weeks later the smith was hard at it. It was mid morning and he still had a full day in front of him. Among other tasks, he had to repair one of his rigs.

Impatient for the apprentice to start, he had orders ready. "Boy, you work the fan on this fire. I need a good one today. Add some coal and make me big hot bed of coke!" The smith turned away to attend to customers.

"Ah, hello. Good to see you again. How are you doing these days?"

Joe muttered, "Don't talk about our being here a while back. These other folks don't know that and don't need to." He winked and the smith nodded slightly. "Alright. What can I do for you?"

With that, Joe looked over his shoulder at Dale, Ella, and Chari who stood near the door. "We need a team and wagon for a week or so. We're looking at property out south." He winked again.

"Well, I have to weld a wheel on the rig you had, my best one. I do have a wagon and team that is stout and reliable. It isn't as new as some others but is all I have today. Will that do for you?"

"Alright. Go ahead and get the team hooked up. We have a ways to go and the sooner the better."

By the time the foursome got going down their route, it was afternoon. For a change Ella was entranced. She looked at the ground alongside the turning wheels. "Look at that shadow!"

As they drove, a long shadow followed the rumbling wagon. The dark outline dogged the wheels as they climbed over rocks and cactus and dropped into low spots. It clung to the wagon as if fearful of the open country. "I could watch that for hours!"

The autumn sun sat a little lower on the horizon as the weeks passed. The day had remained clear and sunny. Even so the temperature was cool. Boulder had been left behind hours ago. The rig headed north by northwest. The goal was somewhere up around the Wyoming state line.

The four riders rolled along. The rig was neither a freight wagon nor a carriage. It was really a cross between a flatbed hay wagon and a buckboard with seats. Whether it had been intended as a freighter or a people mover wasn't clear. In any case, it rode rough.

Ella was still feeling and talking like a poet. "You know, from a distance, the prairie looks like the sea, flat and boringly uniform." She glanced around to see no one really listening. She didn't care. "But up close it is anything but. All the rocks and hills and washes and brush sure cause this wagon to jounce."

Still no one responded. Joe was driving and he had to change directions often, weaving through the landscape. The riders were enduring the slow progress. No one but Ella was watching the sun and shadows. No one was looking at the weather.

Dale was not entirely sure how they came to be going on this 'scouting' project. Each of the other three knew why they were there. The motives and reasons differed. Even though these four were 'partners', what little sharing was done was shallow. Each kept their reasons and motivations to themselves.

One wheel of the wagon dropped into a little ravine or a big ditch, Joe wasn't sure which. Whatever the gash in the land was called, they all got jostled. Dale wordlessly grabbed Joe's shoulder with one hand, the seat with his other, just to keep from being thrown out. Joe caught Dale's eye and spoke softly.

"I hope this isn't a mistake. I really wanted you and me to come check this out first. You and I really should have done that, come here before we brought Chari and Ella out. We need to assess it first."

He hauled on the reins. "Whoa! Look at that big gully and big boulders. I had better get a closer look before we try to get around it." He walked around, looking, and figured a good way.

Climbing back on, he slapped the reins and negotiated around the chasm. He continued, not missing a beat. "But we let the girls in on the deal, the secret. We should have known better. First thing they wanted was to go see the property. How could we not let them?" He looked over at Dale.

"And we sure shouldn't have made a big show of leaving. What were we thinking, all four of us going to the stables? And hiring a big old elephant of a wagon. May as well have put out a sign, 'follow us, we're up to something!' And then we pulled up to the store and loaded on a week's worth of supplies. Talk about making a stir. I'll bet they are still talking about us. Wondering who we are and where we are headed. And why." He shook his head disgustedly, wishing he could kick himself. Then he glanced over at Dale, sitting next to him on the driver's bench. He grinned sourly at his partner and went on.

"Well, at least we talked about heading south. And we did head that way when we left town. No way a person could know where we're really going unless he followed us. And I've been watching. No one is hanging back there."

Dale was of mixed mind. He wanted to keep the deal secret, keep it off the street. But he wanted all four, especially Ella, to see the place. She had to see it to get on board, to really back the venture. He knew that she had questions and doubts. Frankly he had some as well.

Trying to keep it low, Dale responded. "Well, I think that things started alright. We got the wagon and the gear loaded without too much fuss. Then we likely could have slipped out of town with no one noticing. Just another wagon headed out somewhere."

Dale frowned. "But then Ella had to make a comment on the horses. It kind of put a bad taste in my mouth, starting out like that, and I know it did the smith's. He darn near took the wagon and team back. Can't blame him for taking it personally."

He shrugged, then continued. "I thought he said something about he expected better from you. Said that you liked his horses fine a few weeks back. That you two went out south and returned it a while later. And that you had good things to say to him."

He looked thoughtfully at his purported partner Joe. "So you two went out somewhere. How do you know this guy?"

Joe thought fast. He hadn't expected Dale to pick up on that stableman's mutters. He sure didn't want Dale or anyone else to know he and Chari had already been out there.

"I must have rented from him before. Yeah, I think I was in there a while back. Half a day on a horse, you return it healthy, and the guy thinks you're a hero." He glanced at his companion. Dale nodded, seeming to accept the explanation.

Ella had zeroed her ears in on the men when they started talking. She was focused on the first part of the exchange, about why she and Chari were there.

"I heard your remark a few minutes ago, Joe!" She smiled but her voice was crisp. "Just why shouldn't Chari and I take a look at this supposed rich outcrop? We have just as much at stake as you two men."

She glanced at Chari. "And God knows you don't have all the answers. You don't even have all the questions. The more eyes that can look this over, the better we can do."

Having told Joe what she thought, Ella then turned to Dale. "I heard what you said about me and the horses, Dale Smertz."

She glared. "The first team he gave us, one of the poor horses had bridle sores and one was half lame. I had to tell the owner about them, and get some salve and get the one replaced. A healthy team is a must, not a luxury. So I insisted. None of you would. We sure didn't want to start out with a weak bunch of horses. Last thing I want, we want, is to have an animal go lame or sick on us. We don't want to get stranded out wherever it is that we are going."

Chari glared at her. She was already slightly bruised. Sliding around on the hard seat and the jostling ride weren't making her happy. Plus, she was first too warm then too cool. All in all this was not a relaxing or comfortable trip. The further they went, the more she dreaded a long week with these people. She added fuel to Joe's fire. "Well, they sure know about us now. We made a grand exit there."

Ella flared. "Someone had to take the reins." She smirked at the play on words. "I mean, shouldn't we make sure we have a good solid outfit before going out? Or maybe you want to get out in the middle of the mountains and have things go bad? Do you want to nurse a horse back to health just to get home? Do you even know how to nurse an animal? At some spot no one knows where we are? On limited supplies?" These questions had been addressed to the wagon in general.

She then turned and snarled at Chari, "It is easy to criticize, hard to get things done."

Chari shrugged and pointedly ignored her. She turned to Joe, and for their partners' benefit threw a snit. "Joe, you never have told me where this place is. Or how far it is. Or anything else about it. Just where are we going and what will we be doing? For that matter, why are we out here? I should be sitting in Denver taking tea with friends!" She gave him a quick, 'go for it' glance.

Joe looked off in the distance as if gathering his thoughts. In fact he was, but it wasn't to answer Chari. This entire play was hers and she darn well knew about the place and everything else. He weighed his words. The thing was to get Ella excited and behind the effort. And he also wanted to cement Dale's commitment. He talked carefully, as if sharing secrets.

"Well, like I told you. There are supposed to be rock outcroppings up here. They are, I'm told, of the same rock found in the diamond fields of Africa. I got the location from, well, I can't tell you. But we—Dale and I—have every reason to think this is the real deal."

He looked at Dale. "Right, Dale? You have looked at maps and some geological charts and you are an engineer. It looks good, doesn't it?"

Dale nodded. "I have some training as an engineer. The formations and layers sure look the same as maps show in southern Africa. I want to see it for myself. Hey, maybe this will be the next Cripple Creek!" He smiled warmly, greedily, at Ella.

She wondered about all of this, and said so. "What geological layers and outcrops have gems?" She looked at the men, but got no answer. Her concerns came out, a creek in flood.

"The big question I have: Why have these rocks gone unnoticed for years and years? How about all the sharp eyed prospectors? How was this place overlooked by the 59'ers during the Pikes Peak Gold Rush? They went over every rock, valley, and creek in Colorado. Surely someone saw and checked over these 'outcrops'?"

The unstated question: what was in it for her and Dale? And what did Joe get out of it, and Chari?

As Ella started to speak she half noticed a wagon track, a mark where a wagon had recently gone, off to the side. It struck her as odd since Joe said they were going where no one had gone before. The thought flew through and out of her head. She focused instead on stating the goal of the trip.

"Diamond territory. If this place really does have diamonds and other gems, we need to keep it under wraps. And we need to figure out how to make it work."

Chari was waiting for that to come up. Her tone was dismayed. "Joe, darling, we can't do this alone." She glanced at Ella then Dale. "Nor can the four of us. We'll need other investors. Even if we each put up some money."

"We're not putting in a dime, not promising anything, not until we see the property." Dale got that said before Ella.

"Oh, I agree. I was just thinking ahead. Best to have some idea of how to proceed if this does pan out." Chari knew very well how it would pan out. She was certain that they would find gems soon.

Ella glanced at Dale and said what both were thinking. "It is fine and dandy to be talking investors and putting money in and all that. But that is just cotton candy. Let's not get ahead of ourselves."

Dale jumped in, finishing the thought. "We need to get a good look at the area. If it is promising we go from there. Of course we want to keep it secret. We don't want competing claims. If we do bring others in, we need to keep them quiet. Maybe we should make potential investors sign something, a no-talk agreement before we bring them in to look."

Joe felt that Dale and Ella were firmly on board. *Time to let things stew*, he thought. "So, let's all agree. For now. We need to solemnly swear that we keep what I have told you and what we find out here entirely to ourselves, just we four. Not that I don't trust everyone, I do. It is just that we need to keep this quiet. No one can find out where we are or what we have. Someone could get in before us and take it away. So, again, we need to promise to keep this to ourselves."

He looked at Chari and Ella. "Please promise you will tell no one about what we learn on this trip. I know we are being hard on you, but this is important." He glanced at Dale as he said this.

Chari nodded, and played her part. "What could there be out here hours and miles from anywhere? And who would I talk to even if I wanted to? And I don't want to. Your precious secret is safe with me. I will keep it under my hat. Whatever this 'secret' is."

Ella nodded as well. "We are out here to find ourselves a fortune. I know that much. Why would I share that with anyone? Of course I'll keep this to myself." *But*, she thought,

I may have to share a few unimportant tidbits—nothing anyone could use—in order to get investors interested. We'll see....

Chari and Joe shared a lightning quick glance, relieved to have that possibly awkward session behind them.

Dale spoke. He almost visibly swelled with excitement and pride. "We're going to the Karat Top Field." The others wondered where on earth that came from. No matter. He was just getting started.

Ella truly didn't make the karat-gem connection. "Where did you get kerataw? That sounds like one of those dinosaur fossils geologists are finding."

Before Joe could think, he snarked, the sarcasm dripping. "It comes from the tops of carrots we'll be feeding the horses when we get there." Chari stifled a laugh.

Dale didn't hear that. He was worked up, half standing and gesticulating. As he did, the wagon wheel went up and over another rock. One side of the wagon abruptly rose and fell about a foot. Dale almost fell out. He forgot about the Karat Top name, instead making a grand announcement about what could come next. To his credit, he stayed in the wagon and didn't miss a syllable, nor a wave of the hand.

"On this trip we will survey the area. When we are sure of the best spots I think we should stake and mark a mining claim. If the prospects are good we may want to each file individual claims too. We want to lock this lode up, not let anyone else near it. With a little luck it will make us rich."

Ella was flabbergasted at the thought of a claim in her name. Could she do that as a woman? Could she own property? Wouldn't Dale have to file it in his name? She'd have to be sure to get an ironclad agreement. Make sure that it was hers and hers alone. She pretty much trusted him, but she didn't want to push that too far.

Chari was not concerned with that. She would get her share, she knew that. Again, she asked, "Where is it?"

Joe answered. "It is another day or so northwest of here. So I am told by—er—my source. And the map I got from there. We'll find it, I'm sure. The place is probably nearer to Laramie Wyoming than Boulder." He looked at all of them. "I know you wonder, I did too, why no one had found it yet. It is isolated, that's for damn sure." He looked around for emphasis.

"The country has shown no potential for gold or silver mining. There are no high mountains or big rivers, no passes or roads. The terrain is rolling with few prominent points to use as landmarks. It is difficult to stay on track and easy to get turned around. This is hard country to find your way in. You really have to pay attention. It'd be easy to get lost. No doubt that has scared people off."

He winked at Chari. "Isolation is good. When the time is right, we intend to change that!"

Outwardly, Ella was kind of paying attention. Inwardly she was thinking hard. *Laramie, huh? Why, the Union Pacific runs right through Laramie. I'll bet they could run a spur south on a moment's notice. Or maybe we can get Moffat to run us a spur north from their line....*

Ella's mind was no longer on women owned claims or lame horses. She was thinking about iron horses and how to put this place on the map. And making big money, whether from investors or from diamonds. She was lost in thought. *Yes, a juicy mine prospect claim in order to attract a railroad spur. That may be worth pursuing.*

XV

MIK WAS FAIRLY CONTENT WITH THE TIME HE HAD IN DENVER. The air down at only a mile above sea level wasn't so thin it made you gasp. Having real food and seeing friends was good. And the companionship.... His days there seemed awful short. Time now to leave. At the station an engine sat, spewing smoke and cinders, impatiently waiting for passengers to board. The engineer fiddled with controls and the fireman stood by, knowing he would soon be working like a sprinter to feed the hungry boiler.

Walking slowly towards it, he enjoyed the feel of Juli at his side. Thoughts of home and wife were pushed away even as he pulled her to him. He held her waist as close as the tracks kept to Yankee Doodle Lake. He should let go, let her go, but couldn't. He anticipated but dreaded going back to 'working on the railroad'. The song absurdly wafted through his mind as they walked.

"I wish you didn't have to go, Mik. You get along with the folks here in Denver. Can't you wangle an office job or something closer to home? I'd love to have you here. Why do you have to go out to some tiny little mountain station?"

This question was just waiting to be asked. He had rehearsed and was ready. Words were about to start when he saw his friend Cam. He was flabbergasted. Spotting Cam in town was akin to seeing a moose ambling down the street. Both were creatures in alien surroundings. He wasn't supposed to be here in Denver! His place was up at Corona, running the road.

What really surprised Mik was, Cam was talking with that Joe Eggers character! Taken aback, his embracing arm dropped. Without a word he strode towards his friend, more abruptly than intended. Juli gaped then followed along.

THE TWO MEN WERE FOCUSED ON THEIR CONVERSATION. CAM was hardly aware they had arrived at the station. One of the three great motivators was their subject. It wasn't sex and it wasn't power: money, wealth, riches was the theme. Specifically it was mineral wealth in the west, who had it, where it was, how to get it. Joe had been explaining some intriguing and tempting ideas.

"You know, Cam, the real way to it is to get in early. If you aren't in early, you have to work for someone else. That, or sell shovels and beans to other latecomers. Seriously, look at those who get in on the ground floor, or I should say, get in on the surface. Think about those who get in before a handful of dirt is moved. They are the ones who reap the riches."

Joe hinted at projects. "I know of some lodes and veins. Gold, silver, lead, even precious stones. The thing is, Cam, that the days of hitting it big with a gold pan in a river are gone. Now you need industrial equipment and big time funding. Getting mother earth to give up her treasures isn't easy or cheap anymore."

Cam couldn't tell if this guy was chasing blue sky or what. Did he have concrete plans and prospects? It almost seemed as if he was looking for partners or backing. While Cam wasn't in a position to invest, somehow Joe got him thinking. It was almost as if there were ways he might be able to participate, might be able to team up.

Inside Cam, the tough old railroad man was aflutter. He thought, dreamily and improbably, of joining forces with his new fast talking friend. *Maybe I can scrape up several hundred dollars and can get in on things early. I'll bet Joe....*

"Cam! Hello!"

Mik interrupted his financial fantasy. The comforting and silly idea of gold falling out of the sky into his pockets evaporated.

Cam had two quick reactions to the interruption. First was surprise at seeing Mik here, a fish out of water. He was used to seeing the guy at Corona, dressed for work and focused on railroading and freight tonnage. He was not used to seeing or even thinking of Mik as nicely dressed and at ease in town. Not to mention being at ease and acting familiar with a woman! Cam didn't even know he had a steady.

The second reaction was shame. Not really shame, but a sense of disloyalty for talking to Joe. After all, not long ago Joe had been an antagonist to him, Mik and the railroad. Maybe by now he wasn't an outright enemy. But he probably wasn't a friend. The man's loyalties and motivations were not clear. On top of that, Cam felt a little taken in. He was chagrined at how easily he had bought into Joe's grand plans for getting rich.

He shook those feelings off. Quickly he got into railroad foreman mode. He dismissed Joe, half turning away even as he put out his arm to shake hands. He spoke quickly and in a low tone. "Mr. Eggers, nice to see you again. Best of luck in your ventures." He was turned entirely away by the time he finished.

"HELLO MIK. GOOD TO SEE YOU." EYING JULI, HE HOPED FOR an introduction. "It looks like you have had a good time here in Denver." With a grin, he asked kiddingly, "City life seems to be treating you well. Are you going soft? Or are you ready to get back to work up at Corona Town?"

He didn't know how torn Mik was, that he enjoyed his work but he sure liked being with this woman. More and more he found he truly liked being able to dress comfortably. It was very enjoyable to go out to dinner on a whim. And to breathe clean air: what he really disliked about work was the pervasive stink of coal smoke and cinders. On the other hand, there was something about building a railroad through the mountains....

He ignored Cam's barbs and turned the questions back around.

"Cam, what are you doing here in town? How did you get away from the job? Shouldn't you be up on the hill? Don't the crews need your supervision and help to get ready for winter?"

He paused but Cam said nothing. So Mik asked the questions he really wondered about. "And wasn't that Joe Eggers? What is he doing here? I thought he would be long gone. I figured he would have hightailed it to a mining town or some other place."

Neither man noticed that Joe Eggers was hanging around the station entrance. He was discreetly watching them and Juli.

Mik suddenly realized Juli was standing at his elbow. "Cam, this is my friend Juli. Juli, Cam is foreman of the job up on the hill." They nodded, making appropriate 'nice to meet you' noises. She watched, interested in the subject matter and fascinated at the interplay between the two.

"You love every second of that job on the hill. I'm surprised you left even for a day!" Mik continued in a mock serious tone. "How will the trains run if Cam Braun isn't out on the tracks?"

"Well, they'll manage somehow I reckon." The big man grinned. "Steu is back from his break in town, and he's keeping an eye on things. It'll all be alright. Like he said, it really is good for all of us, me included, to take a break now and then."

He turned to Juli. "And I hope you think we are treating Mister Mik well. He does good work for the road." She nodded silently.

"So, Mik, you are right. Winter is around the corner. The snows will come soon. The big storms, leaving many feet of snow. We have already had a dusting or two. And that will make our lives harder still."

He paused, thinking about coming challenges. "But for now, I want to get home. I need some warmth, if you know what I mean." Cam smiled shyly.

"Oh yes, I do." Mik glanced at Juli and her blandly innocent expression almost made him laugh. And in a way it made him wish he didn't have to leave. "Of course it is good for you to go home for a few days. The Road will no doubt survive without you."

"Yeah, I may have to pick up the pieces when I get back." He shrugged and chuckled. "Seriously, the guys will do just fine!" Cam grinned, then got back to business.

"The ride down was good. Gave me a chance to ponder, and to look at the road and operations. I was watching and thinking as we came down from the mountain and through tunnels. So far the road seems to be holding up well. I didn't see any glaring problems or even potential ones." He stopped, realizing he was on vacation and needed to forget the rails for a little while.

"Where are you headed? Are you two going home or somewhere to relax? Or are you headed to Sixteenth Street?"

Mik and Juli had had their time. She was seeing him to the station before she ran errands or something. They were both dreading the last moments before parting. At the same time, each was somehow anticipating the freedom of being alone. It was time again for them to have their own lives.

He answered. "Back up the hill. Why do you ask? Do you have something you want done at the main office?"

Cam took a list out of his shirt pocket, as if rehearsed. "No, not really. These are a few notes I made on the way down. Actually they can all be handled out at Corona Town or by telephone. No need to go down to Sixteenth Street."

He handed the list to Mik. As the piece of paper passed, Cam had a curious sense of a load being lifted from his shoulders. He was actually glad to have someone else take the burden if only for a while.

Mik took it, scanning it. He was so intent on railroading that he scarcely noticed that Juli edged away then left without a word. He might have been more interested if he saw Joe talking with her as the two of them left the station.

Cam wasn't satisfied that Mik could read the list and draw the appropriate conclusions. He felt the need to explain and provide direction.

"The thing now is winter." He reverted from practical foreman to the learned, academic Cam. This was a side of him few ever saw. Actually, Mik knew and liked the learned Cam.

"Like Napoleon learned in Russia, winter makes even commonplace tasks awfully difficult." He continued. "We won't have to fend off Cossack attacks like he did. And we won't have his worry about the natives scorching the earth so we have no shelter and nothing to eat. Not that there is anything I'd want to eat up there anyway. In fact, the earth up there will be frozen, not scorched."

He paused, glancing around as he gathered thoughts. "But like Napoleon found, we sure will have to worry about snow, cold and wind. To cope with all that, we will need protection. That means snowsheds. And we'll need to move snow, which means snowplows. They will let us keep the way clear to bring in lumber and hardware to build more snowsheds." He stopped to tally the number of cars likely needed to bring in timber and boards for one of those simple but sturdy structures.

"And of course we'll need winter clothing and snowshoes for crews. And increased food supplies, to keep everyone functioning. And extra stocks of everything for the times if, or when, we get snowed in. Winter at the elevation of the pass is comparable to winter in northern Canada or Russia. Except the air is thinner up at our altitude."

There was no change in Cam's expression or demeanor. Even so, the learned Cam returned to his library. No more talk about the gifted French narcissist who sent his army to freeze and die in Russia. The railroad Cam was now back and talking. "We could probably use them—snowsheds—over most every mile of the above timberline trackage. That would be one crackerjack construction job. And maintaining that big a building...."

He looked off in the distance, imagining what could go wrong. "Hell, if we have one long shed and it starts on fire, the whole shebang will be gone. And the road would be closed for who knows how long." The shudder he felt was almost visible to his friend.

"Not to mention the expense. Even Mr. Moffat can't afford to build a six or eight mile long building. But we will definitely need some sheds. Will have to look real careful, pick and choose where. To start, we ought to build them near the Needles Eye and the Giant Slide."

In his mind's eye Cam saw a long forty foot wide ledge carrying rails, with steep rocks above and below. And these spots were in the lee of the land. Such places slowed the wind which made it drop the snow it carried. For a railroad, those sites were trouble because they collected drifts quickly. If that microclimate wasn't somehow interrupted the snow would soon be deep, too deep to drive a train through.

"And plows. You know the snow will soon be deep enough to hide a locomotive in! Whole trains could be swallowed by drifts and banks. I am not sure. Did the line ever acquire a snowplow? I know the muckety mucks on Sixteenth Street were talking about a swap or lease or something. In any case, we'll need snowmovers of some kind." He grinned. "And I don't mean an army of men with shovels, although it may come to that. Actually, I expect we'll need not just straight out plows but a rotary too."

A rotary snowplow, Mik knew, was a specialized and expensive piece of equipment. It was a huge fan, twelve feet or so tall, mounted on the front of an engine. The blades were hardened and specially shaped to scoop up snow. Sitting on the front of an engine and turning hundreds of times a minute, it made an impressive, noisy show. The driver drove the engine ahead, sticking the whirling fan into a pile of snow. The fan sucked the snow out then threw it away to the side. At least when everything was working right that is what happened.

Some rotary snowplows had their own motive power. One engine moved the plow and also powered the blades. Some units had a rotary but no motive power. They could move snow when up against a drift, but had to be pushed into the snow by a separate engine. Either type of set up could clear the way for trains running over the Hill.

A rotary plow cleared a path just wider than the width of the tracks. It could sweep snow up to eight or nine feet deep with little problem. If the snow was deeper than the height of the fan, problems. Then, Cam's army of men with shovels would have to go to battle. They would shovel or blast the snow on the track so it was not too deep for the equipment. Too deep a snowbank would choke or even stall a rotary. A stalled snow mover stopped traffic just as much as a derailment or dry tank.

Mik weighed in. "I agree. My money is on needing at least one of them, maybe several." He paused. "Maybe they can borrow or lease some from other lines. Many of the smaller lines are willing to work together for that sort of equipment interchange. Mr. Sumner or someone else will need to agree to that."

Business attended to, they were done, and shook hands. Cam walked out and turned towards home. Mik climbed on the train.

A few moments before, where Cam now walked, a conversation had taken place.

"Hello, Mrs. Mast." Joe took a guess at Juli's status. He wasn't on target but was close enough.

She was intrigued by the man who she saw talking with her man's friend. He wanted to talk. She was not intimidated by unusual situations. She came right back.

"Hello, Mr. Eggers."

XVI

I<small>T FELT LIKE FOREVER FOR THE FOUR RIDERS TO GET TO THEIR</small>
new mine.

Ella rode easily, relaxed, not even half awake as the wagon
crossed the roadless prairie. Brain hard at work,she was mulling over financing, bringing a railroad to the mine, and gems
themselves. Her eyes got heavy and uneasy sleep came. She
found herself sitting in a giant pan covered with corn kernels,
the kind of corn that popped white when roasted. Popcorn
kernels were popping all around, gently and continuously.
The lift of the pop made her jostle and roll from side to side,
even front and back. It was a marvelous and luxurious ride.
One big kernel exploded with....

She came out of her popcorn dream. Her eyes opened
and she saw the front wheel was riding up and over a boulder. She hoped the bottom of the wagon would clear it, that
they wouldn't get high centered. That would be a heck of a
problem, way out here. The rig they were able to hire was in
pretty good shape, but old. It had seen better days. When she
first saw it she suspected it had carried 59ers across Kansas to
the Pikes Peak gold rush.

The sudden jolt made for tiresome travel. A smooth fast
trip like those she enjoyed on a railroad it was not. From

Boulder to this supposed diamond mine was a long lingering ride. She had seen no people or livestock. For that matter, she hadn't even seen a playing antelope. The area was, well, the word sparse came to mind. Suddenly she wondered if there were robbers or even mountain lions watching them. Was coming out here risky? No one knew where they were. Why hadn't they left at least a letter to be opened if they didn't return?

The spooky loneliness was all the more reason to get a railroad spur in to the mine. It would help to keep the miners and product safe. Ella tried to put the worry aside. She strove to think it all through.

Her thoughts tumbled. *It isn't a mine yet. It is just a place that we hope can be turned into one. Darn, I surely hope it really does have genuine outcroppings. That would be good. I just hope it is, for a change, a viable deal. Not just one more of Dale's 'investment opportunities'. As he says, if people are going to put money into something, it may as well be through us,* she thought wryly.

Of a sudden, she started. Kind of. With the jostling and jarring she didn't really physically move; the wagon's motion took care of that. Ella had just remembered something important. Her thoughts raced.

There had been a scam somewhere, she was pretty sure. There was a story she half remembered about someone sly. They salted a field with some high grade ore, literally putting it out on the ground and just under the surface. They brought in investors who raced forward when hearing of it. And then they plucked those people of their money.

The memory made her uneasy. Wasn't it awfully odd that all of a sudden there were supposedly diamonds or other gems to be had for the picking? Was it too good to be true?

On the other hand, if she was involved, better to be a plucker than a pluckee. It was all so confusing....

Her thoughts raced. *Well, the California gold rush started with people picking up gold nuggets. Off the ground and out of creeks, thousands of nuggets. For real and truly. Lots of fortunes were made and lost in those days. There's no reason something like that couldn't happen here.* Still, the whole picture seemed too rosy. She couldn't remember if gems had ever been found like that. Keeping her guard up, being skeptical, was the thing to do.

I have to see who the players are. Who are the puppeteers, the folks pulling strings for this? Who is really behind this supposed mine? Who controls the money? What does Joe have to do with it, if anything? And Chari? No, she is just a tea sipping society girl. She doesn't have the imagination or guts to run a scam. I really can't see her involved. She seems miserable out here today. So, who is it? I need to find out who is running this, who benefits and who doesn't. I need to learn this before we get too far into it, she promised herself.

Dreams of popping corn were gone. Visions of diamonds receded. Hard questions came to her mind. Turning to her companion, she spoke softly. The tone made him pay extra attention.

"Dale, I know we have discussed this. I know you have answered some of these questions. But please remind me again."

She sighed and gave him a thoughtful but doubting look. "You know, riches don't just jump into our pockets. Not to throw cold water on this 'mine', but I am skeptical. Why we are going up here in the middle of absolutely nowhere? Is it really to look at a few rock formations coming out of the ground? To see how far from everywhere it is?"

The thoughtful look turned to a squint. "And for that matter, who told you or Joe about this, anyway? How did you come to learn of supposed riches just laying around for the taking?"

Dale eyed her. "Josephus Eggers is the source. I learned of it from Joe. Believe it or not, Joe saw some newspaper clipping or article or talked to someone. I'm not really sure just how he got wind of it. Anyway, he followed up on that lead."

He paused. Hearing it out loud, he realized just how implausible it sounded. He stuffed his doubts and went on.

"Somehow Joe looked into the story. After some detective work he found the guy who started it, some old geezer. And he talked to the guy. It seems he was an old man who had spent his life prospecting in the mountains. Said he knew of a diamond lode. Joe found him just in time. He was on his deathbed in a hovel. Someplace around Denver, I guess. Anyway, Joe helped him out, got him some medicine. And they got to know each other. The guy said all his friends and partners had died and that he had no family. He was the last one left, he said. The guy finally opened up. Said he couldn't do anything with it, but he didn't want the secret to die with him. So the old guy told Joe about it. He even had a few diamonds to show."

Ella was incredulous. "So you two drug me and Chari out here on the strength of that? A dying beggar's word, backed up by a few rocks he flashed at a new acquaintance?! Dale Smertz! If he hadn't been about to croak, I'd say he was conning Joe. Do you know, does Joe know, that the guy really was dying? What happened to him? Do you even know? What did Joe have to give him for this information? Has anyone asked for money? Is it costing you—us—anything to get access to this place?"

Dale smiled, relieved. "No. That was my first thought too, Ella. It just seemed too good to be true. But the guy did die shortly after Joe met him. He asked Joe to take care of his burial. Joe told him he would see to it, and he did. He later showed me the pauper's grave. It has no gravestone marker or anything but Joe did see him get planted." He paused a moment, melancholy at the memory of the unmarked mound of dirt.

"And since then, no one has contacted us. At least not me, and Joe hasn't said anything about anyone. We, well, not I but Joe, has been watching to see if he is followed. No one has contacted him about the old coot. Or about anything the old guy may have talked about. No person has suddenly appeared with an interest in diamonds or gemstones or mining of any sort. No one claims to be his grandson or long lost niece or such. Far as we can tell, no one has come up here on the sly. Or any other way." He shrugged and smiled.

"So at this point the deal feels like it is on the up and up. I can't see how it is bogus. No one is asking us for money, or anything like that. And the information seems to be real. We hope."

He paused again. He saw what looked like two parallel lines in the ground. They ran for a few feet then disappeared. It occurred to him that they almost looked like wheel tracks. They disappeared before he could process what he saw. For a moment he wondered what they were and how they got there. Focused as he was on the diamond mine, the thought flew out his ear.

"We have had descriptions of the area. Now it is time to see and learn the place. The lay of the land, other formations, signs of other people, and so on. Joe and I need to find a reliable route to it. And we want to learn the size of things. And

check the terrain out. And we want to gather some samples. "
He didn't hear that this to-do list had tasks only for the men.
Nor did he think how that sounded to Ella.

She bristled. The 'Joe and I this' and 'Joe and I that'
made her want to yank the reins from Joe's hands and take
control. Quickly she cooled off. It was time to do some research. She had to look into that old scheme she had read
about somewhere. This old geezer's gem mine could all be on
the up and up, but it never hurt to check and double check.
She had to see if they were being played. Or if she could play
someone. Dale continued, unaware of her concerns.

"Plus, you and Chari deserve to have a 'before and after'
view. Right now it is just a patch of ground, nothing more. I
understand that it is a place of rolling ground, scattered pine
trees, and rock ledges and outcrops. One hill nearby. This
is lonesome high prairie country. I understand, and it sure
looks deserted. There ain't another person or animal for
miles around."

That is what concerned Ella. Maybe it was too deserted.
If no one ever came around, maybe it was a genuine find, a
bonanza. Either that, or it was a perfect place to convince
people of things. She had to get back to town to renew some
old contacts and do some digging and checking.

Dale was going on, convinced the information was
sound and that they stood near the edge of a pile of money.
He droned on. "But when Joe and Chari and you and I bring
investors in here that will change. It won't be dry deserted
scablands. It will be a city. This place will be as crowded and
as busy as Cripple Creek or Dawson City. And we will own
the city lots and the main lode. With any luck at all we won't
need Mr. Harriman or David Moffat. You just wait!"

They had been creaking and bumping along for quite a while. The wagon came to a small creek.

Joe had been listening, intently but not obviously. He felt that Dale was on board, ready to go sell the project. Ella, on the other hand, would take some work yet. She wasn't quite convinced. Joe was sure that when she saw things at the lode, she would be sold big time.

For some reason as he listened to Ella he was reminded of that woman Juli. The one he had briefly talked to back in Denver. She too had street smarts and a healthy skepticism. He kind of liked her and hoped to see her again.

The small creek brought Eggers out of his reverie. It was time for a break. He snapped the reins and got the team to slow. Loudly he announced, "Let's take a rest here and give the horses a break. Good for them to drink and graze a bit. Us too!" He glanced over at Chari. She too had been unobtrusively listening. Their smile was meant for onlookers to be one between friends and lovers. It was a private agreement of their progress.

"Chari, I'll bet you are ready to get off this hard seat. I know I am. We can stretch our legs here and have a bite." He pulled the reins again. "Whoa there." The horses stopped. They were ready to break the monotonous rhythm of pulling a load across roadless country. All climbed down, slowly and stiffly. Joe and Dale worked to unhitch the team from the wagon, and then from each other. Joe thought a moment, eying the few trees around. "Do you think they need to be tethered?"

Dale shook his head. "Nah. They'll stick close. Horses are gregarious and like people. If there are any predators they'll stick extra close. There's lots of good grass in close here. If one does start to wander we can go after it."

The two couples walked separate ways. They had been sitting close for hours and everyone needed space. One pair went by the stream, down from the wagon. The other strolled up a small rise nearby. The wagon and perhaps thirty yards of space separated them. There were plenty of rocks and even a few fallen logs to sit on. Mostly they stood, walked, and stretched out for a minute or two. Finally each sat. It felt good not to be rolled side to side and bumped over the surface.

Ella had been thinking the deal over. She had covered as many aspects of it as she could imagine. Dale's saying that all four should get investors crystallized things in her mind. She had a plan. For now she would keep it to herself. She intended to work it in part by helping other people to have ideas. The trick was to plant seeds so people took her ideas as their own. That was good leadership. And done right, it got things going the way she wanted.

She got herself comfortable on a rock, just the right height for a bench. She savored its solid flat surface.

"Dale. Listen. I like the idea of bringing in investors. A mine like this is too big for the four of us. Like you say, if people are looking to put money into a venture, they may as well give it to us." They both smiled at that.

"Let's think this through. With four of us we should each use our own strengths and skills. Each person has something to add to the pot. We should capitalize on that, get a variety of contributions." She watched, trying to gauge his reaction, then went on.

"I think Joe and Chari should be the primary ones to recruit and sell investors. We can do it too, and there are some people we should approach. If nothing else, just to keep a hand in." He listened silently, making a 'let's hear it' motion.

"But I think you will agree, they are connected in ways we aren't. The two of them seem to know, or know how to find, people who have money. She was telling me she sits on a committee for girl students or some such. People who can afford to send daughters to school sure have money. Folks like that can afford to put money into a diamond mine. He hobnobs with people like that too. So, I think it makes sense that they should take the lead in that part of the arena. They would be good at finding cash to start this up. You and I, you and I can make other contributions."

Dale was careful to keep a poker face as he listened. He thought, *Oh boy, EQ is on a toot. Starting to divvy up the work already. I wonder what she has cooked up.* Out loud, he acknowledged. "I'm not sure I totally agree. But you may be right. Tell me more."

"You mentioned that this will be big. Lots of people, lots of the activity they bring. Hotels, boarding houses, mills, stores, assay offices, saloons, women, house building, so on. Even security men. Working for us, imagine!" She grinned at that thought. "We'll have paying mines with supplies coming in and ore going out. Now, what did the big camps like Cripple Creek, Aspen, and Central City have? I mean, besides all that stuff?"

Neither said anything. She hoped she had his interest and he would answer. He suspected what she meant but wanted to hear her thoughts. The chess game continued.

Ella spoke first. "Railroads, that's what. Successful towns are on the rail grid!"

He thought how railroads had tripped over themselves in the rush to get a line in to each of those towns. Railroad men knew better than anyone that the first to get tracks in would make the most money. He was starting to see her scheme, but still played it a little slow.

"Yes. So?"

"So? Don't you see? If we do it right, we talk to them, stir up some competition. Railroads like the Union Pacific and the Moffat will likely do all they can to get here. And there may be others in the region who would be interested."

She warmed to the subject. Ella was starting to fire up. "The UP already has a main line fifty or sixty miles north, in Cheyenne and Laramie. Moffat will have a line about that far south, near Kremmling and over to Steamboat. And there is the Colorado Central. Not to mention the other roads coming north out of Denver."

She talked faster as she went. Dale had to concentrate now to catch her ideas.

"I bet we can get investment funds from them. From one of them or even from both. And better yet, tracks. That is what we want, tracks, and a piece of the land grant action." Her eyes got big. Land along the right of way was sometimes granted to railroads by Congress, to encourage growth and settlement. Could they get in on that!? Such an idea had not even occurred to her until just now. She paused, almost stunned by the opportunity.

Dale too saw the enormity of such an arrangement. "Yeah, and let's keep that idea quiet. No need to spread that around. You and I will be able to retire to Newport if this works out!"

Ella brought herself back. "Seriously, if we do it right we can play Harriman off against Moffat and maybe others. Let's see who can build the best and quickest spur to—what do you call it, the Karat Top mine?"

Dale smiled. "Good idea, E. Maybe we should tell Joe and Chari."

"No!" Ella was not smiling. He was startled at her quick response.

"Its not that I don't trust them, although I'm not sure I entirely do. It is that if you and I have a good idea, let's just sit on it for a little while. Think it through, be sure it really is a good one."

She looked at him with her best 'come hither' expression. "Dale, you and I have been through a lot together. This one could be big. Before we get generous with our ideas, let's agree it is us first. You and me, then the others." She stopped and smiled. "This is an opportunity to do it right. Let's just you and me make sure we skim some cream from this. At least for now, until we see how things start to play out. Don't tell anyone else. No one. Please?" She fluttered as she said this last word. The ploy worked.

"Well, alright. For now. We can wait and see. I think we should tell them, I really do. But if you really think so, I agree, put it off for now."

As if they are telling us everything they have planned, thought Ella. She stepped to him.

They sealed the agreement with a deep but not too quick a kiss. He was in the unusual position of wanting less of it than she. Usually she broke it off before he wanted, but not this time. Ella was kissing but was also thinking.

I have no idea if this diamond mine will pay out. Doesn't matter. I will find an angel, get some seed money no matter what I have to do for it. And I will decide how that money gets spent.

DOWN THE HILL, ON THE OTHER SIDE OF THE WAGON, JOE AND Chari were also enjoying the stationary seating and firm ground. Joe absently watched the horses munching grass along the small creek.

"Joe, did you see our tracks from when we came out a while ago? I saw them several times."

"Yes I did. They didn't. At least I don't think either one saw anything. Neither one reacted or looked hard the few times I saw our tracks." He blanched. "At least I hope the tracks were ours. Did you see any others?" He tossed down a stalk of grass he had been half heartedly chewing on.

"No, I didn't. Still, good point. We need to keep an eye out for intruders or claim jumpers."

"Right. About Ella and Dale, we have to be careful. They think no one has been this way recently. God knows very few have, ever. This really is desolate country. In any case, we'll have to be sure to deal with that before we bring others out here. We want people to know they are among the very few who know about the deal." He plucked another stalk of grass and nervously bit it. "Say, another thing. Are you sure our rocks look as if they belong?"

She nodded, glancing at the others to be see if they were out of hearing range. They were.

"The outcroppings at the site are much like formations in the rich African mines. At least from the descriptions and pictures I have seen they are. I don't think they really hold a thing, but at first glance they look like they do. And we were careful to cover our tracks. So yes, the rocks will look natural."

She grinned wolfishly. "After one of them finds one, it won't matter. They'll be off to the races then!"

Chari then turned and gazed over at the other couple, smiling and giving a quick wave of her fingers. "Not that these two will know. Who knows how a genuine diamond field looks? Anyway, like I say, when they find one or two stones all logic will go away. You just watch."

Her expression was friendly but her sentiment was not. "And these two are practiced, cynical operators. They'll pick up on what's in it for them. They'll be chomping at the bit to bring in development. Just wait until we start telling people about it. We will have so many investors we can winnow out the small ones and go for the really rich ones."

He nodded. "Hey, Chari, how do you like the name for it? You remember, the rocks there are a deep red color. That is why the name, Karat Top. How do you like it? It is a joke but few will get it."

Chari was still looking in Ella's direction. She rolled her eyes. "Well Joe, I do. Very cute."

She turned to face him. "So far, the decision to bring in Dale and Ella seems to be a sound one. They are getting excited, or he is at least. And I can see the wheels turning in her head. She will try to work her own schemes, you watch. Still, I think they will add credibility and bring contacts."

"Yes, he can talk about his engineering experience. I'm sure he'll not volunteer that it isn't mining work. That is fine with me. Any way to bring in investors is good. And Ella, he says, is his partner. He insisted she come if he came in. You are probably right, she's the one we'll have to watch."

A chilly breeze blew up. After a while, the four put on coats, rehitched the team, and went on towards their destination.

XVII

SUMMER MELDING INTO FALL IS EXQUISITE IN COLORADO.
Weather is calm and clear; days are warm; nights are cool.
Mik stood at the door, looking out from Corona Town. On
a day like this it felt like he could see halfway to New York.
Enjoy it while you can, Mik, he thought. *Soon the storms and
snows will come. Then, I'll be lucky to see halfway to the end of the
building.* The view out over the valley seeped into his soul,
warming and nourishing him. He wrenched himself away
and went inside.

Inside, the calendar on the wall showed September 1904.
Cam sat delving into some diagram or report. The title was
'A Study of the Use of Rail Spikes'. The authors considered
pluses and minuses of alternating the 'fill every hole' pattern.
Such a change could cut use and cost of spikes hugely. He was
skeptical, though. It might reduce expense up front, true. But
using even a few less spikes might allow or cause the rails to
wobble. Loose rails equaled slippage of the road. On the flats
out east maybe that wasn't life and equipment threatening.
Maybe. But up here it certainly would be. Here in the Rockies the terrain climbed steeply above and dropped sharply
below the roadbed. Loosening the rails would be akin to
playing Russian roulette.

"Hello, Mik." Cam was glad to be done with such non-sense. "I didn't get a chance to hear, how was your break in town?" Before Mik could respond, he continued. "Say, your friend seems nice. For some reason I never knew you were with anyone. You keep a secret well! I'll bet the two of you had a good time."

He grinned, savoring the memories of his own time down below, with his wife and family.

Mik's time with Juli had been good but short. And he regretted not saying a proper goodbye. He stuffed that thought. "Yeah, it was a good break. Too short as always." He smiled. "Say, when I first saw you in the station you were talking with that Joe Eggers. He sure had your attention." The unstated question hung.

For a quick moment Cam wished he was still reading about railroad spikes. He shrugged and faced the issue.

"Yeah, that guy could charm a snake out of its skin. He was telling me, hinting actually, that he knew of a lode of diamonds, or more precisely, precious gems. Supposedly somewhere around here. He of course never did say where or anything specific, just hints, rumors, and suggestions. For a few seconds I half believed there was a diamond mine over the hill."

He smiled, making fun of himself. "Looking back, I see that I wanted to believe it. That's what I mean by his charming a snake. He has the gift, if you can call it that, to make people hear what they want to hear. That kind of man can be a fun storyteller or a quick buck artist. He is the latter."

Glad that the subject was out in the open, he then changed the subject. "Mik, I'm not sure if you know, or if I should say anything. But that day in Denver.... I had just left

Eggers and he went off somewhere. Then I met you and Juli. You and I got to talking like I said, and she slipped away."

Mik nodded, remembering.

"I remember now that out of the corner of my eye, I saw Eggers approach her and say something. It seemed a conversation not simply a greeting. Then you mentioned a culvert or switchbacks or something and I jumped back in to railroading. I just remembered this as you asked me about Eggers, and I wanted you to know."

Mik gazed at him, his mind working.

"Thanks, Cam. I appreciate your telling me."

He made a mental note. *This is a good chance to follow up, to connect with her. Maybe she'll tell me what they talked about. I'll have to send a telegram since she doesn't have a telephone.*

Cam watched the wheels turn in his friend's head and made a good guess what was going on. Rather than ask, he turned to road business.

"When I ride the Denver to Corona stretch it is hard to just relax. Coming back this time, like when I came down to Denver, I took notes. I can't help it. Since I helped build it from Utah up to the end. It is my baby, and I look whenever I ride the line."

'Utah' was the railyard named 'Utah Junction'. Located about two miles north of downtown Denver, it was the Moffat Road's mile point zero. All distances on the schedules, plans, and specifications originated at that point. As everyone at Corona knew, the Denver Northwestern and Pacific Railway started building from there in summer 1902.

"Say, speaking of Utah. I'm sure you know, but I have to talk about it. The spur we ran into downtown from there, Utah. We were expecting to tie in to others' lines and stop at

Union Station. But the big money boys back east are so intent on hurting Mr. Moffat that they won't let us tie into the main depot. Instead we have to stop at our own station two blocks away. Passengers are forced to walk. Baggage and freight have to be transferred by horse and wagon. Isn't that a heck of a note?!"

He rolled his eyes. "Ticks me off. That would never happen if us railroaders were in charge instead of the money men." He paused a second, considering that statement, then went on. "Anyway, returning to work, it was good to eyeball every inch of the line. This time I was looking at the uphill pull, thinking about maintenance and the operating needs."

He grinned. "I was thinking that, from Utah to top of the Hill looks different than when coming the other way. But when I say it out loud, it doesn't sound at all insightful. Hell, it sounds silly and kind of stupid. Well, anyway, things along the line still seem to be working well."

Mik nodded. "Maybe it isn't profound, but it is commonsense to look at the road from both directions. And yes, I agree. I looked close at things on the way back here myself. The rails and bed and drainage all seem to be sound. I have to say we did a good job. And the crews running the trains every day are doing a good job."

Nodding, Cam took this in. "Now, we've laid track over the top. We're running trains downhill for the first time since we left Denver over two years ago! We've got track over the summit, across the crest of the nation! We're running all the way over to Arrow already."

Arrow was the small town near the head of construction. Actually it was just a settlement out in the national forest, not an official town. Usually along a railroad someone organized a townsite company and sold lots wherever the train stopped. That wasn't the case with Arrow. It just kind of sprang up. There was no mayor, no sheriff, no orderly and planned street grid.

Mik wanted to go there.

"Let's us take the run down to Arrow today. We both need to eyeball the line. And I want to see that loop. I have seen it and drew a sketch, but I want to ride and look it over again."

A loop was how the surveyors and engineers handled a steep stretch. This loop was unique. Viewed from above (not that anyone but God and ravens could do that) it resembled half a pretzel. The tracks came down along the ridge above timberline. They crossed a draw, called Rifle Sight Notch, on a trestle. Then the road made a big loop. The grade dropped the whole way around it. At the end of the loop the tracks went under a hill, through the Loop Tunnel. The tunnel ran at right angles to and went through the hill, under the trestle.

Cam nodded. "Yeah, I want to ride over the trestle and go through the tunnel." He could already smell the smoke and feel the pang of cinders on his face, looking out over the trestle.

"The tunnel isn't reliably stable. I hear it keeps closing in, kind of a slow motion ooze. It isn't the hard rock we had on Eldorado Mountain or the Needle's Eye. That spot will need to be shored up somehow." He smiled in anticipation. "I really am looking forward to riding the giant corkscrew!" He did a quick mental rundown of what had to get done this day. Most he could delegate and the rest could wait, he decided.

Excitedly, he repeated himself. "Yup, I watched the trestle going up and look forward to riding over it again."

The settlement of Arrow was a few miles past Rifle Sight Notch. From Corona, it wasn't far, about nine road miles. As the crow flies the two were less than three miles apart. The village sat quite a bit lower in elevation, well below the tree line. Down there weather could be a problem but not like up above timberline.

Mik wanted to see the layout and the situation. Plus he wanted to view the progress of the road. For his own sake he needed to fill in the picture. And he knew he would get questions from the owners, so he wanted to be up to date.

"There are no regular freight or passenger trains to Arrow yet, are there, Cam?"

"We do have a few scheduled runs, yes. But you and I can ride down on a construction special. I know we have a load of supplies and rails going over this morning." He thought for a moment. "There isn't much call for paying loads going to Arrow, yet. But, with luck we might ride back on a loaded freight train. There are loads of lumber and cattle coming out already. Not a lot, but some. Early days and all. For now that is probably most of what we'll see coming from the Fraser valley. There just isn't much else out there that Denver might need."

The two men considered the prospects.

The broad valley to the west was called Middle Park. Ranches and one tiny city called Fraser accounted for most of the activity there. There were a few settlements but no other towns in the vast, high valley. Fraser lay just across the main range. As the crow flies, it sits only ten or eleven miles west of Tolland. The commercial center of the area, Fraser even had a doctor. This was cause for comment only because the doc was a she. Doc Susy was skilled and had a good reputation. A doctor is a small mountain town was a good thing.

A business possibility occurred to Mik. Maybe hauling hay and feed would pay. Snows would be deep over in the Park and wouldn't melt away until April or later. Livestock eat too. Cattle need their hay and horses their oats. Carrying in livestock feed might be a paying proposition, in addition to hauling people's bacon, coffee and flour.

He made a mental note to ask around about it. Any way they could avoid empties was a positive. Towing freight cars with nothing in them was a dead cost. Hauling hay out to the ranchers might not pay for itself but would at least help cut the losses. And he was sure there would be freight and passengers coming the other way, towards Denver.

For some reason he remembered a meeting with a ticket agent of some railroad, a while back. The man had gotten off on a tangent, on a subject near to his heart. Mik recalled that the man was from Boston or nearby. He had the noticeable accent. Why a Bostonian would know anything about ranching was a wonder, but the man did. He was suddenly was transported back in time, listening, half to the subject and half to the accent.

"Ranch faa-milies definitely need to have theyah caat-tle and sheep hawled to maah-ket. Every mile an aanimal is hawled instead of haa-ving to waalk puts money in theyah pawckets."

Mik knew that the ranchers of Middle Park—most of them anyway—were happy to see the train come. It would connect them with the outside world. Sure they had the stagecoach line over Berthoud Pass. But that couldn't compete time or expense-wise with the train. The coming of the railroad meant that moving people to Denver wasn't an epic, difficult trek. Plus, and it was a big plus for the economy, getting the cattle to the stockyards was easier and cheaper.

As soon as the tracks got there, ranchers wouldn't have to drive their cattle up to Laramie Wyoming. That trip took a lot of work, time, and wear and tear. The railhead at Laramie was a good hundred miles and several mountain passes away. By the time the cattle walked that far, those that survived the trek and predators were smaller. They had less weight, stringier meat, less fat. So they brought a lower price. Not to mention the time the cowboys had to spend driving them. They had to be fed, paid and looked after too.

Mik had pretty well sold himself on the benefits of the railroad coming to Fraser. It was good that he was at a stopping point because Cam broke in. He was into the subject of Arrow and environs, not the Fraser valley.

"I hear that the station house at Arrow is built, or at least is far enough along to be used. And the road progresses. Grade is cut and rails are being laid on down towards Fraser."

The men readied to go on over the hill to Arrow. The engineer tooted the steam whistle, indicating he was about ready to pull out.

Cam wrote out notes frantically, as he also talked to an assistant, ticking off the jobs he wanted done before he returned.

Mik was impatient. "We gotta run. Let's go, Cam. Grab your coat. Its September and you never know."

Jacket in hand, Cam clambered into the cab of the engine. Mik was there already. With the engineer at the controls and the fireman shoveling coal, it was crowded.

Mik glanced at Cam. "Maybe we should give them room to work. Let's go to the passenger car." One passenger car was attached; the rest of the makeup was freight cars. They carried rails and building materials to be delivered to Arrow.

"Right, but let's go to the caboose. I want to look at the grade and rails. Can't really do that from a passenger car." They climbed down and walked back to the end. The conductor was a regular who they knew and liked. As they climbed in, he gave them a glance.

"Taking a ride down the hill are you? Come on in, there's plenty of room. Cam, I'm guessing you'll want to look at the rails as we go. Take a seat over there. Can I get you coffee?" In the middle of the car stood a small potbelly stove with a coffee pot on top. The flames kept the room warm and coffee hot. "Here, have a mug. Mik?" He looked inquiringly; Mik nodded. The conductor poured one for Mik and topped his off then set it down. "I have to go signal. You're here. We're ready to go." He grabbed a lantern and left.

Both men watched as he swung the lantern. It was a mix of fast and slow overhead and sideways movements. Whatever the combination, the engineer understood. He blew the horn. At the same time, the conductor set foot on the ladder to get back on and the train started to move.

They were looking forward to the ride. The train emerged from the snowshed building out into the sunlight. Mik knew that the Corona Station snowshed would be essential in the winter but now there was scant need for it. Riding inside the caboose was good and allowed for an open view. The road headed west for several hundred yards then veered to the southwest. The line gently descended, the slope at the mild two percent gradient. Soon the sides of the mountain ridges they traversed dropped away, fairly steeply. The grade remained as the train neared timberline.

Mik reviewed a page of his sketches. Not on paper but in his head—Corona Town was near eleven thousand seven hundred and valley floor was about eighty eight hundred. So the road had to drop almost three thousand feet.

Top to bottom measured in a straight line was five miles. Three thousand feet in five miles was six hundred feet per mile. That was around a ten percent grade, way too steep for anything but oxcarts with hefty oxen. The road would have to snake around a whale of a lot and cover much more than five miles to do stay at a reasonable steepness. As it looped and swooped, the road remained high on the side of the mountain, dropping but not too fast.

As the car swayed, Mik remembered something he wanted to mention to Cam.

"I heard there were gold diggings at a settlement a ways north of Steamboat Springs. A place called Clark Peak or somesuch. Not sure the size of the lode. It may be a flash in the pan, we'll see. I think we'll have to watch the area north of the road. There may be opportunities to make money with a short spur.

XVIII

"Mining north of Steamboat? Gold mining? I hadn't heard that. Are you sure it was Colorado?" Cam paused. Things clicked in his head. "That makes sense, now that I think about it. "

Cam thought back to Joe Eggers' hints about mineral finds. He wondered if any of those were related to the area around Steamboat.

"What do you mean, now that you think about it? What do you know that I don't?"

He chuckled. "Not a lot, Mik, not a lot. Its just that supposed precious mineral lode I heard about while I was down in town. You know, I told you, it was Joe Eggers. You can imagine, I half expected him to pull out a bottle of snake oil to make his tip go down better. I check, recheck, and look again at whatever that man says. But if you heard tell of a strike of some kind too, maybe there is something to it. Let's find out more and maybe we can take a look."

Nodding in agreement, Mik absently watched as the mountainside slid by, apparently rocking and clicking a little bit with the train's motion. Thoughts of obscure gold mines receded and his entire attention was focused out the window. Tree line wasn't far below and looked to be approaching

193

gradually as the road held to its mild grade. Bobbing and weaving, the track went in and out of draws and canyons. It could have been a sidewinder rattle snake, all esses and fluid motion. In one or two places the road made tight turns. Then he could look out from the caboose and see the engineer across the way. If you averaged out all the twists and turns, they were headed to the southwest.

As they came out of a stand of trees into a clearing, Mik saw the track veer around right to northwesterly. A tall trestle carried them over a gap probably two hundred feet wide and seventy feet deep. This was the 'Rifle Sight Notch'. From a distance the dip in the land looked like the V shaped rifle sight the gunsmith put out on the business end of the barrel. The tracks ran over the trestle then dropped around to the right. The rails completed the circle and went through a tunnel which went under the Notch below the trestle's supports. The track continued southwesterly. Across the country, postcards were already on sale touting this railroad marvel.

"The loop is quite a sight, isn't it? I worked off the plans and helped build it, but still, it really is something to see!"

The loop's circle was a half mile or so in diameter. The purpose was to lose altitude quickly and compactly. Mik had heard of a similar altitude eating loop, carved entirely as a tunnel inside of a mountain. Surveyors of the Canadian Pacific Railroad laid out and crews carved that masterpiece up in the Canadian Rockies.

Cam had seen a similar loop and trestle by the Colorado mining camp of Georgetown. He had to think that this was every bit as spectacular. Maybe more so, given the altitude above sea level and the isolation of the site.

He couldn't help himself. "This is magnificent railroad engineering and construction! On a long train the engine could be heading down into the tunnel while the caboose is still crossing the trestle...or vice versa! And this is standard gauge, not narrow gauge like above Georgetown. Really something!"

He paused. "You heard right, Cam. We are seeing some slippage in that tunnel. The interior makeup of that mountain within the notch is different. It isn't the hard granite we usually see. It is some kind of compacted clay or gravel or something. When exposed to air it oozes or flows very slowly. It is hard as the devil to keep that bore open. We have to constantly monitor how wide and high the opening is. Sometimes it starts to slump and become misshapen."

He frowned at Mother Nature's audacity. "We'll have to reinforce that somehow. Either steel shoring or cement walls should do the trick."

Taken together, the trestle, loop, and tunnel were a creative solution to a number of challenges. Moffat's men had to aim the tracks to come out at a chosen point above Fraser. And they did their best to keep the grade of the road to two percent. The contortions of the loop and the localized drop to and through the tunnel let them retain that goal. There were a few parts of the road over Rollins Pass which had steeper stretches. But not many.

The two marveled at the road, and at the view. They could see west out over Middle Park with its grasslands and meadows. Chains of mountains were everywhere, generally running north and south. Those mountains, while still formidable, got smaller and lower further west and north. With the pass and soon to be tunnel, the road builders were past the highest and most difficult barriers they would face. The road would run through the country they overlooked, all the way to Salt Lake City. But first it had to descend from the loop down to the valley floor.

"You know, Mik, this is one heck of a view. Look at all that country out there, ready to be settled and put to use. It is wonderful! This place sure is beautiful." Conversation ebbed as they savored the view, then Cam started up. "It is also one heck of a difficult place to build and run a railroad. Keeping any line open and running has its challenges. Keeping this one going through the winter will be tough and expensive."

"True that. The tunnel under the mountain will make things easier. And cheaper. Running the road over the top may eat up most of the profits for a while. Let's hope the tunnel gets done and open pretty quick. You know, I was talking about it with Mr. Sumner."

Horace Sumner, the Denver Northwestern's chief engineer, was an experienced and knowledgeable railroad man.

"He says there are several different ideas about where to dig. Most start somewhere near the Giant's Ladder." The Giant's Ladder was the series of switchbacks on the east side of the pass.

Cam observed. "That makes sense. Depending on where and how high they start, the tunnel could be as short as two or as long as six miles."

"Sure. If they start at a higher elevation the tunnel under the mountain will be shorter. But, as we know, the higher the tracks the harder to keep them open in the winter. I guess the muckety mucks will decide on how to make that tradeoff."

"Yes. The sooner they get a tunnel done, the sooner we can run several miles under this mountain instead of twenty five or so miles over it." Cam was eager to get the road on a solid, paying basis.

Slowing the rig, the engineer adeptly rounded a corner and neared a village. A jumble came to view, a mixture of buildings, tents, and stacks of construction material. It was Arrow, the reason they were riding the iron this day.

The settlement had sprung up near the railhead several weeks ago. Of course the railhead was further on now, down almost to the valley floor. Arrow still served as gathering point and place for workers to eat and sleep. The builders and a growing number of shippers used it as an assembly place and marshalling point. There were even a few 'full time' locals. A motley collection of loggers, trappers, cowboys and even a few sheepmen were around. Occasionally a traveler or hopeful prospector came through. Gossip, drink, and the occasional fight helped pass the time.

The whistle hooted as the train came to a full stop.

"Come back some time when you can stay!" The conductor smiled, knowing that the two men would ride with him from time to time.

"Hey, thanks for the coffee. We enjoyed the views and got a real good look at the road as we came down." Cam had a thought. "I know you watch things like we just did. And that you speak up if you see a problem. I want to thank you for that and for all the work you do."

"Happy to do it. I can't believe you pay me to come ride on a train every day! Seriously, I am watching the tunnel at Rifle Sight. The rock there seems to expand when it hits air.

Something needs to be done with that. Otherwise, we seem to be making good progress towards Fraser and beyond."

"So noted. Thanks. We may see you on the return run."

Mik and Cam got out. Each had a mental checklist of items to look into, and went separate ways.

Cam eyed the construction supplies amassed there. He collared the first railroad man he saw.

"Tell me, who is in charge of these stacks of construction supplies?

"The station master is. He is in that new building over there. The one story made of stacked logs."

"Thanks. How long do items sit here before being sent on to the railhead? As a rule?"

"I really don't know, sir. You will need to talk with the station master."

Cam wanted to follow up on this. He wondered how much was accumulated before being forwarded to the rail head. And how often was it sent on? Now, with the railhead down in the valley, did things even need to be stored here? Why not send them closer to the actual building work? How much inventory, and money, was tied up in supplies just sitting here? These questions were important, even if they didn't involve actually grading and laying rail.

For his part, Mik was interested in the town. Who was there? Just what function did Arrow accomplish? Should it be encouraged, made a permanent stop on the road? Or was it just another ephemeral railhead settlement, here today gone in a month or a year? Could this be a good transfer point for shippers? What if anything besides timber and livestock would come through here? Maybe ore if mining took hold, but that was unlikely. The mines seemed to be east in

Boulder County, or south, Summit County and beyond. This part of the state seemed to miss out on the mining, at least so far. So, Arrow's future hinged on how loggers and ranchmen used the place, or not.

He looked around, wondering if there were other sources of business to be tapped. He wandered into a tent with a hand printed 'general store' sign in front. He sought the owner.

"Tell me, who are your customers here?"

"Some loggers, some cowboys. Mostly gandy dancers and other rail workers. They spend their pay like water, most of them. Mostly at the saloon, not here, I might add. Why?"

"I'm with the road. I just wonder if this will grow to become a town or stay a temporary, rough house railhead settlement."

"I've wondered that too. Your railroad could bring in people from Denver. They could come up and enjoy the mountains here. Cabins, fishing, sleigh rides, nature hikes... all could be done here if people would come and stay."

"Yes, I suppose so. Are there cabins or a hotel for travelers now?"

"No." The man looked at the tent they were in. "Mostly now Arrow is tents. The station master has a log building. It just got put up."

"Thanks." Mik turned to leave, musing on Arrow and the road. Who would or could be persuaded to provide business for the railroad here?

The railroad men met up outside the new station master's structure. As had been hinted but not stated, it was not entirely finished. The log walls were up and sturdy, doors and a window in, and the roof was on securely. But there was no chinking. Daylight was visible between most of the logs.

The walls could have been a ladder with massive, close spaced steps.

   With a glance at the sky, Mik thought that such a building would be chilly and drafty until someone got the gaps filled in or sealed up. *Much to be done and never enough time*, he thought.

XIX

THERE WAS MUCH TO BE DONE IN THE WILDS BETWEEN BOULDER and Laramie too. First the group had to get to their destination.

Chari shivered. "I'm worried, Joe. We're way out in the wilds and no one knows we're here."

"Yeah, well, that's good. We don't want anyone to know where we are. It can feel lonely but that is a good thing."

She went on as if he had said nothing. "And cold, I'm cold! Look out there. Clouds are blowing in and stacking up. And all of a sudden the air has turned frosty. Look, I can see my breath!" She pulled a blanket tight around her shoulders and blew rings, like smoke rings. That brought a smile. "This is fun. Even if it hurts my lungs, watch how I can to puff these circles!"

Joe wasn't happy. Trying to mask his concern, he chuckled. *It looks like we are in for a storm. At least we are almost there. If the place isn't just over this rise, we had better stop anyway. We need to get into shelter.*

He looked over at Dale. "We'd better get a move on. I think we are about there." Joe knew; Dale too was optimistic at Joe's statement. He sure hoped they were in fact just over a hill from the site. He noticed a curiously notched and bent tree and noted it for future reference.

To reinforce the group's respect for his acumen, Joe went on. "I believe our spot is just past that hill from what I can tell. Lucky for us because it looks like weather is coming."

"Yeah. It may blow through, but I don't think so. Soon as we can, let's rig a shelter. If there are outcrop ledges we can use them. Or we can rig up a lean to off the wagon or something."

"I was thinking the same. Something to keep us dry."

Preoccupied as she was with feeling cold, Chari was still aware of what the others were saying and doing. This was the critical time. She would watch the others closely, hoping to see excitement and acceptance. They were pulling up over a hill and this was the place. The weather and being cold were just annoyances right now. Whatever the conditions, they could cope.

It was Chari's hope that Ella would wander around a bit when they arrived. It would be really good if some evidence of the lode was found by her. The way the clouds looked, that would have to happen pretty quickly.

Chari silently urged the team on. They couldn't get there soon enough. Everyone was stiff and ready to get out and move around. Whatever their reasons, she wanted Ella and Dale to walk and see and find. *Please God*, she prayed, *don't let us get quick inch of snow! Let the ground stay clear!*

It was all she could do to not be obvious. Her will power was shredding with the effort not to stare at the ground. She didn't want to look where she and Joe had recently done some work. The one quick glance she allowed herself told her their old tracks didn't show. Sweeping the ground with a tree branch before they left did the job. It leveled the ground and the only thing she saw now were some deer tracks. It looked like humans had never been here. Even as all of this ran through her head, she practically willed the others to hurry out and walk around, as soon as they stopped.

Over the small hill trundled the wagon. Dale was impressed that Joe's memory was good. He didn't know that it wasn't from clues told by a geezer on his deathbed. Joe remembered the location from a few weeks back. Sure enough, there were eight or ten unusual formations of rock. They were dikes, a geological formation.

These rock structures protruded above the ground. Long ago they were molten and pressure forced the lava into the surrounding rocks, into their cracks and crevices. That surrounding rock was softer than the dikes and had since eroded away.

Chari was struck how the scene reminded her of Stonehenge. She almost said so but realized that would divert attention from their looking at the ground, so bit her tongue. Truth be told, she hadn't seen the British ruins. She had merely read several accounts with sketches.

All the dikes were distinctly colored. Some were reddish, a few rust colored, and some almost copper in color. A few had small pockets, bat sized caves, and holes.

"It looks almost like someone built a number of freestanding adobe walls." Ella looked with interest. "And then painted or dyed them!" The New Yorker in Chari wasn't sure just what adobe was, and was curious how Ella knew about it. Gazing at the formations, Ella didn't see Chari's surprised expression. She went on.

"These are amazing! They're huge. I'll bet they are up to fifteen feet tall and a good two feet thick. And look, up there, the corner. The hole looks like a needle's eye." The silence as they took it in was broken only by the wind.

Dale couldn't help but share his thoughts. "Yeah this is really something. The longest is a good forty yards long. Look, one is taller than it is long."

Only too ready to get out of the wagon, Joe pulled the reins. The team halted and everyone jumped off. The odd formations continued to rivet their attention. Joe and Chari pretended to be awestruck. They shuffled around, one eye on the rocks and one on Dale and Ella.

Chari gently nudged Joe and each started to wander a little. Looking at the ground, they acted like they were checking out places to rig a tent. Soon they were happy to stop acting. The clouds were scudding and the temperature dropped like a wrench off a shelf. It was time to find shelter.

Ella felt another gust and shivered. She too started to evaluate the rocks for a place of refuge. She saw one which seemed to have a cave or protected spot. Focusing, she walked intently, paying scant attention to her footing. There were a lumps under foot and all around. She scuffed on one and almost tripped. Whatever it was felt about the size of a walnut. Stopping, she caught her balance then looked down and picked the thing up. It was a strange stone, unlike any she had seen, but she figured it was just a rock. Opening her hand to drop it, she remembered why they were there. Pulling it close, she examined it minutely.

"Look at this odd rock," she called. "It is smooth and flinty, not rough like most stones. And one side…." She stopped talking, looking at one side which showed clear and crystalline. A shriek tore from her. "Is this a…is this what we're looking for?!"

Dale ran over, grabbing the rock. He held it up to what little light was offered by the lowering sky. "By God," he yelled, "By God, this sure looks like a diamond to me!"

Joe and Chari were a ways away. They wanted to check campsites, yes, but they also wanted to give room for Ella and Dale to discover. The two shared a triumphant glance. A resounding *Yes!* ran through Chari's mind. *They found one!*

Caution ruled Joe. *Now we have to be excited but skeptical. They have to convince themselves this is the real thing. Have to go limp, let them take the lead and make the case.* He prayed that Chari was thinking along the same lines.

Dale was exultant. "Ladies, we seem to have a gem here!" He paused, suddenly too excited to speak. Words came. "I present to you the Karat Top Mine! You see it now, before anyone. Remember this! Now it is just a few ledges in an obscure valley. If this...." Here he looked down at the rock in his hand. "If this is any indication, soon it will be a booming town. And WE will own it! Just look at this stone! Tell me it isn't a diamond."

He danced a jig, kicking and scuffing. That uncovered another similar stone. He fell to his knees, scrabbling in the dirt. "Look! More! We've hit the big one, the big one!"

Joe hurried over and grabbed the stones from Dale. He made a show of examining them then held one out to Chari.

"No, it couldn't be, could it? Diamonds?!" He looked at Ella then Dale. "Are you sure? Can it really be?" He sorrowfully shook his head, and gazed at the ground. "I can't believe it." After a moment he brightened, and stood up straight. Grinning, he set the hook. "I guess maybe the old coot knew what he was talking about. We really have something here!"

The excited talk held everyone's attention. The wind lessened and a cold mist started to descend.

Joe glanced up at the weather. "In a year or two, as things prove out, this place will be a town. Who knows?" He looked at Ella, then Dale, then Chari, smiling. Then he got serious.

"For now, though, we need to make some shelter. This storm may blow through or it may settle in. Either way, we want to stay dry." He walked over to a formation he and Chari had been looking at. It was eight or nine feet tall and maybe thirty feet long.

"We can use this like a tent ridgepole—drape the tarp over it. It will give shelter. And what the heck, to pass time, we can take assay samples off of it. And after we get shelter set, I want to walk around some more."

Shivering, Chari forgot precious stones and agreed. "Let's get that shelter up. I am freeezing!"

Ignoring her, Joe looked at his compadres. "Dale and Ella have found stones. Let's mark where we find things, to make us a map." He looked at the couple and they nodded. "Maybe you and I, Chari, can look later. Man oh man, I sure hope this is what it looks like!"

The big canvas tarp was unfolded and draped. Smaller rocks were found and set on the corners and along the sides. They held and the canvas didn't flap in the wind. It felt secure. None too soon: the mist had turned to a gentle rain. Soon it was sleet then snow.

"Dale, what about the horses?"

"They are alright, Ella. Joe and I loosely tied them in that aspen grove." He nodded towards a copse a little ways off. "Shelter and forage. Water. Green grass. It is almost as good as a tarp over a ledge!"

Ella agreed doubtfully and banished thoughts of horses. Was this really a lode of diamonds? In a way it seemed too good to be true. You don't just stumble on diamonds on the surface. It just doesn't happen. Then she remembered, again, the early days of the California gold rush. There, the newspapers said, miners simply picked up handfuls of gold nuggets.

Out of streams, and off the ground, no digging or hard work. Maybe this was the real thing! A grin helped her to relax. It was dry and comfortable under the canvas. A fire just outside provided extra warmth and cheer.

IN THE HIGH MOUNTAINS MANY MILES TO THE SOUTH AND west of the gem seekers, the weather remained stable. A change was coming but for now the temperatures were pleasant enough. A few mild breezes wafted and the sun shone through the trees.

The railroad men met briefly at the station agency then wandered Arrow some more. Mik was struck by the tents. There must have been twenty or so. Some were square and taut, like a sergeant had arranged and approved them. Had they been wood not canvas they could have been part of a regular town. Most of them looked like living quarters. But. Mik noticed several tents, often at the end of a row or off by themselves. These weren't as tautly rigged. Those tents seemed to have a lot of coming and going. Those definitely weren't living quarters. They looked like gathering places. Saloons? He chuckled and mentioned it to Cam.

"Funny how public houses and women show up at new settlements. In any of these places, you can buy a drink or companionship real quick."

Cam smirked. "I'll bet those are open and skinning money from the workers before you can buy nails from the blacksmith or supplies at the general store."

"How much do you think those guys water down the whiskey? It has to be rotgut to start with. And I have to wonder if they even have any kind of a license. You know they likely don't have the approval of the district Forest Ranger. Or anyone else."

Cam shrugged. "You're on the money. That's why they're in tents, so they can fold up and move on. If the law tries to land on them they can be gone in an hour. I'll bet their business is good, though. What else is there to spend money on in Arrow Colorado?"

"Not a lot." Shivering, he looked away from the tented streets and changed the subject. "Say, Cam, does it seem to be getting cooler? I sure feel colder than I did." Mik looked west. "Those clouds were on the far horizon when we left Corona. Now they have blocked the sun and are closing in. Maybe we ought to talk to the station manager about spending the night. The building is new—we could be his first guests."

A mist started and it soon progressed to a gentle rain. Following the cloud bank's cold air mass, it wasn't long before the rain drops turned to snowflakes. For a while they were big and soft, falling out of a still sky. Then a breeze built in from the west and the flakes began to come in sideways.

The two men approached the local railroad boss in his new station house. He of course knew and had been expecting them. "Mik, Cam, good to see you. How was the ride down? That Rifle Sight Notch is really something, no?"

"Yes, we were in the caboose. I got a kick out of looking down on the tracks below us when we crossed the trestle!"

"Quite a structure. And now, we're laying rail down towards Fraser. Iron is all the way there, almost. A few townspeople have come up to see the place here. There is a doctor there in Fraser, a woman doc! Can you imagine? Goes by 'Doc Susie' she told me. Said since I'm rail boss at Arrow, I should be sure to call her if someone is hurt up here. I guess she is a good doc, doesn't lose many patients. That really is the sign of a good doctor!"

He paused and glanced out at the weather. "Looks like winter is making a try at us. So, did you have any surprises or problems on the way down here?" He couldn't let talk of the tunnel go. "How about that loop, isn't it something? Last time I came down, I was riding in the caboose too. Darndest thing it was to look down on the engine pulling me along. It came around under us and it was like riding on the tail end of a big snake!"

"Yes, it is quite a piece of construction." Cam was proud to be part of a railroad which could perform such feats.

"To answer your question, no, we had no surprises. The line looks good from Corona down, and we made good time." He addressed the station agent. "'I do have questions for you, though: How long do materials sit here before being sent on to the railhead?"

"Depends on the material. From two days to two weeks. I can check and give you specifics if you want."

"Do that. Also, tell me, how far down valley is the grade ready to take ballast and ties? How about the actual laid track? You said you were near Fraser. How near?" He knew about how far the progress was, but wanted to see what the station master had to say.

Mik changed the subject. "Railroad talk aside, we need your help. The weather is changing. That's September: nice as gold then nasty as a rodeo bull."

He smiled and gestured at the clouds. "You have two beggars on your doorstep! Seriously, we'll need a blanket and a cot tonight, it looks like."

"Not a problem. Come on in!"

Mik mentioned the saloon tents. "Someone is making money off of our labor gangs. Is drinking a problem?"

"No, not really. These guys need some way to blow off steam. Occasionally someone wants to fight or bust something up, but not often. That is when we could use a sheriff, but we don't have one since we're not a real town. Now if I can't handle the guy I need the help of the Forest Ranger. That is, if I can find him or get word to him. Of course he has things to do besides helping me run this station and babysitting drunks. He has licensing authority for commercial operations here in the National Forest but hasn't pushed it. Far as I know, none of these saloons have applied for one."

Cam asked, "So what is being done? Has he just turned a blind eye to those barkeepers?"

"Yes. I expect he thinks Arrow will come and go pretty quick. When the railhead reaches Fraser this likely will be just a whistle stop with an emergency water tower. So he lets it go. If there is a problem with belligerent workers, he has the power to close up the saloonkeeper as well as break up fights."

Snow was falling heavily now, and the wind increased steadily. The breeze which had started was by now pushed out into Kansas somewhere. The three looked on as a few snowflakes started to filter in through the unchinked logs.

The manager grinned then opened the potbelly stove and put in another scoopful of coal.

XX

THE WEATHER CLOSED IN ON ARROW AND STAYED THE NIGHT.

Railroad men, barkeeps, and other citizens of Arrow awoke under a twelve inch winter blanket. Dry and fluffy snow came, typical of the early season. Later in the winter snow usually dropped wet and heavy. Pretty much everyone in town found a dry and warm place to wait it out. Most were in tents. Some buildings were virtually weather tight. Some were not.

Mik slowly woke, confused. It was snowy. Didn't he bed down inside the station agency? He distinctly remembered falling asleep on a bench, snug in a blanket. As he dropped off, the glow from the potbelly stove filled the room. This morning, he blearily looked out. Flakes were swirling and dancing! There were small snow drifts in the room's corners. He considered this a moment, and was interrupted by the aroma of hot coffee.

Motivated by the pleasant smell, he rose. Pulling his trousers up, he grabbed a boot. He looked at it a moment, then on a hunch turned it upside down. Snow fell out and he took the other boot and emptied it as well.

To his just wakened brain and feet, the boots felt like anvils which had been in the ice house all night. He looked at the station agent, smiling wryly.

"You were right to be concerned about the weather. I guess it is no surprise that the snow sifted in the building through the unchinked cracks. It even found its way into my boots! Good thing I thought to shake them out."

Being a 'glass half full' kind of guy, Mik said the most cheerful thing he could think of. "They're cold and stiff but at least my feet are dry." He was just talking, not addressing anyone in particular. Cam and the station agent looked his way. The agent filled a cup with coffee and scooted it towards him. Mik took a slurp of the hot bitter nectar. Warmth and caffeine kicked in; he started to come alive.

Cam shrugged. "We'll see lots more of this. Get used to snow finding its way into places you don't want it!" He paused thoughtfully. "Even down here in the trees this storm is big enough to cause drifts, in and out. Makes me ask, what's going on up the hill? I wonder if the telegraph lines are up." Looking at the agent, he asked, "Any indication?"

Mik cast a speculative eye out to the tracks. "Let's send a wire and see. I'd bet that the road is open already, or they're working on it. This storm caught us out. It shouldn't have, but it did. This day will no doubt see our first use of the snow plows."

The station master cleared his throat. "I have a theory about all that...." Neither said anything, just looked expectantly at him. Rummaging at a desk, he found a map of the State.

"A look at the map tells us we can likely expect this winter. Corona sits atop the mountain at the easternmost stretch of the continental divide. The divide runs north and south here for thirty or so miles. Then it veers northwest to the north, and southwest to the south." He pointed. "So the terrain at Rollins Pass acts as the mouth of a funnel. And, Corona sits at a low point in the divide; north and south the mountains climb to over thirteen thousand feet, and the ridge stays higher than it is at the pass. The effect of this unique topography is to put Rollins Pass, Corona, and our train tracks smack in the bullseye of winter winds."

He sketched it out, and summarized his theory. "Winds carry snow. The mountains here act as a funnel to direct and speed the winds over the divide. Which means drifts of snow will be dropped on the exact spot where the railroad runs and where Corona bravely sits."

Cam took the map and studied it. Mik nodded. "Yup, we may as well have a target painted on the station up there. We're in for it. Say, can I keep this? I have a sketchbook of the Road and this would be a fine addition to it."

"Sure, take it. Glad to contribute."

Up at Corona crews worked to open the road. Until now keeping the way clear meant moving fallen boulders or scaring balky herds of elk. With the cold season the problems would arise—or fall from—other sources. Accumulating, wind driven piles of snow would be the bane of the Denver Northwestern and Pacific Railroad.

This storm marked the season's first use of snow clearing equipment. It seemed a monumental amount of work was needed, and immense amounts snow had to be moved. Nobody knew that the storm wasn't large or vicious by Rollins Pass standards. Months and years later, people would look at such a storm as an annoyance, a mere inconvenience. This day, with no perspective, everyone at Arrow and the crews at Corona thought they were coping with a major weather event.

Up top, Steu Wentz directed the work. He was in charge since Cam was gone. Early in the morning, he looked out the window to see drifts and limited visibility.

"Wire Tolland. Send up a plow." He figured that should solve the problem. Then he realized he was responsible for more than just miles of track. "And send some men out to shovel the drifts away from the entrances and exits to the snowsheds. I want any train to be able to come in or go out unimpeded. And send someone out to check that the chimneys aren't blocked. We don't want stoves pushing smoke out and choking us in our rooms." He figured the winds weren't enough to blow down telegraph poles or wires. He'd know soon enough if so.

The dispatch man was about to send when his incoming started to hiccup and chirp. Steu had tried to learn Morse by ear but simply hadn't mastered it. He had to wait for the operator to translate.

"Mr. Wentz, Tolland on the line. They have started the plow up. It is watering at Jenny Lake."

The incoming chattered again. "This is Arrow, from Braun. He wants a short report."

Steu glanced at a map of the line, and took things up in order. "That plow is stopped at Jenny Lake? That's well below the four percent and the Needle's Eye tunnel. Damn, I wish we had snowsheds along that stretch." He knew the expense of such a structure was prohibitive, but he could dream. "And it is too far to send someone out in this weather to look to see how drifted that stretch is." He thought a moment. "Ask Tolland when we can plan for the line to be cleared. And then wire Braun that we're clearing the building entries by hand and awaiting the plow from Tolland."

The 'four percent' was the stretch of line above Jenny Lake. It was less than a mile long and had the steepest grade on the entire system. The locating engineers had no choice in this stretch. They had to go steep in order to gain the pass. Even in good weather it added to the difficulty of moving a multi ton train over the continental divide. In weather like this, well, they would all learn a few things about the Hill in winter.

The operator spoke, breaking Steu's quick mental review of the line's steep spot. "The engineer tells them that drifts are six feet past Jenny Lake. He figures he can be here in two to three hours."

Steu had seen snowplows in operation down in town. He was skeptical, but nodded.

"Good. Let me know if you hear anything. And pass that on to Braun." He again looked out at the wind and drifts.

A WORLD AWAY, MILES TO THE NORTH AND EAST AT A LOWER altitude, the weather was kinder. Not a lot, but some. The four 'miners' had wrapped themselves in blankets. Even though they slept on the ground, all were warm and dry. The crag supported tent had served them well. Ella tossed, less than half awake, fuzzily reviewing her night.

Wow, what dreams! I remember someone was laying tracks. They had to be moved because the ground was too hard and lumpy. And a crow kept dive bombing us, but it wasn't me and Dale. It was me and someone, I think a man, a rich man whose face was blurry. And when he clapped his hands it sounded like hammer on rock.

She shook herself fully awake. The weird dreams receded. Her first thoughts were related. *We do need a railroad here.* Then she saw and heard Dale chipping at the overhead rock with a hammer. That certainly explained part of the dream.

The need for a railroad was confirmed as she lifted a corner of the canvas and peered out. White, deep snow offset by red rock formations was pretty. Trees cast exquisite shadows. Stormy conditions had passed and now the air was dead calm. The clouds had cleared and the sun was brightly shining, low in a blue sky.

It was pretty if all you had to do was lay in bed and admire it. But a foot or more of snow meant that the four explorers would have to stay put. They were trapped until the ground dried.

Chari yipped. "Stop that pounding! Can't you see I'm trying to sleep?"

Loudly muttering, Dale didn't care if she heard. "Tough potatoes, honey. Your sleep isn't my problem. I want to see what is inside this rock." He didn't even slow his hammering at the dike.

"Dale, what are you doing?"

Ella wondered if the man was bored or angry, hitting the rock like that. She didn't much care if Chari went back to sleep. She was awake; no reason others should lounge in bed. She looked around and corrected herself. Not lounging in bed, but on the ground. Fancy it was not, but it was comfortable enough.

Dale clinked again, having some success. He held up an apple sized piece of rock he had knocked off.

"Taking samples. They need to be assayed. We need to know what we have here. I know a good chemist who can keep his mouth shut. He will analyze these and others I've collected including those on the ground. That should tell us their potential." He looked Ella in the eye with that, communicating his desire to be sure.

"Well, I can tell you one thing," said Ella firmly. "Diamonds and minerals or no, this place is going nowhere. Not until we get a good road and a good railroad. Look out there!" She pointed outside. "We are stuck here. We are going nowhere. Not today and probably not tomorrow. Even if we got the horses and wagon hitched up, the snow is too deep."

Chari was quiet, still wrapped in her blanket, listening while feigning sleep. Joe was up, excitedly drawing charts and maps. He had been listening and made a quiet mental note to reassure Dale of the find. He caught Ella's eye and nodded, smiling.

"You are right, EQ. We need to find a better way in and out of here."

Ella was taken aback but also complimented that he used Dale's pet name for her, EQ. Somehow she found her skepticism thawing a bit. Her feelings veered to kind of liking the man. Maybe she could find a way to halfway trust him.

Joe acted oblivious to this, although it was just what he intended. He made a show of looking back and forth between his sketches and the terrain.

He pointed. "Look at that draw by that low, gradual hill over there. The sun hits that spot and is already melting the snow. We may be able to get out across that route by early tomorrow." He looked Ella in the eye. "That may well be the start of our road out of here!"

With that he shrugged on a coat and stuffed his pants into the top of his boots. "I'll go check it out right now. I ought to look in on the horses too."

XXI

SEVERAL WEEKS LATER IN DENVER, JOE AND CHARI SAT AT A white clothed table. The Benelux Hotel had superb service and a good reputation for a downtown establishment. They savored a leisurely breakfast.

"This has been a good hotel for us, Joe. I'm glad our rooms are in Denver now. I've enjoyed our stay, especially after escaping that storm up north."

"Yes, this place has worked out well." Joe had stayed here before. He found the staff particularly helpful, concerned, and cheerful. "You know, there is one clerk in particular who looks as if he is ready to break into laughter whenever he sees me. I'm not quite sure why. What did I ever do to amuse the guy? I vaguely remember him from previous stays but I sure don't recall anything unusual. I guess it is good that he and other staff members wear smiles."

Chari idly wondered how stolid old Joe could make a clerk laugh. It was a fleeting thought. She had heard these lines before and was really just waiting to have her say.

"Boy am I glad to see sun and warmth again." Chari smiled. "After that early storm up in the hills last month I was thinking you had lured me to the Arctic! That morning I was afraid we would be stranded for weeks under that awful canvas stretched over a big rock. Suspended in time with Ella and Dale." Her smile vanished as she considered that nightmare.

"Those two were of course worked up about the gems. At first it was hard to act like we were too. I have to admit, before long, I didn't have to pretend. It was exciting. But there were many reasons for us to be excited, not just the thrill of finding a nice rock!"

She looked knowingly at Joe, and smiled slyly. "But you got us out of there the next day, much earlier than I thought. I really did think we would be stuck for some time."

"You know, Chari, I think I could have gotten us out that same day. But there was no reason to rush. Had we forced the issue, it would have been muddy and messy. Three of us would have had to push in a few spots, and that would have been dirty. So I waited a day to be sure."

"Pushing. Now that would be a sight: you, Dale and Ella up to your ankles in mud!"

"Who said I would be in back shoving on the wagon? You're a strong woman...." His tone of voice said he was joking, but his smile said maybe not.

"Ha. I will mutiny before I ever push a wagon through mud. Or anywhere else for that matter."

"I'll bet! Seriously, I know that Ella and Dale were worried about being stranded too. There was another reason I waited a day. I wanted to show them I was the guy who knew how to get things done. I want them to think of me as the one to turn to when problems come up."

"Yes. That's a good precedent to set any time, but especially with those two."

She paused to nibble on a piece of apple. "I'm glad Ella found a rock right away. It was almost like she was following our script! And then they each found more. I think they convinced themselves of the lode. Of course we had to act skeptical, disbelieving. I hope it was enough to reinforce their certainty. After finding the second stone, they were no longer trying to figure things out. They felt they knew, and they wanted us to believe too." She paused, smiled, and continued. "And we do, we do, more than they know!"

"We sure do. Now is time to heat things up, don't you think?"

"It is." Chari nodded, frowning. "Ella tells me they have been cautiously talking up the Karat Top. Not singing it to the treetops, but hinting to some people who have money." She thought a moment. "I don't like that. We need to keep this under wraps better until you and I are ready to move."

She stared thoughtfully across the room. Funny, she had never before noticed that the window overlooking the street was not square. The top was almost an inch wider than the bottom. Odd; for some reason it jumped out at her today. She idly mused how one notices details like that when not concentrating. She shook her head, clearing out the wooly thoughts.

"Their talk has to be stopped. Cold. Do you want to tell them, or me? Or each of us, separately?"

"Both of us should say something, probably more than once. This needs to be controlled. You and I, Chari, it is we who need to decide who learns about this and when. The thing is to feed out just enough information to attract and keep money. We can't have others telling people things. Controlling who knows what is absolutely essential."

Joe was working himself up.

"Soon enough, it will be time to take some investors out to see the field. And I want us to pick them. I don't want them—Dale or Ella—to have any say about that. Nor should they have any tagalongs, any people we don't know and approve of. Don't you think?"

"Yes. We don't tell every warm body about this. Be choosy and keep it exclusive, is what we need to do. Otherwise we'll just have the place overrun and the whole deal spoiled. We need to target four or five, no more than ten men. Men who can put up big money. Big like fifty or one hundred thousand dollars. Each."

She turned to face him, all thoughts of breakfast gone. She too was building a head of steam over the project. "Can you get in to see a banker? Or a railroad man? We don't want a mine owner. Anyone who knows about rocks and formations is off the list. Bringing someone with no business experience would be good."

A greedy and none too friendly grin contorted her face. She repeated herself.

"No, we don't want any miners. Steer clear of them. Money men and merchants, that's who we want. Ooh, and can we get a rich second son from Scotland or Ireland? That would be the best investor ever!"

Joe gazed, admiring her energy and insights. "I agree. A banker or better yet an eastern investor would be a great foundation piece for us. Let's get some solid old conservative businessman to buy into it. Then so many will want to follow that we'll be able to pick and choose!"

She fidgeted. She would have liked to stand and pace, but one doesn't do that in a restaurant.

"So the plan is, we get ten men to put in. Thirty, fifty, even one hundred thousand each. You know, there are women with the resources to do that too. Having a woman sign on would give us credibility. People figure if a woman signs on it must be good."

"Do you know anyone like that? In your womens' teas, there must be some crazy rich heiresses...."

"Maybe. I'll think on that. In any case, ten people at fifty or one hundred grand each will give us over half, maybe close to a full million. That we will call seed money for us to 'develop the site'."

She smirked. "We need to be careful not to smile when we say 'seed'. Not that anyone will be thinking like that. When we get them in they will believe this is the richest find since Sutter's Mill."

Joe nodded. It took a moment to recall the story of Sutter's Mill. A Swiss emigrant named John Sutter owned a ranch and sawmill near Sacramento. Gold was found near the mill in 1848. Word of its discovery set off the California Gold Rush. Had Joe known, he would have grinned at the irony. Ella had repeatedly used Sutter's Mill to justify her own belief in the Karat Top.

An idea came to her. "I think Dale ought to be the man for that."

"What?"

"Development, the front man for 'development'. He is the one we need for 'improving and exploiting' the property. He should be the man the investors expect to develop the mine. And Ella can help him. Of course we don't really want to develop much. At some point we need to do something. He would be good to move a little dirt, nail together some lumber, dig a hole, make things look like they are progressing."

She picked up another slice of apple and nibbled. "Things will be progressing, just not like the investors expect. I'm glad now that you brought Dale and his friend Ella in. With his engineering background he can talk a good game, enough to convince the investors. And we should have him actually do something harmless. You know, scrape a wagon trace, and put up a building or two, talk about bringing in a railroad, while carefully seeming to keep it all secret. In a while maybe he can really do some work, using a little of the seed money. We'll put him in charge."

Joe wasn't so sure. "I don't want anyone else in charge of anything."

"Joe, Joe. We won't really put him in charge. But to the investors he will seem to be. Remember, his and Ella's names are on the papers. Ours aren't. So, on paper he will be the man. He is a natural to do that minor development work. But ever and always, you and I hold the reins."

Charity finished the apple and licked her fingers. Dramatically and being silly, she smacked her lips then closed her eyes in pleasure. Opening them, she looked lustily yet dreamily at Joe. "And while he is scraping a few roads and digging a hole here and there, we fade from the scene. Lay low in some nondescript city for a while. Then, retire to Cuba. Or San Francisco. Wherever we want, with new names and new lives."

She giggled. "While we're doing that, Dale and Ella will be busy 'developing' for a while. They won't even know what is happening until we are gone. They get to hold the bag!"

Her eyes glowed excitedly. "Joe, this is a plan we discussed years ago. It is finally coming to be!"

Joe was excited too, but he was also clear eyed and skeptical. Constantly, he was working and evaluating angles and courses of action. "Getting fat investors is all well and good. But think about it: A man—or woman—smart enough to have fifty or one hundred grand sitting around to invest will be sharp and dubious. Each person we approach will have to be handled slowly and carefully...."

He tailed off, stopping to think things through. "It should be alright for Dale to be front man. It makes sense for him to supervise the work on the ground. And he can keep Ella busy with helping him. She needs to be kept busy, out of our hair. Chari, you're right. This is a good use of their talents. But you and I need to recruit the investors. I don't want Dale or especially Ella anywhere near them."

Details of their plan settled, breakfast took center stage.

Chari had an admission to make. "Denver isn't the cow town I expected it to be. It isn't New York but it isn't so bad—we even have fresh fruit year around!"

"Thanks to railroads and the new refrigerated cars you can even get fresh seafood here. The railroad has sure made life easier."

"Yes it has." Picking up her fork, she went at her omelet as if it might run away.

Joe returned to business. "Dale is seeing the assay man this morning. I need to see him and stop their talk. I will do that today."

―――――――――――――――――――

ACROSS TOWN, DALE WALKED SLOWLY BUT PURPOSEFULLY. Ella kept close. This part of town was safe enough during the day. He knew this street was no place to be after sundown.

Pawn shops, bars, and comfort houses lined the streets. It was early and few people were about. It took several tries and a few wrong turns, but they finally found the address they were looking for.

"You come in and wait in the lobby, alright, Ella? Don't move, don't talk, just sit and wait for me. I'll be twenty or thirty minutes. Call for help if you need to. You will be alright." Unusually for her, she meekly nodded. He turned and went in.

Soon he found himself on a beat up wooden chair. It creaked with his every movement. The room was smelly and hardscrabble. From where he sat in the corner, he guessed the place had been a store. Now it seemed like a cross between a kitchen and a mechanic's shop. The room was clean enough. It was definitely a work space, not for leisure or day to day living. There were hints, echoes and odors of work done. These traces and the makeup of the room affected sight, smell, even the taste of the air.

A man sat at a table in the middle of the room. On it rested several pieces of rock. He tested and pored over them, examining and hefting them. One, he dropped one into a cup half full of some fluid. Then he put drops of some other liquid on that and another rock. All the specimens were now out and drying off, lined up like toy soldiers. The chemist glanced at him, a thin smile on his face, and spoke.

"Well, Mr.—uh, what did you say your name was?"

"I didn't. What have you found?"

The assaying chemist didn't expect to get a name, but it was worth a try. People came in all the time with samples, some valuable, many not. Very few were willing to give any clue of who they were or where they got the rocks. He continued, not missing a beat.

"Well sir, as I was saying, this is interesting." He paused for effect. "You have diamonds here! These seem to be small and not the finest grade, but they are diamonds nonetheless." He tried to read Dale's expression. Dale had his best poker face on, so stoic as to seem deaf and nearly blind. He gave no reaction.

The assay man wondered if Dale either already knew about the diamonds, or was so surprised that he could say nothing.

"This type of gem might have a use in industry. It might also be something used in a rich woman's bauble. You have brought only a small sample. I have found some indication of large, cosmetically fine ones in this group. I am not a geologist, but there is no reason your formation couldn't yield them."

He gazed at his customer, trying again. "Where did you say you got these?"

"Oh, up in the mountains," Dale breezily answered quickly. He had no intention of giving the tiniest clue to the assay man. "Tell me, do you think these samples can give us a paying proposition?"

"Well, yes and no. Are you looking to fill the need for small, coarse diamonds? The low end of the market for gems? If so, it looks to me like you have a winner. It is possible that you have bigger and finer stones in the same location. But like I said, I need to see a larger sample to give a good answer to your question. " He looked at Dale, trying to read him.

"Were you hoping for big diamonds? Like DeBeers has by the bushel in Africa? I can't tell you one way or another. Like I say, more samples are needed. In fact the best way for us to find things out is for me to examine the site in person."

He hoped Dale accepted transition from 'you' to 'us'. He was trying hard to get in on this deal. If it was at all legitimate it was literally the opportunity of a lifetime. Aside from the greed fever he felt, he was truly curious.

Assay chemists were often handed samples. Some indicated riches; most were a waste of time. But he had never before here in the west seen a local diamond. Diamond fever made him feel warm and giddy. He hoped it didn't show since he was trying to be cool and make an ally, a partner, of the customer.

The chemist's repeated requests and probes were ignored. Dale stood up.

"Alright, thank you. When can I expect the written report? I'll settle the bill when I stop in to pick that up, this afternoon. And of course you will keep this strictly to yourself as we agreed."

His expression and tone of voice were commanding and self-assured. Dale was confident the chemist would keep his word. Both knew that an assay chemist who didn't keep confidences, who talked or tried to jump claims, was not long in business. In fact the few assay men who finagled found themselves not long for this world. The mining business was fast moving and unforgiving.

Dale gathered up his samples. He made sure to retrieve all he had brought in including the one the chemist had partially destroyed in the analysis. He stuffed them back in a drab, unremarkable bag and tightened the drawstring.

"Good day."

Getting out of the seedy building was a relief. He was glad to see Ella in the lobby.

"You took more than twenty minutes! Oh Dale where were you? I was worried!" She got control of her mouth. "Well?"

A deep breath tasted sweet. The street air was by no means pristine but it was better than the chemical reek of the assay lab. "Boy, am I glad to be out of that stinky place," he muttered.

Looking Ella in the eye, he grinned. "The Karat Top is a winner!" Ella squealed. "Now, don't get your hopes up, EQ. He said what I had is industrial grade and small jewelry grade stones. Wanted to 'examine the site in person' to see if there were bigger rocks. Yeah right. As if. But who cares?!" He looked around to be sure no one could hear, and leaned close to her. He grinned. "We have a diamond mine!"

It was what Ella had been hoping to hear. Her thoughts raced. *It is time. We need to find money. Money and access.* Aloud, she was more specific. "Now, Dale, now we all get to work. We need to find investors. Joe and Chari will want to do that, fine with me. They know people we don't. You and I need to plan the development of the mine and town. Of course if we know a likely investor, we can approach him."

She thought for a moment, taking in the news. "We don't want to tell people too much. The trick will be to say just enough to milk money out of them. Of course, where the Karat Top is has to remain secret."

They walked, almost ran, they were so excited. She added the ever present thought.

"You and I will need to get a rail spur out there. Not too soon, it will be later, but we'll need it. We need to talk to the UP. And the Moffat people. And the Santa Fe People. We can talk generalities for a while. Sooner or later we'll have to take people out and show them."

Dale nodded, still grinning. "Nothing spells success like a mine with a town and a railroad. That will draw more money. For us."

XXII

MIK SAT WITH CAM AND STEU IN A DENVER OFFICE. THEY were reviewing the early storm that had hit several weeks back, having a 'lessons learned' session. It was important to assess performance and make needed changes. Everyone knew this was the first act of the winter drama. Events and weather would become more demanding as the calendar moved through December into spring.

The three men were grateful Mother Nature had granted a breather. Now conditions were fine. Since there had been a freeze it was officially Indian summer. The skies were clear and temperatures seasonal.

"It seemed bad at the time, didn't it? Looking back now, the weather wasn't too harsh, as Colorado snowstorms go. As first of the season, the storm seemed a bad one. It is easy to forget after a summer of warmth and green." Cam had an grating habit of repeating himself. "I've certainly seen worse, as no doubt you have too." He paused, looked at his companions, and went on.

"Even so, we had some problems. Communications, delays at unexpected locations, keeping the snowplow running, size of drifts…. What did I miss?"

He continued, almost grim, certainly focused. "We want makeups to have a smooth and on time run over the Hill. We need to improve. If we don't, we will have darn few smooth, timely runs. Which will attract the wrong kind of attention."

Steu chimed in. "That, we don't want. We really don't want people to expect that trains coming over the Hill will be hours late, like some of our competitors. What did people start to call the Denver and Rio Grande Western, the D&RGW? The 'Dangerous and Rapidly Getting Worse'? We do not want some name like that hung on us."

Mik chortled. "Yeah, and we don't want to run through a house like they did! Did you see that in the Rocky? A D&RG train actually ran through a house up on rollers, being moved across the tracks. No one was injured, thank God. But some poor fool now owns a big pile of kindling which was once a home. Woo hoo!"

"No, I didn't hear about that. What was that engineer thinking? Or was he?" Cam guffawed. "I admit that we do have delays and obstructions over Rollins Pass. But one thing is sure: we will find no unexpected houses across the tracks up on the Hill!"

The three shared trade gossip and some snide remarks about industry personalities and companies. After a few good laughs, Cam brought them back.

"Seriously, we need to find ways to avoid drift holdups. To start, we need to get the plow out and running earlier in the storm, not wait until it is done dumping white stuff on us."

Mik and Steu nodded at this. Cam made a note to give appropriate orders, then went on.

"If we don't keep the tracks clear ice can build up between the rails. If that happens, the wheels could run right

off. That means a derailment. Needless to say, that's bad anywhere. It could be disastrous on the shelf road."

He almost shuddered with dread, then went on to other
issues.

"I shouldn't need to say it again, and you guys know it,
but I will..."

Steu rolled his eyes and muttered, "Water."

Cam ignored him and repeated himself. "There is no
reason our experienced crews should run out of water and get
stranded. Tell 'em to fill up every chance they get! Better to
stop and top off even if it is hard to get moving again. That's
still better than starting up the hill on half a tank."

Mik smiled tiredly. "You're preaching to the choir, Reverend. What we need is to make it easier for the guys to do
that, to fill up more often. Simple, yes. Easy, no."

Cam shrugged in resigned agreement. He then looked
around, asking silently for their ideas and advice. Getting no
immediate response, he moved the discussion to new ground.

"Sometimes you just have a 'whatever can go wrong,
does' type of season. Maybe that'll be this winter for us. So
let's get it out of the way. Talk to me. What do you see as
problems? How do we handle, avoid or lessen them?"

Mik half smiled and nodded. "Starting with the storm.
You and I were at Arrow, spent the night and woke up to snow
drifts in the manager's cabin. Remember that?" With a shrug
and a grin he followed the thought. "We need to be sure every structure, every engine, every car, is physically sealed and
ready to withstand blizzards. An engineer doesn't need to
battle drifts inside the cab as well as on the mountain."

"You're right. That is a basic step we haven't always
taken." He wrote, 'In addition to normal maintenance,

be sure all new buildings and structures are chinked and caulked. Also check the sealing or caulking in all the rolling stock. Maintain as needed.'

Mik went on. "That morning at Arrow, I looked up the line, with everything buried under a foot of snow. I remember wondering how things would run under those conditions. I thought, ready or not, here is a dress rehearsal for the season."

"I was in the hotseat up at Corona that day." Steu grinned ruefully. "I called for a snowplow, thinking that would do the job, quick and easy. At the time we had no rotary. Didn't see the need for one." He glanced at Cam who nodded.

"So we trotted out the butterfly plow, the big plow mounted on the front of an engine. It got through to us in a few hours. But the engine had to work hard to bust through drifts. The engineer darn near ran out of water before he got it over the top and down the hill to a tank. I'm sure glad he didn't. First storm of the year, we didn't want a stranded cold train out away from Corona. That's the last thing we needed!"

He paused. "I think this winter, we ought to consider running an extra tank car with the snowplow. Of course another tank of water wouldn't be light, and would take more coal to haul. But I think pulling the extra tonnage would outweigh..." Here he grinned. "so to speak... would outweigh the risk of running dry and stranding a train."

The image an engine running dry up somewhere above timberline in a storm hovered in the room. A stranded train full of paying customers and freight was not a happy thought.

Mik glanced at Cam. "That is an idea we need to look at. Question is, will it take more coal to haul a second tank than we can afford? For that matter, can we afford not to add that extra insurance? Heck, I don't know. But I do know that I'll take it up with Denver."

Steu went on. "That storm really was just a mild one. And a good thing! The drifts across the track were only a few feet deep, and not too long." He looked at a piece of paper he had scrawled on during the storm and the breakthrough. "The notes I took say the biggest one we had to break through was fifty feet or so long, six feet deep." He looked up. "Fifty and six. From a small storm. What will we see in February or March?"

"Whatever it is, we had better find ways to get through." Cam's voice was steely.

"We will. We learned from this, and came up with a few new tricks. For example, we put two engines together, back to back. It looked crazy and a little silly, but it sure worked. If they couldn't break the drift with the butterfly plow on the front, the rear engine could pull the plow engine out for another try. That setup will work whether the pull is going up or down hill."

Cam nodded. "Fortunately we didn't need a rotary plow that day. But those bigger storms are coming and I am sure we will need one of those big old snow throwers. They'll do the work of fifty men, fast. A rotary running at full tilt can cut through drifts up to twelve feet deep no problem." With a frown, he admitted, "We don't have one. But I think the white shirts on Sixteenth Street have arranged to borrow or rent one. I know they have one being built, but it hasn't been delivered yet. I can't imagine the cost, but I guess that isn't our concern."

He looked around the room. "Snowslides. How do we avoid them?"

Mik jabbed again. "Reverend, a snowslide is an act of God. We can't avoid them, all we can do is live with them."

Cam ignored the interjection, glancing coolly at Mik as he continued.

"Do we want to send crews out to blast or dig away big overhanging drifts? Have the engineer stop and blow his whistle, hoping to trigger the slide? Keep crews out knocking the drifts down? For that matter, do we even know when a slide is likely or how they form? Is there a naturalist or scientist of some kind at the University who could help us? Help us anticipate avalanches, or even help forecast the size of storms?" That was a new idea for him, consulting with an academic expert. He made a note to follow up.

The questions and problems continued. "How about smoke in Corona? If those rooms are all buttoned up to keep snow out, they will keep smoke in. What about that? And do we set up a crew or standby arrangement of some kind to go rescue folks when we do have a derailment or stranding? I hope we don't, but we may well. If we have to go out, we need a plan. Just in case. Your thoughts?"

The brainstorming went on an hour or more. At last they pretty much exhausted the what-ifs. No one could think of every unwanted, unanticipated problem. Everyone knew such a beast would show up all too soon. The meeting wound down. The three men gratefully broke away to relax.

WHILE THE THREE RAILROADERS WERE TALKING OPERATIONS, Joe had his own form of operation going.

On the streets of Denver, he could have been just another businessman or traveler. He blended in pretty well even though he had been hanging around the same few blocks for most of the day. His hope, his plan, had been to run into some acquaintance near First National Bank. That was the focus of the day. After all, Mister Moffat officed there. Technically it wasn't railroad headquarters but he knew decisions were made there. Having been up and down the block for several hours he felt conspicuous. He wanted to blend in, so stopped to buy a paper.

"Give me the latest edition of the Rocky, please."

"Sure thing, that'll be a penny." The news man looked searchingly at him. "Pretty nice day, isn't it? A good day to be downtown. Hanging around for hours."

Joe ignored the dig, paid his money, and took the paper. It was time to quit and go home. He warmly anticipated seeing Chari.

Three men came out of the building, looking weary. They talked a moment then split up, each going their own way.

Joe recognized them as the crew from Rollins Pass. Cam, Mik, and what was the third guy? Steve? He thought a moment, made a decision. Joe stepped off and swooped gracefully in next to Cam, matching him stride for stride.

"Mr. Braun, good to see you!"

"Eggers." He nodded. "And what brings you to Sixteenth Street in Denver this fine evening?"

"Oh, I was in town on business. I just finished and was considering whether to go dine, but it is early. So I thought I'd head for home. Then I saw you and wanted to say hello. Would you care to join me for pie and coffee? My treat."

Cam had been looking forward to a home cooked meal. He was about to decline then remembered the conversation the last time he had seen Joe. Joe's allusions to mineral riches came back to him in a rush. He was curious and felt the greed bug stir in his chest.

"Why yes, let's."

Little was said as they dodged traffic crossing the street. Some horses shied when a pedestrian walked by and some did not. The trick was to stay agile, not to get in the horse's way. Not to mention the occasional automobile which erratically chugged along, scaring horse and pedestrian alike. They entered the restaurant, ordered, and were served before the conversation resumed.

Joe knew that Cam was not well off. He also knew the man was well regarded in the industry, not just at the Denver Northwestern and Pacific.

"How are the trains running over the mountain up there, Cam? The job keeps you plenty busy, I imagine."

"Sure, Joe, always lots to do." Cam smiled. For a long time he hadn't really trusted this man. For some reason he was warming to him. Joe somehow seemed a bit more reliable, less oily, than he used to.

"The trains? Well, we're keeping them running. I have to say that this winter will be a test for us. Even in the summer season, the weather and conditions at those elevations make life difficult. And winter hasn't fully hit yet." Joe wasn't sure if Cam was nodding to him or to himself. "We'll get the passengers and freight delivered, I have no doubt. But there will be hard times and problems. All we can do is take it one day at a time when the storms come. We shall see."

Joe nodded sympathetically. "Yes, I can see there will be challenges. You seem to love railroading, and I understand the allure of steam and cinders. It gets in your blood, doesn't it?"

His eyes glowed with remembered adventures and fun times.

"But I well know there is a price for such an exciting and dynamic life. The pay is alright, I imagine. But the action is out on the tracks, not in town. The excitement and sheer fun of it keep you away from home and family."

The waiter brought drinks. Joe raised his coffee cup in a mock toast. "There must be easier ways to make a living."

He tried to read Cam's expression without staring. Cam did not disagree with the last statements.

The man was open to an offer, Joe figured. He leaned forward conspiratorially, speaking softly. "You no doubt remember we talked about gemstones."

Cam wordlessly nodded.

"Well, I have done more research and we have run tests. And I have visited the lode. Up north. There are diamonds and perhaps other gems in abundance! My associates and I are preparing to gather a syndicate to exploit...."

Cam's was jubilant for a moment, then realized. His thoughts whirled. *Well, there goes that. I don't have the big money to join a syndicate.* Joe was still talking but he didn't hear at first, lost as he was in dejection.

"...the find. We want to gather enough funding to properly work it into a full-fledged mine." He stopped, saying nothing and looking down at his cup of coffee. He let the silence build a moment.

"We want to bring in a variety of participants. Big money men, yes, but also regular people, every day folks. Of course not everyone is in a position to join a money syndicate. There are people with valuable knowledge and contacts who simply lack stacks of cash. I mean people like you, Cam. People who can help us." He smiled.

Cam brightened a bit but tried not to show it.

"We are prepared to pay a substantial finder's fee for a referral to someone who does invest. For example, if you were to clear the way for us to speak to a qualified, reputable businessman, and he invested, we would pay you five hundred dollars."

Joe took a sudden interest in his slice of pie. Actually it was pretty good. He loved cherry pie. Cam was silent as well, deep in thought as he slurped his coffee.

When pie and coffee were gone, the two men looked at each other.

Joe asked, "Might this proposition be of interest to you?"

"Rather than cash, how about an interest in the mine? A small one to be sure, but, say, a percent or two? For every investor I bring in who ponies up money? Who as you put it is 'qualified'?"

Joe was surprised at the shrewd move. This wasn't in the script! Although he didn't show it, he was trying to come up with a credible response.

"That is a good question, Cam. I can't see why not, but had better first discuss it with my associates."

He reached for the bill and stood up. "I needn't say that this entire conversation is highly sensitive. You will of course keep this to yourself, won't you? We don't want people trampling all over our sparkling future, do we?" Joe winked and smiled, then left to pay for the pie and coffee.

Cam remained sitting, looking at but not seeing the empty coffee cup. Conflicting ideas and feelings surged; thoughts churned, in no particular order. *This is my chance to hit it big. Is this diamond mine for real? Much as I love railroading, this will let me retire. I can be with my family. Not bad for a guy with a few years of schooling. Joe says there are diamonds! But wait a minute, this is the guy who turned his back on coworkers a year ago, and left them high and dry. Can I trust him? Who are his so called associates? But he says it is the real deal! Maybe I should hint about this to someone, someone with money.....But is this a true find? Diamonds, in Colorado?*

Joe walked towards his rooms, eager to bring Chari in on the conversation. His thoughts too churned. *Cam had that hungry look in his eye. And he seems willing to come in at no expense to us. Of course we'll give him a piece of paper which says he owns a percent or two! We'll be happy to promise him a small part if his referrals put up money! I hope he is a way into the bank and business community....*

XXIII

As people said, the first snowfall was just a teaser. Soon big storms marched through the Rockies and across the continental divide every few days. Each one dropped lots of snow with big winds and bone snapping cold.

By the calendar it was spring, but by weather winter ruled. This morning, outside it was still and clear. The latest storm had passed after having dumped feet of the white stuff. The winds made drifts almost up to the eaves. Again.

Cam gazed out a small window. Windows were few in Corona Station, so he took the opportunity to look out whenever he could. There was a calendar on the wall next to the view of blue sky and pure white summits. Every day in the month of March, 1905 was xed out except today, the thirty first.

Mik followed his gaze. "It may be spring on paper, but this place won't see warm days and flowers for quite a while." He knew that down on the plains it was that gentlest of seasons. There the weather was warming. Instead of the snow blanketing the mountain, rain dampened streets and lawns. Tulips and daffodils were up and tree buds were swelling. But up here the drifts were deep and deeper.

He changed the subject. "A crew is working the drifts down towards the Needle's Eye, right? This is the second time we had to do that, or is it the third? Anyway, the guys aren't crazy about drift work there. I don't blame them. Who wants to stand on top of a snow drift cheek by jowl with an eight hundred foot drop? That would be spooky. To have to stand there and dig at your footing would be unsettling, even frightening."

A man came in the office, clothes white with snow and ice. It was Johanssen. A while back he transferred from being a security guard. Now he was a gandy dancer. That term, gandy dancer, made him chuckle. He knew he was just a railroad worker, fancy name be damned. In a rare attack of curiosity, he asked around about the term. Seems that back before machines laid track, men had to tamp down the earth as ties then track were put on the fresh grade. The image of men stomping, or dancing, along the progress of the rails made him laugh as much as the term itself. The taciturn Swede was a proud gandy dancer.

Johanssen scuffed his feet and peeled off his gloves, looking around the room as if it were a palace. The bedraggled figure then walked over to the pot belly stove and got close to it. Steam rose from him like bonfire smoke. The heat clearly felt good, so good that he visibly savored it. After a moment he looked around the room, nodding to Cam and Mik.

"Good Lord. That is a hard job, yah. Growing up in the flatlands, I never thought I would be high in the mountains, digging at the tops of snow drifts. And I started doing security work so I wouldn't have to go out in a storm and do such things. Imagine, digging down so the snow over the rails is only twelve feet deep. 'Only' twelve feet! The work isn't too bad going across flats or small hills. But it is damn tricky, even scary, on that shelf road. One slip and you could find yourself falling into the next county." He edged closer to the stove. He took off his now almost dry coat. Steam rose from his shirt almost immediately.

The dry warmth of the stove revived him. Looking at Cam, he reported. "We opened the way past the Needle's Eye. After our work, the rotary was able to clear the road, never having to back up and make a run at a drift. It worked fairly fast all the way up to the station. The way is open for now. We didn't have to dig the last hundred yards so we got to ride it up to here." He grinned, relieved to have the job done, at least for the day.

"You're sending it on over the hill, down towards Arrow, right?"

Mik demurred. "No, they have a rotary working up towards us now. I expect it soon. The snow fell just as deep on the west side but the drifts aren't as bad. The wind took a lot of that snow and deposited it where you just stood on it!"

Cam finally spoke. "Good work, Johanssen. Tell your crews that, too. I know that is a hard, endless job but it has to be done. Good thing you got it open. We have a trainful of hay going over to the Fraser side, and several cars of cattle coming from there to the stockyards."

He gave himself a satisfied, imaginary pat on the back. "The trains are moving!"

Johanssen wasn't completely dry but he was warmed. He picked up his coat, hat and gloves as he stepped to the door. "I will pass that word, thank you. Now that I'm not sopped and shivering, I'll be heading to my footlocker. It is high time to get some dry duds on. I'll see you later."

Cam watched him go. A thought he had kept with him for a while came to the surface.

"Hey, Mik. Can I talk to you about something? Something we have to keep between the two of us?"

"Sure. What's up?"

"I've been stewing and thinking on this all winter. Haven't told anyone but I need to get it out and talked over and figure it out...."

Mik looked, expectant, and Cam spilled. "You remember Joe Eggers, the character who seems to have money but no job? The guy who kind of helped us back when I delivered that deed?" He stopped to open the front door of the stove. He looked in and grabbed a poker. After a vigorous working over of the coals, he nodded to himself, closed the door, and set the poker aside.

"Even then I thought he was kind of a glad-hander. A guy who is ready to meet anyone and tell them what they want to hear, you know what I mean?"

"Yes, I do remember him. Fairly knowledgeable about railroads. At least he could put out the rail talk pretty well. I'm not sure he has ever actually touched a rail or ridden in an engine." Mik grinned and kept talking.

"The guy sure has the gift of gab. So what? Hey, I also recall seeing you two talking at the station last fall. The reason I remember is that you looked star struck at something he told you." Mik paused, hoping to hear what Cam had been told. Cam stared at the stove, silent, so Mik kept on.

"I agree, the guy is personable. But I'm like you. I feel like I have to count my cash after he leaves. No, that is too harsh, but you know what I mean. I just don't feel like I can trust the man. Not that you asked me. Sorry, I'm babbling. What about him?"

"Funny you bring up trust. He told me, and like I said this can't go anywhere, he told me about a mine opportunity. Says he has a diamond mine, an actual mine. Here in the region, up north somewhere! And he wants me to help him find investors. Says he'll give me part ownership if I bring in men with money."

"Oh?" Mik was skeptical. But the idea of diamonds was alluring. His friend had a contact. To his chagrin, the first thought was a greedy one. *Maybe he can get me in on it too!*

"Yeah, Mik. It sounds good. Sometimes. But when I stop to think, it sounds too good, know what I mean?"

"Yeah, I do. I have to tell you, my first reaction was skeptical. Then my second reaction which came with a rush, I'm sorry to say, was that I wanted in on it. Third reaction is, it probably is too sweet to be real, Cam. Nibble carefully. I'll bet there is a hook in there somewhere. Diamonds out here in the west? I have never heard of such a thing. Have you? And have you seen this property? Does it really exist?"

"I don't know, man. I don't know." Cam looked out the window, eyes unfocused. "Can you help me check this out?"

"Of course. Find out what you can about where it is. The best thing we can do is go have a look for ourselves."

"Alright. I have tried and all he'll tell me is 'It is several day's travel away'. Won't say anything but 'it is up north'."

"Probe him. We can always go out on our own. Find out what you can. Not only where it is, but who else is involved. Try to find out who he has gotten to invest, if anyone." Mik stood up, thinking, then grinned. "If you get pressure, tell them I might be interested."

"You don't have big money."

"Too true. But he doesn't know that. Hint that my old man is an eastern bigwig. That I am the estranged younger son, the black sheep. That ought to perk him up."

Cam looked at him, deadpan. "And all this time I thought you really were a poor neglected orphan. Can you tap your old man to buy us another rotary plow?"

Mik stepped towards the door, and ignoring the sarcasm. "I want to check the cattle train coming over from Fraser." He stopped and looked around, making full eye contact. "And Cam, if I criticize Eggers and his mine, I am just looking out for you, my friend. Don't take anything I say about the matter personally."

Cam nodded thoughtfully. "Thanks."

Mɪᴋ ᴡᴀs ʀɪɢʜᴛ. Iɴ Dᴇɴᴠᴇʀ ɪᴛ ᴡᴀs sᴘʀɪɴɢᴛɪᴍᴇ. Cᴏᴜᴘʟᴇs walked in the parks, sharing laughs and confidences. People enjoyed the flowers, trees leafing out and soft rains. Plans were made for the summer to come.

Joe and Chari sat on one side of the table. Dale and Ella faced them. They were all sipping cups of coffee; two had also enjoyed a pastry. The pleasantries were over and now it was down to business.

Chari wanted to jump in. She struggled with it, but decided it was better if Joe seemed to be in charge. She was willing to let him take the lead. Joe, now Joe looked at it differently. He didn't want merely to seem to be in charge: as far as he was concerned, he was in charge. He opened the conversation with a smile.

"The weather is clearing. Isn't it nice to go out without gloves and a coat over a sweater? Finally, warmth. What does this mean to us? Spring is investor season! It is time to take potential backers to the property." He looked each of the others in the eye, then continued.

"Chari and I will do it. We've talked it over, and what we'll do is take them one at a time. If we take two, they might compare notes. And then they might blab, especially later when they're back in town. People will overhear and we can't have that. A man going out alone will have no one to discuss it with."

Chari started to say something then stopped. She coughed to cover up her almost interruption. Joe looked her way but she stayed silent.

"And I—we—want to keep a lid on things. The less the investors know about where it is, the better. We need to blindfold them or put them inside a closed, curtained coach or wagon. We can't let them see where we are going. We can't have any word of where or what this is, leaking out.

"But how can we develop the site if we won't let anyone know where it is?" Ella wasn't sure she liked how this was starting out. "We'll need roads, a rail spur, and buildings in addition to the mine plant itself. The sooner we can start building the better for us owners!"

Chari nodded, finally trusting herself to speak. "Yes, Ella, you are right." She smiled. Chari didn't often smile. She knew she should more, but she just didn't. Hopeful that her smile now would put everyone at ease, she went on.

"Before we can develop any road, building or drive a tunnel, we need money. But even more than money, we need to be sure no one else muscles in on this. We have to keep it under cover. This is the once in a lifetime shot we have all dreamed of and waited for!"

She glanced at Joe who nodded and smiled but said nothing.

"We have a banker signed on. At least he says he wants in. The thing is, he has a commitment back east this spring. So he can't go visit the site until later. So he is a probable but until we have a check or bearer bonds, he is just talking. We do have several other businessmen who have agreed to put money up if they like what they see. We will take them in one by one. Like Joe says, the country is or will soon be dry enough that we can start."

She looked directly at each of them in turn. She gazed until Ella then Dale looked away. *God, I love this. It is almost too easy to make them do what I want*, she thought. She continued to smile sweetly. They smiled back, apparently in full agreement.

Joe reaffirmed. "I'll set up the first visit. Dale, can you arrange for a wagon we can close up so no one can see out? Better yet, an open wagon. We'll blindfold them. Have the wagon available at the Sulfur Flats, Wyoming whistle stop of the UP. It is located west of Laramie. I'll let you know exactly when to have it there as soon as I can."

Dale was surprised at that. "The UP? Sulfur Flats? Why not go from here, like we did?" Underneath his surprise, he took umbrage at having to do the errand.

"Because for us starting by rail is easier and quicker. Plus, this way we can keep them guessing where they are. We head up to Cheyenne then blindfold or shut the investor into a blind car. He won't know if we're heading north, south, east or west from there. The better to keep him guessing."

"Oh. Makes sense, I guess. Alright, let me know. I will have a wagon and team waiting there."

Joe continued, "And don't tell them anything about why we need it or where we're going. If they insist, tell them some hooey. Like, we're working with some Ivy League university. Some longhair professor wants to look for those dinosaur fossil bones or some such. Tell them the man's diggings are somewhere up north of Sulfur Flats."

Resentment boiled. "Jeez, Joe, how dumb do I look? You don't have to tell me to keep this quiet. I know that. Didn't miss Chari just tell us the same thing?" He picked up his coffee cup and slammed it down, hard. "And why do I have to be the errand boy to get the wagon? You want to go there, and don't want me and Ella to go there with investors. So get your own damned wagon!"

Ella was surprised at Dale's outburst, and frankly agreed. She was about to jump in when Chari spoke.

"Now Dale, no insult was intended. It is just that Joe knows you are good at those important details and he isn't. He's sorry, aren't you, Joe?"

"Yes, Dale, she's right and I am sorry. I really do apologize. Didn't mean to be ordering you around or anything. Like Chari says, you're good at this kind of arrangement. I'm not, I'm terrible at important details and at picking out horses. Can you please handle it?"

"Well, alright. If you put it that way. Let me know a day or two ahead and I'll do it. But before I do it, I want to know the name of the investor you're taking out."

Joe and Chari exchanged glances. Joe relented. "Dale, you have a point. Tell you what. How about you and I take the man out. The women will stay here. Is that alright?"

Ella was angry that 'the women' were excluded, but at least Dale was going. She got in her two cent's worth.

"That is the least you can do. And I too want to know the name of the investor."

Each of them looked uneasily around, unsure if the disagreement was small or major. Of all people, Chari giggled. Ella then the men smiled and relaxed.

"Here's to success!" breathed Ella. The other three nodded. Joe stood and the rest of them followed suit. All headed for the door.

XXIV

THE WESTBOUND TRAIN CRAWLED ACROSS THE BLAND PRAIRIE. Under the blue bowl of Wyoming sky the engine and cars were humble and tiny. A toy set running under a Christmas tree came to mind. The plains were drab with only a few scrubby shrubs as points of reference. The smoke poured from the locomotive and the cars moved, but it looked and felt like they never got anywhere.

They were three: Dale, Joe, and a middle aged businessman. Unfolding slowly, the trip was both bizarre and interesting. Bizarre, because of how the businessman was treated and interesting because it was the first effort at show and tell for the mine. To Dale, the investor was a man to be wooed since he had money to invest. For the record, Joe agreed. But certain precautions had to be taken.

Dale reviewed their route so far. From Denver they rode north on a Denver Pacific makeup to Cheyenne. From there, things got weird. To start with, the investor was blindfolded. Then they all got on a Union Pacific local and went west. It was a first for Dale and Joe both, and definitely for the businessman. Before they even got on the train, before it started to move, the man with the money was unable to see which direction they were going. Some way to be greeted at Cheyenne!

"Mister Moneybags' is the nickname Dale gave to the investor. He never said it out loud but that is how he thought of the guy. Just as well: Joe had not introduced them despite his promise to do so. Dale was hesitant to make a scene, so Mr. Moneybags it was.

The party got off at Sulfur Flats. A scrubby little place several stops west of Laramie, it barely rated a dot on the map. There was no settlement and no one was there full time. One small dilapidated structure with a makeshift sign marked the place. The stop's purpose was that it had a water tank kept full by a windmill operated pump. Dale knew how important water was to the train's engine. Not to mention the people and animals on the cars it pulls. Most travelers never gave it a thought, but the tank's overflow was a real boon for the areas coyotes and antelope.

The three of them watched and listened as the train pulled away. Silence washed over them. Of course the unseeing Moneybags didn't react. Dale found Sulfur Flats underwhelming. There was sagebrush as far as the eye could see and not much else once the tracks were out of sight. If not for sunrise and sunset, there was no way to tell directions, no landmarks, nothing.

The wagon Dale had arranged was waiting. The wrangler who brought it out untied his horse from the right rear wheel, swung on, and rode away with not a word. Joe and Dale manhandled Mister M into the back. As they climbed on, he leaned against one side of the bed, snarling.

"By Damn, this mine of yours had better be good. You are treating me like a hostage. It had better be damn good is all I can say."

Joe snapped the reins and the wagon trundled off in a southerly direction. It took them a day, a needless dawdling day in Dale's view, to come up to the dikes and crags.

For now, Dale understood and more or less approved of this charade. He agreed that they didn't want anyone to know just where the Karat Top was. When he, Ella, and Chari had come out with Joe, it was a straightforward two day wagon ride northwest of Boulder. But this trip was not as long, at least the wagon ride part of it. To the blindfolded man bouncing in the wagon it was no doubt plenty long. Dale hoped the anonymous money man would be impressed when they finally got there.

The outcrops were in full view as they topped a small rise. Joe pulled the reins; the horses dutifully slowed then stopped. "Alright, sir. Let's give you a looksee at this place." He untied and slipped the blindfold off. The man shaded his eyes as he looked around.

"It sure is a far piece to get here. Where are we?"

A tug of the reins told the horses to start up and go. "At the Karat Top Mine. Somewhere in the western United States. You will understand when you see what we have. We do not want every Tom Dick and Harry to know about this. For the security of your and our investment, we intend to keep this a tightly wrapped secret."

They were near the outcrops now and the horses stopped. Joe looked Mr. M in the eye. The man with big money did not like being told what's what. He looked like he wanted to argue, then he relaxed and nodded. Glad they had skated by a confrontation, Joe continued.

"You may want to stretch your legs. Take a walk through these crags, look things over, and we can talk in a bit. Me, I'm real ready to get off this slab seat and move around."

Joe caught Dale's eye and signaled they should stroll away. The man eyed the crags and walked the other direction, towards one of them.

"I'll bet, Dale, that he finds some rocks just like you and Ella and Chari and I did. This place is a wonder!"

"You built it up well. And I really like your explanation of why you can't tell him where we are." Dale paused, thinking of developing the site. "That was a long ride in a bumpy wagon. A railroad into here will be real good. Seems to me we have options. We could approach our friends at the UP for a spur south across that godawful prairie. Or we could talk to the Moffat people about a spur north from their line. Which do you think is shorter?"

"Seems to me that...."

An excited whoop echoed off the basalt and granite. For a moment they were alarmed.

Joe faintly smiled, then deadpanned. "I guess someone found a rock. Or two."

The money man came around a crag, moving fast for a stocky older man. He was waving a fist around like a prize fighter celebrating a knock out. "My glory, look at this! We're rich!" He opened the fist as he neared. In it were three rocks, each about the size of a large grape. "I found these just lying on the ground. Just sitting out in the open! If this is just on the surface, imagine what we can find below! Look at the sparkle, and the colors!" He was breathing fast, Dale figured it was probably just because he was winded from his jog over to see them. At least he hoped that was all it was.

Joe looked at them. One rock was clear, one red, one green. *Good*, he thought. *The man found just what I hoped he would.*

His face opened with a wide smile. "Yes, this place is really something, isn't it? I found some like that my first day out here too! And like you say the beauty of it is, we haven't even started to mine yet!"

He scuffed the dirt with his toe. "Imagine what we will find when we get underground! My associate here," nodding at Dale, "is already working on plans to develop this as a model of efficiency and industrial might. We'll have a town, roads, a railroad, churches, and schools, everything anyone could want."

His face became serious, businesslike. "But we need money, seed money." Since he didn't remember Chari's giggle at the term he didn't have to stifle his own. "Yes, seed money so we can grow this opportunity. The Karat Top can make us all wealthy. But we need to make the most of it. Don't you agree?"

The man was looking at the stones in his hand. He looked up and nodded dumbly, then looked back at the rocks.

"So can we count you in for one hundred shares? At one thousand apiece that is a bargain. As you can see."

The day was getting late. The afternoon sun was low in the sky. The man shaded his eyes and looked at Dale then Joe. His breathing had slowed. He was calm even though he had a fire in his eye.

"Yes, I will sign on and will write you a check as soon as we return. And no one will learn anything about this from me."

"Good! You will not regret it, partner!" They shook hands all around.

"Let's get camp set up. Then, a toast or three. To the Karat Top, of course, to new friends, and to our partnership!"

For good measure they shook hands all around again. Then Dale got to work pitching the tent. Joe saw to the horses, tying them loosely in the nearby aspen grove by a small creek. Mister M. gathered firewood and soon a tall blaze warmed the site.

They were off to a good start. After dinner, the hefty man couldn't simply sit around the fire. He was jumpy and excited at the riches around him. He wandered and found a few more gems that evening. Joe could see his mind ticking over, counting the wealth soon to be his.

Come morning they broke camp. Joe held a bandanna up. "I'm afraid we'll have to blindfold you again."

"Yes, I understand. But this time give me some blankets to sit on in the bed of that wagon."

Two and a half days later they were in Denver. True to his word, the investor ponied up his oath of silence and one hundred thousand dollars. The Karat Top was off to a good start!

ABOUT A MONTH AND A HALF LATER, THE TWO COUPLES MET over dinner. Savoring the meal, each pondered the next steps. Progress on the mine scheme dominated their talk over dessert and coffee.

"Now you have taken out, how many, six or seven investors?" Ella looked at Joe. Chari answered. "Yes, seven. After the first that Joe and Dale took alone, Joe or Joe and I have taken three trips of two investors each."

"Two!" Ella couldn't believe her ears. "You told us you wanted one at a time to maintain secrecy. Why two? Why didn't you consult us? Have any of them talked, leaked word?"

Chari expected the question. "Yes, we did say that. But we had to speed things up. We really need to get money in the bank. Don't worry, though. No shortcuts were taken. We've been extra careful. No one has talked."

Ella didn't want to let it go. "How can you be sure?"

Looking at Joe, Chari responded. It was important to make Dale and Ella comfortable. She glanced back and forth between Joe and them. "Joe made sure to pair up people who didn't know each other. Right, Joe? So they wouldn't come back and compare notes, is what you said. And didn't you talk with each man afterwards, to be sure he paid up and signed a silence agreement?"

He nodded. "Yes, extra steps were taken to send out only strangers. And we kept them apart as much as we could out there. The thing is, we need to get people out to look so they commit their money. But we do not want anyone but us telling people about this mine. By the way, every man we have taken out has signed on. Not a one has hesitated or backed out."

Dale and Ella exchanged glances and she spoke, low and serious. "So if you have seven investors on board, why is there no money? The agreement was that Dale and I would start to develop, at least make serious development plans by now. What gives? Where is the money? What are you doing with the fat checks and bearer bonds these investors hand over?"

"The funds are in escrow in a major bank." Joe responded in a voice just as businesslike and intense.

Dale jumped in. "We need some of it. We can't even talk to an architect or engineer with no money!"

Trying to head him off, Chari spoke. "It is too soon to talk to architects! We don't have our portfolio full yet. Until then we can't move forward."

"Who are you to dictate if we can move forward? Not only can we, we will." Ella tensed, almost as if to jump up and come around the table. "If we are going to make something of this we need to get roads in there. If we don't have roads the costs of freighting will eat us up."

Joe and Chari anticipated that this would likely come up. They made a plan to finesse the ruffled feathers and negate the objections. Joe spoke calmly and reassuringly.

"Let's not get ahead of ourselves. Of course we need roads. But we don't want to tell a road builder about it yet. We need to wait until we have a full portfolio of investors and a full fund. That should take only another two months or so. It would be easy to jump the gun. We all need to be patient."

Patience was not her strong suit, Ella knew. And she knew she was done. "We have poked and played around this for months. I for one have had it. It is time to act. If you don't release some money to us, we'll take our own investors out there. And then we will start building." She glared at all three.

Dale was taken aback at her intensity. At first he was thinking she should tamp it down, but somehow her words fired him up.

Chari glanced at Joe. He could see alarm in her eyes only because he knew her well. She spoke; the velvet of her tone did not disguise the steel of her answer.

"Remember, Ella Queue and Dale Smertz, we brought you into this. If not for us you would probably be working for the Podunk Branch Railway in Dogbone, Kentucky. Or worse. Now, remember, we all agreed early that Joe and I make the financial decisions. We will stay out of your development work. When we can finally release money, we will not second guess your decisions in the development stage. It simply is not time yet." She stared the two of them down like she had done in the past.

Ella, unsure and feeling alone, nodded. Her loneliness was short lived. The spark of intensity Dale burst into flame. Being third or fourth fiddle was frustrating, and he erupted.

"Yes, we so agreed. We will wait a while yet. But we—all four of us—need to move on this. Four more weeks, one month! That is all Ella and I will give you. If you don't release funds to us by then we—the two of us—just may recruit our own investors." He in turn stared Joe and Chari down. He almost blinked when Chari stared back, but held on. She looked away as Ella and Dale stood up and left.

Ella barely kept up as he strode away, angrily and purposefully. "Wow, Dale, you hit a home run there! You sure told them what's what. I agree, it is time to get going." Ella snuggled up against him as much as public decency allowed. "Let's go celebrate, you and me and a bottle of wine."

THE SMUDGED COFFEE CUPS SAT UNAPPETIZINGLY. THE SCHEMERS remained at the restaurant. Joe eyed Chari and Chari eyed Joe. Each waited for the other to speak.

"Well, Joe, they seem to be rushing us. Hurrying us before it is time to move Damn, I don't like having my hand forced. Even so.... We may have to act before the ideal time, before we have harvested all the money we can."

He said nothing. She shrugged. "Bringing in those two yayhoos seemed to be a pretty good idea. But maybe it was a mistake. All of a sudden they're uncontrollable. Mr. Dale and Mrs. Ella will not follow our lead or be patient. They think this is an up and up deal. Of course we can't tell them how it really works. I just hope Ella doesn't figure out that this is really a plan for you and me, and they are window dressing."

She angrily shoved a cup and saucer away. It rattled but didn't fall and break. "If they get their way now about taking in their own investors, the game is done. Word will get out and some geologist will swarm the area. No telling what they might say but it won't be good for us." She gazed around the room, then into Joe's eyes. "What do we do now?"

"I have been thinking heavy on that. Seems to me, we have two options. One is serious and one really serious. The really serious choice is crazy, and I am not sure I even want to say it out loud."

Chari made a 'come on' motion with her hand. He sank back in his seat. His eyes were screwed shut, as if that helped him pretend he wasn't saying it. He spoke slowly and in a low tone. "Two people we know have an accident. Our partners' sudden and sad demise will be a shock to us. And it will be good publicity to attract more investment. And it would free us to run this as far out as we can." Even as the words came out, he couldn't believe how cynical and evil he sounded.

His plan didn't surprise or shock her. Chari just nodded. "And the other?"

"The other is the serious but I think smart option. We move the schedule up. Stall Dale and Ella on development. Step recruitment up and bring in as much money as we can. And we make our exit. If we do that in the next month or six weeks, it would only be two or three months sooner than we originally planned."

She again nodded. "You are right. The easy thing would be to shut it down early." The way she stared into her coffee cup, Joe had the silly notion she was reading instructions inscribed in it. Frowning, concentrating, she spoke. "But still. Still, there is real money to be harvested yet. We won't get another chance like this, you know. This Karat Top is literally a once in a lifetime deal. We ought to work it for all it is worth."

Chari took a deep breath, mentally crossing a line she never ever thought she would even come near. "The more I think of it the more I think the crazy serious may be the way to go." She paused, eying her partner. They looked into each other's souls, drawn and repelled at the same time. The attraction won out.

"Let's go celebrate, you and me and a bottle of wine."

XXV

Nightfall and two couples were celebrating in Denver. A partner, a big decision, and emptying a bottle of wine made for a fine evening.

Away from them in their own part of town near the tracks, the railroad men were talking. The subject wasn't a celebration. It wasn't really the railroad either. Nonetheless it was business.

"Johanssen told me a friend of his works as house help for one of the rich men here in town."

Mik looked up at Cam, deadpan but with a smile in his voice. "And how does this friend of the Swede like buttoning up another man's vest? This surprises me. Johanssen doesn't seem like the type to hobnob with domestic help."

His grin broadened. "But, I'm sure there is a reason you feel I should know this. So, what's the deal?"

"Ha ha Mik. Very funny." Cam paused a moment to find the best way to start. "You know, most butlers and maids are invisible to their bosses. Generally they are treated almost like they are furniture or something. The exception is when the boss woman or her man wants something. I couldn't work like that but it takes all kinds. Anyway, I...."

Mik interrupted. "So who cares? The bosses pay the bills. They get to act as they see fit."

"Yeah, they do. But get this. This guy—the butler—hears all kind of stuff. He hears about upset stomachs and mouthy wives or husbands and such. Mostly it is boring domestic stuff. But he hears other things as well."

With a wicked smile, Cam got to his secret. "Now, get this. He—the friend—told Johanssen something interesting. Seems that his boss just got back from a strange trip."

"What, did he go to ballet school or something?"

"Be serious, Mik. This is important. This trip the big guy went on, it was supposedly to check out a business opportunity." He stopped and gazed at Mik for effect, as if to say, 'listen to this!', then went on. "This big opportunity is a diamond mine. Johanssen's friend couldn't help but hear his boss going on about it. Do you think maybe this diamond mine is Joe Eggers' deal? The one he tried to bring me in on?"

He considered the possibilities a moment, then answered his own question. "This boss is a major money man. He has bags of the stuff. More than you and I will see in our lifetime. And he is a good businessman. You know, one of the relatively honest ones who makes money with most everything he touches."

Mik knew of the man in question. He agreed that the guy was an able entrepreneur and a leader. He thought a moment. "If Eggers has him on board maybe there is something to it. Can we learn something about this supposed mine, and where it is?"

"That's the thing! The story gets better. The butler overheard a bunch and told Johanssen all about it over beers. The story rings true. I don't think it was the beers talking."

Cam smiled. "You know how a little alcohol can make a jack-ass seem like a hero."

"True that."

"Anyway, listen to this description, man. It was a long train ride from Denver. The man was blindfolded! He got to watch as far as Cheyenne. Then his eyes were covered, a thick dark cloth. So he couldn't be sure what direction they went. But they boarded a train and rode for quite a while from there, then got off somewhere. He did not hear the train cross any big rivers or trestles, you know, with a different sound and all. Said it was windy and a little blowing sand when they finally got out."

"Windy and blowing sand?! Hell, that description could fit anywhere within five hundred miles."

"Yes. But this guy didn't get rich by accident. He noticed details and small clues. I guess he bragged to his wife while Johanssen's friend was in the room. He said that maybe he couldn't see, but he could still figure some things out. Said that he concentrated on what he could hear, smell, and feel."

Cam shuddered, trying to imagine being blindfolded for hours. "After some time on the train they got off. Apparently it was at a whistle stop, pretty quiet, not like a busy station. Then he was helped onto a wagon. They went off, at what felt like a slow pace, like the wagon was drawn by one or two horses, no more. And it must have been open, not covered. Because, in the morning he felt the sun on his left shoulder, then his face and head. Later on the warmth was more on his right. So he figured that they were heading south from the train."

Mik was following the story closely. "So that eliminates everything north of the railroad. And a day or so out of

Cheyenne, but we don't know if it was east or west. That still leaves western Nebraska, all of Colorado, and part of Utah."

Cam impatiently nodded. "Wait. He said the wagon ride seemed flat. For most of the day, the country they crossed had no big rises or falls. Just the normal small obstacles, rocks and gullies. Still heading south far as he could tell. Went on for quite a while, probably until mid-afternoon from the feel of the sun. Then the way became hilly and rough. He guessed the time was getting on. And it turned out he was right. Late in the day they finally took his blindfold off. First things he saw, when his eyes adjusted, were trees, hills and a number of rocky outcrops."

"That pretty much eliminates Nebraska. Plus, no mention of the wagon crossing a big river. The tracks run north of the Platte River in Nebraska so it wasn't there."

Mik thought on it. "But if they didn't cross any big gorges anywhere, then they didn't cross the Green River either. So they likely didn't get into Utah.... Sounds to me that maybe we're talking somewhere in northern Colorado or along the border with Wyoming."

"Yep. But here's the best part. The area where they let him see and walk around is full of gems! They told him to go stretch his legs so he wandered over by a cliff. He found three or four gems, laying on the ground or barely covered with dirt. A diamond, a ruby or at least a red stone, and some other jewel. Just there for the taking!"

"It sounds too good to be true, Cam. Diamonds and rubies, just lying on the ground? I'm no geologist, but I have never heard of those being found together. Much less lots of gems lying out in plain sight." He paused, thinking. "We need to go see this for ourselves. Let's get out a map...."

CHARI WAS ANGRY. THE VEINS STOOD OUT ON HER NECK AND her left cheek. Joe had only seen this once before. He recalled that scene with a cringe. A woman had made the mistake of trying to brazenly use and humiliate Chari. Not in private, but at a social gathering. That spectacle and how Chari responded were, well, they were memorable.

She spoke. "Dammit, those two will spoil everything. I thought they said they would wait a month before we approved spending and took action. Didn't they? Didn't they? Dammit, Dale or maybe it is Ella is like a kid in a candy store. They just can't be wait."

"What are you getting at, Chari? What happened?"

"The two of them are getting ready to take out an investor, out to the Karat Top!"

Joe frowned. "We can't let them do that. We just can't let that happen. Did you talk with them?"

Chari thought back. This morning she had 'accidentally' run into Ella on the street. She wanted to chat but wanted it to seem casual. Plus, she didn't want the men in on it.

Timing her walk well, as hoped she ran into her colleague.

"Oh hello, Ella! Good to see you!" She had started out cordially. Ella looked surprised to see her. Her eyes widened and in a moment the pupils turned tiny and dark. Chari had once watched the eyes of a rattler just before it struck. She was reminded, and horrified, of the similarity.

"Don't you 'hello' me Charity Hovus. Shameful, it is shameful how you and Joe are. Secretive. Manipulative. Tightfisted. You tell us nothing about investors or finances or the status of the project. You treat us like children too stupid

to understand anything. I tell you, we are ready to start building. It is time to start improving the site. But, no, you say we
can't. You control the money. You and Joe think you control
everything."

Her glare could have melted the snowdrifts around Corona Town.

"Since you won't let loose of any funds for us to start,
we're taking matters into our own hands."

"What matters, Ella?"

"You know perfectly well."

"No, I don't. Please tell me. We're in this together, especially you and me. The men think you and I are too delicate
and irresponsible to do anything. They want all the credit."
She paused. No answer.

A quick jab might get at least a response. "Dale didn't
tell you to do anything rash, did he?" She suspected Dale
didn't ever try to give orders to Ella. But the question was
worth asking. She hoped it would get a rise. It did, quick and
definite.

"Dale doesn't rule me! I decided, I, Ella Queue decided,
to take control. You get this into your head, Hovus. I don't
need approval from him or you or anybody else! No one, get
it? He and I are taking an investor out, hopefully tomorrow.
From him, we'll get some money on our own. Then we can
start improving the site in spite of you two!" Too much, she
had said too much. There was more on her chest but she re-
sisted, literally biting her tongue. Chari's response was of no
interest to her at all. Ella angrily marched off, ears ringing.

The accusations and the audacity of it still grated. Chari
nodded as she spoke to Joe. Relaxed on an easy chair, he
gazed and waited for her.

"I didn't talk to them, I talked to her. It was like talking to a rancher who thinks you've rustled his cattle. She's mad about having no money. I'm pretty sure she told more than she wanted to. I learned that they plan to take some potential investor to see the Karat Top. She said 'hopefully tomorrow' so who knows. Maybe she was bluffing but I doubt it. She was sure angry. And determined.

Joe stood as abruptly as a private called to attention. "We have to stop them. They'll ruin everything. Word will get out. Then some private eye or geologist will snoop. The gems will be picked over and identified and...."

Her eyes looked into the distance as she mused aloud. "We need to head them off somehow. Like we talked, we need to, what, silence them? Buy them off? Kidnap them? Joe, we have to do something."

"I agree." The hard choices made his expression grim. Ideas glimmered and a plan began to form.

"Alright, here's the plan. You and I need to get out there. We have to scurry out there and be waiting for them. And do what we have to do. That decision, what do we do, can wait until we see them and their 'investor'. But I hope it doesn't go bad. I sure don't want to hurt anyone."

An idea along that line came to him.

"How about we discredit them in front of their man? Treat them like the underlings they really are. Disclose their background as paid agitators for a railroad. Call them the hired help. Scold them for bringing someone out without our permission. Reveal they have no credible mining or geology knowledge. And so on, we can come up with plenty of ammunition."

He smiled, thinking it through.

"If we do it right, we'll get them clear out of the picture at no cost to us. They'll run off with their tail between their legs. No one will get hurt. Best of all, you and I can pick up another money man!"

EARLIER THAT MORNING, ELLA HAD GONE OUT FOR A WALK. As Chari discovered when they 'accidentally' met, she was in rare form. When she returned, she quietly slipped into the room. Dale looked up, surprised. No grand entrance usually spelled trouble.

"Hi Ella! How was the morning stroll?"

"I met that Hovus woman. She acted all friendly but I lost my temper."

"Oh, E. What happened?"

"I just couldn't help myself. I scolded her and Joe for bring secretive and tightfisted and not giving us money to build with. I read her the riot act."

"Well, that was probably justified." His eyes widened. "You didn't tell her...?"

"Dale, it just erupted from my mouth. Yes, I told her we were taking an investor out. I even let slip we hoped to do it tomorrow. I'm sorry, I know I shouldn't have run off like that." She almost teared up. "That cow looked so smug, so in control, so condescending. I hate that."

He walked absently around the room, hands clasped behind his back like a professor rehearsing a lecture. "Well, they won't be happy with that. They may try to interfere, or worse."

"Worse?"

"There is a lot of money in play here, Ella. How much? We don't know for sure. But let's figure. They have taken seven men out that we know of. If each of them has kicked in seventy five or a hundred thousand dollars, our friends are sitting on a big pile of dough. They could have half a million or more. People have been hurt or even killed over less. And they are real closed mouth about it. They resist when we ask questions or try pry some of it away. For some reason they don't want us to touch even one dollar."

He stopped walking and gazed at her. "We need to be extra careful. When we go, I'll pack a rifle along with my .45. You should take your Derringer."

He motioned to her to come to him. They hugged then stepped apart.

She took over. "Let's you get packed and make arrangements for the wagon and so forth. I'll get to our man and tell him to be ready to go first thing tomorrow. And I'll remind him again to keep all of this to himself. We need get the three of us out of here as soon as we can, before they find a way to stop us."

"Alright. Watch carefully and don't let yourself be followed."

ACROSS TOWN, CAM AND MIK WERE LOOKING AT MAPS OF southern Wyoming and northern Colorado. "There are no towns to speak of for quite a ways west of Cheyenne and Laramie. I guess there are a few whistle stops." A question occurred to Mik. "Cam, you know engineers and brakemen, even on competing lines. Do you think there have been an unusual number of stops at one of those pipsqueak stations lately? Can you find that out?"

The big foreman stood and bowed dramatically, sweeping his arm up. "Great minds think alike!" Smiling, he sat back down, cleared his throat theatrically, and spoke.

"Funny you should ask. That occurred to me too. I looked up an old pal and asked him. We kind of trade favors, know what I mean? Nothing dishonest or wrong, just helping each other out now and then. He and I broke into the railroad business together. He stayed with brakeman and operations work and I went into the construction end. We have stayed in touch even though different men pay our wages these days."

"Too much information, Cam. Did he tell you about activity at stops on the line?"

"Yup." He pointed to a spot on the map. "Sulfur Flats. He tells me that more stops have been made there the past months than in the previous two or three years. Usually a morning stop going westbound where just a few folks get off. Then, like clockwork, several days later, the eastbound stops and picks up the same small party. It is always just a few folks. Like he said, you wouldn't notice this type of thing once but repeatedly, it sticks in the memory."

Savoring the story, he relaxed back, then sat up again.

"Almost forgot. He got curious himself and mentioned it to a wrangler friend. The guy often has a wagon and team rented out by someone, to be waiting at Sulfur Flats. Go figure."

With a grin, Mik summed it up. "I'll bet that is the stop we want. The times and distances make sense, and the recent activity there cements it."

Trying to make sense of it all, they were silent. Mik spoke first.

"If we go out there, can we get off the train a mile or two before or after the stop? After would be better. That way we can see who gets off, and get the lay of the place. We don't want to raise suspicion. We can head south from where we get off. Then if we veer over, we can look for their tracks. Wagons make ruts, and they should be easy to spot. And we can follow them to this so called diamond mine."

XXVI

THE FIRST WINTER WAS OVER. IT WAS SUMMER 1905 AND THEY now knew that passengers and crews could and did go over the Hill. True, they went safely but not always comfortably. Trains ran; the line held. Much was learned about operating in snowstorms at altitude. Procedures were developed to avoid derailments. As expected, Corona Town got snowed in a time or two but never for long.

Cam was in Denver to discuss the lessons and problems revealed. He was reporting to Horace Sumner, chief engineer of the Denver Northwestern and Pacific Railway. Mik sat in on the meeting.

"Overall the road did alright. I am satisfied that trains ran fairly well from Denver over Rollins Pass to Fraser. Sure there were bad days or stretches, especially with weather. There were times it was 'all hands on deck' especially early on. As the season progressed those times came less and less often." Sumner nodded but said nothing. Cam continued.

"Much was learned this first season about coping with storms, isolation, and crew burnout. We found ways to give stranded passengers safety. It wasn't easy, but basic comfort and wellbeing were assured. The tracks and roadbed survived the trial very well. There are no major problems in that area."

"And we are looking at making a lake or pond near the top of the pass." Mik glanced between Cam and Sumner as he said this. "Several sites are being considered. As we know, it is essential to have a place for engines to water after the tough trip up."

Sumner grunted. "So you would say, all in all, that it has been a difficult but manageable season up there?"

"Yes, that's a fair summary." Cam nodded at Mik's interjection.

The discussion then veered to progress beyond the harsh environment high on the divide.

"Iron has been laid through Arrow into Fraser and on past. Trains run all the way there now."

"Arrow still has a station stop, water tank, and a post office, does it not?" Sumner hadn't been over this part of the line since the fall.

"Yes, Arrow is still a viable settlement. Never did organize as a town. It is dwindling though. I'm not sure it will ever be a main stop for us. Many of the tent owners who were there upped stakes and moved closer to the new head of construction. The workers there have money but nowhere to spend it, so the saloon men like to be nearby. They're happy to take the gandy dancers' pay!"

Mik stated what the chief engineer and construction foreman already knew. "So now, the town nearest the railhead is Fraser. And the crews are making grade through the mountains west of there, past Granby and into Byers Canyon."

The gorge which carries the Colorado River as it flows west from Middle Park is Byers Canyon. The namesake was William Byers, first owner and publisher of the Rocky Mountain News. He owned a ranch downstream of it, near the settlement of Hot Sulphur Springs. That town was the county seat.

Mik had one more dead horse to beat. Of course Sumner and Cam knew this, but he had to say it. "From there the road will follow the river west, past the settlement of Kremmling, through the Gore Canyon then branch northwest towards Steamboat Springs and Craig."

The name Gore Canyon brought memories to everyone. The Canyon was a potential choke point for the railroad. Cam and Mik made great efforts to keep it clear. They had been involved in delivering some paperwork needed to do that. The deed Cam delivered ensured that the Denver Northwestern and Pacific Railway would be able to build through the Gore Canyon. They all thought the matter was decided.

No one knew it yet, but the question of building the railroad through Gore Canyon was not closed. Eastern money interests were still looking to build something, anything that would block the canyon. It would be a long saga. Even President Roosevelt would get involved before the matter was settled in Moffat's favor.

All items were discussed fully and the winter review meeting broke up. The railroad men walked out of the building and headed down Sixteenth Street. Talk turned from snow and railroads to a lighter subject: their efforts to locate and visit the diamond mine.

"Cam, did you talk to your ex coworker? Weren't you going to get us a ride in the engine up to Cheyenne?"

Mik's question interrupted his daydreams. Cam had returned to thinking on the Gore Canyon and northwest Colorado. It took a moment to get back in the present. He had in fact talked with an engineer he knew over at another line. The man had arranged for him and Mik to catch a ride.

"Yes and no. No passes or papers needed. We just need to talk to Samuel on the train. He's the conductor who'll get us situated in the caboose. That'll be more comfortable than the engine. As you know, conductors pride themselves on their coffee. There's always a pot going on the potbelly. Plus we can get up in the cupola and see who gets off and on. And they can't see us."

"Sounds good. When are we going?"

"Pack your bag. We need to be there in..." he pulled his pocket watch out, shook it ceremoniously, and read. "...an hour and a half. We want to be on before passengers start boarding. It probably doesn't matter, but that way we know who is on board. And no passengers will know that we are on the ride too."

Mik glanced at a carpetbag he carried and smiled. "I'm ready."

———

As the engineer opened the throttle and gained speed, the caboose swayed. They were on the way to Cheyenne. The forward motion of the hundred ton train, the clack of the wheels on the rails, and the rocking of the car combined in their gentle tango. This pervasive and almost luxurious sensory backdrop always captivated Mik. He bathed in the sensations for a moment.

"We left the station per the timetable, on the second. Impressive." He knew Cam was competitive, and was hyper-aware of the punctuality too.

"Yes, that does speak well for this crew. I'll be interested to see if we get in on the dot or not." He paused. "But you want to know what I really wonder about? Why are Joe Eggers and his woman friend on this train?" His quizzical expression, intense and focused, almost made Mik laugh.

Cam wasn't trying to be funny, and his questions came rapid fire. "Why are they headed to Cheyenne? He supposedly has a hotshot mine about to go public, right? Why is she along? Is she in on the mine? If so, why aren't they taking someone to look at it, like he did Johanssen's friend's boss? Or maybe they are on an innocent excursion. Who knows?"

"Good questions, Cam. Maybe they really are taking a pleasure trip. Or they could be going to Chicago or San Francisco to drum up interest and find investors."

"Maybe. What they do in Cheyenne will tell us, I guess. If they get on an eastbound up there, at least they are out of our hair."

"Yeah, if they get on our westbound we'll really have to watch them. I wonder if they'll get off at Sulfur Flats."

Cam frowned. "If they don't, if they go west and stay on, they will see us get off at the next stop."

Mik thought, then smiled. "If they do remain aboard and see us get off, probably it means they have nothing to hide. It sure will make them wonder what we're up to! If they do get off at Sulfur, we'll find and follow them to their 'diamond mine.' Either way, things become clearer for us."

With that he caught the conductor's eye. "I know you have more to do than look after us two visiting freeloaders, but I have a favor to ask."

The conductor had hosted his share of visitors. He smiled, knowing what was coming. "You want me to alert you, wake you if need be, before we get to your stop, right?"

Mik smiled in turn. Conductors were like sergeants. It didn't matter which unit they were in, they knew the score.

He did a mock salute and answered, "About ten minutes before we hit Cheyenne, please."

"You got it. Make yourselves comfortable. I have a train
to look after so I'll be in and out. Grab me if you need me."
With that he walked to the front of the caboose and entered
the next car. He needed to keep an eye on cars, freight and
passengers. This was the first of his many tours to check on
each car the length of the train.

UP IN THE DINING CAR, JOE AND CHARI CREATED A STIR. THEY
were dressed not formally but roughly. No coat and tie or
dress for them, but clothes for the back country. Each had on
canvas trousers and plain wool shirts. Needless to say, they
stood out among the white table cloths and silver. Others
sitting at dining tables wore garb stiff and prim. Suits, full
dresses and hats were the order of the day. A few women even
fiddled with boas or other light shoulder wraps.

The miners knew they stood out. They pretended not to
notice, but really they reveled in it. Joe glanced at Chari over
the menu he was more or less reading. "I didn't see anyone of
interest get on there in Denver, or since, did you?"

She didn't look at him or say anything. The rhythm of
the car's movement was quite enjoyable. It lulled her. She associated this calming feeling with trips. Trips, she associated
with freedom. For another moment she savored the motion,
then spoke.

"No, and we were among the first to get on. So I think
we saw every passenger as they came out of the station. No
Dale, no Ella, and no obvious money man they sent ahead to
wait for them in Cheyenne."

Chari stood up to get the kinks out of her back and legs. As she stretched she turned completely around, able to see the entire car. She wanted to take another quick scan of her fellow diners. No one stood out, at least not so far. She wanted to keep an eye on anyone who moved around. Plus, any new passenger getting on between Denver and Cheyenne would be worth a look.

Reassured, she saw no cause for alarm. And, frankly, she enjoyed feeling everyone's eyes on her. It was fun to flaunt her garb to all of the oh-so proper men and women in the dining car. Who cared if she wasn't dressed 'like a lady'? She was sick and tired of worrying about such things. Soon she would have more money than any of them!

The waiter approached to take their meal instructions. She was hungry so she sat down and ordered large.

FINE TABLE CLOTHS AND WAITERS WERE LACKING IN THE caboose. But the high perch and windows did give a good view. "Cheyenne is Denver but without the mountains and river," observed Mik. "They have planted trees too, in an effort to green things up. But the backdrop is just windswept plains, north south east and west."

He looked around as the engine coasted into town, slowing its speed to safely enter a lively railyard. There were passengers walking and running everywhere. Freight was being moved and loaded, workers hefting boxes and crates. Cattle were being prodded in to or out of stock carriers. Cars were being switched as new trains were made up. Over and throughout, steam, cinders and noise assaulted the senses. The conductor who had greeted them in Denver was nowhere to be seen. He had a job to do, bringing his train into the yards without mishap. Mik left a note of thanks as Cam climbed down the steps, talking as he went.

"I don't want to make too much of things, but let's keep the cars between us and the passengers. That way we can see who is around without them easily seeing us. My contact for this westbound trip isn't the engineer or conductor, but the postmaster. Or whatever title for chief of the mail car is now, since it seems like it is changed every month."

Hearing the sound of a big crash several tracks over, he winced and looked around. "That doesn't sound good. Anyway, this time we get to ride in the mail car. Oh, and I was able to arrange for two horses. They'll ride in a stock car, going west with us. We can take them off when we stop ourselves, won't have to wait around."

He led off confidently, having been through the Cheyenne yards a number of times. They found their ride easily.

CHARI IGNORED THE BEDLAM OF THE CHEYENNE YARDS. SHE was focused on being the first person out of the dining car. She particularly enjoyed pushing her way past one or two people, people who particularly acted as if they were entitled to respect. Self-important, well dressed passengers did not impress her. Some of them had earlier given her the fisheye. Those folks got an extra dose of the icy treatment as Chari shoved past.

"Come on, Joe. We need to get a good seat near the door on the westbound." Joe figured it would be alright if they weren't the first in the train. "Relax, Chari. We have time to get on. And we needn't hurry. We are ahead of Dale."

"But are we ahead of Ella, is the question. I wouldn't put it past her to double cross even her pal Dale." Chari had long suspected that Ella played for her own benefit, not the team's. Since Charity Hovus looked after herself first, she expected Ella did the same. "Hurry up!"

MIK STOOD IN THE MAIL CAR. THE SIDE DOOR WAS OPEN AND he could see the entire station area. He took care that he was behind a work table, in the shadows. Cam was off somewhere, renewing old acquaintances and trading railroad gossip. Taking the extra caution to remain unseen was rewarded. He saw Chari hurrying from the Denver train towards the same westbound unit he was on. Joe walked behind her, trying to keep up without appearing to chase her. The yard was noisy. He picked up a few words but couldn't tell who said what.

"...get there first...." "...show them who is boss...." "...their money...." "...We don't...."

Not long after they passed, Cam returned. The smile on his face confirmed the whiskey on his breath. The ninety proof in him rhapsodized about his visits. "It is always good to see old friends, now competitors and old competitors, now fr...." He saw the concentration on Mik's face and stopped mid phrase. "What's up, compadre?"

"I overheard a little from those two. I couldn't exactly tell who said what. They were walking by, or I should say, he was walking fast after her and she was practically running."

"Oh? Were they running to catch another train or just in a hurry?"

"In a hurry. And get this, their tone of voice was, well, frankly it was hostile. Against who wasn't clear, I really couldn't tell. But I'm pretty sure someone is in their sights."

"But where did they go, which train did they board?"

"I guess if forgot to tell you. Eggers and the woman climbed onto this westbound. Looked like they got into the dining car. I'm not positive of that, but they definitely got on this one."

"Alright, let's be sure they stay on. And then we'll see if they get off, and where. If it is Sulfur Flats or thereabouts, we try to see where they go. And either way, we pull a whistle stop around the next bend."

"Cam, there are no bends in roads across Wyoming."

"You got me! That is true, sad but true. So we don't wait for a bend, but for eight or ten minutes to pass. Then we can pull the cord to stop. That will be far enough that they won't see us get off."

Mik sprawled on the work table. "I'm tired, gonna get some shuteye. Wake me when we leave the station. You're going to be sure they stay on this train, right?" With that he rolled up his jacket, stuck it under his head like a pillow, and closed his eyes. He was quickly sound asleep, and was making sounds aplenty. The thrum and rhythm of his pal's snores reminded Cam of the noises made by mating alligators. It brought back childhood memories, growing up near the swamps in Louisiana.

Soon, but not soon enough for Cam and the mail master, the train jerked and started moving. Mik was roused and told that their diamond miners were still on the train.

A ways past Laramie, an hour or more out of Cheyenne, the mail man spoke up. "That siding you asked about, Sulfur Flats, should be coming up in the next fifteen or eighteen minutes. We've stopped there a lot lately." He looked Cam with a glare and a smirk. "Is something happening there? Something I should know about? I have to wonder why a foreman from a competing line is interested...."

Cam smiled and shrugged. "The Boss Man made me get out of town for a while. I really can't discuss it." He hoped that a mysterious answer would send the gossip machine into overdrive.

The mail master wasn't sure what to make of that. The west was full of strange and unexplained schemes and events. He decided to let it go. "Alright. You tell him to keep up the good work."

Fourteen minutes later the train slowed. The mail man simply grunted, "Sulfur Flats." Mik went over to take a look. He opened a slat which covered a three by fifteen inch view slot.

"They're getting off. Our folks are on the ground, Cam. Just the two of them." He was careful to not to give information the nosey mail man could use. "Now they are climbing into a wagon. It is pointed the direction we thought it would be." He didn't want to say it was headed south.

As the train lurched forward, Cam checked his watch. After eight minutes, he found and pulled the stop cord. Someone in the locomotive sounded the steam whistle. That signaled to the crew and passengers that the train would be stopping for a passenger to get off. The two men gathered their bags and coats, and climbed out. Their horses were in the next car up so it took little time to tend to them.

"Thanks for the ride."

"It is the Union Pacific's pleasure. Good luck with wherever you're going and whatever it is you can't discuss!" The mailman slyly grinned as he said this.

The westbound engineer sounded the whistle and the train started slowly. Soon the dark swallowed it.

"I am glad it is a fair night, little wind and many stars. We can navigate easy."

Mik spoke extra soft, knowing that voices travel in the country. The background hum of the city is pervasive. One doesn't hear it, but it covers many sounds. With the train gone, there was absolutely no background noise. He quietly stood, calming the horse and waiting for his eyes to adjust to the dark. He knew when that happened he would be able to see almost as well as if under sunlight not starlight.

"Yes." Cam spoke clearly but softly, mouth close to ear. "I say we head east by south and look for their wagon tracks. We'll need to keep extra quiet until we see what's what."

Mik nodded and they set off.

Both men kept the North Star over their left shoulder, just at the edge of their vision. This kept them going the direction they wanted. Mik tapped Cam on the shoulder. Coming close, he whispered. "If they went more or less due south, we ought to cross their tracks in twenty or thirty minutes. I figure that we're traveling about a third as fast as the train did for those eight minutes. And we have a little farther to go than back to Sulfur Flats since we are heading south as well as east. Agreed?"

Cam nodded, looking for any trace of wagon tracks and hoping he might hear voices.

A FEW MINUTES BEFORE THE RAILROAD MEN LOOKED UP AT THE stars, Joe and the Chari were loaded up and ready to go. He snapped the reins. As the wagon started, he got the North Star behind him. Then he looked to find a distinctive constellation straight ahead. No matter its name, he gratefully drove the wagon right towards it.

As usual, the bumpy country made for a fitful ride. It was hard to get rest riding on the buckboard seat of a wagon going cross country. Chari forced herself to relax. She needed to be fresh. First thing was to look the site over and make sure it hadn't been disturbed. More to the point, they had to be ready to confront Dale, Ella, and whoever they brought out to see the place.

She did rouse herself once. "Joe, are we sure they are coming soon? Today or tomorrow? We don't want to be stuck out here for days."

He spoke softly. It made her lean in to hear.

"Ella told you they were bringing out their own investor 'soon, maybe tomorrow'. That was yesterday. We got on the first train we could and I think we have beat them here."

He looked her full in the face. "Now, let's not talk. Sound carries a whale of a long way out here. If they are already at the Karat Top we don't want to give ourselves away."

Driving in silence under the Milky Way, Joe marveled at the universe. Light from the millions of stars was so good he could see hills looming up to the south. Not too much longer and they would be there. Almost before he knew it, they were.

He pulled up next to the big outcrop they had once used as a tent pole. The site was undisturbed and no one seemed to have been around. That, he was glad to see. Since it had been their headquarters in other visits he expected that Dale would use it too. The massive crag provided shelter. The line of sight there was limited. They could see just a small part of the field right in front, nothing else. Since no one else was around, neither Joe nor Chari considered a field of view important. They were too tired to bother.

"I'll unhitch the team and tie them up where they can graze. We have a few hours before daylight; let's get some rest. We ought to sleep as long as we can. They can't possibly be here for another day. We need to be alert, and maybe will have to stay up while they're around."

"Alright, that makes sense. Good night!"

With that, she rolled up in a blanket in the back of the wagon. Joe intended to sleep out under the stars. He couldn't resist bathing in their light, even as he slept. Plus the grass was softer than planks in a wagon bed. Seeing to the horses took only a few minutes. He grabbed a blanket and stretched out.

CAM WAS FIRST TO SPOT THE WAGON TRACKS. MIK SAW THEM A half a second later, just as Cam pointed silently. They pulled up and conferred in low voices.

Mik knew his night vision was better than Cam's. "Let's stick close until we see where they lead and where the people are. That way we ought to keep on their trail. Johanssen's friend said there were hills and crags, right? That's where we need to be extra cautious, when we see hills and crags."

Cam nodded and made an 'after you' gesture. Off they went.

XXVII

THE SKY BURST WITH GALAXIES AND WAS SPICED BY THE occasional shooting star. Its beauty faded as Joe dropped off. His sleep wasn't restless nor was he dead to the world. After a while—he wasn't sure how long—there was something: voices and a resonating horse whinny. He came half awake, sat up and looked around. For a moment he was lost, then remembered: This was the Karat Top! It was alright, it was just him and Chari, all alone, forty miles from nowhere. He told himself it was just his horses, or a dream. Drinking in the unimaginable distance to the stars, he laid back. Soon he had his fill and tumbled into a deep, sound slumber.

IN FACT, A HORSE HAD WHINNIED, AND IT WASN'T ONE OF JOE'S. Cam was in the lead as they came over a hill and sighted the crags. He wanted to stop short. The adrenalin was pumping and he yanked the reins abruptly, harder than he needed to. His horse was a townie. She usually spent her nights in a stable with a horse for company in the next stall and a bucket of oats to snack on. Being a worrier, she found this mysterious quiet wilderness unsettling. Plus, she didn't know her rider.

All that was bad enough, but she really didn't like being out in the country in the dark. She smelled cats and bears and did not like it one bit.

She whinnied in protest when Cam jerked the reins but she did obediently pull up. Cam eased up the rein and patted her on the neck. "Sorry, girl. You're doing good," he whispered. Mik pulled alongside. They leaned close to talk.

"Looks to me like the tracks go behind that big crag over to the right." Mik looked over and Cam nodded. "I think we ought to take the horses over to that grove of aspen off to the left. They can graze while we look things over. Carefully!"

"Agreed. We have an hour or so before dawn. Maybe we can get the lay of things without them knowing it." He paused. "Sorry. I got a little muscular with the reins and the horse protested. Hopefully no one heard."

"Forget it. They have horses. It could have been one of theirs. If they even noticed."

Cam's worried mare and Mik's horse were quietly stashed. They were loosely tied next to the team which had pulled the wagon. The agreement was Cam would work around clockwise and Mik, counterclockwise. The plan was to meet back behind the area in half an hour or so, and compare notes. There was a gray smear low in the east. The sun wouldn't appear for some time, but daylight was coming.

Walking on grass or sand was surer and quieter than on rocks, at least for Mik. As the dark slowly died away he warily picked silent footing. He came to a fair sized patch with no grass which looked lumpy. It was almost as if someone had strewn marbles or gravel around and covered them just a bit. They were close enough to the surface to be noticeable even in bad light. He knelt and ran his fingers through the dirt and sand. A hard, pecan sized rock came to him. Looking close, it had a bit of a sparkle, and was green, deep green. Jade?! He stood up and walked further. Now the area was smooth. He walked on and found another field of lumps. Stooping to pick one up, he suspected he knew what they all were. It was a stone not a carved gem. Even so it had a glint. Was it a diamond? Unsure, he pocketed it with the green stone. There were several other fields or areas which were studded with small rocks. He scuffed a few and they looked much like what he had in hand.

Coming the other way around, Cam saw no lumpy ground. He softly went past where the horses grazed. Two of them glanced up then went back to their quite grass munching. Then there was a wagon, and it looked like the one that Joe and the woman had driven away in. Next to it, on the ground a person was rolled up in a blanket. Wheezes and snorts told him the person was sound asleep. Whoever it was, his or her snores didn't hold a candle to the rip roarers Mik had filled the mail car with.

Cam smiled to himself as he quietly backed up and skirted the sleeper. Behind the next crag standing in a crevice were two rods, one metal and one wood. Each was about the size of a broom handle. The ends were muddy like they had been poked into the ground. He took the metal rod. Evidence of a sort, and it would be a good silent weapon. He might have to whack someone but hoped not. Rod at the ready, he stepped out from the crag. Standing silent and watchful, he sensed no movement, no surprises, and he breathed easier.

Not a minute later, Mik loomed out of the dark. A maniacal grin split his face. He had to concentrate to whisper not bellow, he was so worked up.

"There sure as hell are gems around here. Look what I found!" Digging in his pocket, he held out the two stones. "There are fields of these things, all mixed up and just under the surface. You can scuff them up, easy as stomping a spider."

Cam held out the rod, muddy at one end. "I found this leaned up against the rock back there." He held it up, looking closely at the muddy end. "This is too cute. I'll bet this rod was used to plant the rocks. And there's another one back there, too."

"You're probably right. We need to have an expert look this area over. Can you believe these jewels are around for the taking? There is no place on earth where this has happened before. At least no place I've ever heard of."

Cam had focused on finding the mine. Once found, he had wanted to look it over from a practical, skeptical point of view. He wasn't a miner but he was a working man with a similar outlook.

Now.... Another aspect of it all suddenly occurred to him. "I have been blind. If this is real it is a windfall of unimaginable wealth. But if it is what we think, a scam....Big money has or will be put into this. But if there are no jewels, the backers will be the winners. The only winners, and they'll do anything to avoid being exposed. I sure hope Mr. Moffat and his friends haven't done anything foolish. And we need to be darn careful now that we know."

Mik nodded. He murmured, "The light is growing and we can be seen. Let's saddle up and get out of here."

Joe was coming awake. This time he was sure there were voices. Or was it the wind in the rocks? The hour before day break emboldens doubts and fears. Was he falling prey to the pre-dawn frights? Rolling over, he willed himself more or less awake and forced one eye open. Stars were dimming and the Milky Way was barely visible. No movement to be seen, he was sure. But it sure sounded like people talking. Nah, it was probably the wind. After all, they were forty miles from nowhere.

Mik and Cam walked lightly back, each circling on around. They saw the rest of the crags. Cam nearly stumbled on the artfully littered gems. He wondered what other evidence of 'natural' gems there was. His horse again whinnied when he got on. Waiting with two strange horses had eased her worries not a bit.

This time, Joe was sure he heard a horse. It came from near where he had pegged his horses, but maybe a little off. Were the horses loose? That would be disaster! Or possibly there was a cat or other predator lurking. Either way, not good.

Instantly alert, he sat up. The blanket ended up in a heap. Now, Joe had done his share of country living. Usually when out in the woods, he made sure to shake his footwear and clothes first thing. You never knew what might have spent the night in a nice warm dry spot. Not now. He hurriedly tugged at his boots. What—or who—was he hearing out there? He stood quickly and stepped towards the sounds.

As it turned out a scorpion or some crawly critter had taken refuge in one boot. It did not take kindly to having something shoved at it and took a defensive chomp. The jab of pain made Joe yelp. He sat right back down and pulled the boot off.

In the wagon bed, Charity stirred then sat up. "What happened, Joe? Are you alright?"

"Some damn bug in my boot stung me. Aah! Man, that hurts." The foot throbbed. It was quickly swelling, noticeably larger than normal already. "I heard someone or something out there. I'm almost positive. But I can't go look. Get up, Chari, and go see, would you? Seems like it was off in that bunch of aspen trees. A person or an animal is out there. Or maybe a horse is loose." He nodded off to where Cam and Mik were just now starting to move out.

She grabbed her derringer and quickly climbed out of the wagon. Having slept fully clothed, hiding bugs were not a worry. Silently she looked around then stepped away from the crag.

Looking back, she reported, "Two men on horseback. Leaving, I think. Or maybe it's a couple of deer." She squinted. "Too dark to be sure. Something is out there, going away." She turned towards the intruders, aiming the pistol. Yelling "Stop!" she pulled the trigger. Of course she did not expect to hit anything, but wanted to punctuate her order.

Before Chari played Annie Oakley, Cam was talking nice to his horse, trying to calm and urge her on. There was a yowl of pain back by the wagon. Through it all, Mik heard Cam murmuring and saw him stroking his steed's mane even as they hurried out of the aspen grove. Then someone yelled something, a single word, followed by the pop of a small caliber pistol. No more shots rang, to their relief. Cam's horse settled down. They all four, men and horses, got serious and fled.

These horses are pickin 'em up and puttin 'em down pretty good, Mik thought gratefully. *We'll be over the horizon in no time.* They were half a mile away from the crags now, heading north as fast as they could. They had been seen, no point in stealth or silence now.

SOME TWENTY MILES NORTH (JOE'S FORTY MILES WAS AN EXAGgeration) the morning westbound approached Sulfur Flats. A man and woman debated, whispering and gesturing. Behind them dozed a man, middle aged and a little overweight. They both knew his name but didn't use it. Instead they called him 'The Investor.' The car was almost empty. The Investor sprawled over two seats, his tie loosened at the neck and one cuff unbuttoned, sleeve flapping. He rasped a little bit but did not snore.

"I still think it is a bad idea to stop this train and make a big deal of getting off in broad daylight. We should have waited and taken the afternoon westbound. Letting him see the way is a mistake. What if he tells others?"

Ella frowned. "We've been over and over this, Dale. We agreed time is short. And that we need to get our man out to see the place before Joe and Chari try to stop us. I tell you, she was not happy when I told her we planned to bring our own man out. And besides, we'll have his money by then. Why would he let others in on the secret? If he does, its just more for us."

The man stirred. She continued, glancing back. "And I think we have beat them to it. We'll be out there and back before they know what we're doing. It was too bad we couldn't get a wagon out here. We'll be alright, though. No wagon but I was able to arrange for three horses and a mule to be waiting."

"So I have to pack a mule? Lash on our tent and supplies when we stop? Great, I can't wait."

"Oh stop your whining." She leaned close to him, her 'come hither' eyes inviting as she whispered. "If we play it right we can get our man..." here she glanced back, glad that he was still asleep "to put money up. Maybe even today. Then we can start building soon, and we'll be on our way to a fortune! And no one can stop us then! Even if Joe and Chari drag their feet."

The conductor came through the car. "Next siding, Sulfur Flats. Aren't you folks getting off there? We'll be there in...." He pulled out his watch, fingering it lovingly as he flipped the cover. "We'll be stopping in twelve minutes. You need to be ready to get off and get your baggage seen to. We can't spend all day at a half penny stop like this." He tipped his hat, scowled, and went on to the next car.

They got off as quick as they could. With packing and all, over an hour had gone since the train whistled and started away. At last the three saddled up, pulled the mule's rope, and headed out. The investor felt small and all alone. Wyoming was known for open space and not many trees, he knew. And he knew that it is hard to judge distances with little to gauge by. Still he tried.

After a while, The Investor shaded his eyes and looked south. "There are hills and crags there, you say? Are you certain we're headed the right direction?" This last question was directed to both the others. He looked sharply at Dale then Ella.

"We will be there before you know it, just a few hours. Don't fret. Of course this is out in godforsaken country. No one else comes around. And that is why we have such a bonanza." She looked him in the eye and smiled. "It is one that you just might be lucky enough to buy a share in."

It was all Ella could do not to criticize his horsemanship. She did not approve of his spurs. Today of all days, out here forty miles from nowhere, with this person, she bit her tongue. She told herself that the horse didn't seem to be hurt, and truly it didn't. Still she felt bad for it.

The Investor said nothing. For a moment he silently pondering Ella's explanation. But his attention was drawn from talk of a bonanza to a small dust cloud out ahead of them. He pointed at it, curious, excited, a bit apprehensive.

"What do you think that is?"

Dale jumped in. "Probably a dust devil. Its a small whirlwind which picks up sand. Very common out here. They don't get big and usually play out after a minute or two."

Ella looked. She hoped Dale was right, but something told her to look twice. It was a strange dust devil. It wasn't spinning, and there were two specks below it. And they were getting bigger. "Why, it is two riders, coming towards us!"

Astonished and concerned, her mouth got the better of her. "Did Joe and Chari get out here? Why are they coming towards us now? So fast? What do you think they want?"

Dale too was surprised. He laughed to cover it up, and to make light of her babble. He turned to The Investor. "We don't expect to meet folks up here, you understand. This is probably our two colleagues in the Karat Top and I'm sure they have good reasons for being here."

CHARI'S GUNSHOT AND THE YELLING GOT EVERYONE GOING. The two men and their horses moved as if the pistol shot was the start of a horse race. Fearing pursuit, they sprinted away from the crags. Once over the horizon they slowed, taking turns to look back. For the time being at least they weren't being chased.

"Let's keep a look back, I will for a while then you. They'll kick up a dust cloud if they come."

Mik agreed. His eyes were fastened on the horizon in front, but he didn't see it since he was deep in thought. "Yes, good idea. And we need to get a geologist out here. That may be a legitimate diamond mine. Who knows? I sure don't, but someone independent ought to look it over. Fields of diamonds, jade and rubies? Who has ever seen that?"

Cam was thoughtful. "You're probably right." He looked over his shoulder, pleased to see only sagebrush and sky. When he faced forward he was surprised. He wiped his eyes, not sure what he was seeing. There was a dust cloud out there to the north. He squinted. Under it were three or four specks. Were they horses and people?

He looked again to be sure. Then, nonchalantly, he nodded that direction. "It looks like we have company, Mik. I hoped we wouldn't have trouble. Maybe we won't. They could be just folks out riding." Even as the words came, he heard how naive and silly they sounded.

"Yeah, right. Maybe they're coming out to serve their grandma high tea." Mik pulled his Colt .45 out and spun the revolver. He confirmed it was fully loaded before he put it back in the holster.

Cam did the same, and checked the rifle in the holder next to his right leg. Both were ready if necessary.

Dale recognized the oncomers first. What he didn't realize is that he wasn't just thinking, he was also talking out loud. The others heard what he said. "Why, there is that damn Mik. And his friend, is it Gabe? Chaz? I forget. But I know that we have met these two before. What in God's name are those two scamps doing out here?" He turned and spoke aloud intentionally. "Ella. Do you see that?"

Ella's reply and deft explanation astonished him. "Yes, Mik and Cam." She caught The Investor's eye. "These men were out checking the security of the site. The plan was that they be done before we all came out, but perhaps something has come up. Excuse us please while we talk with them. I ask that you stay here, and hang on to the mule's lead. We don't want him to wander off."

With that she nodded to Dale to join her as she rode out to meet the two men who warily approached.

Recognition dawned on Mik. "Cam, its those characters Dale Smith or Smuts or something and the odd woman, Ella. The one that dressed as a man."

"Yes. And there's another man. Lord, that there mule is carrying enough gear for a cavalry regiment."

The two had briefly discussed and agreed what to do if they met someone. Cam reminded Mik and himself. "Remember, we're just out doing some business for the railroad. We know nothing and say nothing."

Mik couldn't help himself. "I'd bet a year's pay those two skunks are involved in this diamond scheme. It is just like them to be in on some crooked deal."

They continued toward the oncoming pair who also approached them. The third person hung back, holding onto the mule's rope. "Remember, we're just out here on road business. No more, no less."

Ella was pleased with her reaction. She had to crow. "I'm not sure how that quick idea came to me. At least now it doesn't look like we got surprised. Money men don't like surprises. Speaking of which, I wonder what these guys are doing out here."

"I don't believe in coincidence. They are out looking for the mine, I'll bet. The question is, what do we do? We can't eliminate them with The Investor watching."

"Maybe they're out looking for our mine, maybe not." She smiled and relaxed a smidge. "You know, Dale, they are just railroad men. Probably just a couple of guys searching out possible routes. Roads do sent out scouting parties, all over the country. Anyway, we don't need to tell them why we're here. I say let them go. If they ask, we're just out on a business trip. That's all they need to know."

The four riders carefully approached, each holding reins in one hand. This wasn't a display of horsemanship. It was to keep one hand ready. Each lightly laid their free hand near, very near, the handle of their holstered, in Ella's case, pocketed, pistol. They warily watched as the other, unexpected riders pulled up about fifteen feet away. The horses fidgeted, sensing tension.

Mik surprised them with an off the wall question. "You guys got any water? This country is dry as a Kansas County!"

Dale glanced at Ella. They had been ready for hostility, or curiosity at least. But a request for help? "Uh, yes. We have some. Are you in need?"

A compassionate reply was the last thing Mik expected. In fact his canteen was full.

Cam jumped in. "Nah, we're alright. But you want a topped off water keg if you're going out there. This patch is parched as hades. Like he said, dry as a Womens' Temperance meeting."

That was enough word play for Dale. He cut to the chase. "We sure are surprised to see someone. What are you hoping to see out here? Where have you been?"

"We're here on business." Mik pointedly looked back at the mule. He knew the prominent Denver businessman holding its lead, and tried to mask his recognition. He was pretty sure it didn't show. "You?"

"The same." Ella saw a glimpse of something, not clear what, on Mik's face as he looked at the mule.

The Investor was closely watching and listening. Ella glanced back as he suddenly spurred his horse. She winced, feeling the kick as if it landed on her own ribs. He trotted up, mule in tow. Authoritatively he handed the rope out. Dale took it without thinking.

"These are not your security men." There was steel in that statement. "I know them. They work for the Moffat Road." As he spoke he sidled his horse over by Cam and Mik, facing Dale and Ella. "I'm not sure what your business proposition is, but I will not be lied to. I won't stay with people I can't trust and believe. Especially out in godforsaken country like this. Take my name off your list. I want nothing to do with this so called opportunity."

Looking at Mik, he raised an eyebrow and spoke. "I think I should go back to Denver."

Mik understood. "Of course, you can ride with us."

Before Dale or Ella could protest, it was over. The three spurred their horses and headed north at a fast trot.

XXVIII

Joe tended to his foot. He hobbled over and found a spot in the creek. It wasn't much, maybe eight inches deep. The cold water first made him shudder and it quickly deadened the pain. Even the swelling went down. At the rate it was shrinking, pretty soon he could get his boot back on.

"Who do you think was around camp this morning, Joe? We weren't followed here, we both paid attention to that. And everyone who we've brought has been blindfolded. So no one knew how to get here." She thought. "Maybe someone heard rumors and put two and two together."

Concentrating on his foot, he was only half listening. "Are you sure it was people on horse and not wild game?"

She bristled. "Yes. I told you what I saw. Plus, I went over and saw hoof prints, prints with shoes, going up the hill. Deer don't wear shoes! It was two people on horseback, like I said." She looked over to where the riders had disappeared. "So, what do we do? Was it maybe Dale and Ella?"

"No, they wouldn't have left. They would have come down and talked with us. And there would have been three. They were bringing some money man out here, remember? No reason for just the two of them to make the trip."

"Well then it was somebody else." She stood and turned in a circle, looking the site over, deep in thought. "We have to think this through. Maybe it was cowboys? Or it could be someone on the lam. Indians? Whoever, I hope it was just an innocent encounter." She humphed in disbelief. "Maybe, but I doubt it."

The frown deepened. "I think we have to plan for the worst. I have to assume it was someone scoping this place out. To invest? Or maybe someone wants to take it from us? Or even worse, someone will go spill the beans and people will come. We sure don't want a crowd." She jumped as if someone jabbed her. "My God, we don't want a mining engineer to come poking around."

Joe thought out loud, trying to make sense of things. "At the very least someone knows where we are. If they tell, we're sunk. I agree, we should assume the worst. If someone wants to take it over, let's find a way to sell it to them. If word gets out on the street, or if it looks like it will, we got trouble. Chari, I think it may be a good time to fold our tent. Case Z."

CAM, MIK AND THE INVESTOR TOOK OFF NORTH, MOVING LIKE scalded dogs. Dale and Ella stared in shocked disbelief. It all happened so fast! A few minutes ago things had been well in hand. They were on their way to show an eager investor their mine. A fortune was within reach. But the moment those railroad men came over the horizon…. The plan frayed then unraveled in a hurry. Of a sudden their life was like a tangled pile of yarn in the dust.

She spoke first. "Well, we're almost there now. Let's go spend the night at the Karat Top. At least there are trees and shade there. We can go back to the train tomorrow."

Dale absently nodded, still trying to come to grips. He didn't like sudden changes. "Yeah, I don't want to chase those three to the train. If I caught them, I'd likely do something I shouldn't."

The horses were urged on and Dale kept hold on the mule's rope. The slowpace gave them time to reflect. Resentful disbelief changing to anger, he lashed out.

"You just had to bring a man out here, your own investor, didn't you, Ella? You just couldn't wait for another week or two." He scowled, upset as hell and confused. An aching shoulder from pulling a mule along certainly didn't help.

"We could have waited a few days and gotten money from Joe. Now The Investor will go back and tell everyone that we lied to him. Worse, he knows where we are. The place will soon be crawling with prospectors. We will lose out. Great, just great."

She was in a foul mood herself. "And how was I to know we would meet two men he just happened to know out here? God, this has to be forty miles from anywhere." She stopped and with a free hand, pointed at him and yelled. "If you're do damned smart, why didn't you see that coming?" Calming herself, she started her horse ahead again. "And you could have refused to come along, you know. That would have ended it right there. I wouldn't have tried to bring a man out here by myself. So don't you blame me, Dale Smertz."

The exchanges got less bitter and loud although they lasted several more miles. As arguments do, this one ran its course.

"Hell, Ella, neither of us wanted this."

"You're right, and I'm sorry I pressed to come up now."

"That is done, forget it. And you are right, I could have refused. I shouldn't blame you and I apologize. The thing now is, how do we handle it? How do we let Joe and Chari know? How do we patch it up with The Investor?"

They crested a hill and saw crags. Ella's face fell. "I don't know about all that. Right now I can't worry about it. Look, there are people there at the Karat Top! What now?"

JOE AND CHARI CONTINUED TO BRAINSTORM THEIR NEXT moves. Whoever said there are no coincidences got it wrong. By pure chance, after a few minutes, Chari looked to the north. She saw an approaching dust cloud.

"Here they come. Or here comes someone, who is anybody's guess. I expect we'll find out real soon. Who they are and what they want, I mean." She reloaded her derringer. She couldn't tell for sure what was approaching. She could see several dots, riders and animals, under the cloud.

Joe put a telescope to the oncoming riders. "Well. Here come Dale and Ella. Just the two of them. If there is a third person he is well hidden. I see the two of them on horseback and a pack mule. Boy, that must be one stout mule! It looks to be carrying supplies good for a month!"

DALE SAW THE PEOPLE BY THE CRAGS TOO. HE HANDED HER the mule's lead and pulled his rifle out of the holster. "I say ride in. I want to find out who they are and what they are doing at our mine. I don't know about you, EQ, but I am mad and frustrated and ready to take a swing at somebody. They had better have a good reason to be here, or I just might use this baby."

He hefted the rifle as he said this. With that, he galloped away.

SOME TWENTY MILES NORTH RODE THREE FATIGUED AND dusty men on tired horses. Lucky for them, the train was a few minutes late. The horse carrying The Investor was a nag and had a little trouble keeping up. He was a portly load and most any animal would have tired under him. But it all worked out. They arrived in time to flag down and board the eastbound. It pulled a stock car and there was room for the horses. The men were able to find an empty compartment and settled in.

"I guess it is only fair that I pay for the horse that I rode. Some stable ought not be forced to take a loss because those two scoundrels lied to me." The Investor was experienced in business. His habit was to give fair and expect fair in return. He settled into his seat and gave the two men across from him a penetrating look.

"Alright, gentlemen. It is time to come clean. What were two railroad men doing out there in the middle of nowhere? Why, you two were running like the devil himself was after you. You were really moving when you came over the horizon. What gives?" He stopped and waited. After a moment he continued.

"Before you talk, let me tell you why I was out there with them. Those two said they had a business opportunity. Said they had a mine of some sort and needed investors. Wouldn't tell me much about it no matter how I asked. They said I should see it for myself. Substantial amounts of money would be needed, they said. Of course, they wanted me to commit to put up a large amount. It sounded intriguing and lucrative, so I agreed to see it."

The red in his face started rise, his expression sour and angry. "I was taken aback by how easily they lied to me. Telling me you were security for them. If they lied about that, I have to wonder, what other stories were—are—they telling?"

Mik glanced at Cam. They both knew this man by reputation. The Denver circles he ran in were out of their reach. Cam shrugged microscopically. Mik took that as agreement they should share what they knew. He started in.

"Well sir, our being there is a long story." Cam nodded but said nothing. Mik felt the hardness of the two stones in his pocket. Gathering his thoughts, he decided not to show them yet.

"Your investment would be in a diamond mine." Mik read his reaction accurately. The man somehow knew that. He was clearly surprised that Mik knew it too. "You are not the only man to be approached about this. Most men taken to see the mine have been blindfolded. For some reason you were not." He tried to read the reaction to that. Poker face on, The Investor merely gazed back.

"So, apart from the promoters, it is likely that only the three of us know where this 'mine' is. Or to be accurate two of us know exactly where it is and one of us has a good idea." The Investor briefly thought on that and smiled his agreement.

Cam spoke. "We know the promoters. We aren't sure how many they are, but we do know at least some of them. We don't know their experience for certain. But we do know that their background isn't is mine development, or engineering, or geology."

He yawned. It had been a long several days, and he was exhausted. Stifling a second yawn, he continued. "I was approached personally to recruit investors among railroad managers I might know. That seemed a little curious at the time. But I thought on it and could find nothing dishonest about it. I never did introduce anyone, nor refer any potential investors to them." Cam looked embarrassed. Now, he kicked himself for the way he felt giddy and greedy at the time of the offer.

"We heard rumors of this 'opportunity' and how men were led there blind. That seemed odd, hardly the way to promote a legitimate business. So Mik and I figured a way to try to find the place. By good fortune, we figured right. We got out there last night, late."

The Investor's poker face cracked. "What did you find? Is this a genuine mine? Are there diamonds there? Why were you running when we met?"

"Oh, we found gems." Mik pulled the rocks from his pocket, extending his open hand to display them. "Like these I picked up. There seem to be diamonds, jade, and other valuable rocks galore. All around. Just under the surface."

The rocks felt hot in his hand, and the idea of quick easy riches overtook him. Greed coursed through him. It was almost a stirring in the loins. He lost focus on his surroundings and the sensations took him over for a brief moment. They evaporated when he heard a questioning voice.

"All around, you say? Just under the surface?" The man started to reach for the gems, then stopped. "May I look at them?" Mik nodded.

To their astonishment, the man reached into a pocket and produced a jeweler's loupe. He expertly flipped it open with one hand as he took the stones. With the glass pressed into an eye, he examined each rock.

Mik look at Cam, raising an eyebrow. Cam shrugged and grinned.

The man took his time, examining each specimen several times, turning them over and around. He moved to another seat then returned in an effort to get different angles of light. The businessman turned gemologist certainly seemed to know what he was looking at. Finally he took the glass out of his eye and stowed it back in his pocket. He chuckled as he looked one last time at the stones.

With a 'humph' he handed them back. Then he folded his hands and sat. Schoolboys and girls had sat like this for generations, hands folded in the lap and eyes front. The man said nothing and seemed to be concentrating hard. Soon he appeared to doze off.

Mik repocketed the gems and sat back. Soon sleep overtook him as well. Cam went forward in the train hoping to find old railroad buddies.

ELLA SAT ON HER HORSE, INCREDULOUS. WHAT WAS DALE DOING? Kicking and spurring the horse, he charged towards the crags, straight at the people. He hoisted the rifle over his head like a hero in a western novel. She was sure the man had gone mad from the stress of the day. It wouldn't have surprised her if he broke into a whoop and holler. Expecting the worst, she waited for the people he was charging to shoot at him. Ella dropped the rope holding the mule. She half turned her horse. In a moment she would have to decide, flee or join him in the fight.

From her distance she saw him abruptly rein the horse to a stop and holster the rifle.

"Now what?" blurted Ella. Her horse didn't answer and the mule ignored her. The dropped rope was all he needed. He sauntered off left, towards the green grass in the aspen grove. Even if someone noticed they wouldn't have cared. Ella started forward to join her partner.

Dale stared at the man over his stopped horse. Joe stared back.

"Damn, Dale, you just about got yourself shot! You came on the attack and I didn't know what you were going to do." Joe had aimed his weapon, finger on the trigger, ready to fire. As the rider closed in his face came clear. Fortunately he pulled up before Joe had to decide, shoot or not. As Joe spoke he lowered the rifle. The rush and the adrenalin made his heart thud loudly in his ear. He shakily sat back. Of a sudden his foot hurt again. He felt woozy.

Confusion and surprise swirled in Dale. The day had brought too many strange and unexpected encounters! He sat limply in the saddle, trying to get his head around this latest one. He focused on the familiar face looking at him, wide eyed. He looked past the armed man and recognized yet another face.

He was able to utter a question. "What the heck are you doing out here, Chari?" Dale ignored his would be killer and focused on that person.

"Yes, I want to know, what are you doing out here, Chari?" Ella had quietly ridden up and stopped behind Dale. The cold question echoed off the crags.

Chari was as astonished as the others at the sudden approach and near shooting. She forgot Ella in the moment. Even as Dale came on and stopped, she didn't anticipate Ella's sudden, icy appearance. Less than a second passed before she calmly recovered.

"No, the question is, what are you doing out here?" She smiled, and jabbed, "Why didn't you charge at us like your man? And where is the fancy investor you told me you were going to bring out?"

"You came out here early didn't you? Were you going to help us present Karat Top?" Ella's eyes narrowed, again like a coiled rattler's. "No, you didn't tell us you'd be here. You had other things in mind." She paused, then it came to her. "You were not planning to help us. You were going to harm us, try to ruin our efforts, weren't you?"

Chari was mute for half a beat, long enough that Ella knew her shot hit home. Enraged, she went into full toot mode. "You would sabotage us! And you wanted to poach our investor! You were going to try to get rid of us!"

Ella was so worked up that she pulled the reins hard right and her horse spun around once before she let the reins slack. Facing her opponent again, Ella spat her wrath. "I never have trusted you Charity Hovus. You and your Joe Eggers are not to be believed or relied on!"

"We? We are not to be trusted? You have nerve! You, Ella, you have undermined me since the first time we met. Always finding fault. Always complaining you couldn't have money. Always wanting more. And now you are bringing out

an investor we don't know. And you would tell him our secrets! I damn the day we agreed to let you and your man in
on this plan!"

Dale and Joe took in this exchange of bile. They heard
the toxic words fly, becoming angrier and more intense with
each sentence. In a few words and phrases the careful work
of a year or more started to crumble. To Dale, his straightforward plan still seemed achievable: make big money, gain
friends and influence by helping others do the same, and finally, establish himself as a respected member of the community. Joe too was concerned that the fury would spill over
and spoil his plans. They appeared to parallel Dale's but were
all about amassing and taking money quickly. His plans were
straightforward but hidden from sight.

The bickering and rage continued.

The rifle Dale had waved like a charging Cossack came
back out of the holster. He pointed it straight up and pulled
the trigger. In the sudden silence all heard the shot echo off
the crags. The horses shied and even the mule grazing in tall
grass looked up. Seeing no one near, he settled back to serious munching.

"Goddammit, enough!" The yell was as loud as the rifle
shot.

"You two"—he looked at Joe and Chari—"snuck out here
without telling us and I won't even try to guess why. Then, on
the way in here, Ella and I met two men who probably spied on
the place and on you two. Did you know that?" Joe and Chari
traded uneasy glances. Dale gave them no chance to speak.

"They are on the way out and are likely on the train by
now. Odds are they will tell everyone about this place. When
we met them, our investor left us and went back with them.

No doubt they are comparing notes. Big problems, enough for us all. And what do you two do?"

He glared at Chari and Ella—"You are fighting like mink over a dead fish. ENOUGH!"

He stuffed the rifle back in the holster. The tirade not only stopped the fight, it gave new information to everyone. Ella had overlooked the obvious, that the railroad men had been here. Joe and Chari thought someone had been around and now were certain. And the investor leaving them sure wasn't good news.

After three or four seconds of stunned silence, Joe started laughing. Ella looked offended, then she too giggled. Chari was about to make snarky when she saw Dale grin, then laugh. His goofy expression made her chortle. Soon all four were gasping for breath and wiping away mirthful tears.

The snickers and cackles finally faded.

"That felt good." This simple statement set off another minute or two of giggling and snorting.

Joe finally caught his breath. He stood up as best he could. His foot still hurt but could bear some weight. At least his heart was no longer thudding against his ribs.

"Alright. Alright, let's get down to business." The others calmed and looked to him.

"Yup, Dale is right, we have problems aplenty. Time to pull together. Somehow we have to get back to Denver and put a cork in those three guys. We aren't ready for the public to know about this." Chari nodded as did Dale. Ella wondered why the public shouldn't learn about their fabulous mineral find but said nothing.

"Thanks to a scorpion or spider, I'm gimpy as hell." He glanced at his foot. "We really do need to get back and deal with all these sudden problems. How about this: Chari, you and Dale, get on the horses and get going. Ella and I can follow in the wagon."

With this he accomplished several goals. First, he wanted to separate the women. They had relaxed and laughed. Even so, the accusations and insults would continue to sting. They would be remembered and avenged.

More importantly, he wanted Chari on the scene in Denver. She was good at damage control. Plus, if need be she could ready their plan of action. They had a bail-out plan, a plan they came up with to use if worse came to worst. They called it, as he had said earlier, Case Z. Neither really thought it would have to be used, but there it was.

"And Chari, ride hard. You may get tired, but you can always get some zees on the train." He grinned and looked her in the eye. The grin was to make Dale think he was simply concerned for Chari. She knew what he meant; she looked back, smiled, and nodded oh so slightly. Ella watched the exchange thoughtfully.

Dale knew Ella. Even though she said nothing, she was thinking hard, running through options and scenarios. Should she go or stay? If she went what could she do to help them? How would The Investor react? What did those two railroad men see and what would they do? Her hesitation grew to an uncomfortable length. Dale was afraid she would erupt and destroy the feeble truce and Joe's humpty dumpty plan. He was trying to think of something to say. With surprise and relief, he watched as she reluctantly swung out of the saddle and held the reins out in the other woman's direction.

She avoided looking Chari in the eye. Chari did the same as she took them. Like Joe feared, unforgotten slights would be avenged, later. Dale and Joe were glad to see Chari adeptly take the reins and swing up into the saddle.

"I'll see you at the hotel, Joe." With that she yelped, "Let's go!" Before Dale could get mounted up she took off to the north. At first she galloped but shortly slowed for him to catch up. They settled into a ground covering, sustainable lope.

XXIX

ON THE EASTBOUND, THE MAN CALLED THE INVESTOR remained seated. Motionless, eyes closed, hands folded, he
looked for all the world like he was meditating or praying.
The portly, inert body moved slightly with the train's rocking as it chugged through Laramie towards Cheyenne.

The railroad men sat nearby and talked in low tones.

"Do we go to the Sheriff with this?"

"How? Why? We have no proof of wrongdoing. All we
saw was some stones in the ground."

"Yeah, I see your point."

"The Sheriff can't do anything with this. But the press
could. Or a banker or the mayor. We need to tell someone.
This needs to be out in the sunshine."

Options and ideas were explored. After a while they ran
out of steam and fell silent. The Investor stirred and came
out of his near trance. He looked up at them and cleared his
throat. "I want to talk to those two imps who lied. And I want
to go see the place."

"Well sir." The man's indignant stance back when they
met came to mind. Mik was surprised.

"Someone with your experience and wealth does not
need advice from us. But in fairness, I tell you that we have

reason to think this scheme is not on the up and up. You will want to tread cautiously."

After a nod, he went back to his silent schoolboy posture, dismissing them from his world. This time his eyes were open but he stared vacantly.

The train coasted into Cheyenne, smoke billowing and sparks flying. Mik stood and stretched. "I think we have two or three hours before a run leaves for Denver. That'll give us a chance to grab a decent meal."

Cam nodded. "I'll go see that the horses are taken care of." The Investor had climbed out of his deep well of thought. He sat still, alert, looking with interest at the train yard. Cam tapped him on the shoulder. "You said you wanted to settle up, pay the stable for your ride. Do you want to come with me now?"

"Yes, I need to do that." He too stood and stretched. The two men climbed down out of the car and left. Mik sat back and relaxed, falling into a doze. They would go eat when Cam returned.

"Mik, wake up!" Mik was dodging dust devils in sage-brush fields and at the same time, chasing giant jewels rolling through the streets. Cam's voice harshly penetrated his dream. "If we want to eat, wake up. Soon it'll be time to catch the afternoon run to Denver."

After climbing out of the car, they walked across several sets of tracks. Cam brought him current. "We got the horses to the stable. The Investor paid separately for his." He mimed pulling something out of his pocket. "You should have seen the wad of bills that guy had. Anyway, he says he is staying here. He doesn't want to go on to Denver with us. Says he'll stay in Cheyenne for now."

"I guess that is his business. Best of luck to him." He glanced over. "I figured out what we can do. It came to me as I dropped off to sleep. Let's just go back and act as if we ourselves found a bonanza. No need to involve the sheriff or go tattle to a business leader. We'll just 'accidentally' tell someone about it, someone with a big mouth. People will soon know where it is and how the place is littered with gems."

"I like it! If the place is real, a lot of folks will get rich. If it isn't, the fraud is exposed." Each had a big grin as they shook hands. Then they went in search of a meal.

BACK TO THE WEST, A PAIR OF HORSE RIDERS CAME THROUGH the sagebrush, headed home from nowhere. Chari and Dale made fast progress to Sulfur Flats. By good fortune, they timed their approach well. The smoke from the afternoon train was visible to the west as they rode up. Dale got off the horse and walked to the tracks. Standing astride the tracks, he signaled for the train to stop. The engineer saw him and slowed immediately.

Looking around, Dale quickly noticed a problem, and told Chari. "There is no stock car on this makeup. We'll have to leave the horses here. We need to do something with them."

This was the last thing she cared about, and her tone told him so. "Tie them up in the shade of the shed." To call the rough structure a shed was charitable. It was more like a falling down lean to. There was no station master at this seldom used whistle stop. The railroad had provided minimal shelter for anyone using it.

She softened. "The next train will probably have a car. If not, the following one will. Anyway, Joe will be here with Ella by morning."

"I don't know, Chari. Leaving them out in Wyoming weather seems cruel."

"Dale, our plan is in danger of coming apart. Those railroad men will spill the beans on the Karat Top. If we don't get to town quick, we lose everything."

She eyed the horses, appraising their condition. "Tie 'em up. They'll be fine here for twelve or fifteen hours." An idea, a compromise, came to her. "Tell you what, let's ask the conductor to fill the water tank so at least they can drink."

That seemed a fair arrangement. Her saying the plan was in danger made him think. He could practically see his new found wealth flying out the window. "Alright. That should be good enough."

Soon the train pulled away, Chari and Dale sitting in comfort. The horses had been unsaddled, watered, and picketed in what little shade the place offered. Any concerns about the horses' welfare soon disappeared. The engine chuffed towards the sunrise side of the State.

Dale mused. "This country is so big and empty. Not a tree in sight! It hardly seems the train is moving. There is nothing to give you a sense of motion."

"Well, we're moving fast. I'll bet the engineer has us going twenty five or even thirty miles an hour!" She smiled at the thought of such speed. Her smile faded as she considered the problems and turmoil they were speeding towards.

"Dale, we need to find those two railroad men. And then we have to muzzle them. That is, if they are saying anything about Karat Top. Maybe, I doubt it but maybe they really were just out there on business. Maybe they were simply scoping out a possible new route. They may have no idea what we have out there at the mine."

His expression was a grim half smile, eyes hard and unhappy. "Sure, Chari. That is about as likely as President Roosevelt wiring me for advice." His expression changed to hopeful. "But I suppose it could be. In any case, I'll find them in Denver. Those two are people I kind of know."

Her antenna were up immediately. "Oh?"

"Yeah. Long story. I'll tell you someday. For now, let me handle it. When we get there, I'll find them and see what they are up to. Even if they were really on train business, I want to know." He paused. "And, we need to find The Investor. He left with them. God knows what he heard or where he is now."

AT THE STABLE IN CHEYENNE, CAM AND THE CHUNKY MONEY guy men settled up the bill for the horse rental. The Investor reiterated that he wanted to see the two 'imps' who had lied to him, and that he would be staying. They amiably parted ways, Cam going to find Mik. The other man wandered the streets around the railyard, thinking and planning. He walked the length of most every street in the district, some of them twice. After a while, he knew what he wanted to do. So then he headed for the waiting room in the train station.

Most train waiting rooms looked pretty much alike. This one could have been a station in any medium sized city. The benches were hard and stiff backed. The layout brought to mind tombstone rows in a Civil War cemetery: precise lines, hard cornered, and severe. He shook that macabre thought off. After a brief study, he chose a seat. It was on the end of a row. The seat allowed him to see everyone coming and going from the room and tracks. He wanted to see his two imps as they came in, before they saw him.

THE RAILROAD MEN ENJOYED A NICE DINNER BEFORE BOARDING. Content with full stomachs, they ambled through the station to catch their ride to Denver. Mik almost walked right by The Investor. When he saw who it was, he stopped to speak.

"Are you positive that you don't want to come to Denver with us tonight?"

The man was deep in thought and seemed startled. "Yes, I am sure. There are some loose ends I need to tie up and here is as good as anywhere."

"Alright." Mik looked at Cam who raised an eyebrow. "Well, then, we'll go on. Best of luck to you." Hands were shaken all around. The railroad men found and boarded their train and were soon on the way home.

The Investor patiently waited. He knew that Cheyenne was one of the busiest stations in the region. Eastbound and westbound makeups came through day and night. Watching the flow of people, he figured his lying imps would show up before too long. The way he saw it, Dale and Ella would hurry to get back to the Sulfur Flats stop and return to Cheyenne. They likely wouldn't be on the next eastbound to arrive. But they could well be on the one after that. He sat for an hour or so, watching the hubbub and enjoying the organized chaos.

Out of the crowd appeared a familiar gangly man.

Sure enough, there was Dale. But that wasn't Ella with him. Where was she? Dale was talking with a woman walking alongside of him. By their manner, she was someone he knew. The woman was not an acquaintance from the train he was merely chatting with. Concentrating, neither saw The Investor as they walked by.

"Dale." The Investor called out.

Deep in conversation with Chari, he was surprised to hear his name. No one in Cheyenne knew him, he was sure. The rangy man was surprised, looked around, and stopped. Caught flat footed, he almost stammered.

"Well sir. I uh, I didn't expect to see you here." He couldn't think of anything else to say.

The tone in reply was stern, even steely.

"'I'm sure you didn't. Dale, you and I have some business to finish. You and I and Ella. She is the one I first talked to about this project. Where is that woman?" His glance told Chari she was an interloper, and it put emphasis on the question.

She surmised this was the man they brought out to invest in Karat Top. This was better than she could have hoped for! It was the perfect opportunity to get into the conversation. Without seeming pushy or strange, she jumped in.

"She is helping a friend." She extended her hand as a man would do when meeting an equal in a business setting. "Hello, I am Charity Hovus. Dale and I are two of the mine's associates."

"Nice to meet you, Mrs. Hovus." He did not take her hand nor introduce himself. Insult to injury, he also ignored her frown at his assumption she was someone's appendage, his Missus.

The man focused on Dale, reiterating. "We have some business to finish. You supposedly have a commercial opportunity. We were enroute to see it when we were interrupted by those two railroad men. I left in a huff and regret it. Dale, I want to see this place of yours and hear your plans for it."

"You do?!" This was unexpected. Dale forged on, glad he didn't have to explain.

"That is a good decision on your part, one you will not regret. We need to sit down and discuss this further." He smiled and shrugged. "The thing is, I can't right now. I need to get to Denver and find those two men. Those two men showing up was, well, something of a surprise. I need to talk with them."

The money man sized up the couple standing in front of him. He hadn't budged from the bench. The crowds surged. Crowd noise and engine clangs washed over them. He realized Dale and the woman honestly did not know why Mik and Cam had gone out there. So he filled them in to suit his purposes.

"Ah yes, those two men. Let me tell you. The three of us talked at length on the train. They were just out scouting territory for Moffat's railroad. They were actually glad to encounter someone, they said. They talked a lot about how the country is dry and desolate."

He tried to read their reactions. In his judgment they bought his tale. "Actually they are quite limited in their outlook, if you know what I mean. I heard all about two percent grade and drainage culverts and keeping timetables and water tanks and enough train talk to last me into next year."

Chari glanced at Dale, then asked, "They didn't mention seeing other people or crags or anything unusual?"

"Oh they said something about crags, but it was in passing. I think it was something about whether to cut through or go around. Truth be told I was only half listening by that point."

Dale gave a slight nod to no one in particular. Chari noticed the gesture. She took it to mean he wanted to find the two railroaders and confirm this version of events. She too was skeptical of the story. The mention of crags meant they could have seen Karat Top. She wondered if this man was telling them everything. The Investor noticed the gesture too. He took it that they bought his story.

Dale nodded again. "In any case, I had better get to Denver. There are those and other people I need to see, and the train is leaving shortly. Good to see you again. We will talk soon. I will send a message boy around." He started to edge away but didn't leave.

Seizing the opportunity, Chari told a story of her own. "Well sir. Dale and I, and also Ella, are associates of equal standing in our effort. What he knows, I know and vice versa. So you can talk with me as you have with him and Ella." She paused to read his reaction. It was neutral, showing neither disbelief nor eagerness to talk with her.

She pressed. "What is it that you want to know about our opportunity? How can I help make you comfortable with it?"

She turned so only Dale could see her face, and winked. "Dale, I agree. You should go on to Denver and take care of business. Go and tend to the work we discussed. I'll stay here and answer his questions."

He hesitated. "Alright then, I'm off. Chari, I will see you tomorrow or the next day. Send a runner around when you get to town. I should have my work done by then and we can compare notes."

He had a funny feeling as he boarded the train. Shouldn't he be the one staying here? It should be he who answered this investor's questions. He and Ella had located, qualified, and brought him into the picture. Yet here he was, leaving the man to Chari. Somehow she had managed to insert herself between him and the man he and Ella had brought in to the picture.

Well, after all, things had gone crazy. They were a team, right? Everyone had to think fast and improvise. This was probably the best way for them to handle it. He just hoped things got straightened out soon. He really didn't want Ella to hear about him going off and leaving The Investor with Chari.

CHARI AND THE INVESTOR WERE THE LAST THING ON ELLA'S mind. Roadblocks and complications to developing the Karat Top occupied her thoughts. Some of them were new facts and items she had learned only in the past several hours. Mind spinning, she went over what had been said and what had been left unsaid. These ran in the background even as Joe was talking to her. With an effort, she focused on him rather than rehash the previous twelve or fourteen hours. He droned on so!

"Ella, I can't hitch the team up to the wagon. My right foot hurts where the bug bit me. And my other knee aches. I have put all my weight on it to favor the hurt one. So now I can barely hobble around. I simply can't get the rig ready to go. You will have to do it."

"Well, alright, I guess I can do that." Many times Ella had had watched the harnessing and rigging of a team and wagon. She had handled reins occasionally after the rig was set up, but that was all.

"I have never done, er, harnessed a horse much less fastened a wagon. You will need to talk me through it."

He chuckled in spite of his jangly foot. "Yes, I will. You don't fasten a wagon. You rig it. Here's what you do...."

It took several tries, undoing and redoing. Between them, the wagon was finally ready. The horses were hitched in the right order and the wagon was loaded. Holding on to her elbow, Joe was able to get over to and up on the buckboard. Before she could walk around and get on, he grabbed the reins. She started to climb on when she remembered dropping the mule's rope.

"I forgot, that darn mule is loose! We can't leave the poor thing here."

She got back down and approached the now happily engorged animal. Not surprisingly, he took a dim view of giving up his freedom, and shied away. She got her hand on the rope several times before getting a good grip. Joe waited for probably twenty minutes as she and the mule matched wits and strength. After a while the critter tired of the game. He allowed himself to be caught, pulled over, and tied to the back of the wagon. The entourage complete, they set off.

Ella was tired from all the work, but was full of anxiety and anger. A nap was in order but she would not succumb. Something had been eating at her and she wanted to know. Weighing her words, she looked steadily at Joe. He tried to ignore the eyes boring into the side of his face. Finally she spoke.

"I heard you say something to Chari that I have been wondering about. Just what does 'getting some zees' mean, Joe? I heard you use that phrase in passing. It sounded innocent but the look you two exchanged.... The words and the way you said them sure seemed to mean something to her."

Joe was surprised, even shocked. He didn't think Ella was smart enough to be suspicious, much less see that something was going on. Was she really that astute?

In his haste to get Chari going to Denver, he wasn't positive she had picked up on the phrase. It wasn't a warning, really, just a 'heads up'. He had meant for her to be ready to bolt if need be. Of course he intended that they would leave town together, them and their money.

Well, strictly speaking, the money belonged to the investors, not the two of them. As far as Joe was concerned, it was simple. They controlled the money which had been freely given to them. It was stored safely away. So he considered it theirs.

This all ran through his head in a flash. He had no good answer prepared, no answer to deflect and reassure Ella. *Stall*! ran through his mind. So he did what he could, hoping to buy time to make a good response.

"Ouch! My foot got banged when we went over that bump! Here, hold the reins a minute." This he would regret. He grabbed at a foot and made a show of massaging it.

More than happy to take the reins, she yanked them, stopping the wagon. And she held them tightly. "I'm not stupid, Joe. You are massaging your good foot, trying to think of something to say. Now, tell me. What does it mean?"

"What does what mean?"

The icy voice brooked no more delay. "Zees, getting some zees."

To show she meant business, she delivered a kick at his bad foot. The pain was stunning. A second kick doubled him over. She grabbed the pistol from his holster, putting him entirely at her mercy.

"Now, you tell me what is really going on. Or, I can stomp on you all afternoon. I know you and Chari have not told us the whole story. Talk." She pulled her foot back for another blow.

He looked at her, incredulous. "My God, Ella. You hurt me."

The whining tone killed any patience she had left. Brandishing the pistol, she cocked and waved it in his direction.

"This is your last chance. I mean it. Talk to me."

THE RAILROAD MEN IDLY LOOKED THROUGH THE CINDER smudged car windows. As the train headed south from Cheyenne, the high prairie rolled by. The Rockies lolled in the sun, magnificent and eternal. Denver was over an hour away yet. The scenery floating by was but a backdrop. Their focus was not sightseeing. What to do with their new found knowledge took their attention and energy.

Cam and Mik agreed, causing a big splash wasn't appropriate. Neither of them wanted to run into town and make accusations or point fingers. Still, they had information. If it were their money at risk, they would want someone to tell them if the scheme looked fishy. What they knew simply wasn't something to be withheld. After much discussion, a course of action was reached.

Drawing on his good ol' boy southern roots, Cam tidily summarized the strategy. "If you want to start a pile of brush on fire, you can take matches and light up five or eight small branches. Or you can prepare a ball of paper and small twigs under it and get it going with one match."

They decided on the one match approach. They would tell Johanssen what they saw. He would spread the word to his buddies. Telling the butler was a surefire (so to speak) way to get word to other domestic help, and to the boss. Johanssen would be the first to learn the news but soon every stable boy and housekeeper in town would hear it. Before long the story would be on the street and everyone would know.

"Besides, we have a railroad to run. We can't spend time telling every fat cat boss that his investment in a mine is likely a con game." Mik was again, still, thinking of the coming winter on Rollins Pass.

"You're right. I'll run Johanssen down and plant the seed." Cam grinned. "Speaking of planting a seed, something I heard or read gave me the seed of an idea for one of our chronic difficulties."

"Oh? Is this your annual contribution to our fine railroad?"

"Very funny. You know how we have problems with water? Engines running dry or darn near so while climbing up to Corona?"

"I know that all too well. It is your favorite subject, Cam. You forget that I have helped rescue a dry engine. It was last winter, February I think. Me and another guy, we traded off. We each had to climb inside a cold boiler. We had to push and pull the grates to reposition them. So we could get the boiler fired up again. We did that while the tanks were being filled with water hauled up by special train. So they could restart the beast and get the passengers and freight where they wanted to go. It was a cramped, dirty and very cold job. My worst enemy shouldn't have to do such a thing. It was awful. Yeah, I know about problems with watering engines. So, what do you have?"

"I know what you mean. I have some boiler crawling time under my belt too." Cam paused, reliving the grubby task, then went on.

"You know that little swale up on the pass? The one just west of the summit? It's a dip with a small, very small, creek running through it. Anyway, here's what we do: Build a dam there, impound the creek and make a pond or small lake. Then we put a pump station there. We can fire it with coal. We have plenty of that. With the pump, we pull water up to a tank by the tracks. The new water station will be less than a mile from the top of the pass. So we can water engines coming from either direction. Problem solved!"

"You know, Cam, I think that is a hell of an idea!" Mik slapped his buddy on the back, then pulled back like he had a mind boggling insight. "Now, Cam, just because you finally have an idea that makes sense, don't let it go to your head," he deadpanned.

Cam smiled. "And how long have you tried to solve this problem, Mik?"

"Touche! Hey, I know. You can put Johanssen in charge of it. That is a good reason to hunt him down and talk to him. After he tells his friends about diamonds he can jump on this. And he'll do good. That way, we can get two birds with one stone and all that."

XXX

BACK AT THE KARAT TOP THINGS WERE NOT GOING JOE'S WAY. The wagon swayed as Ella waved the revolver. Another kick came, hard. Daylight faded and Joe felt himself swirling and spinning into the abyss. Fighting it, he kicked and clawed his way out. Foggy and dull, he at least kept consciousness.

His ankle throbbed from her kicks and his pride hurt from her questions. Not only that, but a loaded gun was being waved in his face. The waver was angry and unstable. Joe flashed back to Dale doing the same thing several years back.

That was unpleasant. This, today, was downright scary. He'd have to tell her something credible. It was not an option to push this suddenly volatile woman. Unpredictability and a loaded gun were never a good combination.

Josephus Eggers took a deep breath.

"Alright, alright, Ella. Calm down. Stop kicking."

She stared at him a moment, nodded, and sat down. The reins stayed in one hand and the gun in the other. For the moment the pistol was aimed at the floor, not him. "Talk," she commanded.

"A while back, I got a letter out of the blue. It was from Chari...." Ella paid close attention. The sun beat down and the mule tied to the wagon started to kick and pull. He was

335

ignored for all his effort and after a while he gave up. Joe talked, Ella listened. Time passed and the story got told.

Joe finished up, or at least he thought he was done with it. "So she had bags full of gems. I don't know how many. She and I came out here to northern Colorado or Wyoming. I honestly don't know exactly where we are. Anyway, we found this place. Then we salted the field. We used two of her bags of diamonds, rubies, jade, and some other, I'm not sure just what. Starting a mine was too big for us so I decided to bring Dale in. He was interested but simply would not get involved unless you did too."

At this Ella did a silent, mental fist bump. Small nagging doubts about Dale's loyalty vanished.

"We showed you two this place. Then Chari and I went out and started finding men with money. And we showed the mine to those marks. And we collected their money, on deposit of course." He grinned in spite of the situation. "I mean investors, we have investors, not marks. And that money is safe in Denver."

"Where?"

"Where what?"

She raised her foot, ready to kick again. "Where is the money?"

Joe suddenly felt like he was floating above this wagon, watching someone else being hurt and interrogated. With that question, this person's life shattered and pieces started to floated away.

He came back to reality in half a second, and fervently hoped he could get to Denver and that Chari would be there with the money. And that they could get out of town before angry men—or Ella—came to them demanding it.

Her booted foot lashed out again. The pain again almost took him under. Unbelieving, he looked as her then at his foot. At least it was still attached to his leg, not broken and swinging loose.

"Joe. Who has it? Where is it? Who else knows?"

Ella was savagely satisfied to see him wilt as his will seemed to break.

"In a suitcase behind the wash stand in our suite."

She drew her foot back again.

"Only Chari and I know. No one else."

Her foot stayed back, locked and loaded. She stared hard. He stared back. She decided she had the truth.

The horses had been restive, shying at the tension, the kicks, the moans and screams. They hadn't moved much and the wagon was still stopped.

"Get off." The pistol was waved in emphasis.

"You can't do this to me, Ella. Please!"

"Get off. Untie the mule. You can have him."

He stared in fear and incomprehension.

Ella pulled the trigger, aiming a round over his shoulder. "GET OFF!"

Limp with fear and barely able to move, he did, carefully. His eyes were big as he hopped, cringing, ankle screaming in protest. His shaky hands required several tries at untying the mule. Joe was well and truly waiting to feel a bullet tear into his side or back. The longer he fiddled with the rope the more he expected it. She waited silently and barely patiently. As soon as the animal was loose she snapped the reins and wordlessly left. He watched the wagon and sole rider trundle off to the north.

Joe could stand no more. He dropped to his knees, keeping hold of the mule's rope. For several minutes the mule heard sobs of fear and self pity. Soon there was anger. Fury gave him strength to stand. Wobbling on his good leg, he opened the pack saddle. In moments he pulled most of the contents and tossed the items to the ground. What he left in was water, some food and a knife. At the bottom, he found an unexpected treasure. There was a little derringer pistol! He didn't know why it was there. It was the one that Ella had stuck in while packing, 'just in case'.

He leaned against the beast. It didn't shy or pull away, sensing that the man was in trouble.

"This is one hell of a note, Mr. Mule." Joe let out a very unamused chuckle, and talked more to his new friend. "You need to let me get on, and you will carry me north, to the train. I hope you got a good night's rest, because you're going to need it."

He went silent, leaning against the animal he hoped would save him.

Soon Ella was over the horizon. She was shaken, ashamed. She felt bad, but also felt justified in hurting Joe. She almost enjoyed it, and that was horrifying. Being a mark in a con enraged her. She had believed that it was a legitimate mine, a real opportunity! Being used was the one thing she really hated. The fury boiled up again. It was a good thing that Joe wasn't in front of her then. She wasn't sure what she would do. For sure it would have been more than a kick and a scolding.

Progress with the big four wheeled rig was slow, too slow. She stopped. Remembering Joe's instructions, she worked them in reverse to unhitch the horses. Seeing nothing of use in the wagon, she left it. One horse was a little bigger than the other so she climbed on, keeping a grip on the reins of the smaller one. The big guy would probably do fine but she wanted to have a ride if he went lame. Plus she simply wouldn't leave a horse in the desert to fend for itself. Headway was faster without the wagon but still it took time. Hours passed before there was a plume of steam and coal smoke off in the distance. And then she saw the horses Dale and Chari rode off on, just tied up and left!

Seeing those poor animals tied to a shanty enraged her more than everything else. It was bad enough that Joe and Chari had played her and Dale for suckers along with so many 'investors'. This neglect and cruelty were too much! She was sure that Chari had somehow forced Dale to abandon these horses. As she got closer she saw that at least they had water. Maybe it wasn't so bad. This brought her back to the main problem.

Ella needed to get her hands on the money. Joe's pistol might come in handy. She hoped not, but realized she was willing to use it if need be.

Of a sudden, doubts about Dale arose. Was he in on this too? Was that why he and Chari left? Why he permitted the horses to be tied up out in Wyoming weather? Were he and Chari in a hurry to go to Denver to get the money? No. She and Dale had too much history, too much time together. She simply couldn't see Dale betraying her. Chari must have lied to Dale or made him do it. He wouldn't do such a thing to an animal, would he? That act alone was reason for her to find Chari and get even. Those poor horses!

She missed the train she had seen from a distance. As she approached Sulfur Flats it came and went. With an hour or so to kill, she tended to all four horses, hers and the abandoned ones. That calmed and focused her, and kept her busy. She was so wound up in caring for them that she didn't worry about suitcases of money or Chari or Joe or Dale. In due course another train came; it had a stock car and she was able to have all the horses loaded on.

Sitting alone on the train, she spoke to no one. Fuming and sulking, she plotted her moves. Before she knew it, Cheyenne was on the horizon and the train started to slow.

DALE ENJOYED THE RIDE FROM CHEYENNE DOWN TO DENVER. He was still a little concerned about leaving Chari alone with The Investor. There was no choice; he knew that. One thing he did want to be sure of was, never let Ella learn about that. She wouldn't understand....

It was good to be back in Denver. First he bathed, then had a hearty meal. With desert dust and train soot washed off and his stomach full, all was well. He felt good, so good he was ready to.... Come to think of it, he wasn't sure what he was ready to do. Should he try to find Cam and Mik? Or wait for Ella and Joe? Or Chari? He decided to go walk. Fresh air and exercise always helped him think. He strolled down Sixteenth Street, pondering, absently watching others on the sidewalk. Then he saw the man he and Joe had taken out to the Karat Top. Once home he had enthusiastically written a big check.

"Hello, Dale. How are you?" The man smiled, obviously happy. He quickly looked around. Sure of privacy, he winked conspiratorially. "How is our project coming along? Are we about ready to break ground? I am surely looking forward to those dividends!"

Dale did his best not to show his relief that the man was jovial. No way was he about to bring up the problems and complications of the past two days. He put on his best boomer's smile. "Well sir. I am glad to say that things are progressing well. I was just in the area and talked with my associates. I am sure we will have good news for you shortly."

"If there is anything I can do, of course you know how to reach me. I will do all I can to help. I probably shouldn't tell you this, but I might even put more money into it." The man smiled. They shook hands and he went on his way.

Dale turned and ambled the opposite direction. A course of action came to him. The decision: do not rock the boat. Just leave things as they are, cool and calm and predictable. The investors were docile. If the one investor was pleased, they probably all were. The guy clearly hadn't heard any ugly rumors or anything about problems. The encounter would have been entirely different if he had.

Reaching a decision was a welcome relief. This way, he didn't have to go find or confront anyone. Whatever fallout from the railroad men could wait. There might not even be any. Anyway, problems or issues that arose from those two guys could wait until Ella and Joe and Chari came back. Dale felt he had made a sound decision. This was a good time to lay low and let things develop. His pace quickened. He returned to their rooms, missing Ella. It was time for a siesta.

"...AND SO MIK AND I DECIDED YOU AND YOUR FRIEND NEED to know what we saw at this 'diamond mine'."

Johanssen's eyes got big before Cam even finished the story. He was enthralled with their adventures and what they had found.

"You mean to tell me that mine is a hoax? And that them fancy gemstones were brought in from somewhere? And then poked under the ground? Put there on purpose to look natural? Just to fool the fools who came out there?" He doubled over with laughter. "That is a good one, yah? Those tricksters are trying to put one over on the supposed smart businessmen!" He laughed some more.

Cam was of two minds. He was a little surprised at Johanssen's coldhearted reaction. In a way it was kind of funny. Big time businessmen who supposedly could take care of themselves were getting taken to the cleaners. Still, he was sympathetic to many of the men who had put money up. Many of them had come by their riches honestly.

He responded.

"You know, Johanssen, it does serve some of those businessmen right. A few of them would trip their grandmother for a buck. Them, I am not sorry for. But there are some good men with money in there. Like the boss of your friend who told you about it. You need to tell him and others about this."

"Oh I will, I will. And we will all have a good laugh too! Yah, a diamond mine. My left foot!"

Cam started to tell about the plan to build a lake atop Rollins Pass, but Johanssen was already headed for the door.

"I'll go see him now." And he was gone.

Cam finished his sentence to an empty room. "...reduce down time and expense and I will talk to you about this later...." He smiled too and left.

THE STATION IN CHEYENNE WAS NOISY AND BUSY, AS EVER.

The newly met man and woman faced off. One stood, one remained sitting. Both knew that another person in the picture would change things. The question was, how to work it to their advantage?

The Investor looked Chari up and down. And up. Aware of the leer, she decided to disregard rather than challenge it. He spoke.

"Let's you and me have dinner. We can talk and you can answer my questions about this mine."

She disliked his pushiness. But, one way or another she was determined to salvage the situation. By God, she would milk an 'investment' out of this man. Most of all, she needed to obtain his silence about what he had seen out there, forty miles from nowhere. Whatever it took. If need be, she could even flounce around a little bit. She smiled.

"Alright. There is a good restaurant here in the station, and we can get a private booth."

He nodded and stood up. "After you."

Perusing the menu, their standoff was the backdrop to small talk. The weather, the size and comfort of seats in first class railcars, labor troubles at Cripple Creek and the like were discussed.

After ordering, he came right out, beating her to the punch. She was put off her questions for him.

He fixed her with a stare. "Where did you get them?"

"Them?" She smiled. "Oh, my husband knew Dale and Ella from business. He thought they would bring talent and energy to the project." Her expression belied that. He let her talk on.

"I may have stretched the truth a bit when we met. Dale and I are associates in the project, yes. But I am senior to him. My husband and I found the site and the two of us control the investment and development."

"Oh?" Using this one little word was a surefire way, he had found, to draw people out.

"Yes. I said we were equal to put you at ease. But in reality Dale is a junior member, and Ella is even more so." This wasn't necessarily so but she wanted to build herself up in his eyes. And it made her feel spitefully better. "Only my husband or I can make money decisions."

"So Dale and Ella were brought in at your husband's insistence?"

For some reason she felt she could talk to this man. He pushed the door open a bit with that question, and out gushed answers. "Yes. And they were useful in bringing possible investors to us, and in sharing out the many tasks that need done."

Her smile turned into a frown. "But Ella is now pushing us. She wants to hurry the development. But we are not ready. She insists she wants money let loose, direct to her. As if! Sometimes it is almost like she has something else in mind. In fact I am starting to wonder what she and Dale have...."

She realized there was no reason to share this with a man she had just met, especially someone she was wooing as an investor. Stopping mid-sentence, she gazed at him.

He fixed her with a smile. That puzzled her. What was so funny or positive about Ella being a pushy, manipulative witch?

"No, Mrs. Hovus. Not Ella and Dale, although what you say tells me a lot about the whole Karat Top scheme."

His smile broadened. "When I asked about 'them', I meant where did you get the rocks?"

She was immobile for half a heartbeat, but the recovery and response was worthy. "Oh, you mean the gems?"

He nodded, smirking.

"Why, they are naturally occurring around the crags of Karat Top. That is why we seek your investment. With it we can make you an even richer man! Do you have friends who may be able to join in? We need more seed money before we can break ground. That is the argument with Ella I was telling you about. You see...."

He interrupted her with a 'humph' sound. It wasn't loud and no one in the restaurant reacted or looked over. She wasn't sure if it was anger or a laugh. He paused half a second, then spoke. His voice was clear. It wasn't loud. No one in the room could have heard his words.

"I know that they are naturally occurring." His sneer brought her up short. "They occur as uncut, second rate stones in a jeweler's wholesale shop."

Chari gazed silently. Either he was onto something, or he suspected it and was fishing. Listening carefully, she hoped he would give her enough to destroy him.

"I was a jewelry buyer in a previous life, Chari my dear." His smile and tone told her he was holding the reins now. "The rocks your Karat Top has strewn around must be a new kind of gem. They do not occur naturally together. Diamonds aren't found with jade which is never near sources of ruby. The rocks I saw from your mine are sad, even pathetic. They are uncut discards. I saw the like a thousand times in New York and Antwerp."

"Ah, I...." Nothing came to mind. She could only stare open mouthed, like a landed perch.

"You don't know what to say. I understand." He let her stew.

"Well, before you say any more, hear this. First, I am not the law. It is up to you how you run your business schemes and who you have pay for them. I do not care. Second, those two guys know. No, that isn't exactly right. They don't know for certain. They suspect. They strongly suspect that the ground there is salted."

"They even found the sticks you poked them into the ground with." His tone of voice seared. She couldn't believe she and Joe stupidly kept those sticks around.

He leaned back, meeting her gaze. She knew how a butterfly felt, pinned to a wallboard. She started to speak but stopped when he held his hand up.

"Third. The word is about to hit the street. I pretended that I was asleep or thinking, and that I did not hear them. But I was really listening closely. Those two railroad men are going to blow the whistle on your Karat Top Mine."

He leaned back, hands behind head. He nodded, a nobleman giving a serf leave to speak.

Suddenly dry and hoarse, Chari croaked. "What do you want from me? From us?"

He simply stared at her, long enough that she fought not to squirm.

"Chari, we are now partners." He paused, a hint of a smile playing over his face. "We, that is you and I, will take the money you have collected for this Karat Top Mine. I will take sixty percent of it. You will take forty. What you do with your share is up to you."

"That isn't fair."

"Neither would your going to jail for fraud. Years behind bars with violent lonely women doesn't sound like fun. Or, maybe you would get off light. Would it be fair for people to take their money back, then strip you and your 'associates', dump tar and feathers on, and run you out of town?"

He smiled alarmingly. She had never seen a crocodile except in newspaper sketches, but this looked like one to her. "For my part, I will go away and start a new life. Charleston, Havana, perhaps somewhere else." In his mind's eye he was already boarding a steamer for New Zealand. He intended to disappear. The clues were meant to misdirect any pursuit.

The tone of voice turned serious, almost courteous. "You should join me. There are plenty of other schemes and projects you and I could undertake. We could do well together."

He smiled, again looking like a croc sizing up a morsel. "Do you understand and agree?"

"What about my husband Joe? And how about Dale and Ella?"

"Those two you can ignore. Forget them." He waited half a beat. "Joe, now Joe could be a problem. He has access to the money, right? Where is he now?"

Her head swam. She was used to asking the questions, not having to give answers. It took a few moments for her to overcome the eddy of fear and surprise. She knew and dreaded the new order of things. This new person, not she, not Joe, was the one calling the shots.

She blurted what she truly felt. "Yeah, it is fine with me to ditch those two. Ella and Dale have been nothing but trouble. For as long as Joe has known them, they have brought trouble."

She waited a full beat, deciding. Should she wait for Joe and hope for the best? Or hop over into this bewildering lifeboat which had just pulled in from nowhere. Could she really sail away in it? Yes, she decided, she could. And she would.

"Yes, he does know where the money is hidden."

She looked at him defiantly, glad to at last have a little bit of leverage. "No one but he and I know."

She repeated the question. "Where is Joe now? Well, Joe is out somewhere between the Karat Top and the railroad. He was hurt—scorpion bite. He's stove up, can't move hardly at all. Dale and I came back here. You saw us so you know that he went on to Denver. Ella and Joe were to follow from the Karat Top. They were going to take the wagon and the mule when they could get moving. So that is where Joe is."

Decision made, she felt herself flying as she jumped from Joe across to The Investor's lifeboat. It was almost a physical sensation. As she flew, she had several fleeting hopes: That she would land in the vessel. That her new partner knew how to row. And that he wouldn't toss her overboard.

XXXI

CHARI HAD JOE'S SITUATION ABOUT RIGHT.

Somewhere between Karat Top and the railroad he was in a special purgatory. Mumbling to the mule and wincing at his foot, he leaned against the creature. Chari came to mind and he wondered what she was doing just then. Was she wondering about him, where he was and how he was doing? The thought of her gave him strength and hope, and it motivated him to move.

With difficulty, he got up on the beast. He sat astride in front of the nearly empty pack. The pistol he stuffed under his belt. It was a woman's gun. Smaller than the one Ella had taken from him, it was better than nothing.

Looking north, he could no longer see the dust raised by Ella's hijacked wagon. He and his new friend set off, the gait slow and wobbly. Mules move at their own pace. Try as he might, Joe was unable to hurry him. After a few minutes, he realized he didn't care. It was good enough to be riding not hobbling.

Not long and they came to the abandoned wagon but didn't stop. He had what he needed. For some reason he felt bad for the owner. A stable owner somewhere would wonder what happened to the wagon he rented out, and there would be hell to pay by somebody.

As the man and the mule came close enough to see Sulfur Flats, the sun was just kissing the horizon. Any other time Joe would have enjoyed the nice sunset. He was able to guide the mule up next to the shanty and slid off. It felt good to get off his backside. But man oh man did his ankle hurt. He stuffed the pain and stoked up his anger. He was determined to get to Denver and his money before Ella.

He mused over the past day, smiling inside. *I am glad I had an answer ready when she asked where the money was. She will find something there, but.... Hopefully I bought some time to get down there. Chari has prepared for us to get out of town, or at least I darn sure hope she has. I hope we don't have to lam. Denver has been sweet. But I'm am afraid we will. Especially if Ella starts in and gets Dale riled up. Or if that investor squawks. Or if those two men who were snooping round start talking. Yeah, we have to get out of town.*

He munched a biscuit he dug out of the pack, and took a swig of water. It helped although he still felt tired weak and dirty. The eastbound train whistled in the distance. Some would call the sound mournful. Not Joe. To him it was anything but sad.

He was going to escape being left to die, crippled in the wilds of Wyoming. Now he could go get his money. And if he could, he would find his abandoner and exact revenge. He limped as he went over by the tracks, pain forgotten. Waving his arms, he was almost falling down grateful when he saw the engineer slow.

The conductor hopped down, acknowledging the man who had flagged the train to stop. "You are the third or fourth Sulfur Flats party in the last few days. For some reason, suddenly it is popular to go through this god forsaken place." He looked out from under his visor. "Just what is out there that folks want?" He wanted to pry more but something over Joe's shoulder got his attention. "And I see you have an animal to be put on board like the others." The trainman turned away, giving orders to load the mule into a stock car.

The foot hurt bad again as he climbed aboard. The train began to move and the conductor came down the aisle. Joe caught his eye. "What time are we scheduled into Cheyenne?"

He chuckled mirthlessly. "You are on the local, my friend. We stop at each and every cow crossing. If things go well, no problems or derailments, the schedule has us coasting in at noon. Well, really, at 11:57. So you may as well relax and enjoy the ride."

THE NEW PARTNERS IN CHEYENNE CAUGHT THE LAST EXPRESS to Denver. That was better than spending the night and catching an early run. Nor did they want to ride a three AM milk run. The train they took, if on time, would get them to Denver fairly late but not past decent hours. They climbed aboard the parlor car at about the same time Joe flagged down the local many miles to the west.

If Chari was one thing, it was focused. When she had a goal in mind, she went about it diligently and whole heartedly. She talked over plans with her partner. New partner, old methods. She reviewed and rehearsed and thought through snags and tried to anticipate problems.

"I think I should go get the money first thing. I'll go alone in case there are problems. You will want to make your arrangements to leave too. As soon as I have it, we can take the next train out. It won't matter where at first. Anywhere away from Denver will do."

He considered her plan, and didn't like it. It wasn't that he thought her inept. No, he knew she was plenty capable. Events had come fast and he barely knew her. In a few words, he simply didn't want her hands on all the money when he wasn't around.

"I see your point about my making preparations as well. Question: is the money in one place, in a suitcase or carpet bag? Or is it in several lockboxes? Or what?"

"One place. You need to trust me on this." She realized she didn't know him. "What should I call you, partner? Do you have a name?"

"Call me Paul." The answer was off hand, laconic.

"Paul it is." She figured it wasn't his real name. Her pause told him she saw through it.

"Well, Paul, if I go charging in with a stranger we will make people notice. Worse, we might tie things up or cause delays. We need to move fast and not make a splash on this."

"Good point. Alright, you go get it." Unspoken, he intended to find out what he could about the money even if he had to follow her.

The train pulled in on time. They climbed off and stood on the platform.

"So, let's each grab a good night's sleep. I will pack and prepare in the morning and you will too." Her voice raised at the last of this, making it a question. She didn't want to seem to order him around. He kind of nodded in agreement. She continued.

"And I will collect the money from where Joe left it. And I'll meet you here, ready to go, for an afternoon train." She looked up at the schedule boards. "What do you think, the 4:47 to Amarillo? Or the 5:23 to Chicago?"

"We meet here at 4:00, at the ticket window. If we haven't decided where to go no one else can know either. We can buy tickets for several places and use one set, deciding at the last moment."

"Yes, that is good. I will see you then, partner!" The smile she put up was supposed to dazzle him. It didn't but he played along, looking moonstruck. She waved down a cab. The horses clip clopped up and she climbed in. "Til tomorrow!"

He smiled and nodded. The cab left. He quickly flagged another. "I want to see where that woman is going, cabby. Here is a dollar extra for you to shadow her cab. Return and tell me where she is and there will be your regular fare for the trip, plus three more dollars."

As the train chuffed across Wyoming towards sunrise, Ella's rage and mortification built. She really didn't know which was worse, that Dale had allowed the horses to be tied up at Sulfur Flats, or that Joe and Chari had intended to defraud them. It wasn't that she was offended that those two had stolen—or intended to steal—money from other people. Part of those proceeds were theirs, hers and Dale's. They had time and effort invested. It all made her feel betrayed and foolish.

Chari and Joe all along intended to steal our share of the money. And then they meant to have the blame fall on us! These thoughts ran in endless circles through her head and emotions all the way to Cheyenne. And those poor horses that got left tied up in Wyoming weather. At least they had some water to drink. Small consolation!

When the train got to Cheyenne, she saw to the horses. Four were under her wing—the two she brought and the two left by Dale and Chari. Somewhat brazenly but technically truthfully, she said she had rented only horses and had not rented a wagon. The charge for the horses came out of her own pocket. The receipt she kept, intending to wave it in Chari's face and demand repayment.

Ella grabbed the first ride she found to Denver. It was a milk run, a local stopping at every crossing and settlement. It left at 2:57 AM and got in mid morning. She snuggled under a coat and got what sleep she could. The rocking of the train, the starts and stops, somehow lulled her to a fairly restful night.

Joe's eastbound local made unusually good time. A mid-morning sun sat halfway up the sky.

"Cheyenne next, Cheyenne in seven minutes!" The conductor's cry woke him from a not very relaxing night. The man was in a good mood. He spoke to any passenger who would listen and some who didn't. His grin was telling. "This is as early as we have ever gotten here on this run. Today, things rolled exactly right and we had no problems. If you are going on, you will have plenty of time to catch your connections. Me, I'm going home to surprise my wife!"

Joints creaking and eyes feeling like the floor of a rodeo arena, Joe stood. It occurred to him that by arriving early, the conductor might receive as well as give a surprise. Briefly he wondered where that idea strayed in from. A welcome lurching stop told the passengers it was time to get off.

The ankle hurt like Ella was still kicking. Pain was overcome by anger and his desire to get to Denver and the money. He hobbled, hanging on the rail where he could and leaning on the wall where there was none. It hurt but he hurried out the door of the train, onto the stepstool the conductor provided, and across the way to the terminal building. There he bought the first ticket to Denver he could get. He landed a spot on a run just leaving. Despite his pain he moved so fast that he was on the way south before the local he rode in on was completely emptied of passengers. The conductor was flummoxed, and told the brakeman so.

"Damn that guy with the limp. He disappeared and left us with a mule. That is the last problem I want to have. He didn't tell us which stable owns it. I want to get home to mama."

The brakeman was raised around animals. He owed the conductor a favor so he stepped up.

"I'll go and take a look at the bridle and pack. Maybe some item will have the stable's name or some clue on it. With luck, I can get it back to the owner. You go ahead, don't worry about the mule."

He found what he needed and saw that the beast was returned to its owners. The mule didn't get a say. Likely he would have preferred green grass under aspens near crags to a cramped stable next to a train yard.

Joe cared little for the mule's welfare. Nor did he care about what happened to Dale. The main thing was to get to Denver and see Chari. Next moves had to be planned carefully. Chari had to be told that Ella knew the game. That woman had her blood up. She would want in, both for her and Dale.

There was no doubt in Joe's mind that he'd find Ella nosing around. She would she poke around and ask questions.

Likely she would be waving a gun, his gun, and trying to take their money. He had to stop her!

Stewing and worrying, Joe wanted to get out and push to make the train go faster. It rattled south, finally crossing into Colorado. The schedule called for mid-afternoon arrival. Once there, he hoped to get to Chari quickly. If his foot hadn't hurt so bad he would have paced, anything to make the time go by. He knew he was lucky to be alive, and that made him angry at Ella. She left him out there! His anger and anxiety were almost too much.

JOHANSSEN SPOKE WITH HIS BUDDIES WHO QUICKLY SPREAD the story. The tale was heard in dressing rooms, pantries, and stables. Most everyone got a good laugh. The idea of rich men getting taken was amusing. Butlers, maids, and liverymen chortled and guffawed. Even as they giggled, each one pretty much felt that his or her boss was not among the greedy, rather was among the victims. Of course word spread like bindweed in July. Before long every boss and bosses' wife had heard it too.

Cam's one match theory was well proved. The railroad men intended to start a brushfire of talk about a diamond mine. It took off and was soon burning high and hot. There was one topic of talk in Denver that day. In the back halls and fitting rooms, at the city's lunch clubs and around quilting circles, all and sundry were discussing the Karat Top.

THE ERSATZ DIAMOND MINE WAS SCARCELY ON THE MINDS OF the railroad men. Mik and Cam were looking ahead to another winter season on the Hill. They were not anticipating a pleasurable time. Rather, they were dreading it, grimly looking forward and determined to best it. Operating a rail line over Rollins Pass was proving to be difficult and expensive. Not to mention dangerous.

"Snowslides causing derailments. Ice buildup on the tracks. Snowdrifts causing closure. Snowdrifts causing delays. Rotary plows getting stuck. Snowdrifts too deep for rotaries, needing to be dug down to the right depth. Frostbite and snow blindness. Smoke buildup in Corona Station. Cabin fever."

"I think you have hit the high spots, Mik, or should I say low spots. At least this time around we know what to expect. And it looks like we have surrounded and solved the problem of engines running dry."

"Yes. That was a good idea. No more having to crawl into boilers during a blizzard. No more angry riders or shippers. Best of all, no negative attention from Mr. Moffat."

"I wish all the problems you listed could be solved as easily as that one was."

"At least there is a start on digging the tunnel. Once we can go under the mountain those problems will be history."

"Mik, I heard that the crews starting that work have been pulled."

"Yeah, me too. I heard the crews were working about three miles up South Boulder Creek from the start of the Giant's Ladder. They did some good work and dug a hundred or so feet into the hill, just about into bedrock. Then they were pulled off the job."

Mik shrugged and continued. "I guess the powers that be have to juggle expenses. Do they send regular runs over the Pass to serve Fraser and points west? Or do they punch a tunnel under the Main Range? It isn't quite that clear cut a choice. My guess is, the expenses of the road over the top are eating up the money needed to drive a tunnel."

"Well, that is one for the big men to decide. You and me, Mik, we need to think about extending the snowshed on the west end of Corona Town...."

XXXII

Curious to see if or how Paul would keep track of her, Chari glanced back as she climbed into the cab.

"Take me to the Hotel Benelux. Don't go direct. Take me around the site where they'll build the new State Capitol."

"That is well out of the way, ma'am. It will almost double the fare. Are you sure?"

"Yes. Take your time while you're at it."

It wasn't so much that she distrusted Paul, which was true. The thing was, there was so much at stake. She wanted to know exactly what was going on. Watching out the back window, there was another cab that stuck to them, a few lengths back. Just as she thought. Someone was following. Maybe Paul wasn't expecting her to watch and was inadvertently letting himself be seen. Either that, or someone else was in the mix. That was worrying. It didn't matter which, it told her she had to be extra careful. Learning what she needed, it was time to go ahead with her plans.

"Cabby, I've changed my mind. Don't bother with the State Capitol. Go ahead direct to the Benelux."

Shaking his head in wonder, he stopped. Then he turned the cab around mid-block and went back towards her hotel. "As you say, ma'am."

As they neared the hotel, he spoke. "Is everything alright? Do you need help?"

Chari got out and paid the fare. "No, I don't need any help, thank you. Your brief tour of the city confirmed what I thought I would see. Everything is alright, really it is." She added a dollar, smiling. "For your extra trouble."

The suite was a welcome sight. Its comfort and sanctuary had been on her mind since she and Dale left the Karat Top on horseback. Her relief was deep and genuine. It had been a strange and tiring couple of days. Her life was turned upside down. She didn't even look behind the wash stand for the cash case. Later for that. Several layers of travel grime were her target now, and she simply splashed and toweled her face. Dirt came off to soil the towel, but she still wasn't squeaky clean. It was enough. Exhausted, she surrendered and hit the bed. As she laid down, she fantasized about stacks of bills and bearer bonds. A smile played on her face before she fell into an exhausted sleep.

As HE WATCHED HER GET IN THE CAB, PAUL WASN'T SURE WHAT she would do. Would she go to her hotel or go get the money somewhere else? He half expected her to stop by some seedy store or shop and come out with a suitcase. In a way he was disappointed when she headed for the Benelux. Waiting outside in the cab, he watched the entrance. It was fruitless.

After a while he decided Chari wouldn't be coming out. If she really had the case she said was stuffed with money, she was staying put. It was late and the day had been grueling and long. Everyone was tired. She probably was asleep up in her room. Of a sudden that sounded good to him. He gave directions to his room, glad to put an end to the day.

FOR SOME REASON THE GLOW OF THE SUN JUST BEFORE IT CAME over the horizon reminded Ella of the circus. The glow in the east lit up the town as the train pulled into Denver's Union Station. This day it brought to mind her long dead idea to go to the circus winter grounds. Dale had quashed that and she was glad. If they had run off to the circus she wouldn't be here, about to get rich. She was about to seize the money suitcase! As the train slowed and bumped, she felt strangely aware and energetic. It was odd to feel so alive and focused. After all, a lot of not so good things had happened in the past days. By all rights she should be wiped out, frazzled, angry and bleary. Not Ella. She was totally charged up and ready to go.

As the train coasted to a stop, she looked out and saw her fellow passengers pushing and shoving to exit the cars. She calmly waited until the crowds thinned. Then it was easy to walk off and out of the station. Being hungry, she looked for a place to fuel up. The sign in front of a café promised service that was 'quick and friendly.' Since it was close to the station they would be used to women traveling alone. Last thing she wanted was women staring and men leering at her. The sign was accurate. The waiter soon set her toast and eggs down with a warm smile.

"There you are ma'am. Let me know if you need anything else."

"Yes, coffee please. Black. Tell me, do you know the Hotel Benelux?"

He nodded.

"Where is it? A friend is there. I'd like to see her. The thing is, she isn't expecting me and I would like to surprise her."

"Ah. Sounds fun! The Benelux." He noticed the next table over needed a coffee refill and half started to take care of it. "Well, ma'am, after you enjoy our fine breakfast, go out and turn left. Three blocks down, it is on the right. You'll see the sign, it is catty-cornered across that intersection."

"Thank you. Can you get me paper and envelope please? I need to write a quick note."

Pencil in hand, Ella gathered scattered thoughts. Scrawling four or five lines didn't take long. Folding the letter, she stuffed the envelope then addressed it. Still distracted and thinking of the money, she didn't seal it. After simply inserting the flap she handed it to the waiter. "If I don't come back by dinner time to collect this, please drop it in the mail. Can you do that for me?" She put on her best helpless maiden smile.

"Yes, it is my pleasure." The waiter glanced at it. He tried to remember that he should seal the flap. The envelope was addressed to a Mr. Dale Smertz at a local hotel. He folded and put it in his pocket, unsealed.

"Thank you. Here is a dollar for the stamp and for your trouble."

THREE BLOCKS DOWN THE STREET THE MORNING ARRIVED. UP in her room, Chari awoke. It took a moment to orient herself, to realize that she was safe at home in her suite. Well, in her and Joe's suite. She remembered coming in late after a loooong and trying day, concerned about who knew she was in town. Looking down, she saw that she still wore yesterday's outfit. They were the same clothes she wore from Cheyenne to Sulfur Flats out to the Karat Top, a night in the wagon there, back to Cheyenne with Dale, and finally all the way to Denver with Paul. All of that in one outfit? No wonder she felt grubby and out of sorts.

Now fully awake, she listened. What roused her was noise, a low rattle. It sounded like someone trying to open the door. No one but Joe had a key! It couldn't be him—he and Ella were still somewhere in Wyoming. Was it the maid or someone else? Quietly she stood up, smoothing her hair and looking again with distaste at her wrinkled clothes. Carefully and quietly she walked to the door, listening. The doorknob shook like someone was turning a key in the outside slot.

With the tiniest of creaks, the door swung open. It was Ella, and she was pocketing a small metal object. Time slowed, almost stopped as they looked at each other. Chari saw Ella holding what looked like a screwdriver or narrow knife blade. Of course! The sound that woke her wasn't a key! What she heard was a pick being used to manipulate the tumblers inside the lock. Chari wondered how and where Ella had learned to do that.

The frozen moment melted. Time flowed back as it should.

"Ella! What are you doing here? Why didn't you just knock on the door?" Then she remembered, Joe and Ella were following in the wagon.

"Where is Joe?"

"Joe is out in Wyoming, getting his just desserts."

"Just desserts?"

"Yes, he and that mule are out there wandering. He had it coming." Ella, pupils tiny, looked intensely into Chari's face. "I'll see that you get what you deserve, too." She let out a giggle, almost a maniacal cackle as she stepped in, forcing Chari back. "Tell me, Chari dear, where is the money?"

"What money?"

"Don't be cute. Joe told me all about your bags of rocks and salting the field and finding investors and…."

"Ella, where is Joe?"

"For all I care he is rotting in the sun near your precious Karat Top." The pistol she lifted from Joe appeared in her hand. She waved it carelessly. "I am here to get the suitcase of money. That is money Dale and I earned and you will not cheat us out of it. You wouldn't tell us about it and you wouldn't give us any of it. I think that you two meant to leave town with it and give us none!"

Stalling, Chari tried to soothe. "Now Ella, we are partners. Joe and I never intended that. We just couldn't share everything, all the facts, with you at the time."

"Horse puckey!" The strange oath erupted, loud and violent. "Joe told me the plan. He spilled all of it. I had to kick his ankle several times, but he told, oh yes he did. And I kicked him once just for good measure, good and hard, and left him out there! May he rot in the sun like a pile of mule dung!"

She looked to the back of the room. "He said the suitcase is behind the wash stand." Ella waved the pistol again. "Go get it and bring it here."

Chari gulped. "Ella, be reasonable. You and I are partners. We need to talk woman to woman, friend to friend." She made a show of thinking, concentrating hard. "I know! Let's you and me split it. Right now. Like sisters, forget the men! We can do what we want with our own half. Take it all or give some to Dale and Joe. We can each be rich and no one will be hurt."

Ella didn't even nibble at that bait. Her face was as stony as her words were icy. "Go. Get. It." The sound of the hammer being drawn back, cocking the weapon, emphasized the order.

Blanching and trying not to quiver, Chari was out of ideas. She braved out a few moments, then went in and pulled the suitcase from behind the stand. It was heavy!

"Here!" She drug it out and dropped the case. It thudded to the ground. "Take it!"

The greed bug's sting made Ella feverish, almost delirious. She fell to her knees. As she grabbed for the case, the pistol dropped and bounced unnoticed. So focused on the money was she that the pistol slid across the floor almost like she meant for Chari to have it. Avarice shined in her eyes, almost bright enough to make Chari squint.

She wanted to open the case. About to touch the latch, she realized her vulnerability. The pistol was up for grabs. Both reached for it. Chari had a head start and easily grabbed it. She leveled the weapon at Ella who was looking, pasty faced, between the gun and the case.

"Get out. I would shoot you but I don't want to soil the carpet. You and your friend Dale have been nothing but trouble. I wish we had never met. Get out! I never want to see you again!"

Now it was Chari wildly waving the pistol. Ella wondered if she would really use it. Even in her manic mood she didn't want to find out. Raising her hands in surrender, she edged towards the door.

"Now Chari, I didn't really mean anything by all this. I'm just tired and upset. Be calm. Your secret is safe with me, sister! Just let me go and I'll disappear and you'll never see me again...."

Any second, Ella feared, she would hear a loud noise and feel the punch of a bullet. Afraid her days were done, she was surprised and relieved to reach the door. Anger flooded back. Running and ducking to escape, she screamed. "This isn't over, Hovus."

PAUL ATE BREAKFAST AT A RESTAURANT PROCLAIMING 'QUICK and friendly service.' The eggs were superb. Feeling expansive and anticipating being very rich, he left a big tip. An envelope with an address fell out of the waiter's pocket as he took the money. "Thank you sir!"

As Paul left he saw the man stuff the tip in one pocket. The waiter then picked up the envelope like a piece of litter. His expression changed. The envelope must have reminded him of something because he kept it, slipping it into a pocket.

THE THREAT ECHOED AS ELLA RAN AWAY. CHARI TOOK IT SERIously. Quickly she locked the door and wedged a chair under the knob so that only a battering ram could break it in. Hefting the pistol thoughtfully, she wondered for a moment if she should have plugged Ella. Too late for that, but best to keep both the money suitcase and the gun close by. She carried the case into the bathroom and drew a bath. Before she undressed she set the revolver on the vanity, in plain sight and in easy reach. After a long warm soak she felt less jangly, even almost normal.

The encounter with Ella and her revelations were certainly unexpected. She considered Joe's spilling their secrets about the scheme. There could be no sticking around now.

Could she wait for Joe? Really, the question was, should she? One thing was sure: She would leave today, whether with Joe, Paul, or alone.

Feeling clean and refreshed, she stepped out of the tub, toweled off, and dressed. Traveling clothes were the order of the day. She wasn't sure exactly how the next day of her life would play out. No matter what, once she left these rooms she wouldn't be back.

The suitcase occupied the room's center, full of her future, and she glanced its way every now and then. She didn't want to carry or expose it unnecessarily. But hunger gnawed; she needed to eat. And she damn sure wasn't going to leave it unattended in her room. She took the bag to the lobby.

"Yes ma'am," inquired the concierge, glancing at the suitcase she held firmly.

I need you to lock this up in safekeeping for a while. I am going out and do not want to leave it in the room."

"We have no locked safe room. But we can keep it behind the desk and release it only to you. Is that satisfactory?"

She hesitated, remembering the greed in Ella's eyes. "I suppose so. You will keep an eye on it yourself? You personally?"

"Yes ma'am, I will."

She glanced at his name tag. "Alright, thank you, Mister Stevens."

With that Chari went across the street and had a good meal. Each bite helped her put her troubles and plan in perspective. The meal was hearty enough that she felt she might need a siesta. At the desk, she stopped to pick up the suitcase.

"There you are, ma'am. It is right where I put it and no one has asked about you or it."

Chari was too preoccupied to even thank the man. She simply picked up the case and returned to her room. In the hall as she approached, she held on to the bag in one hand and the pistol in the other. Heart in her throat, she checked to see that no one was in the room. Satisfied that she was alone, she again slid a chair against the locked door. With the suitcase sitting in plain sight in the middle of the room, she picked out another small travel bag. It was a carpet bag, smaller than a case but bigger than a purse. The first item she selected to put in it was her last velour sack containing gems. She thought of this bag as 'seed corn'. Making sure the drawstring was tied well, she put it at the bottom. Then in went a few clothes, a bible, and on top, Joe's pistol.

The clock chimed three thirty as she packed. Her meetup with Paul was about here. She looked one last time around the room, smiled thinly, and sighed. Then, carpet bag slung on shoulder, she hefted the suitcase and left.

Across the street from the Benelux, Paul sat in a shadowed recess of a café. Watching the people go by was good entertainment while he sipped coffee. And it passed the time. He was alone, ready to leave town. No one knew where he was. He hoped that Chari would come out soon. Instinct told him she wouldn't try to leave without him. Best to be sure, though, so he watched. If she wasn't going to show at the station he didn't want to go there. He would simply go on with his life. Here, he could see her come out or confirm she didn't. Either way, no surprises. So he thought.

There she was, lugging a heavy suitcase with a carpet bag slung on her shoulder! She walked in the direction of

Union Station. He signaled for the bill, intending to tail her. He would walk where she did, staying a block or so behind.

AS PAUL ENJOYED COFFEE, ELLA LURKED ALONG THE STREET nearby. She comfortably leaned against a tree. Her spot was further from the station than was Paul's shaded table. The angry, caffeine fueled woman had no idea the man she knew only as The Investor was near. Out of context, she would have trouble recognizing him. True, she and Dale had ridden with him from Denver to the deserts of Wyoming. But she was so focused on Chari and the suitcase she had all but forgotten about The Investor. In her state of mind, seeing him nearby would have confused and further enraged her.

How sad and frustrating that everything had blown up when those two railroad men came over the horizon! If only they hadn't crossed paths. Also, it infuriated her that Chari had managed to force her out of her room. Leaving empty handed still seemed unreal. How did she leave the hotel without the suitcase Joe said was full of cash? And Chari had wrested Joe's pistol from her too! Ella was determined to get even with that high society milk cow if it was the last thing she did!

Patiently awaiting her prey, Ella shifted against her tree. She tensed. A woman was coming out of the Benelux. It looked like Chari. Yes, it was her! Looking warily around, she tightened her grip on the suitcase. Shifting a carpet bag hung on her shoulder, she turned and walked away. Where? She could be going anywhere. Ella figured it couldn't be far or she would take a cab. She was almost certain that Chari was going to the train station. She was leaving town, fleeing!

There was a shortcut to the station and Ella headed for it. Through a passageway she rushed, not looking closely at what lay in the gutters. She knew there were small animals hurting and dead in these back alleys. Usually her heart broke but today none of that mattered. After the alley, she cut through another hotel's lobby and crossed a street.

Confident that she beat Chari to the station, she looked inside. She wanted a spot where she could comings and goings. Yet not being too visible herself was also a thing. And she had to be able to get in and out easily.

Scanning the waiting room hurriedly, she saw a group of women. Some of them were youngish, some almost middle aged. They looked worn, like life had worked them hard. All were dressed plainly and similarly, almost in a uniform. Most every ethnic background was represented. They stuck together and were clearly reluctant to mix with the folks in the station. Most of them wouldn't even look around the room, much less make eye contact. They stayed to themselves so intently it was almost garish. Travelers coming through were curious and wanted to stare at them, Ella could tell. But good manners forbade that. People would glance and just as quickly look away.

The women were not sitting but were standing, milling around one of the benches in the center of the cavernous room. A matron who for all the world looked like a basset hound was lecturing them. Ella couldn't hear the words but the tones were harsh. Perfect!

She sidled up to the edge of the group. Looking at her garb then theirs, she decided she more or less fit in. From her vantage point she could scan the main entrance easily, and wouldn't have to turn her head much to see the side doors.

She moved slightly trying to stay out at the fringes of the group. She took care not to be too close, but close enough that she was pretty much invisible to other travelers.

"Don't get too near."

Ella was concentrating on the doors and didn't hear the warning delivered in a voice just above a whisper.

"Don't get too close. You don't want to be mistaken for one of us."

Intrigued, Ella looked directly at the young woman. In a conversational tone she asked, "Why not?"

"We are just released from halls and sanatorium homes in Baltimore. The matron is delivering us to western mining towns, sprinkling us around like bread crumbs...."

The older woman barked, "Quiet, you two!" She marched over and faced Ella. The supervisor immediately and instinctively disliked this person, this hanger on. The matron tagged her as trouble with a capital T. "Who are you? Why are you interfering with this young woman?"

Ella was dumbfounded. The watchdog went on, no longer haranguing the group, now intent on Ella.

"Are you a rabblerouser? One of those muckracking reporters? A Christian woman do-gooder? We'll not have it, not have it! Leave this moment or I'll have the police...!"

Had Ella simply stepped away at the first warning, her camouflage would have remained fairly effective. But she didn't. Now, the loud snapping matron drew the attention of almost everyone.

About the time the matron confronted Ella, Chari approached the station. Outside the main door, she trudged up, feeling and looking bedraggled. She was tired and a bit sweaty from lugging the suitcase Joe said was full of cash.

The carpet bag dug into her shoulder. She wanted to set it all down, but didn't dare until she was in a safer place. She bluntly refused the redcap's offer to take her luggage. Gripping the bags even tighter she stepped into the main waiting room. As she crossed the threshold, the hound dog started to yap and snarl in earnest.

The loud questions and threats cut through Chari's fatigue. She followed the harsh nasal tones and was astonished to see Ella! What was she doing with a group of fallen doves? Chari had feared Ella would try to surprise her on the way over. That or force a confrontation here in the station. But with a group of girls and women being sent to the mining camps? And why was a stocky woman in uniform yelling at her? What a bizarre scene!

Relieved and bemused, Chari stifled a laugh. She took stock of the room then walked around through the crowds, aiming for the ticket window. She didn't see Paul. Didn't matter, she intended to buy tickets. If he showed, they'd go together. If he didn't, well, she had the goods and would do what she thought best.

"Chari!" A voice carried over and through the din. She stopped, looking around. There was Paul at the door, loudly calling her. She wasn't sure if she should be relieved or resentful. In a way she had hoped he wouldn't show up. There he was, so she smiled and nodded. He hurried over.

Ella too heard his call. It was hard to decipher. Mostly she heard the rantings of the matron standing inches from her, scolding and threatening. The worst was her spewing droplets of saliva as she yelled. Wiping her face with a bare hand, Ella turned and saw Chari and a man who was hurrying to her. Who was he? He looked familiar somehow. My God, she thought, is that The Investor?

The matron was incensed. Her voice rose another octave. "Don't you turn away from me young woman! You pay attention when I am speaking!"

Ella ignored the shrewish command. She stepped off, intending to face down Chari and the man. She didn't run but she didn't saunter either. The matron followed right along, keeping up the flow of invective. Like horses following the bell mare, the young women in her charge followed. Some pressed close to their leader. Others held back a bit, but the feminine gaggle moved with her and Ella.

JOE WAS TIRED AND HE HURT AND HE WAS WORRIED ABOUT Chari and more worried about his money. At least he was finally in Denver almost to the station. He was happy at that, after riding a mule to Sulfur Flats and a slow train to Cheyenne and then the regular run to Denver. The train pulled near Union Station. And it stopped. It was dead stopped. He hated that they had to wait for a siding to open up. If his foot was well he would have gotten out and walked the last one hundred yards. He tapped his fingers on the window impatiently.

At last a spot at the station siding came open. The engineer took it and soon Joe was detraining with the other passengers. Limping along, he decided that first order was to find Chari. He'd go to the hotel. Several day's worth of dirt and sweat clung and he wanted to get cleaned up. If she wasn't there, maybe there would be a message at the desk. As soon as he found her, they would pack up and leave. One other thing he was determined to do: avenge his treatment at Ella's hands, or more precisely his treatment at her feet.

As he hobbled over the tracks towards the cavernous waiting room, Joe heard a commotion. The place was always full of travelers and was never quiet. But this was something else. A man was calling, then a woman was nattering. What on earth? There was the rustle of crowd movement then a woman's voice carried over the confusion.

"Hovus, I told you this wasn't over," Ella screeched. She ran the final steps toward Chari, eyes wild.

Chari gaped a moment, then turned and ran as best she could. Fatigue and lugging a suitcase which banged at her hip slowed her.

"Paul, stop her!"

Paul hurried and put himself between the two women.

Adrenalin flowing, Ella charged. She was past Paul like a linebacker juking a rookie. Intent on the case, she grabbed at it. Chari pulled it away.

"By God, this is mine! Get away from me! Paul, help me!"

Paul stepped in and got a kick in the shin from one of them. Ella turned.

"You! Why are you here? You haven't even invested yet!" Ella was het up and his presence made no sense. "Get away. This is between her and me!" But it made perfectly awful sense in a way. He was new on the scene. Was he in on the scheme to defraud her too? She, Ella, had invested tons of time and effort. Why should he even be here and why did he rush to Chari's aid?

The matron had seen enough. She didn't like this woman from the minute she accosted her girls. As far as she could tell, Ella was just a thug and a troublemaker. The matron wasn't about to let this mouthy woman bully people. This wouldn't be the first cat fight she had broken up. She waded in.

"Give me that case!" The harsh nasal tone brought the struggle to a momentary halt. The matron grabbed the case and held it close, glaring at the two women and the man. "This is a public building! Stop it!"

With a roar, Paul grabbed the case and shoved her away, losing his grip as he did. The fighting women both grabbed as it fell to the floor. Ella's hands slid off but Chari was able to get a grip and pull it to her. At the same time Ella felt the hand strap of the carpet bag. She yanked and it came free. In the melee, Chari kind of noticed it fall, but was focused on the safety of the case.

Joe entered the waiting room and could not believe his eyes. He stared, trying to take it in. Chari and Ella! Chari and the witch Ella and some guy, yelling and tugging! And they were all fighting over the suitcase he had stashed behind the wash stand! To add to the scene, a stocky, canine woman wearing a uniform was barking some nonsense in the midst of it! He barely noticed the gaggle of plainly dressed, bland looking women hovering around the scene.

He gaped for a moment, then waded in, painful ankle forgotten. He shoved at Ella. She stumbled, the carpet bag dropping unnoticed. She stared, unsure if it really was Joe or just her overworked imagination. "You aren't real. You can't be real. I left you to die. You can't be here, you can't be!" She turned away, convinced she was seeing things.

She wasn't imagining. He spoke, or rather yelled.

"You left me, you hag, but I am here! And you will pay for what you did." He shoved her again. The contact brought her to her senses. She flailed back at him. "You, you, traitor! We trusted you and you never meant to give us anything! It is all a fraud! You and your woman deserve to rot!" She kicked at his ankle. He fell, grabbing it and moaning, curling up into a ball on the floor. She jumped on him and beat his ribs.

The matron was stunned. She couldn't move but simply watched, mesmerized. Ella's fists hit Joe like a three year old in a tantrum. He tried to roll away but Ella stuck with him. The horrified woman finally stirred, trying to separate the two.

Ella shoved her away with one hand, grabbing Joe's collar and shaking him with the other. The matron almost fell to the floor but caught herself. Out of the corner of her eye she saw the woman and man who started it back away from the scene. They had the case. She herself stepped away from the man and woman rolling and hitting and moaning and sobbing on the floor.

The uniformed woman used her best parade ground voice. "Call the police!" Someone had alerted security when the melee started. They were on the way and uniformed cops were not far behind. Even as she yelled, a railroad security man and several uniformed cops descended on the two people still struggling on the floor.

The fighters were separated and pulled to their feet. Two burly policemen hung on to each of them. They were to be taken off to the police station. The matron watched, her flock forgotten for the moment. The volume of the two fighters had been high, heard throughout the room. The range and sheer creativity of their insults were astounding. She heard things new to her, and she was a hardened shepherd of refugees from the streets. The crowd cheered and watched in awe as the two fighters were marched out.

XXXIII

Business schemes, trains, and storms come and go. The men and women working the railroad went about their lives. The melee in Union Station made for a day's headlines. But it caused not a ripple in the routines and tasks usual to running a railroad.

Cam and Mik stood a quarter mile west of Corona Town. It was summer 1905, a fine day along the continental crest of the Rocky Mountains. They were near a newly built siding, just north and west of the main route. On it sat an engine, drinking thirstily from a water tank. They looked down on a lake behind a newly constructed dam. A twelve inch pipe ran about a hundred yards from the lake up to the tank. Chugging merrily, a coal fired pump pulled water to the tank.

"It looks like your plan to bring water up from Pumphouse Lake is going to work just fine."

"Yeah, Mik, I think it will. One less worry. At least for the summer. We'll need to be sure the line doesn't freeze in the winter."

"Drain it after every use and that should be that. Not your problem anyway. Leave it up to the Corona Station crew. They'll handle it just fine."

The train, tanks full, pulled away from the siding and started on its way.

Waving at the conductor as he rode the caboose by, the two men ambled towards Corona Station.

Cam looked around, drinking in the untamed beauty. "Mik, it is time to move on. The rails run through Fraser to Granby and towards Kremmling. We have already surveyed and soon will be making grade in the Gore Canyon."

"True. The Rollins Pass Route is running about as smooth as it ever will. Making it work over this mountain isn't easy but we have learned to do it. We know the weather and how to fight it. We know how to shove trains over the Main Range, east or westbound. Now the challenge is to get the rails to Craig and on through to Salt Lake City."

Mik looked to the north and west, as if he could see the capitol of Utah just down the hill. His friend looked too, then spoke.

"You and I can base out of Fraser now. We're just in the way up here, keeping the railroad men from their work. Being in a town for a while will be a nice change."

Cam thought a moment, then confided in his friend. "I think I will bring my family up. I hear the town even has a doctor. A woman doctor, can you believe it? She goes by Doc Susie, I'm told. She has a reputation of being quite the healer."

"You should do that, Cam. Bring your wife and little ones out. It is time that you have a life with something besides iron and dynamite."

The train whistled in the distance.

XXXIV

THE EXCITEMENT AT UNION STATION SLOWLY SETTLED. THE passengers and others in the station buzzed as the combatants marched out. Across the room, a man casually carried a piece of luggage towards the ticket window. A woman walked beside him. There was no reason for them to stand out. Paul was firmly holding the case. He tried to blend in, not to look at Chari. A traveler whose only care was buying a train ticket wouldn't be looking nervously at his partner. Somehow they were able to edge away from the near riot while keeping possession of the suitcase. He spoke, not too loud, and not looking at her. "Go buy a cabin's worth of first class tickets. To anywhere. Just make sure we have privacy."

She barely shook her head, looking straight ahead as she spoke. "No, you come with me. We need to stay together at least until we...figure things out." She meant, and wanted him to know, that she wasn't losing sight of him or that case until the money was counted and divvied up. Even as she spoke, something gnawed at her. In the excitement back there, something had happened. She had lost something, or something had gone awry. Something had happened but she couldn't put her finger on it.

Ticket buying went off without a hitch. Soon they were aboard and seated. Chari made sure the door was locked. "It is nice to have the whole compartment."

"Yes, it is, Chari. We can spread out, see what is in the case, and make plans. By the way, where are we going?

"To New Orleans via Albuquerque. But first, I need a nap." A satisfied, weary smile lit her face. "That confrontation wore me out. Who was that woman in the uniform? Was she a prison guard or something? Strange doesn't describe her and what she did!"

A concern still nagged at her but she shoved it back. And she couldn't believe Joe had showed up! She believed he was lost, dead in the desert from what Ella had said. The whole affair confused and saddened her. But thoughts of Joe were overshadowed by the money! Exhausted, she barely had the energy to sit up. She wanted to be fresh and rested to count the money.

She looked at Paul. "After a rest, we'll both feel better. Then we can open this beast and count our assets." She moved the case next to the window, sat between it and him, and draped an arm over it. Then her eyes got heavy.

IN THE YELLING AND HITTING AND THE JOSTLING, NO ONE seemed to notice when Ella lost hold of the carpet bag. It simply fell to the floor. There it got kicked around and scuffed a bit but stayed closed and undamaged.

One of the young doves did see it. She scooched down, avoiding the scuffling and kicking legs, and pulled it to her. Standing, she stepped unobtrusively back and turned away. After carefully opening it she reached in and rummaged through.

A surprised, pleased smile lit her face. Closing the bag securely, she elbowed a friend who arched her eyebrow then looked at the bag. The new owner nodded and grinned, stepping further back. As if by prearranged plan, they drifted away from their peers and the still yelling matron. Everyone was watching the shouting and fighting. No attention was given to two plainly dressed young women edging through the crowd. Once out the door, the new owner of the carpet bag gestured and talked. Without a backward glance the young women walked away, disappearing into Denver.

THE WAITER FORGOT ALL ABOUT THE LETTER. ON THE WAY home he found it in a pocket. That reminded him, he was supposed to mail it if he didn't see the woman who tipped him well at breakfast. He couldn't believe what he saw in the evening paper. There was a photograph of that very woman being arrested! She was accused of starting a riot or big fight inside the station. Wow, that must have been a sight!

Ella's photo caused him to pull the unsealed envelope out. She was in jail so he had to decide what to do now. Giving in to temptation, he stopped mid sidewalk to read the letter. A rough clad man jostled him. The guy had calloused hands and lanky arms. His face was red with an unhealthy glow. The hot complexion could have been anger at the man clogging the sidewalk, or something he drank.

"Jeez, do you think you own the sidewalk? Get out of the way!" He pushed by.

The waiter was reading and didn't even hear the rudeness. A smile played over his face. He double checked the envelope's address, turned and went that way.

LATE IN THE EVENING CHARI WOKE. THE TRAIN ROCKED comfortably, carrying her to a fresh start. She saw that Paul sat across, staring alternately at her and at the case. He had not slept, judging by his expression. By now they were in southern Colorado. She looked out at the coal trains heading from the area going north. For some reason she knew that they were on the way to the steelworks in Pueblo. Why that factoid jumped in her head she did not know. Soon their train would labor over Raton Pass. Adios Colorado, hello New Mexico, hello new life!

Chari sat up and smiled. She laid the case on a seat. "Let's see what we have, Paul."

She got ready to open it and realized her key was in the carpet bag. The carpet bag! Where was it? That was the nagging problem she couldn't put her finger on. She had not missed it until now. In fact she had completely forgotten about it.

The key was in there. With grief and horror, she realized it also held her stash of gems, her family bible, and the pistol! All gone! She almost panicked. The rocks were her safety blanket. Mama's bible was all she had left of growing up. And worst of all, the pistol....She had had some half-baked thoughts about that. She had even just dreamed of it. How maybe she could use it to force Paul off the train, penniless and friendless. And then she could take the money and somehow go get Joe back. But not now. Getting rid of Paul would have to wait.

Of all this, she shared not a bit with her new partner. She simply improvised a quick line.

"I lost the key in the confusion. I'll have to pick it." It took a few minutes. You have to practice lock picking or you lose the skill. At least that is what someone told her once. She was getting flustered when the lock clicked. She flipped the top.

"Pages from the city directory. That must just be padding."

She pulled them out. Under them, spread out, was a layer of bills. There were tens, twenties, and fifties. A few hundred dollar bills peeked out too. There were stacks of them. Jackpot!

She picked several bills up, expecting to see more underneath. But no. Under the bills was a selection of several years' worth of catalogs from Sears, Roebuck and Company. There seemed to be no more dollars, no bearer bonds, no lists of investors.

Apparently, there was nothing there but pages and pages of ads for farm implements, women's undergarments, furniture, and other stuff.

Paul then Chari pulled out a catalog. They tore every one of the books apart. Surely the money must be under or within them?! No such luck. Paul even sliced the case lining with his pocket knife. Nothing. He sliced into the leather outer surface. No. The stack of bills added up to about six thousand dollars. That was nothing to sneeze at, but fortune enough to start a new life it was not.

They looked at each other in anger and shock. They couldn't believe it! Greed had not paid this duo. Chari had run out on Joe. Paul abandoned a successful business career and his family. And now, now, they were on the train to nowhere with a measly pile of money, no friends, no future. Snarls, argument, and sobs didn't change the awful truth.

The engine tooted, signaling that the next stop was Raton, New Mexico. As the train coasted to a stop, two people jumped off. Each had several thousand dollars and a faceful of frown. They hurried to buy a ticket to Denver.

BACK THERE, THE TOWN WAS ABUZZ. NOT DALE, OBLIVIOUS BY nature and more or less in hiding. He had been waiting to hear from Chari or someone. The few days he had laid low seemed like forever. He was tired of napping, killing time, and had cabin fever big time. He hadn't even seen a newspaper! The second day he figured he would pack a bag just in case. What would the two railroad men say? That wasn't clear, but he had a hunch he'd hear about them somehow. Just in case, he wanted to be ready to get out of town.

He looked under the bed for his suitcase. It was there, dusty and scuffed. Oddly, there was also another suitcase there, new and expensive. He pulled his out and set it on the bed. Then he grabbed the other. It was full and kind of heavy. It came out but not easily. It had a tag on it. Dale made out the name 'Joe Eggers', and there was some other writing on the other side. He pushed it toward the light and got on his knees to see what was written. What the heck?

The light wasn't great but he was able to make out the neatly printed message. 'Dale, if you find this, don't tell anyone. I need you to keep this case safe and secure for a few days. I'll explain when I retrieve it. Thanks. Joe'

This was unexpected and baffling. Here he was waiting for one of his partners to surface and bring him up to speed on the Karat Top and investors and those two railroad guys and everything. All along, he was literally lying on top of something Joe had entrusted him with. You never knew!

He laid the case on the bed and looked at it, trying to guess what was in it. Finally he decided to open it. He was a partner, wasn't he? And partners don't keep secrets, right? It took a while to get past the lock. He had no key but he did have picks. The hours Ella spent teaching him this trick came back. He tried to recall her tips and thanked her repeatedly as he worried the narrow metal levers around.

There! The lock clicked. He flipped the lid up. Papers. There were papers with one name and a dollar amount listed. And there was a list with three columns, apparently a recap of the individual pages. It showed the names of investors, amount invested, and percentage ownership of the 'Karat Top Mine Corporation'. On that sheet, he and Ella were named as principal partners and owners. In fact, Joe and Chari's names never appeared on this sheet or anywhere. Why was that?

He moved the list and papers. Under it was a layer of newsprint, one or two pages only, not thick. And, under that... were bearer bonds. Below that, stacks of cash. There had to be thousands and thousands of dollars! After staring in awe, he helped himself. He was careful to take small bills, no hundred dollar notes. He grabbed tens, twenties, and fifties. No one would miss a couple of hundred bucks out of thousands, right? So he told himself as he locked the case and shoved it back under the bed.

This was a new development. Did it change things? How? Or not? He just didn't know. Dale couldn't decide if he should go check things out or what. No, Joe told him to keep the suitcase safe. So that's what he would do, stay here and keep an eye on it. But, man, he was tired of laying low. He needed some fresh air and to see something besides four walls. So he got the idea to treat himself to a nice dinner. He would be rich soon, real rich. He could afford it. Hey, he had several hundred dollars in his pocket, didn't he?

There was a knock at the door.

"Smertz, Dale Smertz. Special delivery letter for Mr. Dale Smertz."

No one but partners knew where he was. Still, Dale put one hand on his pocketed revolver and opened the door.

"Yes? I am Smertz."

"Sir, a woman gave this to me this morning. She told me to get it to you if she didn't come back for dinner. She has not returned so here I am, and here it is." The waiter waved the letter.

"Oh, well give it to me." Dale held out his free hand.

"Well, sir, there are extenuating circumstances. You and I need to talk." The waiter unexpectedly stepped in like the room was his, driving Dale back a step.

"You see, this letter does you no good in the wrong hands."

He stared into Dale's eyes. Dale fingered the pistol, unsure if he should use it. He waited to see what this odd man knew or pretended to know.

"Here, read it for yourself." He pulled the envelope open and handed Dale the note.

Dearest Dale,

I gave this note to a man to deliver to you if I don't come get it by the dinner hour. Since you are reading it, I am in trouble or worse. Dale, there is no Karat Top! Chari and Joe salted the ground to lure investors. They used

you and me and they put our names on the documents.
They used us! Get us as much money as you can and
leave town! I will try to meet you at our agreed spot in St
Louis but God only knows when or if that will happen.
Don't give up on me.

Love, EQ'

Dale folded the letter sadly and set it aside.

"Now, Mr. Smertz, like the letter says, you are impli-
cated in this Karat Top scheme."

Silence. Each waited for the other to speak.

"I have made a copy of this letter. If anything happens
to me, it will be delivered to the Sheriff and to the Rocky
Mountain News."

He had Dale's attention. "And what do you want out of
this?"

"Two thousand dollars. You pay me $2000 and I will go
away."

"You will go away, alright." Dale smiled. The pistol came
out, cocked and aimed. "Get out."

The hole in business end of that barrel looked huge to
the waiter. His eyes got almost as big. Turning, he ran. Dale
locked the door and waited several minutes. Then he went out
for a good meal. Making sure the door was double locked, he
took the pistol with him. Wanting to be sure the creep wasn't
lurking, he looked all around when he left.

"Extra! Extra! Riot at the train station! Buy your paper
here! Extra!" The cry of the news hawker intrigued him.
Dale bought a paper and tucked it under his arm. He figured
he'd read as he ate.

The paper was more than intriguing. The lead story almost made him choke. Ella and Joe fighting? Apparently over a suitcase? A uniformed woman trying to referee the fight? Another man and woman last seen leaving the area with the case? Ella and Joe, both arrested, in the hoosegow? The light dawned: The suitcase! They thought it was the one stuffed with cash back in his room. Or maybe there were two? He couldn't erase the image of the suitcase under his bed.

Dale paid for his dinner. Should he go bail her out, bail them out? Find out what was going on? He was tempted to run down to the jail. But he worried about the case under his bed. A night in the klink wouldn't hurt. After all, they were both under lock and key, and couldn't bother him or come for the case. Everyone but Chari was safe, and he didn't care about her right now.

He had laid low and now he learned what was really happening. It was time to make his next move.

XXXV

Dinner over, Dale returned straight to his room. He lay on the bed, weighing options. He wasn't sure, didn't know what to do. Should he go rescue Ella? Or cut himself loose? How about Joe, behind bars too? And where was Chari? How did she fit in all of this? How about those two railroad guys? This wasn't good. Things just didn't add up.

It didn't take a genius to see that the Karat Top was about to explode. Things were about to splatter all over the front pages. It was a good time to be somewhere else. Maybe he should just get the hell out of town.

But he wasn't sure he could leave Ella.... He drifted off to sleep. After his sleeping brain mulled things over, he would decide in the morning.

After a shave and wash up, he ordered breakfast. And he had the bellboy deliver a paper with it. As he hoped against but somehow expected, the headline screamed, DIAMOND MINE FRAUD!!!

Savoring every bite, he finished his bacon and eggs with coffee, toast and currant jelly. Then he picked up the new suitcase and sauntered to Union Station.

A first class ticket in his pocket, Dale Smertz boarded the train.

Afterword

Trains ran over Rollins Pass starting in 1904. Originally, the route was to be a short lived alternative to a tunnel under the continental divide. Financial and political obstacles delayed the tunnel for years. The Denver Northwestern and Pacific Railway went into receivership in 1913, two years after David Moffat's death. Its successor, The Denver and Salt Lake Railway, ran the line over Rollins Pass.

Terrain and weather caused problems from the outset. New techniques and equipment were developed. Due chiefly to snow, the line was very expensive to operate. Engines running dry was one of many problems. Pumphouse Lake was actually created to address that issue.

The bore under the divide, named the Moffat Tunnel, finally opened in 1928. It is in use to this day. The line over the Hill was kept open for several years as a backup but was not used. Track was pulled in the 1930's, closing the saga of Rollins Pass.

There was in fact a scheme involving a salted jewel mine in northwest Colorado. The schemers had San Francisco businessmen excited and putting up big money. Potential investors were taken out to the area by train. Blindfolded, they rode for a day or two to the 'lode'. There they were encouraged to find gems just under the surface. A skeptical geologist heard of it and was able to piece together where the field was. He and a friend went there, discovered the ruse, and exposed the scam. The con men left town emptyhanded and escaped punishment. This all occurred before the turn of the century.

About the Author

S̲TAN̲ M̲OORE̲ IS AN AVID READER, HISTORIAN, AND OUTDOORS-man. A third generation Coloradan, he is a Vietnam veteran. When not reading up on today's and tomorrow's past, he is traveling, or more likely is outdoors. Exploring the mountains and canyons of Colorado and the Southwest are among his favorite activities. Moore very much enjoys family, wife, children and their spouses, grandchildren, and friends. He makes his home near Denver with his long suffering spouse and the two cats who let them stay there.